Praise for One Night

This gripping crime novel pulled me in from page one! With layered twists, strong female leads, and a plot that keeps you guessing, One Night is a brilliant, suspenseful read that kept me guessing the whole way through. Highly recommended for fans of crime fiction, strong female leads, and intelligent storytelling. Reads on the Road

One Night is a well-grounded read for crime thriller buffs. Mel Hobbs

A detailed plot, twists and intrigue. Recommended. Brenda Telford

A great story that had me turning the pages. Highly recommended to any reader who loves a good crime story that will pull you in. I loved it and I do hope that there are more DS Bec Harpin stories to come. Helen Sibbrit

A tight crisp murder investigation undertaken by the formidable Detective Sergeant Bec Harpin unfolds with two dead bodies, many rabbit holes and a good friendship on the line. Cleverly plotted and set against a Melbourne backdrop, the lights of the city shine on this police procedural and crime infused narrative. Happy Valley BooksRead

Fans of great crime fiction will love this second Bec Harpin story. A clever plot with interwoven storylines sees the mystery unravel at a steady and satisfying pace. Highly recommended. Judith Kneebone – Librarian

Praise for Making Up Amanda

I simply relished this story. A mesmerising and addictive read I couldn't put down. Suspense and surprise as the plot unfolded. What crime story is all about. Bianca Mal Amazon

Had me enthralled from the very beginning. I love an edge of your seat crime story, and this was one I couldn't put down. Sarah Amazon

A must read for crime thriller buffs. I could not put it down once I started reading. Highly recommended. Mephie Amazon

Refreshingly different setting ...a most satisfying read. Readinghighreviews

Great read. Kept me in suspense until the end. Lovereading Amazon

Fast paced and well written with its criminal construct delivered seamlessly. Happy Valley Amazon

A very engaging read. Emma Moon Goodreads

An intriguing story with great characters. Recommended. Ballaratti Amazon

Praise for The Piano Woman

What a fabulous read this was. It's dual timeline entangling the past and present with a nice twist. Happy Valley - Books Read

A real page turner in terms of story and plot. The gradual unravelling of ancestral secrets across four generations is skillfully executed. Chandani Lokuge author of 'My Van Gogh.'

It was easy to get lost in this well written multiple timeline novel. Dabble in the present day and take a step back in time with memorable characters, it's a guaranteed great read. Mrs B Book Reviews

Read the book in one day. I could not wait to see how the mystery unfolded. Goodreads

A wonderful story of a writer who is struck by a deep but fractured memory of her grandmother after hearing a stranger play a piano in a mall. I loved it. Amazon Books

Well written endearing characters and an unpredictable plot. Mel's Bookworm Reviews

The end wrapped up beautifully. I even shed a few tears when the whole mystery was revealed. Goodreads

As a fan of dual timeline novels this one hit the right notes. There is mystery and some romance and a well written compelling tale of families, traditions, and personal growth. Highly recommended. Author, Phillipa Nefri Clarke

The structure of the book was very well executed maintaining the suspense throughout. I was hooked until the end. Goodreads.

I'm waiting for the sequel. Goodreads

ALSO AVAILABLE BY ROZZI BAZZANI

Hector – *The Story of Hector Crawford and Craford Productions (non-fiction)*

The Piano Woman

Making Up Amanda – *DS Bec Harpin Book One*

Rozzi Bazzani is an award-winning author who has written scripts, libretti and songs for theatre including two stage musicals. She has been a regular contributor to the Arts pages of the highest circulation newspaper in Australia.

Before writing full time Rozzi worked as a 'session' singer in recording studios. She has performed live on stages across Australia and internationally and used her voice for both spoken and sung commercial work. She has backed some of Australia's best-known singers and supplied voices for anything from soap to sunglasses, face cream to dog food.

After returning to study and graduating from Melbourne University where she majored in Romance Languages, Linguistics and Fine Art, Rozzi's love of reading and history (her first job was in a public library) inspired her first book, 'Hector,' a fully researched biography of Australian TV mogul Hector Crawford which won the Victorian Royal Historical Society Publication Prize and was short-listed for the Ashurst Business Literature Prize.

Longing to write fiction, 'The Piano Woman' a mystery romance appeared in 2021, followed soon after by the first in a crime series 'Making Up Amanda,' featuring Detective Sergeant Rebecca Harpin, and 'One Night' the second book in that series.

Rozzi lives in Ballarat, Victoria, and with her husband and two big poodles is often seen walking the local tracks around Lake Wendouree considering the next plot twist for her newest book.

ROZZI BAZZANI

ONE NIGHT

First Published 2025
Copyright © Rozzi Bazzani 2025

S & B Books
Level 1, 409 Keilor Road
Niddrie, Victoria 3042

ISBN Paperback: 978-0-6456930-4-1
E Book: 978-0-6456930-5-8

The truth is rarely pure and never simple.

Oscar Wilde

Chapter 1

Bec could feel the frustration building and that wasn't good. Normally, running calmed her tension, particularly running through the ancient trees and rocks around her hideaway up here on the mountain, but not today.

She had moved here permanently a few months ago, and already loved the peace and isolation surrounding the little cottage her uncle had unexpectedly left her in his will, especially because it was still held in a family trust, so no-one could trace her to her little piece of paradise.

It would have been perfect except for the phone reception. Her new job in the homicide squad meant she had to be on call twenty-four seven, so the dodgy reception was a major concern. It was also the reason for her frustration today. Her phone had buzzed over and over again. The first couple of times, she had stopped and answered formally in case it was the office with 'Detective Sergeant Rebecca Harpin', but the lack of reception meant she couldn't hear a thing, and she couldn't even see a message saying who the call was from.

It was starting to get dark as she headed up the last hill to her cottage, and she took out her phone again, holding it up to see if she could get any reception. Nothing. A million possibilities crowded in: her new boss getting furious that he couldn't speak to her, a family crisis, something with her best friend, Lyn, then, worst of all, the Rigby family had her new number and the threats were going to start again.

She picked up her pace, running hard to get to the one place in the cottage she seemed always to find a phone signal, the Rigby case flaring in her mind just as the shrinks warned her it would. Being shot at by the youngest scumbag son had sent her to talk to Internal Affairs.

'And did you feel it appropriate to discharge your weapon at that time, Sergeant Harpin?' they'd asked.

'No, I thought it would be appropriate for the scumbag to fire at us in a narrow laneway and for us to just stand there,' was the first answer that had come to mind, but she had summoned all her control to say, 'Yes, in my judgement, my partner and I were at serious risk of harm and there was no risk to civilians for me to fire my weapon at the suspect at that time.'

Although her actions had been deemed appropriate in the circumstances, she had still been required to see a police-force-appointed shrink for months to ensure she was fit for duty.

Finally, as she collapsed puffing against her front door, her phone went off in her pocket, buzzing with incoming messages. She carefully pulled it out, expecting the worst. They were all missed calls from her friend Carolyn Moorhouse.

It was strange for Carolyn to call so many times. Normally, the barrister would leave a single concise message and then wait for Bec to call, but tonight there were over six messages and calls, all within about an hour. Bec's antennae were on full alert as she dialled her friend's number.

Although Bec had known Carolyn for over fifteen years, she had never heard her normally composed friend so rattled.

'Can you come, Bec? I really need your help.'

Bec's brain flashed back to the last time a friend had said that to her. When Bec was fifteen, her best friend, Lyn, had called very late one night begging for help, 'Please, Bec, can you come to my place now?' Bec hadn't hesitated then, and she knew that she wasn't going to hesitate now.

'Where are you, Caro?'

'My chambers. Please, Bec.'

Within five minutes, Bec had changed and was in her car heading towards the city.

It was those words uttered by Lyn all those years ago that had led Bec to join the police force and led to her friendship with Carolyn. Carolyn Moorhouse had been a young prosecutor given the carriage of the shocking family case that arose from Lyn's call. Carolyn had been kindness personified to Lyn and Bec as she had teased out every terrible detail, but then, in court, Carolyn had turned into a sword-wielding Boadicea as she tore the defence to shreds.

Their paths crossed again when Bec was a young constable giving evidence in a case Carolyn was prosecuting and they had struck up a friendship, and now Bec would count Carolyn as one of her few true friends. Not that she had told the shrinks that. According to them, a 'normal' person had a wide range of friends and family they could fall back on during a crisis, so Bec had been forced to exaggerate her relationship with her own family and described several colleagues as 'friends' just so she could fit the definition.

But Carolyn and Lyn were actually the real deal. The people she would always drop everything for. Like right now. Carolyn had never asked for her help before, so Bec knew that whatever had prompted the call had to be serious.

She pressed her foot harder on the accelerator.

Chapter 2

The town hall clock chimed 10 pm as she pulled up in William Street outside the high-rise building where Barwick Chambers held Carolyn's rooms on the ninth floor. She had driven fast to get here. The last thing she'd felt like doing tonight was driving back into the city, but Carolyn had asked, and for her to take such a step, Bec reasoned it was something serious.

Plenty of legal professionals like Carolyn worked ridiculous hours, and there seemed to be more than the usual number on the streets. Bec sat for a moment, resting her hands on the steering wheel and watching the passing parade. Her day had panned out very differently to that of a senior barrister. Cops started early, finished late and worked shifts. Weekends in a big case; a nap in your chair might be all you could get as a rest. She certainly didn't have the luxury of picking and choosing which cases she'd work on. She stepped onto the footpath and walked to the entrance.

Only when she'd been buzzed in, taken the lift and walked past a wall of locked office doors, did something akin to dread wash over her. She shrugged it off as a symptom of her tiredness. The effects of an exhausting day were still playing out in her body, after all.

The door marked 'Carolyn Moorhouse' was closed. She listened for a moment before tapping softly on the heavy wooden door.

'Is that you, Rebecca?' Carolyn spoke from inside.

'It is,' Bec said.

Carolyn wasn't smiling when she opened the door.

'Thank God you're here.' Her greeting was brusque in the way a schoolmistress might address a small child who was running late. Bec let it slide and scanned the room. A dishevelled-looking, dark-haired man sitting stiffly at Caro's desk stared back at her. 'This is Juan Zamora, my pupil barrister for the next six months until he's qualified,' Carolyn said, gesturing with her left hand and slamming the door closed with her right. 'Don't know who this is,' she added, pointing to a male figure lying face down on the floor, who already had Bec's full attention. 'But he is dead. I checked multiple times.'

Bec's senses rushed to overdrive. She didn't move while she took in the state of the room, committing all she could to memory. Clear signs of a struggle: papers on the floor, a chair overturned, files strewn across Carolyn's desk. And lying by the dead man was a large metal Buddha that Bec remembered usually sat on a side table close to the door. She remembered that Carolyn would always touch it for luck before she left for court appearances. Now, it lay on the floor covered in blood. As carefully as she could, she sidestepped along the wall and reached over, feeling for the man's pulse. Nothing. She scrutinised the body closely, absorbing everything that could be important to an investigation. Blood pooling around a blood-soaked beanie and a nasty gash to the side of his forehead seemed to indicate that the dead man had taken a blow to the head, with lucky Buddha the likely weapon. She guessed the dead man was in his fifties, a day's stubble on his face and wearing a cleaner's uniform. A white medical mask still covered part of his face. His skin was a grey colour and was already cold when she'd checked for a pulse.

As the adrenaline surge from the sight of the body waned, the full picture dawned. No other cops. Only Bec at a crime scene in her private capacity. If this was right, then she was out on a limb, big time.

'Are you both alright?' she asked, waiting for Carolyn or her pupil to say something.

'I am now you're here,' Carolyn said at last, and Bec heard a catch in her voice. This was a first. All the time she'd known Carolyn Moorhouse, Carolyn had never been a woman who showed emotion under pressure.

'He put up a good fight.' Carolyn gestured to Juan. Bec noticed that Juan's shirt was torn, and that he certainly looked like he'd been in some kind of punch-up.

'He broke in and came at me,' Juan said finally, eyes downcast. 'I was protecting myself.' Bec heard a hint of a Spanish accent.

'Broke in?' Bec said. 'He's a cleaner for the building, by the look of his outfit.'

'He broke in, I disturbed him, he came at me,' Juan repeated, speaking directly to Bec's face this time.

Bec turned to Carolyn. 'Tell me you've called this in,' she said, even though she knew that if she had, the place would be crawling with cops by now.

'I called you,' Carolyn said defensively.

'You called me over an hour ago, Carolyn.'

'I called you, Bec,' Carolyn repeated, her eyes flicking away from the directness of Bec's gaze.

'And you didn't think to mention that you had a dead body waiting.' Bec breathed deeply to calm herself.

Silence.

'Okay. So, we're here.' Bec raised her palms to acknowledge the mess they were in. 'Who is going to tell me what's going on?'

The pupil spoke first. 'Carolyn was already gone. But according to my phone, I called her at 6.58 pm.'

'It was getting dark when I left,' Carolyn said, 'so it must have been around 6.30. I was meeting a friend at 7.15 – in Fed Square.'

'So, you weren't here when this happened?'

'No, I wasn't. Juan wasn't meant to be here, either.'

'A last-minute cancellation to my holiday,' he said, his voice lacking conviction.

'Can anyone vouch for seeing you, wherever you were?' Bec directed her question to Carolyn.

'I … yes, I think so. I'll need to make a call.'

'You can't call anyone else until the investigators get here.' Bec heard herself talking to her friend like a cop, and her stomach tightened. Bec would have her own situation to explain when those investigators arrived.

Carolyn's gaze turned icy. She stared at Bec as if she were an adversary.

'You called me at 8.30 pm, Carolyn. What took you so long to contact me, or the police? I got here just after 10 pm. That's three hours after the incident.'

Carolyn responded defensively, as if the delay had been Bec's fault. 'I'd been leaving messages for forty minutes before you called back, Rebecca.'

'And you, Juan, why didn't you call the police when it happened?'

'I didn't know what to do, so I called Carolyn. She came back and said that you would know how to handle a situation like this,' he finished lamely.

Did he really expect her to swallow that Carolyn, one of this country's finest barristers, didn't know how to behave at a crime scene in her own chambers?

Bec could only look at each of them in turn. 'So, the best thing you could think of to do between you, was to sit here for hours and wait for me to arrive?'

Silence descended.

Bec grabbed her phone. 'I have to call this in. Then you can explain to the team that arrives exactly why you sat next to a dead body for hours without either of you calling the authorities. And I have no idea how I'm going to explain what the hell I'm doing here! But right now, I need you to carefully get up, and without touching anything, walk down that side wall and around to the door. This scene has enough contamination already.'

Carolyn and her pupil appeared anchored for several seconds before Carolyn suddenly moved forward, carefully placing her feet down as if she was avoiding rain puddles. 'We can wait in the conference room,' she said, glancing back at Juan Zamora, who'd jolted himself forward to trace her steps.

Bec dialled the West Melbourne Police Station and identified herself. After her explanation and hanging up, she spoke quietly to Carolyn, who was waiting outside the open door. 'You know I can't be involved in this investigation now that you've dragged me into it. I can't even work out what you and Juan were thinking not to call it in hours ago. And I have to say, Caro, the three-hour delay is going to have every one of those police officers offside from the get-go. Cops don't like gaps in timelines, just like barristers don't.'

She saw that her friend had gone very pale.

'I didn't know what to do, Bec,' she whispered.

Bec could only shake her head.

Chapter 3

When the police arrived, uniform wasted no time organising foot traffic on the ninth floor, directing anyone left in the building to an alternative route via the stairwell.

'You can't stay here, we need to keep the scene clear,' Sergeant Mick Mallory, a beefy officer with a loud voice, barked as soon as he'd ascertained who she was. Bec thought from the way his voice was ringing along the carpeted corridors, they'd probably hear every word on the floor below. Two young suits appeared from the lift, their eyes widening at the scene of police everywhere, then scuttled away in the other direction, following Mallory's instructions.

Bec had no intention of interfering. The best thing for her to do at this stage was to sit tight and not get in anyone's way. She glanced at Carolyn and Juan, who were both lost in their own thoughts, not talking, seemingly oblivious to the activity going on around them. So many questions Bec wanted to ask. Ten minutes in an interview room and she could sort out what had happened. Unfortunately, she knew any chance of her running this investigation had been blown up by Carolyn calling her in privately. Just the same, she was mounting arguments in her mind to stay on the case, if only to help herself understand why Carolyn called her when a triple zero call would have generated an immediate response. What had her friend expected her to do?

The two lawyers were perched stiffly on chairs with their backs to the wall. Bec sat near them, her body slightly turned away, waiting.

Carolyn was the first to break the uncomfortable silence that had fallen between them.

'Will we have long to wait?'

'Detectives aren't here yet. The uniforms won't question you, that'll be the detectives,' Bec said, quietly mapping ways the intruder could have gained entry to the building. Carolyn's suite occupied the ninth floor, rooms twelve and thirteen, and was situated directly opposite the lifts. It wouldn't be easy to regulate access during business hours in a building like this. Courts of all jurisdictions were only a short distance away, and these chambers were the busiest in Melbourne. Instructing solicitors and their clients came and went all day long. Bec twisted around to face Carolyn and spoke softly. 'Do you know what time night security arrangements kick in?'

Carolyn nodded and whispered back without looking at Bec, 'About 6.30, I think. Goes to pass-card access only after that.'

This explained the timing, Bec figured. Yet, if the intruder had entered sooner before the front doors clicked to pass-card entry, he could just as easily have hidden in a storage area in the building and waited. Either way, the CCTV cameras Bec had seen in each corridor and the lift should help them identify who was in the building at the time.

Mallory's voice echoed through the doorway, confirming that the intruder was dead and declaring Carolyn's chambers a crime scene.

'We could have told you that,' Bec heard Carolyn mutter under her breath.

Juan, his face a deathly shade of white, looked even more ill. He had withdrawn since police had arrived, and hadn't uttered another word. Frozen into silence.

Bec was finding it difficult to remain seated. She got up and stuck her head through the doorway. 'Anything I can do, Sergeant?'

'No. Just wait there, Ms Harpin. Detectives are on their way.' Bec heard the man's intentional ignoring of her rank, reducing her role to that of civilian witness, at best.

*

Once DI McCormack from West Melbourne Police Station arrived with three offsiders in tow, the mood changed. Mallory showed him the body and the overall scene, and Bec heard Mallory saying, 'Male, roughly fifties, blow to the head, no identity on him,' and mention the unusual weapon that appeared to have killed the man. Then McCormack's response, 'Contact the Bar Association and ask them who the cleaning contractors are. They should be able to tell us who was rostered on today.'

McCormack wandered out into the corridor, glanced at Bec and said to Carolyn and Juan, 'My name's Detective Inspector McCormack. If you don't mind, I'd like to hear from each of you in your own words what's happened here.'

'Will this be our formal statement, Inspector?' This was Carolyn trying to take control. In her profession, she knew very well that the DI would need to hear an outline for himself to direct the next step.

'No, Ms Moorhouse, that will come later, as I'm sure you know.' McCormack's tone was friendly but firm. 'Sergeant Harpin, Ms Moorhouse, if you could both just sit tight for now.' He gestured to the other end of the passageway. 'There's a quiet room down there. I'll speak to you first.' He pointed to Juan Zamora.

Carolyn briefly caught Bec's eye, and if there was a message in that glance Bec couldn't read it. Juan got up slowly, and from the look on his face – glassy eyes, shoulders slumped – he could have been walking the plank.

McCormack instructed his officers to completely cordon off Carolyn's office in readiness for the crime scene investigators.

When he eventually got to Bec, he said, giving her a not-too-polite head-to-foot, taking in her straight-leg jeans, rollneck and hooded outdoor jacket, 'And why do I have a detective sergeant from the murder team at the scene of a potential murder before any other copper knows anything about it?'

'Caro is a friend of mine, and she called and asked me to come,' Bec said calmly.

'And you didn't tell her to call triple zero?' He regarded her sceptically.

'I wasn't aware of the circumstances until I arrived, sir.'

'And what time did she *ask you to come*?' He leaned in on the words.

'I spoke to her around 8.30 pm.'

'And yet, you didn't call it in until 10.15?'

'Ms Moorhouse asked me to attend her chambers. I arrived at around 10.10 pm and called it in as soon as I realised what had happened, sir.'

'Call at 8.30 pm and you arrive at ten?'

'I was at home in the Macedon Ranges when she called, sir.'

He rubbed the side of his head. 'And you drove all that way based on a request. Not because Ms Moorhouse told you she had a dead guy on her floor?'

'Yes.'

'I'm struggling to see why on earth you would drive that distance at that hour without good reason?'

'I understand, sir, but it was for the sole reason that a friend asked me to come. And I wasn't on duty.'

'So, let me be clear. When you got here, you found the dead man and cleared the scene, is that right?'

'That's right, and called it in immediately.'

The DI was a man of few words, but he was scrutinising her and weighing the situation. Bec was certain the summary in his report about why she'd been present at an unreported crime scene would not do her any favours.

'Well, Detective Sergeant, although I find your story very difficult to comprehend, it's not me you have to convince. I've called your boss and he is sending the duty team, who, I am sure, will enjoy trying to make sense of your story. Do you see any other way forward, Sergeant?'

'No, sir.'

McCormack signed for Caro and Juan to come back after he'd finished speaking to Bec. 'Homicide detectives shouldn't be too long,' he said to all three of them. 'You'll have to wait they get here and go through it again.' He pulled out his phone and took a few steps away.

McCormack was civil, Bec thought, but they both knew exactly what was going to happen once her colleagues from homicide arrived.

*

Relegated to her seat, Bec saw Detective Sergeant Glen 'Jacko' Jackson and Detective Constable Les Green glance across at her and Juan Zamora during their briefing from Mallory and McCormack. She saw the crime scene investigators troop in, and she watched Mallory and McCormack depart. When the two homicide detectives called her name, Bec stood up.

Green, the shorter of them, seemed semi-amused. 'Detective Sergeant Harpin, you do know that joining homicide means investigating crimes, not being a part of them, don't you?'

'I am an innocent bystander here, Detective Green,' Bec said, knowing he'd already been told of her involvement.

'Accident, was it?' His eyes focused on hers.

'Me being here?'

'No, I'd say that's a fair dinkum disaster. I meant the dead guy.'

'Certainly unplanned, I'd say,' she said.

'And certainly unlucky for him,' Jackson said. 'We'll sort your situation later, Harpin. First, we need to establish what's happened.'

'I'd like to sit in on the interviews,' she said.

Jackson, the senior of the two, stared hard for a moment. 'You're on thin ice here, Rebecca. You couldn't have compromised yourself more. Woman's a friend of yours. That right?'

'Yes, she is.'

'You reckon she's solid?'

'I did, Jacko, but there are too many questions.'

Green snorted, but Jackson nodded.

'Okay. But you have something to say, you say it to me afterwards. Not a word during the interview.'

Bec nodded.

*

Detective Sergeant Jackson directed his first question to Juan. 'DI McCormack tells me that you are Juan Zamora. May I call you Juan?'

A hesitant nod.

'Can you tell us what happened between you and the deceased?'

'I stupidly went out when I heard the door open,' Juan said sharply, finding his voice.

'You mean the door to these rooms, or someone buzzed in from downstairs on the street?'

'No-one buzzed from the street. I meant the door into Ms Moorhouse's chambers,' Juan said, his eyes moving between his interrogators.

'I wasn't expecting anyone,' he said. 'I was alone, working back to catch up. I thought I heard the door but decided it must have been some other office. Then I heard some movement in Ms Moorhouse's room. I thought maybe she had left something behind and had come back, or maybe it was her clerk leaving a brief. Anyway, I opened my door, and there was a man going through one of the drawers of the filing cabinets. When he turned around, I saw he was wearing a mask.'

'Okay, but don't the contractors in these offices still wear medical masks when they work?'

Juan shrugged. 'Maybe. But he was going through the drawers. A cleaner shouldn't be doing that.'

'Okay, a masked man going through a filing cabinet. What happened then?'

'When he saw me, he seemed surprised and ran towards me and pushed me back against the wall.'

'The cleaner did that?' Green couldn't hide his scepticism.

'He ran straight at me,' Juan said defensively. 'I said to him, we don't keep any cash here.'

'And then?' Jackson asked, trying to get the full picture.

'I waited till he turned around to leave and I jumped him,' Juan said, talking with great energy now. 'I can look after myself, you know.'

'That much is obvious,' Green said, his eyes roaming the room.

'I wanted to find out who he was, what he was looking for. We struggled. He was yelling, I tried to twist his arm, but he kicked back. I shoved him hard against the table and everything fell, including the Buddha. He tried to push me away, but I pushed back even harder. Then he fell sideways and hit his head on the statue.'

'Fell and hit his head on the statue that had just fallen in that exact spot?' Green gestured towards Carolyn's office. 'Is that what you're saying?'

'That's what happened.'

Juan glanced quickly at Carolyn, whose facial expression hadn't changed.

'And nobody came to see what the racket was about? With so many people working in this building, nobody heard a thing. No-one came to your rescue?' the senior detective asked.

'I don't think anybody else was working on this floor at that time. A lot go out for dinner and come back later.'

Carolyn leaned forward. 'Detective, the fact is that even if someone was working, these chambers are completely silent. They spent a fortune soundproofing the walls in the last renovations. Can't risk anyone overhearing client interviews, so they made sure nobody can hear what's going on, even in rooms next door to each other.'

'Thank you, Ms Moorhouse. If you wouldn't mind letting me finish before commenting.'

Carolyn leaned back, putting her hands up in apology.

Green turned back to Juan, clearly not buying any of this. 'What did you do then?'

'I called Carolyn.'

'He did call me,' Carolyn confirmed. 'I made it back around 7.50 pm.'

'Okay, thank you, Ms Moorhouse. We seem to have a time gap. Juan calls you at 6.55 and you are with …' he checked his notes, 'with friends at Federation Square. Now, that's what a ten-minute walk? Yet, you arrived at 7.50?'

Carolyn looked sheepish. 'We had a change of plan. I was with a friend in Elsternwick and it took time to organise an Uber.'

Green made some more notes. Bec was impressed at her colleagues' questioning, picking up the hole in the timeline as Bec herself would have done.

'Okay, so you are back at 7.50 to find a body covered in blood in your office, but – now please understand our confusion here, Ms

Moorhouse – you don't call the police or an ambulance, you phone a friend.' He raised his voice on the last three words to make his point.

'A friend who is a senior detective.'

'But you failed to mention to your friend, a senior detective, at the time you asked her to attend your chambers, that your request involved a dead body lying right in front of you. Is that right?'

'Yes, that's right, I didn't mention that. I just told her I needed her to come.' She looked at Bec. 'And she did.'

His face didn't change; his eyes were deadpan. 'Alright, if I allow for your panic, what time did Detective Sergeant Harpin appear on the scene?'

'Around 10 pm.'

Green studied his notes. 'You called at 7.50 pm and DS Harpin returns your call at approximately 8.30. She drove from Mount Macedon and arrived around 10 pm. At which stage, the victim has been lying dead on the floor for approximately three hours and fifteen minutes ...' He let his sentence trail off. 'So, DS Harpin arrives, sees the dead guy, and finally someone does something sensible. She calls us, as you or Mr Zamora should have done three hours earlier, Ms Moorhouse.'

Silence.

Bec knew what was coming. There were too many holes.

'I'm afraid we are going to have to ask you to come to the station, Mr Zamora, to make a formal statement, and until we can verify what's gone on here tonight, you will have to stay with us until then. Ms Moorhouse, we will need you to come along as well to make your formal statement.'

Chapter 4

By the time Bec got home, it was the early hours of the next day. The mountain was dark and still, so dark that she could barely see the outline of her cottage. Low cloud cover hanging like a thick thermal blanket obliterated any light from the stars or the moon. She pulled out her phone torch and used that to pick her way along the path to her door. The house was cold, but it was too late to think about lighting a fire.

After a few hours of rough sleep, she rose at 7 am, took a quick shower and was dressed and on the road again.

Just an hour later, she drove into the security carpark and took a deep breath. 'Give you time to find your feet again in the city,' Chief Superintendent Baker had commented. Bec wasn't aware she'd ever lost her 'feet', and thought her results spoke louder than words. She'd expected a promotion after her last assignment, but instead it was a brief stint on desk duties while the force shrinks cleared her for active duty again. Two incidents involving firearms had them worried something else was going on. In the end, she'd been directed to apply for a temporary senior sergeant position in homicide; six months maximum, filling in for an officer who was already on maternity leave. It felt unfair, like she was having to prove herself all over again. But if that's what it took, she was up for it.

'We don't think she'll be back, though,' Wendy Santos, a chunky senior constable, said on Bec's first day. 'She was really sick, and mentioned a few times that she was looking forward to the change of pace. My bet is she'll take a desk job if she comes back at all.'

Bec had considered what Wendy said, and thought she understood how dealing with small children at home one minute was enough, never mind handling violence from offenders the next. A challenging switch. Bec knew from her own ordeal with weapons – which wasn't over yet – how attitude and energy was everything in this job.

She sat still in her car for a few minutes, trying to shake off that line of thinking, while the replay of Carolyn's angry late-night call on the drive home started up again, replaying every word, with Bec not having to press any repeat button at all. Overwrought and angry, Carolyn had exploded on account of being dragged to the station to give formal statements to Bec's hard-nosed colleagues, Detectives Jackson and Green. 'I don't like being treated like some scumbag criminal defendant,' she'd raged. Bec shouldn't have taken the call, shouldn't have spoken to her. But their solid friendship and her concern for Carolyn's welfare had made her pick up. Despite all her misgivings about Carolyn and Juan calling her instead of triple zero, she hadn't been able to stop herself wanting to help sort out whatever happened.

'What did you expect? A man dies in your chambers, you leave him lying there for three hours, then think you won't have some explaining to do? Seriously, Carolyn, what the hell were you thinking?'

Bec had been forced to remind Carolyn that she too had been questioned with the same sceptical attitude. Why had she agreed to assist a friend without asking for the reason to drive an hour – why did she do that without question? Twice she'd told them, 'Because that's what friends do.'

Green had been unable to hide his disbelief. 'And Carolyn Moorhouse conveniently forgot to mention in her request that a man was dead in her rooms?'

'That's right, Detective, as I have said, she didn't. If she had told me that, I would have called it in immediately.'

The detective, who was known as the 'biggest hard head' in the homicide squad, had nodded slightly, as if he couldn't imagine a criminal barrister of Carolyn's standing, someone who would have seen all the colours of human behaviour in her career, being that stressed about an accidental death, and he'd made that clear.

Bec couldn't disagree with him on that score. But he'd looked hard at her and said, 'Lots of fucking holes in their stories, far as I can tell. Particularly the three missing hours.' And Bec couldn't disagree with that, either.

'Do you think he will be up for manslaughter? He has briefs to complete for me and I—'

'You know how this goes. We investigate and hand it over to the prosecutors, Caro. And, as you also know, I shouldn't be talking to a witness.'

'And I thought we were friends, Rebecca,' Carolyn said angrily and slammed the phone down in her ear. Then, less than five minutes later, she'd called and left an apologetic message. '*Bec, I'm sorry. It's the shock of this. Sorry, forgive me?*'

Bec understood it was a stressful situation. But she also had no doubt that once the Crime Investigation Unit had completed their job, there would be a charge of manslaughter or murder, depending on the coroner's findings. Should Juan's prints be found on the blood-covered Buddha, it would be murder. And in that instance, the man's best chance would be making a case for self-defence.

She shut down the engine. No matter which way Bec looked at the events of last night, something didn't feel right. None of it made sense. What did Carolyn expect Bec to do? Investigate privately to keep her name and reputation clear, a free pass because she was a friend? Or sheet the blame to Juan Zamora? Was he going to take a fall for his boss? That didn't make sense, either.

The one thing that was clear in all of this was that Carolyn had landed Bec into a situation that could affect the rest of her career. Just yesterday, she had been furious that her last two successful cases hadn't led to a promotion, and, in fact, she didn't even have a permanent role. If her involvement in this case was sent to Internal Affairs, she knew there would be a black mark against her forever. 'Didn't she have an investigation into her involvement ...?' Promotion gone. Reputation gone.

Bec sat in her car, trying to control her anger. Her friend had put everything at risk. Well, she couldn't change that, but what she could change was the outcome. Step one, stare them all down. She had gone to help a friend. They didn't believe her. Their problem. Step two, she had to make sure there were no loose ends. If Carolyn or Juan Zamora had told one lie, she would personally nail them up, but if their stories stacked up after forensics, she would make sure they were cleared. And step three, if she could pull off steps one and two, she might just save her career. But she knew that was a very big 'if'.

And even if she wasn't working the case, it wouldn't stop her trying to find out why Carolyn had called her and not triple zero. Bec had stated to Green and Jackson twice that Carolyn was a long-time close friend, but thinking on it now, Bec realised she really knew very little about Carolyn's non-public life. Yes, she could fill in a questionnaire about where her favourite eating haunts were, who her preferred judges and magistrates were, the soft spot she had for certain types of wrongdoers, she knew what made her laugh and which wines she preferred. But the kind of detail she needed now was different. Who was Carolyn Moorhouse really? Did she even have a private life? Bec had always assumed Carolyn's social scene would be slim (like hers), given the prodigious work hours she put in. She didn't wear rings and had never even hinted at there being someone special in her life. Bec's stomach tightened. It didn't sit easily to start digging around, scrounging for intelligence on a friend she'd always trusted. But to understand anything about last night, like it or not, Carolyn would have to explain her actions better than she had so far. But for now, Bec had to face even more questions from her direct boss about her involvement.

She was ready. Gathering her bag, she got out quickly and beeped the lock key.

Chapter 5

A searing pain struck her body, sharp and sudden. Gasping for air, she pulled up, but she soon bent over in agony. Cursing under her breath, she acknowledged the stitch. It hit hard. Nothing to do but breathe until the pain that was driving into her body like a sharp knife subsided. Placing one hand onto her side and the other on her right hip and taking quick shallow breaths, she cursed the wretched 'thing' that was slowing her down and would make her late. Nikki was always punctual for auditions. No-one knew more than her how do or die auditions were when there was a lucrative role at stake.

She grimaced, the pain jabbing at her again. It took a long count of twenty before she straightened and the stitch weakened its grip. She checked her watch. *I can still make it*, she thought, *long as I don't get another one of those*. She rubbed her side, repositioned the shoulder strap of her bag and set off gingerly, before she sped up again. Part of her was excited, despite the hitch – *stitch hitch* her mind rhymed the words, a favourite word game. Another part of her was dreading the long wait, the questions about her experience and coming up with answers, where, to put it mildly, the truth generally became as expendable as last week's tea bag.

The most critical thing was to come across as perfect: flexible, accommodating, sexy. She knew how it went. She'd done it before. The last time she'd auditioned for reality TV – and come to think of it, the time before that – she'd come close. But the worst thing about not being chosen was having to endure the 'special' half-encouraging, half-pitying 'we'll see you again smile' that producers reserved for losers; that was her personal hell – worse, way worse, than the anguish of not being selected.

She was not going to be discouraged though, like when the fast-talking confident persona of the past hadn't done it for her. She'd simply created a new one. This past week, while scrubbing and lathering her body under the shower, she'd practised a 'Marilyn' voice, cooing and purring, all breathy and vulnerable. She'd thrown herself into the part so wholeheartedly that there had been moments when she'd truly believed she'd transmogrified (she was that good) into the blonde bombshell herself.

One thing Nikki knew was, she wasn't a loser. She'd made up her mind. She wouldn't fail again. No way. She couldn't. Her soft, sexy sell was going to break through. It had to.

After quickly getting ready, she paid a fortune for an Uber that dropped her at the wrong place, forcing her to leg three blocks in shoes not built for footpaths, only to find, when she reached her destination, all steamed up and out of breath, a half-minute past the advertised time – she checked her watch – a queue stretching out the door and beyond. The producers were the ones running late. With no other option, she grudgingly found the end of the queue and lined up with the congregation.

Only one big difference between this lot and a flock of birds, she thought. *No safety in numbers here. This was war. Competition at its most ferocious.* Each beautifully made-up, artfully turned out, scantily attired model/actress in front of her wanted the same thing. To be 'the one' cast in the latest TV series of the hit reality show *Love Nest*. Each of these beauties was chasing a fast ticket to notoriety, a gigantic social media platform and the handsomely paid sponsorships that came with victory. She scanned ahead, searching for familiar faces, and seeing no-one she recognised, breathed a relieved sigh. She stood tall, feigning haughty confidence, trying desperately not to grimace because her feet (after all that running) squeezed into shoes too high and a half-size too small (the only pair remaindered at sale price) were throbbing.

'Excuse me.' A long-legged brunette, above-average height, appeared from nowhere. 'I was here first,' she said, taking a large stride to oust Nikki from her spot. 'I just went over there to the loo.' She waved her arm in the direction of the beach that was two blocks away.

'That's right you did, I saw you,' a shorter pink blonde standing two in front joined in to defend her taller competitor, for some reason. They didn't appear to know each other. Perhaps they were just testing allegiances for the show – if it came to that.

Nikki had heard about a skirmish that broke out at a different TV lifestyle audition. One contestant biffed another, the other swiped back and it was on. She'd heard that the producers had to pay to keep the incident out of the news. The last thing she needed was to find herself caught up in something like that. She was in enough trouble. Police from the Fraud Squad had paid her a visit last night, looking for Mark. As if she knew where he was. She'd told those officers that if she knew where he was, she would have beaten them to him. The words she'd used to describe him had raised the cops' eyebrows. And she hadn't even told them about her money. How he'd cleaned out her bank account. Left two dollars just to insult her, she believed. If she ever found him, she was going to put a two-dollar coin somewhere painful.

Her stomach turned. What an idiot she'd been to think it was love. Plain embarrassing now to acknowledge that she'd been 'had'. She was dealing with it – or rather she was trying to. Although lately, tears could pop into her eyes at strange and random times. He had stolen the money earmarked for her attempt at Hollywood. The money she had scrimped and saved for years. All gone.

'It's nothing,' she'd say, if anyone asked what was wrong. 'Same old PMT,' was an easy, acceptable excuse. She knew no-one really wanted to know any more than that. But deep down, Nikki sensed that if she couldn't pull herself together, or confide in someone soon, it might not end well.

'Fine,' she said, tottering backwards without making eye contact with her opponent. The taller one turned her back on Nikki and never looked in her direction again. But nor did she chat to her pink supporter, either.

Eventually, the assistant producer called out her name, instructing her to 'hand over her photo and details'. Nikki took a quick breath and stepped forward.

'Have you auditioned for us before?'

This was how it always went, she thought, staring back at the young woman who was not too discreetly giving her the once-over. They lure you into a false sense of security, enticing you to see this as a friendly process – a place where only good could happen. But Nikki knew this was a lie. Hearts got broken here.

'Of course I have, don't pretend you can't remember me,' was what she wanted to say. Instead, she gave her eye-wateringly lovely smile and said in a sexy-wispy voice, 'Yes, I have.'

'So, you know how it all works,' the assistant said matter-of-factly, persisting with the insincere notion that nothing bad could happen. Nikki smiled some more.

'This way, then. The producers will see you now.'

Nikki felt her heart lift and sucked in a breath. *This was it.* The young assistant, iPad pressed hard to her chest, marched off while Nikki trotted along behind, trying not to stumble in her ridiculous shoes. She needed this part.

Chapter 6

The duty officer called out as soon as she walked through the door. 'DI Griffiths is looking for you – the Moorhouse-Zamora matter from last night.'

Bec hung her bag on her hook and made her way over to the officer. 'Did he say when?' She wanted to begin the intelligence search on Carolyn before Jackson and Green beat her to it.

'Right now.'

*

'Senior Sergeant Harpin, morning.' DI Griffiths glanced pointedly at the clock on the wall of his office, which read 8.52 am.

Bec closed the door behind her. 'Morning, sir.'

'Take a seat.'

She sat down.

He remained on his feet, glancing into the distance – towards the window he was too far away from to appreciate the panoramic views overlooking the rail network and the docklands redevelopment. 'I'm going to cut to the chase, Rebecca. I'd like to know what the hell you were doing in Carolyn Moorhouse's Chambers last night before it was called in?'

'I responded to a call from Carolyn Moorhouse, sir. She asked me to come to her chambers.'

'I've read your statement. She asked you to travel late at night without giving any indication of what she wanted to see you about.'

'That's right, sir. I know it sounds odd in hindsight knowing now about the dead man, but that's what happened. A friend called and asked me to come. She gave me no other information. I had no reason to suspect anything other than a friend requesting my help.'

'Do you make a practice of going out at all hours to people's houses or offices just because they ring you up?'

'Not for just anyone, sir, no I don't.'

'But you went out last night, without knowing why your friend needed you?'

'I did. As I said, sir, Carolyn Moorhouse is a long-term colleague and friend. She called. I went. I was shocked when I saw the body, and when I immediately ascertained the man was dead, I called it in. Sir, I'd like to follow this one through.'

'Jacko and Green don't agree. They think you may be called as a witness.'

'With all due respect, sir, I don't see that my attendance at the scene alters my ability to investigate. If I had been on duty and got the call, my actions would have been identical.'

'That may be true, but how do I know your personal friendship with Moorhouse won't influence you?' He regarded her keenly.

'I freely admit that I have worked on cases with Carolyn Moorhouse over a number of years, sir, but I think that my track record—'

'You don't need to raise your track record, Rebecca. I'm only thinking about how this would look to the media.' He waved off her comment. 'Anyway, why do you think Ms Moorhouse, knowing she had a dead body on her floor, called you but didn't say anything about it?'

'Sir, I just don't know. It does seem strange not to call triple zero. It's entirely out of character. But if I were to speculate, my guess would be that we're friends and she panicked.'

Griffiths lowered his head, a look of scepticism on his face.

Bec carried on. 'I'd be happy to think she trusts me, sir, as I've had good reason over the years to trust her judgement. I could have been the first name that sprang to mind because I've worked quite a few cases with her, going back to uniform days. But the reason I drove in was because I thought she wouldn't be asking me to go without good reason.'

'And that was enough?' He was still watching her carefully.

'Yes, sir, it was.'

'I have to say, Rebecca, seems to me there's something on the nose about a barrister calling a friend and waiting three hours with a dead body on the floor in front of her. But apart from that, I'm not convinced the press would believe you could objectively handle this investigation, especially if your legal colleague has anything to hide.'

Bec could feel the situation slipping away. *So much for my blistering arguments.*

Griffiths sat down and began flipping through pages in a file on his desk. 'I have taken note of your psych report, Rebecca. Excellent – passed with flying colours – so I'm pleased that the counselling our people provided has worked to get you back on the job. And I see there is a recommendation for you to check in every few months. Is that right?'

'Yes, sir, that's their recommendation.' *Nothing more to say there.* She waited.

'Jacko outranks you, and he was the one to take down the official statements. Then there is the question over your impartiality, and, I might say, from my point of view, a question over your judgement in attending without question. So, Rebecca, my inclination is that Jacko should carry on running this.'

Her heart sank.

Disappointment stinging, Bec took the lift down, her mind filled with the questions she'd hoped to have answered had Griffiths allowed her to run the investigation. Why would a cleaner be rifling through files in Carolyn's office? Why would he attack Juan? Why wasn't he carrying any identification? Why the timing gaps? Why did Carolyn call her?

'You right to go, Sergeant Harpin?' the duty officer called out the minute Bec exited the lift.

'Right as rain,' she said, and walked towards him.

'The DI just told me Jacko has Moorhouse, but he told me I'm to give you whatever else I've got.'

'And what's that?' Bec said, irritated that her being passed over was already common knowledge. Wouldn't Jackson be loving that.

'An elderly woman reported dead in her Thornbury flat. Uniforms called it in as suspicious straightaway.'

'Suspicious?'

'She was tied up.'

'Who found her?'

'A neighbour. An elderly bloke rang up. Pretty upset, apparently.'

'Did anyone call the ambulance?'

'Yeah, he asked triple zero for both.'

'What about Crime Scene, have they been notified?'

'On their way.'

'Do we know when this happened?'

He read from the screen. 'Not yet. The old bloke told the attending officers that he gets up early every morning and says hello to her. Only this morning, her door was open and he could see she was lying on the floor. So, presumably, sometime last night.'

'Alright, do we have a name for the victim?'

'Doreen Madden. Address is unit two, one-three-seven Flinders Street, Thornbury. I'll text it to you.'

'And the bloke who called it in?'

'The caller's name is Reginald Cousins. Lives up the road. The scene has been secured and there are several uniforms waiting for you, alright?'

'Who's available?' Bec asked.

'Wendy and Shaun. That's all I can spare today.'

'Alright,' Bec said. 'Give them the details and tell them to meet me in the carpark.'

Chapter 7

A crowd of onlookers had already gathered outside. 'Over there.' Bec pointed to a vacant spot on the footpath, twenty metres along from the taped-off area where officers were patrolling and keeping people back.

She felt her energy rise, as it always did, when she started a new investigation. She wasn't looking forward to informing Carolyn of DI Griffiths' decision. Carolyn would not be happy having to deal with Jackson and Green, based on her attitude when she met them – cool and distant – as if they were adversaries she'd have to face off in court. But Carolyn was just going to have to deal with it, just as Bec was having to handle the ramifications of being called to a crime scene without warning.

Griffiths' comment that something was on the nose in Carolyn and Juan's story had hit a nerve, and Bec agreed. Whatever the truth was, she would get to the bottom of it. Bec had always believed that she and Carolyn would help each other out in any situation. But Carolyn had burned that bridge. Maybe not completely to the ground, only time would tell. But one thing she knew for sure, without trust, relationships dwindled and faded away. Bec didn't want to lose a friend. She hoped Carolyn didn't want that, either. *Things go wrong. Shit happens*, she thought. *Just tell me the truth.*

Bec's disappointment at being passed over for the Moorhouse case was lessening by the minute as she focused on the situation at hand.

'We'll need to speak to residents in the entire block,' she said, scanning the surrounds while waiting for her colleagues to catch up. 'Wendy can you and Shaun make sure that every unit has been door-knocked, and if there's no-one home leave a calling card and ask them to get in touch. It's hard to imagine that nobody saw anything in such a close set-up. Then we'll need to interview other residents in the street.'

'That'll take a while,' Shaun said, glancing along to other similar blocks of units lining both sides of the street.

'Hopefully, uniform has already started the process.'

'This would have been all single houses, once.' Wendy glanced up and down the street. 'It's changed since the last time I was in this area.'

'You know the area, Wendy, great. Let's make a start, shall we?' Bec clapped her hands.

'It was a long time ago, Sarge. Not sure it'll be much help.'

'Well, we can see. We have a dead woman waiting for us, so let's get in and see her,' Bec said, setting off towards the gathering up ahead of police and onlookers.

'Morning all,' said the officer standing by the tent surrounding the entrance to the scene.

'Senior Sergeant Rebecca Harpin, homicide.' Bec flashed her ID. 'And this is Constable Shaun Hanley and Senior Constable Wendy Santos.'

'Leading Constable Danny Waylen,' the officer responded. 'We have a woman deceased in the ground floor unit two, name of Doreen Madden. Pathology is already here, waiting to have a word.'

'Who is it, Avikesh Ahern?'

The officer looked blankly at her.

'Avi, red hair?' Bec prompted.

'I think that was the name for one of them, the male, and yeah his hair colour is ginger,' the constable said. 'Tan skin but ...'

Once most people met Avi, they never forgot the thickset pathologist. 'Avikesh Ahern's the name,' he would happily state to anyone who stared at his unusual hair-skin combination, 'Fijian-born with the soul of an Irishman.' *It would get very wearing*, Bec thought, *having to explain your gene pool to every person you met*. But unfortunately, that was the world we lived in. And luckily for Avi, he revelled in it.

'And the bloke who found her, where's he, Danny?'

'Over there,' he pointed in the direction of the units, 'Reginald Cousins … He's waiting on the chairs I set up outside number one. It's a bit quieter over there.' Bec could see that Constable Waylen had set up a small table and a few garden chairs, as if the occupants were expecting visitors for brunch.

'Alright, thanks. Tell him I'll speak to him in a minute. What did he tell you?'

'Doreen was a lovely woman, according to Reginald,' the officer said. 'He met her down at the local club a year or so ago. They used to share a drink sometimes and play the pokies. He lives just down the street,' the officer pointed again, 'said g'day to her on his walk every morning, and some days – usually Tuesdays – he'd go around to Doreen's place for a cuppa and a biscuit. This morning, when he knocked on her door, he found it half-open, and when she still didn't answer, he went in. There she was, he said, lying on the floor – tied up and dead. He's pretty upset.'

'And what time was that?'

'Just before eight,' he said.

'Alright, I might go and have a chat to him now. Shaun, you make a start on the doors, see if anyone heard or saw anything suspicious last night or this morning. Wendy, start across the road. I'll talk to Crime Scene, then I'll have a word to Reginald. Back here in forty-five, okay?'

'You lot took your time getting here, Senior Sergeant,' the pathologist said, struggling to his feet from a crouching position. 'I've got a lunch,' he announced once he was upright.

'Morning to you, too, Avi. Crime doesn't fit our diary appointments, you should know that by now,' Bec said. 'Another hot date, was it?' She smiled. It was always the same with him. She scrunched her way around the living room in plastic-covered shoes, glancing at shelves and noticing that there were no family photos on Doreen's mantelpiece. She slipped on nitrate gloves and opened a few drawers that at first glance contained nothing but the usual stuff. She would have a closer look later.

'If it was, Rebecca my dear, it will definitely have cooled off by the time I get this done,' he grouched.

Bec liked Avi. He was hard working and thorough, even if he complained that women never wanted to date him again once they learned of his profession. 'It puts them off,' he said once, throwing his arms in the air. 'What can I do? I'm nearly fifty years old. I'm quite a catch, even if I do say so myself.' Bec had laughed, but Avi was right. His job was unusual, dealing with dead bodies all day, but there was nothing scary about him. 'Don't worry, the right one will show up one day,' she'd said sympathetically, while thinking someone could just as easily be giving her the same advice. Blokes who wanted to hang out with a female homicide cop were as thin on the ground as women wanting to date a criminal pathologist, obviously.

Glancing down at the body, she said, 'How long has she been dead?'

'About fifteen hours, I'd say.'

'Got any initial thoughts on what happened? Did the rope strangle her?'

'You know not to hold me to this, but on first impression, I think this poor old love might have had a heart attack. No sign of physical trauma to cause it, plus there's an asthma puffer over on the kitchen table, so that could also have something to do with it. There are gag marks. And as you can see, she was tied up.' He pointed to Doreen's feet, and Bec could see that her hands were still tied. 'It's just possible, you know,' he paused, 'that she died of fright. I mean, tying up an old woman, she would have been terrified … I'll let you know more when I get her back to the office.'

Bec looked away, her imagination running, causing her to push down a rising nausea.

'Okay, Avi, if that's it, I'll let you get on with it.'

'Still no stomach for my profession, Senior Sergeant?' Avi said, regarding her with undisguised amusement.

'Something like that,' Bec said. 'Just let me know when you've got the results we need.'

'I'll get them to you as soon as I can.' He sighed. 'Looks like no lunch again for Avi.'

'Beats a weight-loss program,' Bec said.

'Are you calling me overweight?' She heard the pathologist laugh as she was leaving.

*

Strolling towards the man who stubbed his cigarette on the ground the moment he saw her approach, Bec took in the light-brown jumper, trousers riding up to reveal white socks and slip-on shoes, and hair plastered down in a comb-over. He looked old and dressed old. *Maybe late sixties.*

'Mr Cousins?' she said, smiling and extending her hand.

'Yeah, that's me.' The man struggled to his feet.

'I'm Detective Senior Sergeant Harpin, Rebecca,' she said, 'from homicide. I believe you found Doreen Madden's body?'

'Unfortunately. She wouldn't hurt a fly, Doreen. I dunno who'd want to harm a really nice lady like her. I told the others all I know,' he said, gesturing in the direction of the uniforms who were out of sight, but who could be heard calling out 'stand back' to what must have been a burgeoning crowd curious to know what was causing the disturbance and blocking the street.

'I am sorry to make you repeat yourself, Mr Cousins, but would you mind telling me as well, please,' she said, indicating for him to sit.

'You can call me Reg,' he said, nodding as he sat down again.

'Alright, thanks, Reg.' Bec sat opposite. 'I appreciate that. Can you tell me what happened?'

'It's awful,' he said.

'Take your time,' she said, speaking calmly, 'and at some stage, I'll get you to come down to the station to make a formal statement. Nothing to worry about, just procedure. Are you okay with that?'

'Yeah,' he said, 'that's okay.'

'But for now, just tell me in your own words what happened this morning.'

Reg regurgitated the story of his friendship with Doreen. How he'd just popped in on the way home from his morning walk. 'You know, every Tuesday I drop in for a cuppa, a biscuit and a chat.' And how when he arrived this time, he found the door slightly open. 'Unusual for Doreen,' he said. He called out, and when there was no answer, he went in. 'And that's where I found her.'

'Lying on the floor?'

'Yeah, she was. All tied up. Who would do that to a lovely woman like Doreen? I mean, it's not like she had any money. Apart from a few, we're mostly all pensioners round here.' He grabbed his hanky and pushed it to his eyes. Bec put her hand on his arm and let him cry.

*

Bec waved to Shaun and Wendy, who were making their way down the stairs, and went over to them.

'Anything?'

'Not yet. Most aren't home,' Shaun said. 'And those we did talk to saw nothing and heard less. There are a couple of cameras, but they could be dummies. We'll check with the owners' corporation for their security footage if there is any.'

'We left our details for the others and we'll follow up if we don't hear,' Wendy said. 'But those we did chat to said she was a nice old biddy. No-one knew why she'd be targeted. They're all pretty shaken up.'

'It's going to take a while to cover this,' Shaun said. 'More feet on the ground, I reckon.'

'I'll see to it that uniform carry on with door knocking,' Bec said, not wanting to be asking for overtime or more officers at this early stage of the investigation. 'Could you walk Reg home? He's upset,' she said, gesturing to Doreen's friend. 'See if you can get a bit more about himself out of him. And what he knows about Doreen and her next of kin. He's agreed to give a formal statement, and we'll do that tomorrow. Come back here and pick me up when you're done. I'm going to have a bit more of a look around here.'

'Righto,' Shaun said.

'Do you have someone to make you a cup of tea, Reg?' Bec heard Wendy asking as they corralled Reginald Cousins towards the house he'd pointed to as his. Not really homicide's job to be chaperoning witnesses, but you never knew when someone would let go of some important fact. And in this, a little bit of kindness went a long way.

*

'This is me,' Reg said. 'Number four, home for the past forty-four years.'

'Righto,' Shaun said, studying the block of white brick units that had a red-tiled roof, square windows, typical of the 1950s period. He wanted to be back at the scene, not playing nursemaid to some old codger who was guilty of only one thing – unfortunate timing to have stumbled upon the body. *Errands like this are uniform jobs*, he thought, piqued. 'You right to see Reg to the door,' he said to Wendy, who was looking around, surveying the street. 'I'll see if there are any cameras in any of these places.'

Wendy shot him a look. He was pushing his luck and they both knew it. She was the senior officer. Shaun might be coming up for the training course to equal her rank, but he wasn't there yet.

'You two seem to be getting along nicely, isn't that right, Reg?' Shaun twisted around to see that Reg was already getting his house keys out of his pocket.

'Off you go, then.' He tapped Wendy on the shoulder and winked.

'Cut it out, Shaun,' she said, and pulled her arm away.

He watched his colleague – who was short, Asian and female – walk through the gate and up the path, shepherding Reg as if he were a child. He waited for Reg to fumble with the key and open the door. Then, Wendy walked in right behind the man and disappeared into the house.

Ten minutes later, Wendy came out of the house and closed the door.

'Your loss,' she said cheerfully. 'Lesson one, empathy and patience. Then you would have heard what Reg just told me.'

*

Shaun struggled to keep his jaw unlocked as Wendy replayed her conversation with Reg to Bec.

'Shaun kindly let me go in alone, and as soon as I boiled the kettle, Reg was ready to talk.' Wendy glanced at her colleague and continued. 'Reg said Doreen had a son she was devoted to, Kenny.'

'Well, that's interesting. No photos of a son I could see in the flat. Has anyone else you've spoken to mentioned a son for Doreen?'

'No, and he said he didn't know for a long time, either. He thought Doreen was all dressed up to go on a date at the same time every week. It was only one day when seeing her all done up and heading for the tram stop again that he jokingly asked her that question, which prompted her to confide in him that she was going to see her son, Kenny, who was, get this, in the slammer but due out any day.'

'And when was that?'

'Roughly six months ago.'

'And he's out now?'

'Yes. According to Reg, Doreen was very happy about it.'

'Does he know where this Kenny lives? Did he ever meet him?' Bec asked.

'No, on both counts. Doreen mentioned that she said he could move in with her, but he found a place of his own,' Wendy said.

'It's a bit odd, don't you think, if he was dropping in on Doreen once a week, that Reg didn't meet him?'

'Maybe her son didn't drop in much given no-one else has mentioned him.'

'Let's find what we can about Kenny Madden. If he's done time, shouldn't be too hard,' Bec said. 'Good work, Wendy. Okay, if you two keep going here for a bit, I'll get back and make a start on the background. You know what you have to do.'

Chapter 8

Someone was knocking on her door. *Go away*, Nikki thought and rolled over. She pulled the pillow over her head. But the constant *tap-tapping* kept on, until she leaped out of bed and tiptoed to the door. She was just in time to hear a male voice she didn't recognise say, 'Leave a card.' Then, the scraping sound as a small white card appeared at her feet. The footsteps moved away. She bent to retrieve the card and her heart skipped; police, a phone number and a request for her to call them. Wide awake now, her hands started to shake. And from somewhere outside, the sound of muffled voices talking. She pressed her ear to the door and heard her neighbour, say, 'Yes?' And the same male voice telling her about what had happened in unit one. Nikki held her breath in disbelief as she listened.

'Unfortunately, she was found dead this morning by a friend. We are looking for information. Did you notice anything out of the ordinary yesterday or this morning, Mrs …?'

'Chambers, Ivy Chambers. That's terrible, poor Doreen, dead,' she heard her neighbour say, all concerned.

'Did you know Doreen?' a female voice wanted to know.

'I did, just casually you know, but enough to … She did say once that she suffered high blood pressure – you know, older people talk a lot about their health, don't they? Did that kill her? Did poor Doreen have a stroke?'

'Unfortunately, Ivy, we're not in a position yet to give you the exact cause of death, but we are treating her death as suspicious. Hence our door knocking to try to find more information. Were you home last night?'

'I'm home every night, dear. I did the food shopping in the afternoon like normal, then back here.'

'And you didn't go out again?'

'Not at night, dear. It's a long time since I last did that.'

'And you didn't hear anything at all?'

'I'm afraid not. When *Dancing with the Stars* is on – I watch the quiz shows first, then my dancing show – I have it up loud to hear all the funny comments from the judges, then straight off to bed to read a little romance.' She paused. 'But you might ask my neighbour, across the way, Bianca. She seemed quite friendly with Doreen. She's an actor, you know.'

'Thanks, I'll make a note of that.'

Nikki grimaced, imagining the police officer scribbling something down. She'd played a police officer once and knew the routine.

'We tried, but there's no-one home,' the male voice said.

'That's unusual, she's normally not an early riser that one,' Nikki's neighbour said, as if talking to herself, 'unless she has a "gig" – I think that's what she calls it. If she's not answering, it means she must have a job,' she confirmed. 'She's a nice type of girl. Been in *Home Away from Home* you know,' Ivy said it like it was a character reference.

'That's interesting,' the male officer said, 'do you know Bianca's surname?'

'Oh, goodness me, I'm sorry, it's not Bianca. I was thinking about the last character she played on TV. I knew it was her, of course. She was really good. Her real name is Nikki, Nikki Cardone.'

'You live here alone, Ivy?' the female officer took over.

'Since my husband left a long time ago.'

Nikki imagined Ivy dabbing at her eyes the way she always did at the slightest mention of her husband.

They talked some more, but Nikki couldn't concentrate after hearing the words 'suspicious circumstances.'

Then, as footsteps moved away, she collapsed against the door and started sobbing.

Chapter 9

Bec was already heading back to the city when her phone rang.

'Detective Sergeant Harpin, it's Diana.' DI Griffiths' assistant spoke in her usual calm way.

'Hello, Diana.'

'Can you leave what you're doing and come here right away?'

'I'm in the car heading back now. What is it?'

'The DI would like to see you, so come straight on up. You won't have heard it on the news yet, but there's been a shocking domestic – multiple murder and suicide.'

'Okay, shouldn't be long.'

*

Assuming the incident Diana mentioned would mean her being part of the team to handle this new crime, Bec made a quick decision. If she had to be caught in a line of traffic so slow she could have walked faster with a broken toe, she ought to use the time to call Carolyn about her case. Carolyn would be upset, but for Bec, breaking bad news was a huge part of this job. And she could mostly find the right words to say – apart from the child-abduction case a few years back, where a little girl was found dead and abandoned in scrubland and contacting the family had been so hard that Bec had struggled to contain her emotions.

She had Carolyn's number on speed dial. She used that now and waited.

Carolyn responded after two beats of dial tone. 'What's going on, Rebecca? I've been trying to reach you.' Again, she sounded cross. 'I've been left dangling and Juan is completely distraught, in custody. You said you would—'

'Carolyn,' Bec cut in. 'I'm returning your call to see firstly if you've remembered anything else that might help with the investigation.'

'I have not. And I'm the one looking for answers here. How long does Juan have to stay locked up, for God's sake?'

'I don't know, and even if I did, I couldn't give you that information. At best, you are a material witness, Caro, you know that.' Bec found it hard to grasp how their relationship had slumped to this – Carolyn finding it hard to be civil.

The sheer number of missed calls to Bec's phone from the barrister had caused Bec to wonder again about her friend's mental state.

'You know how these things go,' Bec repeated.

'What on earth am I supposed to do, Rebecca? Nothing like this has ever happened to me before.'

Bec softened her tone. 'And that's the other reason I'm calling, to tell you that the investigation will be handled by two of my colleagues, Glen Jackson and Les Green.'

There was a pause.

'You can't be serious.'

'I am serious. The DI sees my presence at the scene before it was called in as compromising, and he wasn't comfortable with one of his officers investigating a friend. I shouldn't have been at the scene before it was called in, Caro, and that's it.'

'You mean you're leaving me to deal with those boofheads.'

'Not my choice, Caro, so cut it out. And by the way, Jacko and Green are fine detectives. I'd be happy to have officers of their calibre investigating on my behalf.' Bec heard herself praising the two men and wondered if that was in fact her position. She decided that it was. Annoying as they both were, each ranked highly when it came to solving crime.

'So, you'll not be involved at all?' Carolyn repeated disbelievingly.

'No further involvement, do you mean?' Bec said pointedly and heard Carolyn mutter something indecipherable. 'My suggestion is that you wait for the coroner's findings and take it from there, Carolyn.'

'Is that it? Is that what you're offering, just sit and wait?'

'It is. Until you hear from the investigating officers.'

Bec heard a long outbreath of air. 'Alright, alright,' Carolyn conceded.

'But as a friend, Carolyn, I need us to talk about this privately, for the sake of our friendship.' And when Carolyn said nothing, Bec added, 'I must get back now. Are you okay?'

'Not really.'

'I'll be in touch,' Bec said, and ended the call.

Something was seriously wrong. Carolyn and Bec had always spoken about cases, even if they shouldn't have. So, if this was something professional, Carolyn should be able to talk to her like they always had. And if it wasn't professional but private, which Bec now thought it had to be, it should have been even easier. Her stomach churned. One minute she had a good friend in her life, and the next, Carolyn felt like someone she barely knew. A witness who wasn't telling her the truth.

Chapter 10

By the time she was back in the building, Bec had caught the first news flash on her car radio about the three children, the wife and the shooter. Police work didn't make hearing about crimes like this any easier. She got straight in the lift and rode up. Diana turned away from her screen long enough to wave Bec straight in.

'Rebecca, you made good time.' DI Griffiths glanced pointedly at the clock. He wasn't wearing a jacket and his sleeves were rolled up.

Bec closed the door behind her.

'Take a seat.'

'Thank you, sir.'

He paused. 'You've no doubt heard about the incident in Sunshine – family of five.'

'Just now, only the headlines, though, sir.'

'Tough economic times, it's families that pay the price,' Griffiths said seriously, going on to share some more details.

A family tragedy where not a single member had survived meant more than just financial trouble, Bec thought, gathering her questions in anticipation of her next assignment. She was expecting to hear more about this from the DI, but instead of elaborating further, Griffiths just shook his head and changed the subject. 'How's it going in Thornbury?'

'We're underway, sir, checking locals, gathering as much detail as we can till we get forensics back.'

'Summary?' he asked.

'Older woman Doreen Madden, lived alone, found dead and tied up in her own flat, sir, found by a friend. No sign of forced entry. Place wasn't ransacked. She may have died of fright, according to the pathologist. We'll know more when they come back with an exact cause of death.'

'Anyone obvious in the way of a suspect?'

'No, sir, not yet. Son recently released from jail. Trying to locate him to see if he knows anything.'

She prepared herself. Her summary seemed to cause him concern, from the frown on his face. And in a second of panic, she knew that he was about to relieve her of the Madden case, too.

The DI sat down and appeared to be weighing his thoughts. Finally, he said, 'It's not my style to retract decisions without good reason, Rebecca.' He was tapping the fingers of his right hand onto the wrist of his left. Bec steeled herself for the blow. 'But with the complications I'm expecting to arise from the murder-suicide operation that's happening now, I've decided to alter course on who will handle the Moorhouse investigation.'

Bec sat perfectly still, her heart beating faster.

'Due to the nature of the crime at the shooting today, Jacko and Green will be better suited to handle that with their team, which leaves me short-handed elsewhere. So, unless you have any objection, I'm going to assign Moorhouse to you … and your fledgling team.'

'Sir.'

He looked directly at her. 'Against my better judgement, I'm prepared to let it run to see how you go. We are in a tight situation. Not enough experience on the ground.' And before Bec could say anything more, he added, 'But you'd have to manage Thornbury as, well. Can you do that?'

Without hesitation, she said, 'Yes, sir, I can.'

A pause hung in the air.

Bec saw a hint of amusement on his face. What, he thought her response was funny? Thought she was too keen and would likely fall on her face?

'That's good. Very good. I like your attitude, DS Harpin.' He nodded, watching her carefully. 'The Bar Association is driving me mad. When something happens on their turf, it's all rush and priorities.'

Bec said nothing.

'So, despite your friendship with Carolyn Moorhouse,' he said pointedly, 'I'm handing this investigation over to you.' For a split second, his eyes held hers.

'Thank you, sir.' Bec thought Griffiths might be dealing with heat from above himself. He wasn't quite as contained as he'd been earlier, and it was amazing the difference wearing no jacket made. He looked almost human.

'Having said that, if at any time you need to talk something through, do not hesitate. And it may be that sometime you need extra assistance. Again, I can only repeat, do not hesitate to reach out and I'll see what we can do. But we are going to be stretched for the next little while.'

'Yes, thank you, sir.'

'Don't thank me yet, Rebecca. I'm just giving you enough rope. It's up to you whether you hang yourself.'

'I'll certainly try not to do that.' He could be simply looking for a patsy, someone to blame if things didn't go well. She, as the newcomer on a temporary contract, would be just the ticket. She hoped that wasn't why the DI was handing the investigation to her. But she would be watching how things went down.

Griffiths was scribbling notes as Bec closed the door behind her. She took the lift to her floor, and with his words turning in her head, she thought, *Someone might hang themselves by the end of this, but if I can help it, it isn't going to be me.*

Chapter 11

They climbed the stairs to the unit once more, foot sore and tired of asking questions and not getting much back in the way of juice to report.

'So, you watch much TV, do you?' Wendy said, slightly out of breath as she took the last step.

'Who doesn't?' Shaun said distractedly, eyes already focused on the doorway five along. This was their third attempt to catch this resident at home.

'I don't,' Wendy said, expecting Shaun to ask for some explanation. But when he didn't, she walked silently on until they were only a few paces away from their destination.

'Go on, then,' she whispered, 'what are you waiting for? You're the one panting to talk to her.'

After taking down Reg's statement, who had also referred to the same actress Mrs Chambers mentioned – Nikki Cardone – the one who used to visit Doreen, Shaun had pulled out his phone and looked her up. 'There she is,' he said with a smile, turning his phone around to show Wendy. 'Might be all make up and lights of course, but she does look pretty dishy to me.'

'It's just as well I'm here, or you mightn't hear a word Miss Dishy says,' Wendy said, nudging him forward. 'Are you blushing? I don't believe it. You haven't even laid eyes on her yet. Come on, let's find out how accurate that photo is.'

'Alright, alright, here goes.'

Raising his knuckles, Shaun gave three mandatory knocks on the door. Silence. He knocked again. Not a sound. He and Wendy exchanged glances. Wendy shrugged, flipped out a card and wrote on it. She was leaning down to slide it under, when the door cracked open.

'We're looking for Nikki Cardone,' Shaun said to the woman peering out at them – long tangles of blonde hair, eyes swollen, black eye makeup smudged around her eyes giving an appearance that resembled more owl than woman. 'This is Detective Senior Constable Wendy Santos, and I'm Detective Constable Shaun Hanley.' He held up his ID. 'If you have a moment, Ms Cardone, we'd like to have a word with you.'

'I can't talk to you now.' The crack edged towards closed.

'It won't take long,' Wendy said, fully upright again. 'It's about your neighbour Doreen downstairs. We believe you were friendly with her?'

'Doreen? No. A cup of tea sometimes, that's all. She was more of an acquaintance.' Her voice was soft and husky.

'Are you aware, Ms Cardone, that your friend Doreen has died?'

'Ivy next door told me.'

'We believe there are suspicious circumstances involved in her death. That's what we're investigating.'

'I don't know anything.' Her voice grew louder.

'We would just like to talk to you. You may not realise that you saw or heard something important. May we come in?' Shaun said.

'Otherwise, we'll keep coming back until you speak to us.' Wendy ramped up the pressure.

Pause. 'Give me a minute.' The door clicked shut.

Shaun and Wendy exchanged glances again.

'Flushing drugs?' Wendy whispered.

Shaun shook his head.

Some minutes later, the door reopened and Nikki Cardone, in tight jeans, white T-shirt, bare feet and scrubbed eyes, was inviting them in. 'Sorry, I just had to tidy myself.' She brushed her hand past her eyes. 'And like I said, I really don't know anything,' she added, padding away from them towards a small table with four chairs.

'Come through.' She gestured as if it were a grand apartment when the only other furniture was a comfortable couch in front of a huge television screen.

'Thank you. May we call you Nikki?' Wendy asked, placing her phone and pad on the table.

The woman shrugged like she could care less.

Her face was puffy as if she'd been crying a lot, but there was no denying her credentials for glamour roles in TV soaps. In the flesh, she was as beautiful as the publicity photo Shaun had pulled up – even if she looked a bit worse for wear right now.

Shaun sat awkwardly. 'We are detailing the movements of all residents in this block of units on the night Mrs Madden died. It would be helpful if you could tell us where you were the night before last, Nikki.'

'Me?' Nikki pushed her hair so it was tumbling around her shoulders away from her face, and stared at him – forcing him into silence.

'Yes,' Wendy intervened, 'sorry, it's a simple question we have to ask everyone in the units.'

Nikki glanced back at Shaun. 'To be honest, Detective, the night before last, I was here in bed feeling very sorry for myself. You see, my agent had just rung to tell me that I didn't get a part I was counting on. Being a jobbing actor has its ups and downs, you know. Not often there's a regular pay cheque,' she added, eyes moist. 'Can make it very difficult sometimes, if you know what that feels like.'

'I see, and can anyone verify that you were here alone?' Shaun persisted.

'Of course. I didn't get a part I really needed, so I threw a party for a few hundred friends … I was in bed, upset, and to be clear, yes, I was alone. And no, I didn't see or hear anything.' She pushed her chin forward.

'How well did you know Doreen, Nikki?'

'Not very. She was nice to have a chat with sometimes, that's all.'

'Nothing you can tell us about her, or who might have wanted to harm her?'

'No. If I knew that …' She left the sentence unfinished, directing all her attention to Shaun.

'Doreen had a son called Kenny, did you know him, too?'

'Nooo, I don't think so.' She seemed to consider the name.

'It's just we've heard from a few sources that Doreen's son visited her quite often. And since her death, this Kenny hasn't been sighted. We'd like to speak to him, that's all. Even if it is just to tell him about his mother.'

'He'll be devastated,' Nikki exclaimed. 'I mean, any son would be, wouldn't they …? I guess. Sorry, can't help you.'

Wendy shot a look at Shaun, who was mesmerised by the woman. 'So, if I asked if you'd noticed any strangers hanging about the place lately, your answer would be …'

'No,' the actress said.

'Is there anything at all you can think of that might help our investigation, Nikki?'

'No,' she said again, shaking her head.

'Nothing Doreen said in any of your chats over a cup of tea?'

'No, that was all about the weather and the cost of things.'

'Right, well, if you think of anything, you will call us?' Shaun placed his card on the table.

'Of course.' Nikki batted her eyes at him.

'Thanks for your time, Ms Cardone.' Wendy got to her feet. 'If there is anything you do remember, please get in touch.'

Once they were out of earshot, Wendy, mimicking Nikki, turned to Shaun, batting her eyes. 'Yes, Detective, of course I will.'

'She gave us what she had,' Shaun said defensively.

'Is that so, Shaun. Well, I don't happen to agree with you. If you'd been paying attention, it was clear she knew Kenny. And when I asked about her having cups of tea with Doreen, she didn't deny it. She's hiding something, if you ask me.'

Chapter 12

As pleased as Bec was to get the Moorhouse case back, it certainly forced her brain into a heightened state. She'd told Carolyn that she wasn't handling the case and had been shocked at the distance she'd heard in her friend's voice. Now, she wondered how Carolyn would react to this turn of events. 'Fearless, steady and consistent,' were the words Bec would have always used to describe the star barrister. She'd witnessed Carolyn in harrowing court scenes where she hadn't flinched, holding the line of argument in the most hostile of onslaughts and laughing about it afterwards.

'It's all a bit of theatre, Bec,' she'd said.

But the Carolyn she was dealing with now was not that person. Bec wasn't sure she even knew who her friend was anymore.

A red light flashing on her internal phone delivered a message from Jackson. *Hey, Harpin, good luck trying to keep your friend and her amigo out of jail ... dodgy as ... that one!* Jackson's humour was hard to take sometimes.

She pushed 'delete' and called Records to request the Moorhouse file be delivered to her. *Why were her male colleagues always so damn competitive?* she thought for a moment then smiled. They would say the same about her, and they would be right. She was equally competitive. This was the work she loved. And an investigator who didn't care about results – in her view – should look for another job.

Jabbing at the keys on her computer, Bec brought up the list of resident interviews and read through what they'd managed to gather so far in Thornbury. Not much to go on there. She'd already trawled online to search for the name Kenny Madden amongst the most recent prison releases. The system had thrown up nine individuals called Kenny, but as soon as she added the Madden surname, she drew a blank. Carefully, she'd worked her way through more than a dozen name-alike individuals on social media, hoping to find an image or some profile for Kenny Madden. If Doreen was in her seventies, then her son had to be over forty, maybe fifty if she'd been a young mother, so Bec discarded the profiles that didn't match the age range.

With all the other teams on the murder-suicide, there wasn't much activity today in the surrounding offices, and with Wendy and Shaun still in Thornbury interviewing residents, Bec took a moment. Seated quietly at her desk, she realised it would be no easy task to deliver results for these two investigations – especially with only three of them on the team. If she allowed her mind to run through the mountain of tasks that lay ahead, it could overwhelm her, so she went to the mantra that accompanied her on morning runs. Comforting as a cup of hot chocolate. Not only because it sounded simple, but because it was doable; all about the right parameters. *Get stuck in, one step at a time.* The job might not be quite as straightforward as that in certain situations, but as a general approach it'd delivered outcomes for her so far, and that's what policing was all about – results.

*

She dialled Wendy's number and without any niceties said, 'How's it going?'

'Doing our best here, Sarge, not having any luck. Think we'll pack it in out here for today.' She sounded flat.

Bec's first take on her younger colleague was of an officer who rode the swings and roundabouts of investigations hard. Bec understood. She'd had to learn long ago that self-control was critical to the job, and she'd trained herself to resist the high highs and the low lows, just like running the bush tracks. Self-control was also something she worked on in her head every single day. You never knew when this kind of extra preparation would come to the fore – learning to keep your brain clear under pressure, not letting emotion take over. Not even in tough circumstances, like having to investigate a friend.

'That's alright, I'm calling because I need you to come back in for a briefing anyway. The DI has handed us the Moorhouse dead cleaner investigation. We need to get up to speed fast.'

'Shaun, too?'

'Yes. That's the entire team, I'm afraid.'

'Okay, I'll see if I can drag him away from Miss *Home Away from Home*.'

'Who?'

'The TV star. The blonde bombshell who lives in one of the units upstairs – I'll fill you in. We finally caught her at home. We're on our way.'

'Okay, how about our witness, Reg. Did you get his formal statement?'

'We did. Nothing new there.'

'And followed up the security footage?'

'I contacted the Body Corporate. Those cameras are fully operational and they agreed to send footage. Should come through any time.'

'Good. We can check who was hanging around the place beforehand. Might even get a little snapshot of Doreen's killer. You never know.'

'Be nice, wouldn't it?' Wendy laughed. 'Wow, the Moorhouse case, as well. What happened? That shocking domestic clear the others out?'

'Something like that. I just need you two back here as soon as you can, alright?'

'At the car now.'

Bec put the phone down and sat staring at her computer screen. Of the twelve Kennys released from prison in the last two years, none of them fitted her guy. Her head was aching. And she realised she hadn't eaten, which made her think about Josh, her ex. He used to chase her about eating regularly and not skipping meals, as she was prone to do. She took a long draught from her water bottle. Water was an appetite suppressant, just the same as coffee was.

'Sometimes, I think you fancy my chicken soup more than me,' he used to joke. *Right now*, she thought, *he might be right*. Bec had ended things with Josh, and since then the numerous messages he'd left on her phone pleading for forgiveness and understanding saying things like, *It wasn't what you think* and *Please, Bec, you're the one I care about* had left her cold. He'd always stopped short of using the 'love' word when they'd been seeing each other – thank goodness, or she would have known for sure that he was full of shit. And until recently, she'd managed to park him to one side. But the uncomfortable truth was, she had missed his company. There'd been nothing casual about their relationship. She'd been kidding herself on that score. Still, having no romantic partner hadn't harmed her professional life, as far as she could tell, although the shrinks might not agree.

She changed her line of thought. Food was what she needed now, not wallowing in some soft-sell romance. Food and more information: the security footage from around Doreen's building, fingerprints to ID, the body in Carolyn's chambers. Something. Impatience rose in her chest like an ocean swell. *Calm yourself*, she counselled, and breathed out. *Head down, bum up*, she heard her old partner, Theo, say, whenever an investigation stalled. *Go over everything again, revisit the scene –* which was exactly what she was about to do. Not without food, though.

She grabbed her notebook, tucked her phone into her pocket and headed for the canteen.

Chapter 13

'Breaking news?' Wendy said, standing in Bec's office after a slow drive back.

'What happened for the change of heart upstairs?' Shaun asked. 'Weren't Jacko and Green running that case?'

'The murder-suicide got priority,' Bec said casually. Naturally, her colleagues were curious to know why an investigation had been lifted from one team and handed to another. She was experienced enough to know that her being unofficially at the scene of Barwick Chambers would be office gossip. And she was completely sure that the DI would never have changed his mind if he hadn't been short of feet on the ground elsewhere. Jackson and his team were more senior to handle the domestic shooting, but in the end, the reasons Griffiths gave her for his change of heart didn't actually matter. It was theirs to run now, which was why she'd brought Wendy and Shaun back from Thornbury, to work out their plan of attack.

'My view, Sarge, the DI gave it to us because we're really good.' Wendy laughed.

Shaun grinned. 'Yeah, why didn't I think of that?'

Bec smiled too. 'Before we set to work on Moorhouse,' she said, sitting on the edge of her desk, 'can we just check a few things about Doreen's investigation.'

'Like what?' Shaun asked.

'Well, there's no-one on the prison system database called Kenny Madden who fits our profile, for starters. Are you certain that was the name your witness gave, Wendy?'

'Yes, definitely,' Wendy said, surprised and slightly flustered by the question. 'I'll check my notes and sound-alike names.'

'Okay, in a minute. I've tried all of them. It's unusual not to find anything when the bloke's been inside.'

'Fingerprint results would make our job easier,' Wendy responded.

'Okay, so nothing new today?' Bec said, pleased that she'd risen above the sort of door-to-door yakka that went on at the start of an investigation. It was gruelling, and boring sometimes. Yet, good face-to-face work was critical. It required good instincts and acute attention to detail. Bec knew that the team's small observances on visits like these turned into helpful clues that helped end an investigation. And she understood the frustration, too, when there wasn't enough to go on. Sometimes, it did feel like wheel spinning, the engine was running, you were ready for action, but no clear destination in sight.

'A few residents reported seeing a man leaving Doreen's unit from time to time over the last few months. Not very tall, slim, not young, not old, always wearing a hat, no useful description,' Shaun said, scratching his head.

'The son?'

'Could be.'

'Well, doing a disappearing act is certainly putting him in the frame for this,' Bec said.

'Her own son? Tying her up and leaving her? Lord, I hope not.'

Wendy could be overly dramatic sometimes, Bec thought. 'Nearest and dearest are always high on the list, Senior Constable. Even the TV coppers know that,' she added, and the three of them laughed. Not because it was funny, but because it was true.

'True enough, Sarge.'

'Anyway, pathology shouldn't be much longer. They're under the pump.'

'What, and we're not?' Wendy shot back.

'Point taken. But we have to deal with it.'

'Actually, hang on a minute.' Wendy was leafing through her notebook. 'Thinking about what you said just now, I hope Reg said the son's name was Kenny Madden. He said Kenny for sure. But I might have added the Madden. Not sure now.' Bec heard Wendy's embarrassment at this possible error.

'That'd be an easy mistake to make,' Bec said without conviction. 'Need to pay attention to these things, Wendy. Check Reg's statement and we'll see what the prints give us.'

Wendy's face gave her away. The mildest censure did not sit well with her. She didn't like making mistakes. Bec understood. She didn't either. And for this reason alone, she thought Wendy had the makings of a first-rate investigator. Mistakes could mean clues missed or even lives lost in this job, a fact the senior constable appeared to fully comprehend.

Bec got to her feet and moved over to the whiteboard. 'Let's get this down and see what it looks like.' She surveyed the blank space, then grabbed the marker and drew a line down the middle to form two columns.

'So, Case One, Doreen Madden found in her unit early Friday died possibly of a heart attack or an asthma attack brought on by the stress of being tied up. We'll have to wait on the pathology to know more. Evidence says Doreen had a son, Kenny, who has made himself scarce.' Bec scribbled their names. 'We heard from a witness who knew the deceased that the son had just got out of jail and didn't live with his mother. We need to check Births, Deaths and Marriages, employment records, tax office and so on for Doreen. A woman of her age probably wouldn't have been too active on social media, but you never know. Check those things, too. As far as the son is concerned, we can't find any record of a Kenny Madden or otherwise in the prison system that matches our profile.'

'And no clue as to a motive,' Shaun said.

'That's right, no-one has given us any reason for Doreen to be targeted or if her death was intentional. With no clear motive and the son missing, we must consider it may have been something domestic that got out of hand. But we have a mountain of people still to interview, residents from the block of units and neighbours from the surrounding area who may have seen something. And, of course, Kenny might just show up with a strong alibi, but with no DNA for a few days yet, our priority is to do the interviews and find the son.'

'Easier said than done,' Shaun said. 'What age would the son be?'

'He'd have to be what, late forties, early fifties?' Wendy said.

'That was my assumption, too.' Bec wrote the age ranges of mother and son on the board.

'Then there's that actor upstairs, who says she didn't know Doreen or her son, but I think she knows more than she's letting on.' Wendy directed her comment to Bec.

'Maybe you don't like her, that's all,' Shaun responded.

'Alright, Wendy, that's yours to follow up. Go with your gut,' Bec said firmly. 'If you could take care of institutional searches, Shaun, I'd like to go out there again to have another look around. Maybe tomorrow before the scene is closed. I'll let you know. You both right to do that?'

Both officers nodded.

Bec turned back to the whiteboard. 'Our second case involves a male cleaner found dead in Barwick Chambers on Thursday two days ago in the rooms of barrister Carolyn Moorhouse. We have no identity for this man yet. The circumstances are not clear. Moorhouse's pupil barrister who was in the rooms at the time, name of Juan Zamora, is in custody. He claims he startled an intruder that he then struggled with. In the process of that struggle, he says the cleaner fell and hit his head on a metal Buddha that had fallen to the floor.'

'So, an accident?' Wendy said.

'According to Zamora, it was an accident – an unlucky fall – but again, no forensics, no ID, so we investigate.' Bec began writing up tasks.

'Here's what we need to do. First, chase the cleaning company and find who was rostered on to clean Barwick Chambers that day. We need to find out who this man is.'

'Why would Zamora wrestle with a cleaner? Surely, he knew cleaners were going to come into the office. Seems suss, doesn't it?' Shaun asked.

'That's right, but Zamora's statement says the bloke was going through a filing cabinet and he ran at him when Zamora asked him what he was doing. We are looking for a motive here, too. Who knows what the cleaner was hoping to find? Maybe he thought there might be cash in one of those files. Anyway, we need footage of the interior of the building. The Bar Association oversees that, so we need to contact them and ask for their surveillance footage from the building. We should have fingerprints and DNA from the pathology soon, and if we're lucky who knows, maybe even a name. But once we know who we're dealing with, the rest should be relatively straightforward to put together.'

Bec paused. 'Any questions?

From the intense expression on Wendy's face, she was bursting to ask something. Instead, she just sat next to Shaun silently listening.

'There is something I'd like to add, Bec said. 'You may or may not be aware that Carolyn Moorhouse is a friend of mine, and on the night the cleaner died in her chambers, she called me after hours. She asked me to attend without telling me about the dead body.'

'You were there?' Shaun said with a look of sheer astonishment on his face. Bec nodded. 'So, that's why the investigation went to another team.'

'I have repeated this on numerous occasions,' Bec said, annoyed that she felt defensive. 'Just so both of you are clear, I was called to the scene in a private capacity, as a friend. As soon as I realised the situation, I called it in.'

'Geez, some friend,' Wendy scoffed. 'Carolyn Moorhouse is a big-time barrister. She would have known very well the shitstorm she was dragging you into, Sarge. Asking you to attend a late-night crime scene without telling you why. Really?'

Using all the mental power she possessed to stop her face showing how much she agreed with Wendy's words, Bec said calmly, 'Well, that's for Ms Moorhouse to explain at some point.' She smiled convincingly. 'But as I've just said, because of my connection to Case Two, we need to tread carefully. The DI was forced to give us this.'

Shaun and Wendy were appraising her. She needed the respect of her team here. She was a temporary appointment filling in. 'I don't intend to let either the DI or the victims down,' Bec said, 'which means we are going to have to tick every box, cross every T and dot every I until we solve them. Okay?'

They both nodded silently.

'Let's get on with it, then.'

Shaun and Wendy wandered off to their respective stations, talking confidentially, and Bec had a fair idea they would be wondering whether the temporary detective sergeant was about to fall in a hole.

It hit Bec hard to hear Wendy's take on Carolyn's actions. Constable Santos was right. Carolyn called her in that night fully cognisant of what she was doing. Now, Bec returned to the number-one question on her mental list. Why?

Chapter 14

Early morning, nothing outside was moving, and conditions were cold and dark on the mountain. Bec thought she heard a dog howl and turned over, causing an avalanche of paper to slide to the floor. Hauling herself up onto her elbows, groggy still from not enough sleep, she took in the mess of file notes strewn all over her bed and on the floor.

Embers from last night's fire, blackened and dormant, not throwing any heat, seemed to accentuate the cold air. Shivering, she started gathering the pages. Jackson and Green's notes from the crime scene and the sworn statements made interesting reading. She'd stayed up half the night reading through what they'd recorded, and their thoughts on the crime at Barwick Chambers. One line that she'd read over and over stated that neither of them was convinced that Carolyn was telling the truth. Question marks about her statement peppered throughout their notes underlined this scepticism. Not that they thought she'd killed the cleaner herself. Just their feeling that she knew more about his death than she'd let on. Yes, they were prepared to consider Juan's version of events, the accidental push and fall – perhaps because they knew that the pathology team would have the last say on that. But both had made comments throughout on a sense of something 'hidden' about Carolyn. It hadn't made Bec feel any better to realise that a seasoned cop like Griffiths and two hard-headed detectives like Jackson and Green suspected there was more to Carolyn's version of events than she'd revealed. Her heart weighed heavy reading their notes.

Carolyn told Bec that she had not known what to do when she realised what had happened, and she'd reached out to Bec in desperation. But her statements to Jackson and Green read as concisely as Bec would have expected. No confusion, no desperation. Her calling Bec that night made even less sense after reading the statements. What had she expected Bec to do? Bec had fallen asleep pondering that question.

Eager to get on with her day, she pushed the covers back. Her head was thick this early. Her limbs twitched as they did when she needed to exercise, but looking out of her bedroom window, she decided against venturing out for a run. The fog outside was too much like the fog inside her head, trying to make sense of things.

Settling instead for a steaming hot shower, a long-life green drink in a carton and no coffee, twenty minutes later she was dressed, ready with the rudimentary battle plan she'd prepared under the hot water and out the door.

*

Her phone buzzed during the morning briefing, and checking now, she saw another missed call from Josh. She couldn't seem to stop the positive flutter she still got when she saw his number. No time to meet up even if she wanted to. Her resolve never to speak to him again was softening with every call. The shrinks had said that the memories of being shot at and then almost drowning would give her trust issues, but she knew her issues went back before that. A family who had made it clear that they did not approve of her lifestyle and career choice. Bad guys who seemed to be able to get her mobile number no matter how many times she changed it. Walking in on Josh up close and personal with a young employee. Yeah, she had trust issues. She certainly didn't need a shrink to tell her that. She couldn't help how much she missed him, just the same.

But right now, back to reality: Bec had two dead bodies on her hands and precious little to go on to move either investigation forward. Josh, her personal life and trust had to wait. She'd been chasing the cleaning company, Ajax Domestic and Industrial Cleaners, in a bid to get her hands on the list of names of workers on duty the night the cleaner died. But for reasons not immediately clear to her, no-one was returning her calls. And after finally getting through to speak to someone, the manager was stalling.

'Let me ask you again,' Bec said. 'Who was on the roster for Barwick Chambers on the evening the cleaner died?'

'Can't be positive.'

'Surely, this can't be hard for you to answer.' Frustrated, Bec was ready to read him the riot act. 'Surely, you have names and addresses for the staff you employ?'

'Yes, we should have, but the truth is, sometimes we don't.'

'You need to explain how that works.' She spoke calmly to mask her annoyance.

'Look, I don't want to get into trouble with my bosses.'

'This is a choice you need to make, sir.' Her tone lifted. 'Trouble with your bosses or trouble from me. Let's try that again.'

The man on the end of the phone was unmoved. 'Yes, but there's a reason that I can't guarantee who was working that job on the night in question.'

'Alright, let's do it your way. Please, could you give me your full name.'

'Mannix, Ernie Mannix.'

'Mr Mannix, can you explain why you seem unwilling to answer one simple question?'

'Because I can't afford to lose my job,' he responded anxiously. 'I've just refinanced my mortgage.'

'Well, Ernie, I'm not asking about your home loan, I'm asking you to answer a simple question. So, here's your choice and consider carefully,' Bec said evenly. 'One, you tell me who was working, or …' she paused and heard his breathing stop, 'if you prefer, I could come down with a team of uniforms and we can go through every file in your office like a dose of salts.'

'No, please don't do that,' he said quickly. Bec could hear phones ringing in the background, and she imagined Ernie checking his surrounds for anyone listening. 'Alright, alright, but this cannot have come from me, okay?'

'Okay,' Bec said. 'The names, please, Ernie.'

'It's since COVID … right?' He lowered his voice. 'Before that, we had reams of foreign students who loved flexible hours and casual rates, but since COVID, it's just bloody hard to get people to work. Even when we can find someone, they won't stick at it. They let me down, and I'm the one who's gotta deal with customers on the phone yelling at me and asking why the cleaner hasn't shown up.'

'Yes, I see that wouldn't be easy.'

'It's not. So, a while back this young bloke, Ahmad, said to me (at least he had the decency to call), *I can't come, but I've got a friend who can do it in my place. You just pay me and I'll pay him.*'

Bec heard him take a quick breath.

'So, you can guess … I was so relieved not to have to cover another job, I said yes. And that's how it started.'

'How what started, Ernie?'

'We accept substitutes. I don't ask any questions. I just want bodies in place to fulfill our contracts.'

'What you're saying is, you let the people on your books work schedules out amongst themselves. And you have no idea who is working for you?'

'Yes, I guess we know who is meant to be working, but sometimes, not all the time, we don't even know that. We just pay as per the emailed timesheets.'

'Alright, probably more of a case for the tax office or immigration than me. Not part of my case, Ernie. You can relax on that score. Just the same, I'm still going to need a list of all the people who were meant to be working on that floor or in the building on that night. Can you do that?'

'I can, but please be careful if you talk to them. I don't need you scaring off my workforce.'

'I'll be very gentle with them,' Bec said, thinking that Wendy probably wouldn't cut them any slack at all. 'Thanks, Ernie, you've done the right thing. I may need to talk to you again, but I appreciate your assistance.'

'Okay, but remember, the stuff about the substitutes didn't come from me.'

Bec disconnected. It might be a much larger undertaking than she'd anticipated to find out who was working in the building that night. But all the same, she was heartened by the possibility of finding a name for the dead cleaner, even if it meant chasing down every name on Ernie's list.

Chapter 15

The entrance to the Thornbury units was still cordoned off when Bec pulled up. There was just one uniform present logging traffic in and out. The street was quieter today. As Bec had seen yesterday, locals, once they established that what was taking place had nothing to do with them, just got on with their lives. All the sightseers had disappeared.

While they waited for pathology results, she'd decided to go in for another look. To get a better feel for what happened to Doreen and who knew what else; a clue overlooked? Unlikely. But it was too easy to forget sometimes that the scrupulous science of today wasn't always a part of policing. That even before all the modern-day forensics they now relied on, crimes still had got solved. Good old-fashioned police work, of keeping your eyes and ears open, was still worth its weight in gold.

Shaun and Wendy had set off earlier to continue their questioning of other residents in the apartment block and the surrounding street, with two uniforms in tow to help them. Bec parked her vehicle behind theirs, messaged them to say she'd arrived, and walked over to the lone policeman guarding the site.

'Officer, DS Rebecca Harpin, homicide.' Bec flashed her ID.

Overnight, it had continued to niggle at her that she might have missed a clue at the crime scene. Although she'd told Wendy and Shaun to take the running on Thornbury, Bec couldn't let it go.

What had been completely missing from Doreen's home was any feeling of homeliness. No memorabilia. The sort that usually adorned the mantelpiece of a person who lived alone. Doreen's place had no happy reminders; in fact, no photos at all. Where was her story? A woman in her seventies should have special happy pictures of loved ones spread all over the place: friends, pets, parties, holidays, work colleagues – even photos of herself at a younger age. The absence of anything like that in Doreen's unit was strange. Reg had told them Doreen was a devoted mother, visiting Kenny in prison, regular as clock work. Why no picture of him? She obviously wasn't trying to hide the fact that she had a son or that he was in prison. She'd spoken about him to Reg. Could it be a sign of something amiss in their relationship that there was no trace of the son in her flat and that he hadn't shown up in person? This meant Bec had to consider Doreen's son as her prime suspect. The fact that they hadn't even been able to establish what Kenny looked like, much less where he lived or any contact details, meant they were dealing with someone who knew how to fly under the radar. None of the sketchy descriptions Wendy and Shaun had gathered of a man coming and going to Doreen's unit had delivered anything of value.

Bec was chatting to the officer standing guard when Shaun and Wendy rolled up. The uniform gave them what he had. 'Nosy parkers dropping by,' he said, 'but no-one called Kenny, and no-one acting suspicious. We've kept an eye out, but most people just want to know what happened.'

'Let's hope we have something to tell them soon, thank you, Officer,' Bec said, as she and her team pulled on rubber gloves.

Shaun unlocked the door and stood aside.

'Crime Scene has finished,' Bec said, 'so let's give it a really thorough going over.'

In the light of delays from forensics, they had to try to piece together some other possibilities to help direct their investigation. What could she have done to cause someone to tie her up and scare the poor woman to death? It was unlikely to be money related. Doreen lived week to week, from the look of her flat – probably on a pension.

With the flat closed up, no light and the blinds drawn, a combination of crime-scene chemicals and another unidentifiable smell wafted out to greet them. Bec never found it easy entering spaces where victims had died. They walked in slowly, Bec first, then Wendy.

'Leave the door open, and open some blinds, can you?' she said to Shaun. 'You check the bathroom, Wendy. I'll stick around in here. And, Shaun, you look in the kitchen. Take your time and be thorough. Behind cupboards, under drawers, anywhere she may have hidden anything important.'

She stood for a moment picturing how Doreen might have lived in this room. It was a one-bedroom unit. If Kenny ever stayed over, he would have slept in the living room.

She checked the couch first, behind cushions, underneath, then pushing the seat until she felt it start to slide. Made sense – it folded down into a bed. Her next move, the wooden chest that supported an oversized TV screen that dominated the room. Gently pulling the single drawer, she found it stuffed with TV guides and junk-mail catalogues that she had to wriggle and tease out. 'Where's your son, Doreen?' Bec murmured. 'Why doesn't he get a mention anywhere? Were you scared of him? Did he tie you up?'

She was leafing through all the catalogues, shaking out the pages then stacking them on a small table searching for anything, when Shaun called out, 'She had plenty of food stashed, tea bags, biscuits, cheeses, dips, chocolates and tins of everything under the sun. Anyone feeling hungry?'

'The usual stuff here,' Wendy told them, 'An old asthma puffer, tissues, creams, powder and bath salts. Only one toothbrush, though.'

'Shaun, rubbish bins, just in case. I'll check the bedroom, then I think we're done here,' Bec said.

The room was small. Doreen was a tidy woman; her single bed tucked perfectly; a sheet of old-fashioned lace draped over it. *She wasn't keeping any company in this room*, Bec thought, and a flash of sadness for the woman washed over her. 'Come on, Doreen, help us find who did this,' she whispered.

She could hear Shaun and Wendy talking to the officer stationed outside; they were enjoying a laugh about something. Bec went straight to the chest of drawers and began pulling out Doreen's smalls. Nothing stored underneath.

Shoving the contents back, she felt under and behind the drawer then started on the next. Dropping to her knees, she dragged the bottom drawer out and tipped everything down on the floor. Nothing useful.

Turning to the old-fashioned wardrobe, she went through everything and behind. Just as she was about to relatch the door, she noticed a calendar on the inside of Doreen's cupboard drawer. *Helping Hands Mission*, it read. Bec knew it. A charity that helped people get back on track after time on the street, prison, or other difficult situations. With Kenny recently out of jail and this current calendar on Doreen's door, Bec straightened and snapped a photo with her phone. Maybe this could help her trace the missing man.

'Security footage has just landed from the Body Corporate,' Wendy announced, staring down at her phone.

'Okay, good,' Bec said. 'You two finish up here for the time being. I just need to check something. See you in the morning.'

*

Outside, she watched Shaun and Wendy walk slowly back to the block of units and disappear inside, before she picked up her phone. With Juan Zamora still in custody, her plan was to interview him next. She'd punched in two digits to follow up her interview request when the device in her hand began to vibrate. She glanced down at the number and quickly disconnected.

But when it rang again, her finger hovered before she pressed 'accept'.

He spoke first. 'Hello, stranger.'

'Josh.'

'Sorry for the barrage of calls, but I need to see you, Bec. Please.' His voice was hesitant but still gave Bec a thrill.

In the long weeks they'd not seen each other, she had realised one thing. Avoiding a conversation about what happened, at least to hear what he had to say, was hurting more than hearing the truth.

'You mean tonight?'

'Yes, why not?'

'Might not be a good time,' she said, her heart wanting to agree and knowing she couldn't.

'Sorry, that was dumb, always a bad time for a cop, right?'

She heard his voice now masking disappointment. Or was it annoyance?

'I have two new investigations. Files I need to—'

'You're always going to have investigations,' he said abruptly, but his voice softened again. 'I really miss you, Bec.'

I've missed you, too. Bec had found these words hard to say before – now they sprang to her mind so easily. 'Can you just give me a day or so to get settled here? We do need to talk. I've just started a new six-month contract with the homicide squad and it really is frantic. Not payback, I promise. I'll call you.'

Pause.

'Promise?'

'Yes, I promise.' She laughed. Josh had always demanded multiple affirmations.

'Alright, I'll let you off this time. Is that what you say to some of your customers?'

'Not very often.'

'Okay, I'll try to be patient. Please, call me.'

The phone went dead in her ear, but her heart was beating hard and her face was smiling. She had taken a step she never thought she would. Going back on her decision to never speak to him again.

She was still thinking about what that meant when the Remand Centre confirmed she could interview Juan Zamora right away.

*

Hurriedly, she keyed in Barrister's Chambers Ltd, the property arm of the Bar Association. Should there be a problem, she would go there now. Otherwise, time saved, time gained. She identified herself and asked to be put through to the head of security.

'I'm sorry, Detective Sergeant. Mr Sleeman is out on inspection. Not sure when he'll be back. I'm Karen, his assistant. Can I help?'

'Yes, Karen, thank you. This is about the investigation for the man who died recently on your premises, in Carolyn Moorhouse's rooms. I'm going to need details of the security arrangements you have in place for Barwick Chambers, access to security footage, and pass card swipe times for entry into the building and for accessing Ms Moorhouse's floor.'

'What a shocking thing. The entire organisation is buzzing. Nothing like that has ever happened before.'

There was a comment to make about bodies and barristers, but Bec refrained.

'What was it about, do you know?'

'We are currently investigating what happened.' Bec tried not to sound impatient.

'They're saying it was a robbery gone wrong,' the personal assistant continued. 'Surely, whoever it was didn't think there was any money in the barrister's rooms. Even senior counsels are forever crying poor.'

Bec heard the woman laugh. 'We just don't know, Karen. Now, I'm going to need that video footage for the weeks before and since, plus the names and addresses of all the current pass holders as a matter of urgency.'

'Just checking, I believe we've already sent most of that through to the West Melbourne Police Station.

'Thank you, but this is now a homicide investigation. Our unit is based at Head Office in the city. You'll need to resend that information to me together with everything else I just mentioned. If you could send it to this address as soon as you can.' Bec gave the woman her email.

'Yes, of course, I'll do it right now, Detective,' the woman said soberly, recovered from her earlier enthusiasm.

'Thank you.' Bec spoke calmly, which was far from her present state of mind, and disconnected.

Video footage would make Carolyn's and Juan's movements easier to check, to see if their timing worked out. After she looked at that and spoke further to Juan Zamora, she would talk to Carolyn and go through the ever-expanding list of questions she had for her barrister friend.

Still behind the wheel of her car, Bec called Carolyn. When the recording of Carolyn's voice kicked in asking her to leave a message, she did.

'Caro, it's Rebecca. As the investigating officer in charge of the break-in to your chambers. Yes, the DI changed his mind.' She hesitated to measure her words. 'I will need to go through your statement. We need to make an interview time. If it's easier for you, I could come to your chambers. Otherwise, you come to us. And as soon as possible. Let me know. And, Caro, please don't make this any harder than it already is.'

Chapter 16

When the information landed on her screen, Bec nodded in satisfaction. It always paid to restrain any frustration when demanding things from people. The Bar Association assistant had done as she had been asked.

Bec clicked the file open and scrolled through to the street entrance camera, then to the date and time of the crime. Right away, she clocked the arrival of a shadowy figure who was hard to distinguish: beanie pulled down and a white medical mask – to all intents a cleaner going to work. This had to be the dead man. The time of his arrival was right. Her heart was beating faster. Was it the sugar from her coffee or seeing the intruder enter Carolyn's building? Both probably.

Though engrossed in the image on her screen, Bec still heard the steady approach of familiar footsteps along the corridor.

'How's that break-and-enter going, Harpin, need some help yet?' It was Jackson's voice. He didn't stop. Just yelled as he passed her office door.

'Know anyone who could help?' Bec shot back and was rewarded with a burst of laughter.

She'd hardly seen any of that team since the domestic shooting. One part of her was glad not to be dealing with a mother and her children shot dead by the other parent. There were no pretty homicide cases. No investigation was without some shocking element, but none were easy.

She sat for a moment staring at the fuzzy outline of the intruder on her screen. Jackson's comment was probably right – the whole thing could be a simple break-and-enter, an opportunistic grab for cash and valuables that went terribly wrong. But staring at the shadowy figure entering the building, she thought, *No.* Her gut reaction, whose guide she relied on always, was telling her this was much more complicated than that.

'There you are,' she said softly, and leaned forward, watching the man step through the door from the street, past two blokes who held the door open for him. He entered the lift and Bec noted the time it took to reach the ninth floor. Cameras picked up his exit. She replayed the footage several times. The fellow was a pro – the way he had pretended to be searching for his pass card at the front entrance, aware of the cameras. At no point had he lifted his chin even slightly to allow the cameras a good look at his face.

She printed a few still frames of the grainy image, then flicked to the camera in the area outside Carolyn's rooms. The man walked straight to her door and disappeared inside. How quickly he dealt with the lock proved just how experienced the fellow was. Bec clicked on a later file that showed her own entry into Carolyn's building. Watching herself go through the front doors, and re-emerge later from the lift on Carolyn's floor, she found disconcerting. At least anyone watching could see that when she arrived there was with no concern on her face or in her movements, about what she would soon confront. She was flicking back and forth, noting Carolyn's time of arrival and other movements in the building, when familiar voices told her the team had returned.

'Maybe you should get a signed photo of her to hang up at home.' Bec could hear Wendy and Shaun bantering as they exited the lift.

'There would be worse faces to see first thing in the morning,' Shaun said.

'Oh, listen to you, Casanova, she's staying over now.' Wendy laughed.

'I was talking about the photo … oh, forget it!'

Bec got up, went to her doorway, and called out, 'Hey, you two, in here, please.'

Wendy was still teasing as the pair sauntered in. 'Sarge, the seriously good-looking actress living at the Thornbury units, we saw her rushing up the stairs to her unit and I thought for a minute that Shaun here was going to lose the plot.'

'Wendy's exaggerating … as usual, Sarge.' He rolled his eyes but checked Bec's reaction.

'Shaun is smitten. She's twisting him around her little finger.'

'That's enough, Wendy,' Shaun said, glaring like he meant it.

'There is something about her, I must admit. She is a stunner,' Wendy said. 'But I think she was lying.'

'About what?'

'I don't know, everything. I think she was closer to Doreen than she admitted, and I'm certain she knows the son or at least met him.'

'A feeling won't be enough, Wendy. You're going to need more than that to get my attention. Why do you think she knows him, and if she does why would she lie?' Bec said, eyeing them both.

'Just the way she answered when we asked. She paused before she said she didn't know him. It was slight, but then she said, "He'll be devastated."'

'Okay. Why lie about it? Is she covering for him?'

'Don't know, Sarge, but there's more with her. I'm sure it'd be worth you talking to her.'

Bec nodded. 'We can do that. But we're going to have to divide our time with two investigations, so we deal with each piece of information for either Moorhouse or Madden as it comes to hand. It won't be easy. Right now, we have these pictures of our dead cleaner to check. Shaun, if you could get as much background as you can on Doreen?'

'Okay, I'm on it.'

'Also, I've been in contact with the cleaning company for Barwick Chambers, a mob called Ajax Domestic and Industrial Cleaners, who are sending through names, addresses and phone numbers for all the cleaning staff rostered on the day the cleaner died. I'd like you to manage this,' she said to Wendy. 'We'll need to work our way through that list and be careful with our questions.'

'Why so?'

'Apparently, just because your name is on the roster doesn't mean you were the person working. The staff, mostly foreign students, can organise their own replacement when they can't attend, according to the bloke in charge.'

'What does that mean?'

'A bit of substitution going on amongst their workforce,' Bec explained. 'Not our concern if people who get paid are not the ones who show up to work. We just need to know who was on duty and working on that day. Just need to be mindful, that's all. We don't want to be blamed for scaring off their workforce. I only want the name, even though I don't think our dead guy was a cleaner. Watch him on the footage. He's a pro. Doesn't even slow down when he picks Moorhouse's lock. I think he used the cleaner's guise to get into the building. But this is something we need to know in case he was signed on to get access.'

'Okay,' Wendy said, clearly intrigued.

Shortly after, Shaun called out, 'Hey, Sarge, look at this.'

'What is it?'

'See this?' he said, and sat back for Bec to read from his screen.

She leaned over where a document headed Births, Deaths and Marriages showed, *Doreen Madden, born 2 April 1945 in New South Wales registered as never married. One unnamed child, male, given up for adoption in 1967.*

'And that child is Kenny, you think?' she said. 'Are we sure it's our Doreen?'

'Yep, date of birth looks about right.' Shaun looked pleased with himself. 'It doesn't change anything. I mean, we still can't find him. These days, you hear more and more about long-lost children/parent reunions. They must have found each other again, later.'

'It's possible, even probable,' Bec said thoughtfully, thinking Shaun had likely hit the nail on the head. 'I still don't get why we can't find anyone in that block of flats to give us a clear description. If he was visiting Doreen regularly, someone must have seen him. He must have said hello to someone from time to time. And why hasn't he been in touch?'

'Yeah, it's making him look even more like our guy, isn't it?'

'Good work, Shaun. Now that we know for sure we have no Kenny Madden in the prison system, we'll just have to try to check his name in every other way we can.

'We've got more pictures to look at than Movie of the Week,' Wendy said, sitting at her own screen, booting up her computer.

'And more coming,' Bec said.

'Sometimes, sitting too long makes me jumpy,' Wendy added. 'I'm more of your action officer.'

'Okay, Senior Constable Santos, on that note, I'm going to follow another hunch about Kenny. Not sure it'll go anywhere, but you can come with me,' Bec said, and saw trepidation flash on the younger officer's face, as if she feared a reprimand. *She was too jumpy sometimes*, Bec thought.

'After that little find about Doreen, Shaun can you make a start on security footage of the Thornbury units?'

He nodded.

'Shouldn't be long.'

'Yep.' He didn't turn as they left, already clicking on the files. Shaun was good for solid effort. Bec appreciated that.

Chapter 17

The mood was sombre in the car as they drove in heavy city traffic along St Georges Road on their way to Preston.

'I'm not too big, so I pump iron,' Wendy said, to break the silence.

'It's good that you work out, Wendy. I run,' Bec said. 'Can't be too fit in this game. And it helps after a tough day.'

'What makes you think this calendar is something,' Wendy asked, gaining confidence. 'She may have just been given it by someone.'

'Yes, but these people try to assist blokes like Kenny on parole, so just maybe they helped him, and it was he who gave the calendar to Doreen.'

'Right.' Wendy was looking at the photo of the calendar on Bec's phone and starting to read the article on Helping Hands Mission that had been downloaded.

'So, it's worth a few hours of our time. If Kenny did come here, maybe they can give us a description, or better still an address for him.'

'Right,' Wendy said again.

It was a massive warehouse-style yellow brick op shop, signed like a super site, using a big font and bright colours: bargains, clothes, jewellery, bric-a-brac and furniture.

'Hard to miss,' Bec said, pulling into a vacant parking spot right next to the entrance.

'Are they expecting us?'

'Nope, thought we'd get a faster response if we just drop in.'

'Scare them witless in a place like this.'

'Means we'll get faster answers so they can get us off the premises as quickly and quietly as they can. Come on,' Bec said, and got out of the car.

No need to ask for the manager. He found them. The moment they entered the front door, a man of medium height and medium age, carrying too much weight, came bustling towards them.

'Good morning, Officers?' he said brightly. 'I'm Dennis, buck stops here with me. How can I help?' He didn't offer a handshake.

Bec and Wendy presented their IDs and introduced themselves.

'I knew you were police from the way my workforce disappeared as soon as you pulled up. But homicide, oh my goodness.' Bec noticed perspiration on his top lip. He reminded her of Hardy, the old-time comedian from Laurel and Hardy. Bec watched the comedy channel late at night when sleep wouldn't come.

'We are looking for a Kenny Madden,' Bec said. 'Is it possible you may have helped someone of that name at some point?'

'Of course, of course, let me see,' he responded, sailing off towards a corner desk, where there was a computer screen set up. 'We help a lot of people here, Detective. Was he an ex-con?'

'Yes, released about six to eight months ago.'

'Okay, let me see.' The man sat down and began typing, spelling aloud in an exaggerated fashion as he went, which reminded Bec even more of the comedian. 'M-A-D-D-E-N with two Ds. Is that right, Officer?'

Bec nodded.

'Right, seems we did have a Kenny here for a few months. No surname but his "contact" name is Doreen Madden. Has Kenny done something wrong, Officers?'

'Would you have an ID photo, or an address?'

'No, no photo, sorry, and his address is care of Doreen Madden. Our people don't like being photographed. They're trying to fit back into normal life, you see. Many of them, quite a few of them, have done time. Let's say they're sensitive about who sees them. All they need is someone to vouch for them and we give them a chance. I'm sure you understand that, Officer.'

'Yes, but do you take any other details from the people you are helping, apart from their names?'

'Just what they'll give us when they volunteer. Later, if they want to be registered in the workforce, then they must give more information, but we don't worry. We're just trying to help people get back to some sort of normal life.'

'So, did you know Kenny?' Wendy asked.

'I saw him a few times, I think, if I have the right face. I deal with so many …'

'What happened to him?' Bec added. 'You said he was here a while ago.'

'Not sure.'

He stood up and called out to a thin man, skinny jeans, and a checked shirt, straining to lift a floral velvet armchair onto a trolley. 'Lew, you got a minute?' The man stopped what he was doing and strolled over, looking wary. 'You remember Kenny, the fellow who was volunteering at the second-hand furniture place, then came to us?'

'Kenny, yeah, why?'

'The officers here are looking to contact him, that's all. And as they don't really have an address or even a picture of him, they were wondering if you'd be able to give a description.'

'No, I wouldn't. Kenny's alright. Haven't seen him in a while.'

'Do you know where Kenny was living?' Bec asked.

'Not really. From what I gathered; Kenny had a few lady friends. Maybe he spread himself about if you know what I mean? Dunno if he had his own place yet or was crashing wherever he could con a bed.'

'None of the others will be more forthcoming, unfortunately. There's not a lot of love for the police amongst my charges, I'm afraid. Should I contact you if anyone does know anything or if Kenny shows up, Officers?' the Hardy character said, beaming at them, while none too subtly edging them towards the exit.

'If you could,' Bec said. 'Kenny's mother, Doreen, has died, and I'm sure he would want to be informed.' Bec handed him her card.

'Yes, of course. I'm sure he would want to know about that.' He glanced down at the card. 'Thank you, Officers.'

Walking back to the car, Wendy said, 'That's a start. People who knew him by name.'

'Yes, four minutes on the number two-five-one bus from here to Doreen's unit,' Bec said.

'You think he was living with Doreen.'

'On and off, probably.'

'That manager was on edge,' Wendy said. 'Do you think he was hiding something?'

'Who knows. Ex-cons as workers. First names only. Donated goods. He sure doesn't want us sniffing around too much. Let's just hope for his sake he wasn't protecting Kenny working out the back somewhere.'

'Do you really think he was?' Wendy spun around to face Bec.

'No.' Bec laughed. 'I don't. I think that manager would have fainted from the stress of that.'

*

The drive back was easier, moving against the tide.

Bec's phone rang. She pressed 'accept'.

'Shaun, what is it?'

'Sarge, you're not gonna believe it!'

'Try me,' Bec said.

'I got hooked watching the pictures, right, so I started going further back on the security footage from Thornbury. And guess what I found?'

'This is not a pick-a-box quiz, Shaun, what have you got?'

'Nikki Cardone, going through the front gates with a man. The vision's not clear, it's in the evening. Just one week before Doreen died.'

'And do we know who this man is, Shaun? Could it be one of the other residents?'

'No, Sarge, don't know yet who it is. But I don't think it's a neighbour. None that we've spoken to anyway. My guess is it's likely Kenny 'cause they go straight into Doreen's place. No pause, no intros, Doreen just lets them in.'

'Good work, we're not far away,' she said, activating the flashing blue lights and pulling out to take off in the overtake lane.

'He'd do anything to watch pictures of that actress.' Wendy laughed, jumping out just as the car stopped moving and slamming her door. 'I told him she was lying.'

Chapter 18

Wendy rushed ahead, while Bec took a moment to throw her keys and jacket down before she joined the team at Shaun's workstation.

Excitement written all over his face, Shaun clicked 'play' and said, 'This is it,' and the image started moving.

'Yep, that's her,' Wendy said, pointing at the screen.

Bec watched a young woman, long blonde hair, and a bag over one shoulder, push through the gate, talking animatedly to the man beside her. From what she could make out, the two were clearly not a couple, but seemed very relaxed with each other. The man was older, dark clothes, and the 1940s gangster hat on his head disguised his appearance sufficiently that they couldn't see much of him at all. He was not very tall. The three of them watched as Doreen opened her door. They saw her embrace the man then Nikki as she let them inside.

'Poor woman,' Wendy muttered. 'Here one minute, gone the next.'

'Call Ms Cardone, would you, Shaun, while I watch this again. Tell her we'd like her to come in for a chat. And tell her it's not an invitation.' Bec moved into Shaun's seat. 'She can talk us through what's going on here. You can pick her up.'

'In his dreams,' Wendy breathed.

Shaun just shook his head.

If this really was Kenny on the security footage, they were off. Here was a breakthrough at last. They might have finally stumbled onto an image of Doreen's missing son. It wasn't perfect, but it was something.

And they had a woman who knew Kenny, who previously claimed not to know him – and someone who clearly knew Doreen better than she'd indicated when interviewed. Why would Nikki lie about knowing Doreen and Kenny when it all looked like happy families on the tape?

'She's not answering, Sarge. I've left a message.'

'Just keep trying until you get her,' Bec replied. 'If she's still not answering by later this afternoon, we'll have to pay her a visit.'

*

The excitement of having found the image energised their determination to find a key into Kenny's disappearance. Wendy was leaning forward over her desk, on the phone, slowly going through the list of names provided by the cleaning company. And from how she was massaging her forehead, not with any success. Shaun was lost in the security footage again, keen to see what else they might reveal. *The glamour side of policing*, Bec thought, *the boring tedium of checking, searching, and paying attention to every single detail.* It was gruelling work. Yet, without it, there was not a hog's hair of possibility of obtaining a result. *Hog's hair*, she laughed to herself. Where did that come from? Late-night TV probably.

Bec stared at her computer screen. Then, downing the dregs of a bitter half-cold coffee, she pitched the empty cup into the wastepaper bin. Usually, fingerprints returned within twenty-four hours, forty-eight at most. They were way past that and still there was no ID for the cleaner. Not good enough, no matter how much she liked Avi. She punched the speed dial for pathology.

'Hi, VIFM, this is Pip Styles, how can I help?' the woman said in a voice that resembled someone selling undergarments in a department store.

'Detective Sergeant Harpin,' Bec said, holding back her frustration. 'I'm looking for fingerprint results for an unidentified body under the case name Moorhouse, and anything you can give me about a Doreen Madden from Thornbury. Is Avi not around?'

'Detective Sergeant Harpin, I work with Avi, I've just started,' she said by way of introduction. 'He asked me to give you a quick update. I was just about to call you.'

'Must be bad news if Avi won't call himself. Nice to meet you, though, Pip,' Bec said, thinking forensic medicine was one calling she could never have answered.

'Yes, same here,' Pip said pleasantly. 'No, not bad news, it's just we're behind in processing the evidence for Doreen Madden. People are off sick. Only so many hours in the day.' She recited the list of platitudes, which for any homicide detective would fall on deaf ears. 'More overtime going than anyone of us can poke a stick at, and still we're way behind,' she explained. 'Hair samples taken from the site are waiting for analysis, prints yet to be identified, and we're yet to identify even the type of rope that was used.' She paused for breath. 'Avi asked me to tell you that we're experiencing a rather busy patch, and that your body is in a queue.'

I'd like to know who takes priority over a poor woman who's likely been scared to death. Bec sighed inwardly. The first few days after a crime offered the best chance to solve what happened, and this kind of delay was at the worst time for Bec and her team. The problem was the entire squad was stretched across so many crimes, with each one of her colleagues wanting their case prioritised.

Trying not to let this come through in her voice, Bec said, 'That's not what I wanted to hear, Pip.'

'No, sorry, we are doing everything we can to speed things up.'

'Yes, I'm sure you are. Just let me know the second you have something.'

Bec's phone vibrated. She glanced down and smiled.

Chapter 19

After a long day, it seemed to Bec, that she'd been driving for hours. Spinning the wheel as she turned into their street, she relaxed, pleased she'd made the effort and not gone home. It had been a line ball when Lyn had messaged and said, *Why don't you come for dinner tonight?* But Bec realised that the company of her best friend was the best remedy for her fatigue, so she'd said yes without further hesitation.

Lyn's kids, Sadie and Ben, excused themselves early, Bec imagined on account of them not wanting to spend time listening to their mother and her cop friend catching up, when they had important things of their own to do somewhere else in the house.

Lyn and Gary lived in a large home, with five bedrooms and a four-car garage. This outer suburb of Melbourne was one place where the quarter-acre block still held sway. Street upon street of houses with big extensions and pop-up second storeys with gardens big enough for games. Gary had thrown down his dinner hurriedly, given Bec a quick peck on the cheek and told Lyn, with his arm around her, to leave the dishes and he would take care of them when he got home.

'Isn't he the best,' Lyn said, starry-eyed, hearing the front door slam. 'He takes his parent-teacher nights seriously.'

Bec nodded and smiled, lips closed. She saw too much of 'the other'. Parents who didn't care two hoots about their children's education, or what their kids did at night – oftentimes leaving them to roam the streets.

'Bet you never thought I'd end up married to a schoolteacher, did you?' Lyn nudged Bec. 'Me either. Come on over here.' She picked up their wineglasses and headed for the living room, where the TV for once was silent. 'A bit of peace and quiet,' she said, sinking into a generously proportioned, fashionable sofa. The couch faced a glass sliding door that led to a barbecue deck, where a bright exterior garden light shone down, highlighting a large wooden table and chairs. Bec recalled the times she'd sat at that table as a guest, making small talk with Gary and Lyn's neighbours. Lyn dashing back and forth with bowls of salad, and Gary, glass of ale in one hand, turning chops and sausages with the other, talking over his shoulder about football or the cricket. This was the life Bec's mother had wanted for her. The life her mother still wanted for her.

Bec loved coming here, despite her reluctance to embrace the same lifestyle as her schoolfriend. Her enjoyment of seeing how Lyn had built a happy family life never dimmed. At the end of a harrowing day, a few hours with her friend and family was better than ten sessions of therapy.

Perhaps Bec should be envious. Lyn was a born homemaker, and Gary was that rare species of man who seemed to 'get' what it took to run a family and a household. But while she loved visiting and seeing her friend glowing with happiness amongst her family – like a *Women's Weekly* advertisement for stay-at-home mothers – it was not what Bec had wanted. She had chosen law enforcement. Lyn had chosen her life, and Bec had never heard the slightest hint, ever, that she wished she'd made a different choice. She and Lyn both were still happy with their choices, like the old cliché 'horses for courses'. Not that Bec's mother accepted it. Her constant cry over the years had never changed: 'Why can't you be more like Lyn and live a normal life?' Bec had thought about it many times, but the answer always came out the same. For whatever reason, her horizon differed from Lyn's and from what her parents wanted for her.

Maybe it was to do with her growing-up years – the shrinks would probably have an answer for that. Her parents' life had not presented a perfect example of family life. There was some 'uneasy state of mind' that drove them from place to place. Bec had always thought it was a good excuse for her father to say a town clerk needed broad experience when he dragged them to yet another town. 'Your father doesn't want to be a stick-in-the-mud like your uncle Jim,' her mother used to say whenever they were packing to move house again. Nothing wrong with Uncle Jim, as far as Bec could tell. Except, he and his wife had lived happily in the same house for most of their lives. Bec's police training was barely underway when her father announced the move to Queensland.

'This time,' her father said, beaming at Bec and her brother, 'we're headed for sunshine – I should be able to retire up there.' Her parents' expectation that she should just give up her training and move away with them, as if what Bec was doing meant nothing at all, turned out to be the final push for her to move out and stay in Victoria.

After that, whenever her mother said she should live a 'normal life', Bec didn't have any idea what that meant. Given the constant shifting house in her family, she had never known anything resembling the norm others experienced. Old friends, known streets, places that were so familiar you could find them with your eyes shut. This had never been her experience. It was always the rub of the new for the Harpins: new house, new school, new friends that you maybe didn't commit to because you knew you'd be moving away again soon anyway. And her brother, Paul, well, he always went along with what their parents wanted. And when the move to Queensland came up, he said he didn't mind cane toads and cockroaches, and he was happy to move with them.

He thought Bec should just 'grow up'. She and her brother didn't talk much anymore. And when they did, it was just a quick phone catch-up for birthdays and Christmas. She had the feeling that Paul, who was a builder, had no idea of who she was, and never had. Nor she him, if she was honest.

Lyn's voice brought her back. 'Alright, you've heard all our news, so what's happening with you?' Bec saw the little frown on her forehead that conveyed Lyn was trying to, but never would, understand Bec's world. Questions like this had become a kind of ritual at the end of a meal.

'The usual,' Bec said, grinning the question away with her standard reply. 'Chasing the bad guys.'

Lyn's frown deepened. 'Is it worth it, Bec? Really? I see how you look when you're here. I see how comfortable you are in a regular family environment.'

'Oh God, now you sound like my mother.'

'You know what I mean.'

'Kind of. We're just different, that's all.' From her previous attempts, Bec thought it was futile to try to explain what policing was like, even to a well-meaning friend like Lynette. Just easier to stay off the topic altogether. 'It's so lovely here,' she said, 'you've got your perfect life, and when I'm sitting on a stakeout in the cold, you think I wouldn't want my own Gary home cooking me a perfect steak? 'Course I would. But when I hear a judge sentence one of the scumbags, and know he's off the street ...' she paused, 'then for me, it's worth it.'

'Not when you get hit over the head and almost drown – ending up in hospital and having your friends worried sick about you,' Lyn added, wanting the last word.

'Yes, but the scumbag who did that is in jail, too, remember? Three life sentences.' Bec grinned and sipped her wine. One glass had to last with the long drive ahead – even if tonight she would have liked another.

'I thought after that little episode you might throw it in. Instead, what do you do? You apply for a promotion and get it.' Lyn rolled her eyes.

Bec changed the subject. 'I'm finally selling my apartment.' She placed her glass down on the coffee table. 'I'm commuting in from the mountain.'

'Bec, that's miles out. Surely, you're not driving back tonight?'

'Yes, I do every night. It's peaceful. I like waking up there and I can run through the bush. It takes a bit longer to get home, but …'

Lyn shook her head. 'So, now you're telling me I need to worry about you on the road and running by yourself in the bush. I swear, I don't know what to do about you sometimes, Rebecca.'

'Now, you sound exactly like my mother.'

'Well, this time I agree with her,' Lyn shot back. 'I thought you'd be moving in with Josh when you sold up.'

Bec took another sip of her wine. She wanted to talk about Josh, but …

'I don't know,' Lyn persisted, 'I thought after that last assignment, you two seemed thick, you know? I thought you'd stick together.'

The pictures started running through her head again, Bec dropping into his café expecting to see him holding the fort with customers. But when she stuck her head into the kitchen – there was Josh alright, but he was up close with someone else. He saw her – 'Bec!' – a startled look on his face. 'Sorry to intrude,' she'd said, and flown out the door. That was it. *Don't tell me we are trying for something when you clearly are not.* It hurt. For a while, she'd thought he might be the one guy able to deal with her and her job. But she'd ended it and not returned his calls until this week.

'Yeah. He was lovely after that, but it's hard when you're both busy all the time. Let's just say it didn't go the way I expected.'

Lyn regarded her quizzically. 'Meaning?'

'Meaning … I saw him with someone else and ran off, haven't seen him since.' She blurted out the words the way a child would when something stung. No sign of the collected Detective Sergeant Harpin, homicide.

'Really?' Lyn frowned. 'I'm surprised. Wouldn't have put Josh in that category.'

'And which category is that?'

'Oh, you know, someone who says one thing and does another.' Bec imagined what was coming. 'You dark horse. Why do I always have to drag everything out of you, Rebecca?'

'Okay, so I've managed to avoid telling my oldest friend in the world about falling out with Josh,' Bec said, pleased that the conversation she needed to have was being had. 'What will you think if I tell you there is a possible kiss and make-up on the cards?'

'What are you doing to me!' Lyn squealed, bouncing up and down like a teenager. 'Tell me everything,' she said, straightening her legs and leaning in.

'Josh has been calling and begging me for a chance to explain. He said I saw him with his arm around someone in the kitchen, that's all, and that I got the wrong impression. He's asked to meet up. I said I'll call him in a day or so when I have my case load in hand.'

'Go on,' Lyn said, listening intently.

'Go on, nothing.'

'And you have missed him?'

'Yes, hate to admit, terribly. But I'm scared.'

'Of what?'

Stumped for a second, Bec laughed. 'Have you got a better question, like one I can answer?' She took a sip of wine.

Lyn reached out and patted Bec's knee. 'We know how brave you are for others, Bec. Be brave for yourself, for once.'

'I'm scared of getting back with him and finding it was the wrong thing to do,' she confessed to the only person she could confess these feelings to.

'Big deal, what if it is. You'll get over it. And if it's right, you won't have missed out. What's to worry about? Grab love with both hands. Oh, come on, Bec.' Lyn placed her wineglass down and grabbed both of Bec's hands in hers.

'You are good together. He's lovely. Do it.'

Bec gave a smile. 'Is that Agony Aunt's last word?'

'For now. Let's raise a toast.' Lyn poured them both a little extra drop. 'Now, this time, you keep me in this romance loop, okay, until it's all sorted.'

Smiling, Bec agreed.

*

Half an hour later, they'd moved to the kitchen to make coffee, one getting out the instant, the other milk from the fridge, coordinating like the pair of girl guides they'd once been. Lyn was scrambling through a tin looking for cream biscuits, when Bec said, 'You remember Carolyn Moorhouse, the barrister?'

Lyn turned. 'What kind of question is that? How could I not remember her?'

'I meant, do you remember anything about her.'

'Apart from how she helped me. What else is there to remember?'

'It's a case, been in the papers. A bloke died in Carolyn's legal chambers.'

Lyn put her hand over her mouth. 'I haven't seen a thing. That's awful. Is she okay?'

'Yes, she's fine. A bit shocked. I'm heading up the investigation.'

Lyn's eyes widened. She put the milk down, waiting to hear what Bec was about to say.

'The thing is – confidential, right?' Bec raised her hands.

Lyn nodded. 'Cross my heart.'

'I've known Carolyn since meeting her in court at your hearing years ago. Then I met up with her again on a case when I was still in uniform and we just clicked, you know? We've been friends for ages. The thing is, on the night the bloke died in her chambers, she called me. Not in any official capacity, just said she needed my help and asked me to come to her rooms. When I got there, there'd been a scuffle with a young barrister and a man was lying on the floor dead.'

'What?' Lyn reacted, bumping the milk carton over, which started spilling over the benchtop. 'Shit, just a minute,' she said, and reached under the sink for a cloth to start mopping up. 'She didn't warn you?'

'Not a word. I arrive to see her and her student just sitting. She's put me in a difficult position. And until the case is resolved, my presence at this crime scene raises doubts about why I was there.'

'Bec, that's terrible.' Lyn squeezed the cloth dry and threw it down in the sink. 'What can you do?'

'Obviously, we need to sort out what took place, and that will happen in the course of the investigation. But since Carolyn made the call that night, I've been thinking, and you know what?'

'What?'

'I don't know much about Carolyn at all. Not really. Sure, I've known her for a long while, but … I thought you might remember something.'

'That'd be a stretch, like what?'

'I don't know, anything. Like, did you ever get a feeling she had a significant other, anything like that when you used to meet with her?'

'God, I don't know, I was such a mess. And I was young, don't forget. Hang on, let me think. I might have heard her once asking someone about pick-up times. Sounded like kids to me.'

'Yes maybe.' Bec said.

'Strained the friendship now, I think?'

'You could say. Or burned it completely, who knows.'

'I'll bet. Why would she drag you into it?'

'That's what I can't figure out.'

'I don't know anything about the law, but you'd have to say that as a big-time barrister, she must have known what she was doing involving you,' Lyn said, trying to be helpful and failing dismally. 'Sorry, Bec, I wish I could help, but I can't think of anything.'

'Never mind, it was a long shot.' Bec picked up a sweet biscuit and took a bite.

They talked some more about how Gary was going for Head of Senior School, then Lyn said, 'Why don't you stay here with us tonight? You don't have to drive back to the mountain. The kids would love it and so would I.'

'Thanks, but I better get going. Got another big day tomorrow,' Bec said, and stood to leave, searching around for where she'd left her bag.

'Are you sure? We could have more wine.'

'Raincheck, my beautiful friend. Say goodnight to Gary and the kids for me. And thanks for the heart-to-heart, just what the doctor ordered.' She hugged her friend.

'Don't mention it. Anytime. I'm always here for you, Bec.'

'I know.'

*

Bec tried listening to music on the way home, but questions about both investigations flooded her brain. After the conversation with Lyn,

Carolyn's explanations kept coming back to Bec. The timing didn't make sense; three hours. Her statement was that both she and Juan were too shocked to do anything except call Bec and wait for her to arrive. But three hours gave them a lot of time to get their stories to match. Or get rid of evidence. Juan said the cleaner was going through a filing cabinet. Clearly looking for something specific. Carolyn had to suspect something, but so far, she'd given nothing away. And did she really think that Bec would somehow get her out of it?

Her head was still spinning by the time she got home.

Chapter 20

After scouring every document Shaun had gathered on Carolyn, Bec slept badly. Her restless and disturbed brain still wouldn't calm, so she gave up. Flicking the light back on, she started reading again. As if going over the research once more might illuminate something new.

The shock of reading that Carolyn had a daughter hit hard, forcing Bec to contemplate why on earth a friend would never mention something as important as her own daughter? Lyn had sensed Carolyn's family situation. Why hadn't Bec?

Admittedly, Carolyn's daughter, Merrily Baxter, didn't live in Melbourne. Twenty-six years of age now, she was completing a Master of Law at Oxford University in the UK. And at the time of Lyn's case, Merrily would have been in early school. The file also contained details of Carolyn's divorce from Merrily's father, Ian Baxter KC – an Englishman who trained in Melbourne then moved to Adelaide to establish himself there. Bec was completely baffled. And not just because Carolyn hadn't been forthcoming about her personal stuff. Heaven knows, Bec herself had been described as 'tight lipped' about personal things. What had really smacked her in the face was that she hadn't even thought about Carolyn's personal circumstances.

She'd always thought that her finest asset as a police officer – aside from her fiendish work ethic – was intuition; her 'gut', her ability to identify people telling lies or withholding information. But lately, this certainty had taken a jolt: the incident with Josh, Carolyn's behaviour, and now a daughter she'd never mentioned in all the years they'd been friends. These revelations made Bec feel like her intuition had flown off to some distant cloud.

She paused for a moment. *That kind of thinking leads to bad places*, she heard Joan, her first mentor and exemplary police officer, say. *No time for that, no time for self-doubt.* And without wasting another second, Bec was on her feet. Only one way to deal with a head-spin like that.

She set off with first light creeping stealthily through the trees, and broke into a jog. The track she liked to run wasn't far from her front gate, and soon she was pounding away on the dirt path. No-one was about at this hour, not even dog walkers. She settled into a steady pace, focusing on her breath, arms and legs – chilly air biting into the back of her throat with every intake. Once she found her rhythm, she was running comfortably. Breathing in the fresh mountain air laden with eucalyptus was intoxicating, and running beneath the enormous canopy of green splayed like a giant fan was clearing her head with every step. She ran hard for almost an hour.

*

Showered, refreshed and feeling a whole lot better, Bec made herself a pot of tea and sat down to a bowl of cereal smothered in fresh fruit and yoghurt. Her first instinct when her phone started to vibrate was to ignore it.

'Morning, you got home alright?'

Lyn sounded intense, Bec thought, *for so early in the morning.*

'Yes, an easy run with the lights. You're up early.'

'I couldn't sleep last night thinking about Carolyn and what she did to you. Honestly.'

'Sorry, Lyn, I shouldn't have said anything.'

'You should have, and I'll tell you why. I remembered something in the middle of the night.'

'Really, what?'

'I checked with Gary this morning. I didn't tell him why I was asking – that's our little secret. But he remembered alright.'

'Now, I'm on the edge of my seat,' Bec said.

'It was a night out for us without the kids, right? A while ago … maybe five years back. Gary and I are out in the city for a big night, can't remember the occasion, probably one of our birthdays. But maybe we were just out,' she added a little defensively. 'Don't always need to have a reason, do we? Anyway, here we are making our way to the restaurant, when we stop at a posh bar – you know the sort, dim and moody, very glam in one of those little laneways.'

Bec didn't know. The closest she ever got to something like that was Josh's locale.

'So, there we are sitting at our dark little candlelit table, and Gary says, *Keep it nice* and points to a couple on the other side of the room practically making out. You know? The woman is all over this bloke, and he's not exactly hating it, if you know what I mean.' She laughed. 'Anyway, we're sitting there feeling sophisticated sipping our margheritas, when they get up and dust themselves off and start to leave. Then, I see who it is.'

'Who?'

'Carolyn Moorhouse.'

'Are you sure?'

'How could I forget the barrister who worked on my case? It was her. I was shocked.'

'Hmm,' Bec said, 'bet you were.'

'I didn't mention to Gary I knew who the woman was, and after that we left too.'

'Well, never expected to hear anything like that,' Bec said. 'Doesn't sound like the Carolyn I know.'

'No, but after her behaviour towards you, maybe you shouldn't be surprised?'

'Maybe. Hey, and something else you said, I've just had confirmed. This is in confidence, too, by the way,' Bec said, trying to make light of it, although the shock of discovering Carolyn had a daughter, about whom she'd never spoken, had fazed her no end. *I thought we were friends.* It was Bec's turn to repeat those words.

'Heavens, what?'

'Caro did have a child, just like you thought. A daughter, and she was married at the time you knew her.'

'Wow, well there you go. What a secretive person.'

'Thanks, Lyn, and sorry again for disturbing your beauty sleep with all this.'

'Oh, that's alright. I'm glad I remembered. And seeing as you asked, I thought it was worth mentioning. Helpful, is it?'

'It is, Lyn, in a bad way, you sleuth.' Bec laughed.

'I've got your back.' Lyn giggled. 'But seriously, Bec, I think I'm getting a feel for the kind of work you do.'

'Careful or I'll sign you up,' Bec teased affectionately. 'I'll make a note and file it with my profile of Carolyn Moorhouse. I'm not sure what to make of it. But thanks, Lyn. I'm sure it'll come into play at some point down the track.'

'Good, I'm going to make some coffee now. Wish you were here. We could talk about it some more. Love you.'

Bec disconnected and stared at her phone. What next? If Lyn's memory of this story was correct, Bec wondered if she had ever known Carolyn Moorhouse at all. The high-minded, woman she'd known for years seemed so unlikely – at any age – to be carrying on in public the way Lyn had described.

*

Making her way to her office, it was hard for Bec not to feel pleased that the Moorhouse investigation had come her way. Even if she suspected that Jackson and Green, despite being up to their necks in the shocking domestic tragedy that was still dominating the news, would be watching her progress. Griffiths had given her a chance, and she wanted to prove his judgement right. Being involved firsthand was the only way she had to remove the doubt that would be tied to her name, and to find what was going on with Carolyn. *Just bring it on*, she thought.

Chapter 21

She was first in, as always.

Shaun and Wendy arrived a little while later, coffee cups in hand, just as Bec was preparing to leave.

'So, we are looking for Kenny Madden, and Shaun's watching security footage. We need the actress to tell us who she was with in the video, if it was the mysterious Kenny. And you've got the list of cleaners to get through, Wendy. How's that going?'

'It's going.' Wendy flipped the top of her coffee cup and took a sip. 'Should be through it today. Getting nowhere.'

'Alright, carry on, I won't be long,' Bec said, grabbing her phone and jacket. 'We'll regroup when I get back.'

*

It was overcast, the cover of heavy cloud making it a dull day. Bec was legging it along Spencer Street on a mission to the Assessment Centre. She felt her muscles stretch and the tug at her calves as she went through the long list she'd nominated to achieve today. It was ambitious. But as they were losing valuable time with lagging pathology, it was even more important to push on with what they had. She hated the feeling of having no new information. It made her feel she was stuck on the back foot, with no concrete lead for either investigation.

Whenever she looked at the red brick fortress up ahead in the middle of the city, it always seemed to be a warning for people passing of how the decisions you made could impact your life. Especially as right next to where Bec was going, people were boarding trains for holiday destinations. Trips on the big rail network to 'crocodile' country in Darwin, the Red Centre of Alice Springs, the northern beaches of Sydney and Brisbane, or west to the Adelaide wine country and the mining hubs of Perth. Not one of them that Bec could be dragged into, but people were wheeling their cases towards the station all day and night.

Yet, it was a very different story if you were one of the unlucky ones housed where Bec was going. There you would be cooling your heels with all the other criminals; all ages, hardened repeat offenders and newly minted juveniles all locked in cells awaiting their fate.

Bec recalled sliding door moments in her own life – like when she'd chosen to finish her training and not moved with her family to Queensland. She could be sitting on a sunny beach in a floral shirt right now. Doing who knew what? But that went for anyone. Which building you went in depended on which path you took.

She stood outside for a moment to catch her breath and looked up. It was a punch of a building, this Assessment Centre; stark and brutal. She checked her watch. Right on time. Entering the building, she went through the usual security procedures and waited.

Juan Zamora, accompanied by a prison guard, looked dreadful when he walked in. The government-issue green tracksuit was unbecoming on his frame, and the five o'clock shadow, which was a magazine look on some, only deepened his unhappy expression. His face didn't raise a smile when Bec greeted him with, 'Good Morning.'

She didn't believe Juan was a killer. Most likely, his explanation of what had happened was true. An accident in the course of a break-in. His eyes, dark and moody, were full of sorrow; it was plain as day that the experience of being locked up here was having a huge impact on him. One minute this pupil barrister was doing his high-profile job, and the next he was being attacked in legal chambers, which was unprecedented – or rare at any rate – and now he was here in a lockup with no power to control any aspect of his life.

Bec felt sorry for him in this situation. 'How are you going?'

He shrugged. 'How do you think I'm going?'

She paused, weighing up whether to ask after his family. She wanted to but decided not to. From what she'd seen of his circumstances, still living at home with extended family, they would be a mess living this nightmare with their only son in prison, looking at an uncertain future.

Bec opened the conversation with, 'I'm not going to ask you to go through your version of events again, Juan. I'll be running this investigation from here on, so I'll be straight with you. A man died at your workplace as the result of an altercation with you. You say it was self-defence due to an intruder breaking in, and I'm inclined to believe your version of what happened. But ...'

He made no move to interrupt her.

'It could also be a question of murder or manslaughter, which we must rule out, you understand.'

He said nothing.

'I've read the crime-scene reports and the formal statement you gave to my colleagues, Detectives Jackson and Green, and I do have some questions, if you don't mind.'

He shrugged again. 'I have nothing to add.'

'Carolyn Moorhouse said, which you didn't contradict, that on the day this intrusion into chambers took place, you were not meant to be working. Can you give me a little information around that?'

He sighed. 'So, now you want all the dirty laundry as well,' he said.

'I'm not sure what you mean by that.'

He shrugged, took a breath, and looked her right in the eyes.

'I was meant to be going on holiday with my fiancée, Detective Sergeant.' He paused. 'We argued that afternoon. She broke it off. I had a change of plan. No holiday. So, I thought I might as well go to work. I had plenty of unfinished things to do.'

'Go on.'

'When I got in later, Carolyn told me to go home. She hadn't been expecting to see me for three weeks, you see. She left ahead of me. But I took my time. Then the man broke in, and we fought. When I saw that he wasn't moving, I called her. She was shocked, as you can imagine.'

'And you have no idea who that man was or why he would be breaking into your chambers?'

'No clue, both counts.'

'Alright, thank you. Anything else you'd like me to be aware of?'

'No.'

'Alright, Juan. I was notified earlier that pathology is experiencing some delay in producing the results we need to further this investigation, so I'm going to recommend you be released in the meantime, pending investigation.'

'Oh, I can go but I can be arrested again at any time?' Juan said, animated, not in a good way.

'You can remain here if you prefer,' Bec said, and saw him flinch. 'But if your story pans out and pathology confirms the intruder fell onto the metal object in the manner you described, you should be fine. Having said that, head-injury results take a while to produce, as I'm sure you know. But I don't consider you a flight risk, so I'll fill out the paperwork while I'm here and you will be free to go.'

'Pending investigation,' he said.

'Pending investigation,' she repeated.

'Can I return to work?'

'Yes, but you'll need to be available to answer any questions we may have at any time. Alright?'

He flicked his eyes up briefly to meet Bec's and said, 'Thank you.'

She hoped she was right about him.

Chapter 22

On her way back, Bec wondered about Carolyn's reaction to Juan Zamora's release. Could it bring about a change in her attitude? She had no idea. One thing she did know, Juan Zamora was grateful to be released, even with the investigation ongoing. He wasn't a murderer. He might have been in the wrong place at the wrong time, but Bec didn't see him as violent, an explosion waiting to happen, bludgeoning the intruder with Carolyn's Buddha.

Shaun and Wendy both looked up expectantly when she walked back into the office.

Bec spoke to them from the doorway, telling them about Juan Zamora's release.

'He's not being released because he's a barrister in Moorhouse's chambers?' Wendy said tartly.

Bec found the comment so provocative she cut her senior constable short.

'We have no possibility of charging him at all until comprehensive pathology reports are in, Wendy, and without that, we have nothing to contradict his version of events. So, for now, as I said, pending investigation. Are we clear?'

'Sorry, Sarge, just sometimes … That wasn't what I meant. I'm sorry. I wasn't saying …' she petered out.

Shaun came to the rescue of his colleague. 'The DI was looking for you, Sarge.'

'Was he looking for something in particular?'

'He didn't say.'

'Alright, back to work.' Bec closed her door.

*

As Griffiths had left no message, Bec decided to do nothing. If he wanted to speak to her, he'd find her.

She sat down and turned her attention back to her task list. She'd been keeping an eye on the clock after the conversation with the lab yesterday. Avi should have fast-tracked fingerprint results at least for the cleaner by now. Bec liked the pathologist, but enough was enough. How were they expected to solve crimes without all the facts? Oftentimes, Avi didn't pick up when he was overloaded, but yesterday, when he'd simply handed his phone over to Pip and got her to deliver the bad news, this was a new development.

Today, Bec wasn't going to take no for an answer. She was hopeful because there was one thing she knew about the man: Avi possessed an impeccable, almost theatrical sense of timing. Her guess, he'd see her number come up and know he'd have to give her something. Bec pushed the number and waited. Sure enough.

'Avikesh Ahern at your service,' he responded grandly.

'Avi, it's Rebecca.'

'Yes, my dear. How are you?'

'How do you think I am, Avi? Two bodies and no forensics, nothing to go on. And, Avi, please, can you let go of the "my dear" bit? You know I'm not keen on it.' She smiled, hoping some of the brightness made it through to her voice.

'Oh, it's not so bad, is it?'

She imagined the twinkle in his eye.

'Only that it makes me feel old, Avi, before my time.'

'Tick-tock, my dear, it's the same for all of us.'

'That's no comfort. Listen, I know you're snowed under, but at least give us the fingerprints for our cleaner in the Moorhouse matter? It's—'

'Well, as you ask,' Avi butted in, 'I do have something. Just about to call you.'

'Were you really?' she said. Irony was lost on the man.

'Yes, my dear, I was.'

'So, what have you got?' Bec was trying not to rush Avi, even if she thought he needed prodding sometimes, like right now.

'Well, the bang on the head certainly killed him, but I need to do a bit more work to be sure whether he was struck deliberately or fell onto the metal object.'

Six weeks or more, Bec thought, knowing that blunt-trauma head injuries took the longest time to produce a result.

'Can't be more precise than that just yet. His blood wasn't too good. Not a healthy man at all. I'd say he ate a lot of junk food, judging by the—'

'Too much detail, Avi, thanks,' Bec interrupted.

'When I called our fingerprint friends, guess what?'

'Hopefully, they found a name.'

'Yes, exactly so. They found your Buddha man's fingerprints on the database.'

'So, you have a name?' Bec said, fully excited now. Sweating on forensics was not her favourite part of an investigation, but when the science came through, like now, it was nothing short of exhilarating.

'All in the report I am sending you this instant.'

'Avi, what can I say …' she began.

'Yes, I know I am, aren't I?' He chuckled. 'Anyway, this one was quite a busy chappy, I'd say, at one time.'

'What kind of busy and when?'

'In the report, Rebecca,' the pathologist teased cheerfully. 'Oh yes, a right Mr Light Fingers, he was. Read the information through and you can see for yourself. Let's just say he was a regular customer of your break-and-enter team. Sending now. More coming soon. Enjoy!'

And before she could ask about the progress of the DNA results from Doreen's unit, the phone went dead.

Bec shook her head and couldn't resist a smile as the email pinged onto her screen. And there it was. The name of the dead cleaner, found on the prison system, was Aniken Smith.

Grinning furiously, Bec jumped to her feet and called the team in to tell them the news. She started scribbling his name on the whiteboard as she spoke.

'Hip hip hooray.' Wendy rushed in, shoving her hands high in the air.

'So, he's done prison time, too,' Shaun said.

Turning back to her small team, Bec said, 'Yes, so what would your next move be?'

'Get his proper mugshot,' Shaun announced, starting to type.

'Now that we've got a name, we can pull his file and find his parole officer to get a bit of background,' Wendy added.

'Start there. Let's find Mr Smith's parole officer and see if someone can help us fill out more of the picture about who Smith was. Can you take care of that, Wendy, and check the cleaners' list, see if our Aniken Smith is on any roster?'

'That'll be a waste of time. I don't reckon that list is even real.' Wendy shrugged. 'Fake phone numbers, too, most of them not even connected. Absolutely no detail about who was even meant to be working Barwick Chambers or anywhere else. Dodgy as all get-out.'

'Probably right. I'll see what happens when I give them the name of our bloke. Shaun, can you do the electoral role, social media, and the rest of it?'

'Do you want me to leave the footage?'

'No, pace yourself with the pictures, that's all.'

'Okay.'

'Let's get to work.'

'What about Miss Dishy? She still isn't answering our messages,' Wendy said. 'We have to get her to talk, Sarge.'

'Yes, you're right.' Bec paused. 'She'll have an agent. Time to try that path if she won't answer her phone or her front door.'

Bec glanced up and checked the time. *Finally, getting somewhere,* she thought.

*

The afternoon drew on, with Wendy and Shaun working feverishly at their stations.

'It's Rebecca Harpin from homicide.'

'Hello.'

'We spoke earlier.'

'Yes.'

'We don't seem to be getting any traction with your people. We have a name now for the person who died in the barrister's chambers.'

'Alright,' Ernie, the manager, said, as though he wasn't vaguely interested.

'Aniken Smith,' Bec said. 'Somebody on your list has to have information if he was working for you.'

'I did warn you, didn't I? Said it mightn't be easy. Now, you can see how difficult my job is.'

'Yes, thanks, Ernie. What I need to know is which of your employees was meant to be cleaning that day in that building. Once I have the name, I'm sure I'll be able to convince them it would be in their best interest to tell us who worked in their place. Someone knows Aniken Smith and probably even where he lives and a whole lot more.'

'The thing is, Sergeant, a lot of the people who do this job come from places where police aren't trusted. I could put out an email asking for information if you like,' he said doubtfully. 'See if anyone wants to put any names forward. But like I said last time, I wouldn't hold my breath.'

'This Aniken Smith bloke fronted up in the same outfit your people wear, so he knew the routine, Ernie. We have a mugshot, so I'll send it through, and I'd like you to look at it.'

'So, he's a jailbird?' Ernie said. 'Well, that seals it. Even if someone does know him, they're sure as hell not gonna rat on him to the coppers.'

'Just have a look, will you?'

Bec waited a second for Ernie to download the photo. 'You know him?'

She heard some keys being pushed.

'Nothing here,' Ernie said. 'I've never seen him. I hate to say this, Sergeant, but in those big-city high-rise places, all my people need is a uniform to get inside. No-one looks at cleaners.'

Bec paused, absorbing Ernie's words.

'Are you saying that anyone observant may have noticed that a cleaner's uniform was the only requirement to get through security into the building?'

'Anyone with a dark turn of mind could do that, yes. But the other thing I checked was, according to our roster, we only get paid in those chambers on a Monday night. We don't do twice a week. Barristers' chambers are as tight as, which means we don't clean there on a Wednesday. From our point of view, we shouldn't have even had anyone there that night.'

'You could have mentioned this earlier, Ernie, and saved my team a lot of wasted effort,' Bec said, heat rising in her limbs.

'Yeah, sorry, I just realised the other day. I made a note to ring you, but it's just been sitting here. You were on my to-do list, Sergeant,' the manager replied casually.

Time waster, Bec thought, and ended the call.

After explaining the outcome of this call to Wendy, she looked about ready to call the bloke up and give him a piece of her mind. Instead, Wendy grabbed Shaun to get him to go with her to the canteen.

'I need a break,' she said.

He got up. 'Want something, Sarge?'

Bec was still steamed up, but she let it go. 'No, I'm right.'

She watched them leave.

It was frustrating sometimes. But one thing Ernie had done was confirm Bec's thought that Aniken Smith was not only a pro, but he was clever. Had skills, had done his research. He obviously knew cleaners were invisible and could just walk into these office buildings. It probably had been easy for him to dress similarly to the company's outfit, too. At some point, she would raise just how easily Smith had breached all the security. But not now.

Maybe a look through his file might reveal more about the type of criminal he was. Bec emailed archives, requesting that the file for Aniken Smith be delivered to her as soon as possible.

A mid-afternoon slump hit suddenly. Elbows on the desk, eyes closed ignoring the noise of voices talking and phones ringing, Bec allowed a silent yearning for a night with Josh to take over. One where he would pour her a glass of red, and they would eat takeaway, and he'd listen to her complaints about the world then find a way to help her laugh them away. Yes, she wanted to see him. Her mood jarred instantly, broken by retrieving the painful memory of him with that young woman. She sighed and sat up tall once more. Not going to happen. At least not today. She told Josh she'd call when her case load eased. No way that was now. She raised her arms up and sideways like wings on a bird and stretched her back.

The Cardone woman not returning calls was concerning. Nothing to worry about too much at this stage, Bec didn't think. She was confident they would find her. Yet, it was odd that first Kenny and now the actress had vanished. Security footage had placed her with the same man on several occasions. Yet, she'd told them she'd never met Doreen's son. Still, there she was on camera, large as life, going in and out of Doreen's flat. The man had to be Kenny. Why lie? Why disappear?

From what Bec could make of it, the acting profession was one of those fluid occupations, where your next job could be anywhere. The actress could just be away somewhere. It was a worry that both had disappeared so soon after Doreen had died. Cardone was the key. It was one thing for an ex-prisoner to slip off the radar, but for a TV starlet, that could be death to her career. Finding the woman's agent was a matter of urgency. Bec had a strong feeling that once they located Cardone, they would likely find the mysterious Kenny.

Chapter 23

'Hey, cut it out, sweetie, will you?' her agent said sharply.

Nikki, hunched over in the oversized client chair, tears streaming down her cheeks, reacted to the command. She sat up and blew her nose. When Cammy Duval had rung to tell her that the part hadn't come through, that she'd missed out again, Nikki couldn't take it. She'd gone straight to Duval's offices in South Melbourne to find out why. Why not this time? What excuse not to choose her? But then hearing 'the reason' spoken aloud by her own agent was more than she could take.

'Not authentic?' she gasped. 'What does that mean?' More tears.

'It doesn't matter.' Duval rubbed her lips – dark red, a colour that never wore off – together. Pencil-thin, dyed red hair and cobalt-blue nails, the fifty-something woman, former actor who'd turned to artist management, was known for her astute casting, and now presided over a booming business. Since the day she'd crossed over, Duval had dressed exclusively in black and had no patience for weakness. However, Nikki had heard that Duval could still be a soft touch in certain situations.

'It's not life threatening. You'll be back on top soon, don't worry about it.' Duval waved her arm confidently. 'It was your choice to audition, after all. I told you it wasn't for you, so I'd say you've done yourself a favour losing out on a reality TV job. It's rubbish, darling. It's not real acting, and I know deep down that isn't what you want. You need roles that suit your talents. So, dry up those tears and let's focus.'

Nikki stopped crying and directed her attention towards the woman who'd successfully put her up for lucrative roles before.

'This is what happens with that cheap shit.' The agent flung a copy of the latest issue of *Showbiz Insider* magazine across the desk. Nikki leaned over and browsed a few lines.

'Look at that one about the woman in Japan – suicide, contestants falling ill and worse. It's tragic. If we are talking authenticity …' she paused. 'Now, what's the trouble really? Surely this,' she waved her hands, meaning Nikki's tears, 'is not just about missing out on something like that? You're an actor, darling, you get some roles, and you miss out on others. That's the job.'

Nikki rubbed her eyes. 'I know it's not the right thing, but I wanted to get this because I really need the money. Something's happened,' she said, tears flowing again. 'Someone who I thought was a friend has stolen my savings.'

Duval stared at her.

'Every cent. I can't even pay my rent,' Nikki blurted.

'Oh, dear girl,' Duval said, who knew all about hard times as an artist. Nikki had heard her story many times. In a flash, her agent was up and around the other side of her desk, pulling Nikki into an embrace. 'And who was it that did this wicked thing? No-one I know, I hope.'

'No, just a friend who said they had an emergency and needed money,' Nikki sniffled. 'I drew out my savings to help and never saw him again,' she lied.

'And you just wanted to help, you lovely girl.' Duval let her go. 'I might have known this involved a him,' she said, returning to her own side of the desk. 'Look, I can give you a little cash to tide you over, and if you like you can doss down upstairs for a day or two until you sort yourself out. There's a small bathroom in there and a fold-down. I won't be in until ten tomorrow morning. Then I'm in Sydney for a week. Do you want me to speak to your letting agent? I can tell them that we're waiting on a call back, and you'll be on TV again most likely by the end of next month.'

'Oh, could you?' Nikki said, wide-eyed and feeling better already. 'That would be fantastic, but I still would like to hibernate here for a few days.' No need to mention that the police won't be able to find her and she would be away from everything at the flat. For a little while, at least.

Chapter 24

Bec was cooling her heels by passing time in morning traffic listening to a crime podcast. From time to time, she heard a comment that shed light on her own investigations. For that reason alone, she tuned in occasionally, using her commute time as a convenient window to listen to different perspectives on crime. Sometimes the discussions were interesting, but this morning, hearing a well-known social commentator state confidently that economic conditions had only a minimal impact on the rise of domestic violence, she switched off the broadcast, preferring silence, or engine noise to that kind of codswallop.

She'd barely turned her thoughts to Nikki Cardone when the number on her dash screen appeared simultaneously with her phone ringing. She picked up.

'Carolyn.'

'So, it came your way, Rebecca,' Carolyn said, her voice frosty. No hello, no small talk. 'Why the change of heart?'

'Nothing I'm aware of, and it doesn't matter,' Bec said, thinking how they were talking to each other in a strange way. 'It's a situation, isn't it? But here we are. As I mentioned in my message, I will need to go through your statement with you again.'

Carolyn didn't respond directly to that. Instead, she launched off onto a different topic.

'A good move, releasing Juan from custody, Rebecca. He's totally shaken up. I've told him if he's up for it I'd welcome him back to chambers until he recovers his feet. I'm convinced there will be no charges against him. But he can't seem to get "pending investigation" out of his head. Not helpful.'

Probably in this instance Caro meant, as soon as he recovered, she would ask him to leave, Bec thought. Or, he might decide to go voluntarily. It was a hell of a mark against your name as a barrister to have been incarcerated even for a short time. No matter what the eventual outcome.

'More helpful than him remaining in custody for forensics to complete their tests,' Bec responded. Her tone was cool, too. She heard it. Seriously, was it that Carolyn had expected her to let this whole thing go, or help her and Juan fabricate a different story?

'Yes, I suppose so,' Carolyn said, as if she didn't agree. And clearly, the absence of any mention of her being sorry or commenting in any way about what this 'situation' was doing to their long-term friendship spoke volumes. 'Without Juan, my schedule is brutal so would you mind coming here? You mentioned it was an option?'

'Yes, fine.'

They made a time that suited them both and disconnected.

Bec finished the drive in silence, trying to push down the mounting apprehension about Carolyn and her behaviour.

*

'DI Griffiths is not back yet,' a locum assistant told Bec. 'Diana has gone on leave for a week,' and, 'would you like to take a seat?'

Bec shook off her annoyance.

The assistant turned back to her screen.

'Should I come back? You could text me when he's ready?'

'No,' the woman replied, not turning to face Bec. 'You should wait.'

A desk job was something else, wasn't it? Bec thought. A universe she never wished to visit in her law-enforcement career. Manning the door for some fast-track desk jockey who expected her to be on time but had no appreciation for her schedule. A proper copper would understand that she had better things to do than sit around waiting for them to show up.

For a nanosecond, it crossed her mind to leave before she thought better of it, and luckily, before she had to decide how long she would wait, she heard her name called.

'DS Harpin, come in.' DI Griffiths swept past regally and opened the door. 'Sit down.' He nodded at the chair.

Bec sat. She had missed her morning run, and from the tightness in her leg muscles, she would have to make up for it tonight when she got home, if the light was right.

Griffiths wasted no time. 'What have you got on Moorhouse, Rebecca? The Bar Association has been on the phone. They want to know how the investigation is proceeding and the status of her pupil barrister, Juan Zamora? I thought you agreed to keep me up to speed.' His face was stern.

'Yes, sir, I did. But until last night, I really didn't have a lot to share.'

'By that, I hope you mean that you have something worth sharing with me now?'

'I do, sir, regarding Zamora. I've arranged for his release, pending investigation.'

Griffiths stared at her. 'Well, that should stop some of the bleating from the Bar. Good. Anything else?'

'Forensics got a fingerprint match for the dead man. No DNA yet, but we have a name.'

She had his attention.

'Name of Aniken Smith. Done time for break-and-enter, no violence. Mostly, private residences where owners are on holiday, that sort of thing. Released nine months ago after a second stint.'

'Then what on earth was he doing breaking into a barrister's chambers on the ninth floor of a city building?'

'Unfortunately, that's something we've not been able to establish so far. It seems a leap from his normal modus.'

Bec was about to continue when Griffiths spoke. 'Alright, and the woman in Thornbury? Have you got anything there?'

'Not making a whole lot of progress there without forensics, sir. Some of the neighbours said she had a son called Kenny, but we haven't been able to locate him yet. We think, after Shaun found some facts, that this Kenny might have been given up for adoption at birth. Again, some neighbours say he's done time, but we can't find a Kenny Madden in the system. So, haven't gotten any further with that, at this stage. What we do have is some security footage that shows an unidentified man visiting the dead woman. It's not a clear image, unfortunately, but we think he's the son. The footage also places a woman at the units in the same shot. We did speak to her earlier, but at this time, we can't locate her. She's an actor, so probably working away somewhere.'

'Isn't there someone who knows him or can vouch for the man, if he is the son of the dead woman?'

'Not so far. Just the actor. I do find it suspicious that if Kenny is Doreen's long-lost son, he would go missing at the exact time his birth mother dies. Would make him, at the very least, a person of interest.'

'Do you need help, Rebecca? Seems to me you need Green or one of the others to come across to give you a hand. He and Jackson have done a fine job bringing their situation under control ...'

'No, sir, I feel confident—'

'Rebecca, pardon me for saying. You were confident when I proposed you handle both cases.'

'Yes, sir.' Bec feared colour may have risen to her cheeks from the heat that just invaded her body. But speaking steadily she said, 'And I still am. We are getting somewhere now. Just need a little more time.'

'Seems to me, you are not getting anywhere very fast with either of them.'

'Sir.' Bec sat still, fully expecting Griffiths to say Green or someone else was coming onto the investigation.

He watched her, thinking it over. Bec couldn't pick which way he would go.

'Alright,' he said at last. 'You have demonstrated a positive attitude from the start, Rebecca. I admire that, and you have made progress, not a lot, but some. An unreasonably long wait for forensics, I will concede, probably has hindered your progress. So, for this reason, I'm going to allow you to carry on. But do as you say, please, and keep me informed.'

'Yes, sir.' She was doing all she could. Why did it feel like some backhanded bonus to be able to stay on her own investigation?

Chapter 25

Waiting for the lift to arrive, niggling thoughts persisted. Where was Kenny? Helping Hands Mission had confirmed that they knew of him but had refused to give any more. Bec and her team had been unable to find any other trace of Kenny Madden living in Thornbury or anywhere else. Nothing registered in his name – no phone, power, nothing. Was he even a convicted criminal? Was this a story concocted by Doreen? If so, for what purpose? Bec felt she was missing something.

There was no getting away from the mounting pressure Bec felt to have a breakthrough on this. She knew Griffiths wasn't kidding when he said he'd bring the other team on if that's what it took to get a result. *No panic, no jumping to conclusions*, she cautioned herself and repeated the procedures drilled into her: *A good investigation is built on persistent checking and follow-up. Trust the process. And if that isn't working ... yet, trust yourself.*

*

'Let's try Nikki Cardone again,' she said, returning to find Shaun and Wendy busy as bees.

Wendy looked up. 'There's a box from archives that's just arrived.'

'Okay, thanks.'

'Already left a message, Sarge.' Shaun turned around.

'Did you call the neighbours? Has anyone seen her?'

'Seems not,' Wendy said, glancing at Bec, as if she was trying to judge whether Bec had forgotten her suggestion that Juan had gotten out on bail as a favour to her friend Carolyn Moorhouse.

'That's right. Her neighbour Mrs Chalmers said, she didn't think Nikki had been home for more than twenty-four hours. Thought she might have gone to one of those famous all-night parties that showbiz people have.' Shaun smirked. 'Said she reads about them in her favourite magazines, the before photos and the afters, too. Couldn't stop her talking about it. Could we, Wen?'

'And wouldn't you love to be invited to one of those,' Wendy said, glancing at Bec again, trying to engage her in the fun.

'What, and you wouldn't?' Shaun retaliated.

'Maybe if they told me *Bondi Vet* would be there,' Wendy said with a laugh.

'Alright, meanwhile back here,' Bec tapped her nails on the desk, 'parties are a little thin on the ground. Wendy, can you get onto the security company again? See if they've got any more footage for the Thornbury units. We need pictures going back further, another month at least. Let's see what else has been going on at that address. I'm not happy that we can't find Nikki, either. She's the only link we have to the dead woman and the Kenny character. Either she is away for something job-related, or she isn't around for some other reason. Whatever it is, she's had enough time to respond. Mobile phones do still work on film sets. Can I leave the task of finding the showbusiness agent to you, Wendy? Assuming somebody does represent her.'

'Oh, someone will,' Wendy said confidently, 'you can't get those roles without professional help.'

'Is that right?' Shaun laughed. 'Tried, have you?'

Bec cut in. 'So, that's yours, Wendy. Shouldn't be too hard. Shaun, can you carry on with the footage?'

He nodded.

'I'm going to make a start there.' She pointed through the glass to the box sitting on her desk marked 'Aniken Smith' in large black letters. 'And I've made an appointment later to meet Carolyn Moorhouse to go through her statement.'

'Looking for anything, Sarge?' Shaun asked.

'Yes, I'd like her to tell us what exactly she thinks her intruder might have been looking for.'

Chapter 26

Bec sat down at her desk and set to work. Lifting the lid off the box, she placed it down, wrinkling her nose at the waft of stale paper. She wanted an impression of how Smith operated. Reading through all the charges might help a clearer picture emerge. Glancing at one file then another, she kept going until she found one dated twenty years ago and opened it.

It was hard to miss. The name of the defence lawyer was always written at the top right-hand corner of the front page. Bec had a visceral reaction seeing Carolyn Moorhouse's name inserted there. She sat completely still, stunned. What did this mean? Carolyn had been Smith's legal representative and hadn't ever mentioned it? She read the name again. Then leafing through, she quickly read the file. No doubt about it. Carolyn knew the man who had died in her chambers. He had been a client of hers. Blood rushed to her head. Was that why she had behaved the way she had – this connection?

'Wendy, Shaun,' she called out, 'take a look at this.'

'She's been lying the whole time,' Wendy said triumphantly after reading it.

Shaun nodded slowly. 'Looks like she does have more to tell us.'

*

Bec stepped inside Carolyn's rooms, which were uncharacteristically chaotic, with files piled over every surface.

'One of the worst times of my life, Rebecca,' Carolyn muttered, closing the door once Bec was inside. 'The number of adjournments I have had to request has caused a huge backlash. The whole thing's a nightmare. Do you have anything more to report from forensics?' Carolyn said, staring at Bec as she directed her to the only seat clear of documents.

'No, not what we need yet.' Bec noticed Carolyn's hair was greasy and hanging down, unlike her usual immaculate presentation.

'Juan is coming back to chambers, but he's taking a few days to recover – that is if he ever can recover from all this. Can I get you a water?'

Bec declined. She was observing someone she barely recognised. This was not the Carolyn she knew. Agitated. Not in control. Brittle voice.

Bec had asked Carolyn, right after the break-in, if she was alright. She'd responded, 'Not really.' This was not the time to revisit that comment, or to wonder why Carolyn appeared to be blocking all attempts to speak frankly about what happened that night. But one thing Bec knew was they were going to have to have that conversation today.

Unsure of how to regain the communication they once had, she went straight to the purpose of their meeting.

'We're hoping to get to the bottom of this, to end the ordeal for all concerned,' Bec said formally.

Carolyn placed a jug of water on the desk with two glasses. She poured one for herself and offered Bec a glass for the second time.

Bec was trying to picture the Carolyn that Lyn had described and couldn't. She wanted to ask Carolyn why she'd never mentioned to her that she had a daughter, or that she'd once been married? But this was not the time for that, either. What she needed to know as a matter of urgency was why Carolyn had not informed her, or anyone else, that she had known the man who'd died in her chambers. What was she hiding? Did she and the dead man have some other connection? Bec had to draw heavily on her professional training to quell the tension in her stomach.

'I have copies of the security footage from the entrance to the building, and we've tracked the victim from when he entered the building in the lift foyer on the ground floor to the lift foyer on this floor,' she said, watching carefully for any reaction from Carolyn. 'Now, here's the thing. Seems to me that our victim didn't come to your rooms randomly, Caro. He caught the lift directly to this floor and went straight to your office.' She paused to make sure Carolyn understood. 'He didn't try any other doors.' Carolyn took a sip of water. 'So, what I need you to tell me, Carolyn, is why your office? What was he looking for?'

Carolyn shook her head. 'I don't know.' She placed her glass down. 'The filing cabinet Juan said he was rifling through is full of what I call "maybe" briefs. There was no money or anything like that there – just reams of paper.'

'Off the top of your head, is there nothing at all that comes to mind, an original document, something else valuable that he might have been looking for?'

'Nothing I can think of,' Carolyn said. 'No shortage of clients who think they've been wronged by a court decision.' She shrugged. 'Any number of disgruntled defendants from when I was a prosecutor, but there's nothing in those files to help.' Bec noticed Carolyn massaging her right hand with her left, giving an impression of hand wringing. 'So, why he targeted me, as you say, I'm afraid I don't know.' From the tone of Carolyn's voice, Bec thought she could have been a stranger to her.

'What are "maybe briefs"?' she asked.

'Briefs you get sent, then the instructing solicitor says just hold on to it but doesn't do anything. Waiting for fees in advance, more instructions, clients who got cold feet, who knows? So, they go in there.'

Bec nodded. 'Does the name Aniken Smith mean anything to you?'

Carolyn frowned. 'I don't think so, should it?'

Her professional façade was good, Bec thought. *Very good. No sign of any reaction.* 'Maybe,' Bec said. 'Long history of arrests. Couple of stints in jail. Fingerprints for your intruder have revealed that he was a serial break-and-enter guy.'

Carolyn exploded with annoyance. 'Ah, so he's a career criminal. Why the hell didn't you say so sooner? Probably thought I had something worth nicking in here. That explains it, then!'

'I am surprised you don't remember, Carolyn,' Bec paused, taking her time, 'because your name came up in this man's history.'

The barrister's face changed colour. 'Hang on, could you say that name again?'

'Aniken Smith. You represented him years ago as a young barrister.'

'I don't remember even being a young barrister, Rebecca, but maybe the name does ring a vague bell.' Carolyn frowned. 'I mean, for heaven's sake, I was a legal-aid duty defence barrister in the Magistrates Court. Five cases on your docket, you meet the client twenty minutes before, read the charges as fast as you can while you get instructions and work out what position to take, go into court and do your best. Client goes down or gets a rap over the knuckles and a suspended sentence, you shake hands and move to the next one. I don't remember any of them, to be honest. But if you've read the file, what did he get? Did I get him off?'

'Break-and-enter, third time, he got six months,' Bec said.

'Not bad. I did my job, then.' Carolyn expelled a sharp breath. 'He wouldn't be breaking in to kill me over going to jail for six months on a third offence.'

'True, but Mr Smith didn't go to any other chambers, just yours,' Bec said emphasising the 'yours.'

'Hang on, hang on.' Carolyn got to her feet, shaking her hands like she was flicking off water where there was no hand towel. 'Let me think. If he's a professional break-and-enter, there is something.'

'Right?' Bec waited.

'I do have an on-again off-again brief from a firm in Sydney. Got a call from them a couple of weeks ago saying that their copy of the file had gone missing and could I send a copy back to them. It's one of those "maybe briefs" I mentioned. It was sent to me, then I was told not to worry, then called back and told the clients might want to go ahead, after all.'

'What's that file about?'

'I can't say I've read it in detail. Something about Bitcoin, you know, Cryptocurrencies. My memory says, someone smart did something dumb, cost them big time, now they are baying for blood. That's the nutshell.'

'The file in Sydney went missing. Do you know how?'

'No, no idea. I got an email from the instructing solicitor's PA. I mean, it can't be that. It's just a money case. Rich guys suing other rich guys. This whole building is full of those cases. It's how we make our livings.'

'Yes, but I'm going to need a contact for the Sydney firm that briefed you.'

By the time Bec walked out of Carolyn's rooms, she was still trying to work out what had just happened. Carolyn said that to the best of her knowledge, she'd represented him once, many years ago. Bec would have to check that. And while she did concede that people often did look different after a long time, the Carolyn she knew would have remembered.

Or was it that she should ask herself a terrible question. Was Carolyn a consummate liar? The friend Bec had trusted for decades seemed to be able to lie to her without blinking.

Chapter 27

Bec's phone pinged as she was getting out of the car. She looked down. Josh.

... missing you.

She didn't text back. Later. She wasn't up to it now.

Bec went to the canteen, ordered a cup of tea, and sat there waiting for the nausea to pass until well after her cup was empty. She couldn't grasp how she and Carolyn could have been friends one minute and not the next. If everything Carolyn had told the police was true, then why would a dreadful accident affect their friendship? It just didn't make sense.

'Hey, Sarge,' Wendy called out as she came through the door. 'You were right, Cardone's agent was easy to find amongst the online agencies.'

'How did you go with Moorhouse?' Shaun asked as Bec approached.

She filled them in on her conversation with Carolyn.

'The body lying on the floor – she didn't remember his face?' Wendy chipped in.

'Well, he was wearing a medical mask, remember, so not a surprise on that score. Anyway, what have you got?' Bec realised she had left out the matter of the missing file.

'Cammy Duval, Agent to the Stars,' Wendy said, reading from the screen as she scrolled past an endless sea of faces. It was pleasing to see Wendy and Shaun working like a well-oiled machine.

'And there she is, Nikki Cardone.' Shaun pointed to the screen.

Bec stared at the publicity photo that had captured Cardone in a classic pouting pose. She was just as Shaun had said, a naturally beautiful young woman. Bec even vaguely remembered seeing her face on TV.

'Says here she has played different roles in a few soaps, and she was the golden girl in that peanut-butter ad,' Wendy confirmed, reading from her own screen.

That was it, the peanut-butter ad, Bec thought. Shaun had Nikki's profile photo on his screen. Glam photography had a way of making anyone feel badly groomed and inadequate. It crossed Bec's mind that she really should update her wardrobe beyond fitness gear and police clobber, before Wendy said to no-one in particular, 'I think I'm going to get blonde tips.'

'Won't help,' Shaun shot back.

'Oh you! Sarge, did you hear that, he's abusing me,' Wendy said with a laugh.

'Only kidding, Senior Constable. Bad guys will still be scared of you.'

'Just the way it should be,' Bec added to close the conversation.

'Cammy Duval's offices are in South Melbourne,' Wendy read aloud. 'Not far at all, if we need to talk to her.'

'Let's call her and see if she can help.'

Wendy nodded and pushed the numbers in, pressed 'loudspeaker' and waited.

'*Cammy Duval, leave your number and I'll get back to you,*' a voice said after a few rings.

Bec left a brief message.

'I don't think we'll have long to wait, Sarge,' Wendy said. 'Who wants a message from homicide on their voicemail. Especially the way you phrased it.'

Barely two minutes passed before the phone trilled.

Bec identified herself and said, 'Thanks for returning my call, Ms Duval.'

'Please, Cammy.'

'Okay, Cammy. Not meaning to alarm you, but we'd like to speak to a client of yours.'

'A client of mine? Do you know what I do, Officer? I'm not a lawyer.'

'Yes, Agent to the Stars, as far as I can tell.'

'That's alright,' she responded, satisfied. 'But what can I, or any of my lovely clients, have to offer homicide? Good grief, I wasn't thinking. Has someone's parent died?'

'No, nothing like that. We just need to locate Nikki Cardone,' Bec said.

'Nikki!' Duval was shocked. 'Has something happened? I'm in Sydney, but if it's bad news I'll need to come back. My clients can be very fragile.'

'I'm not sure that's necessary. It's just that Ms Cardone is not answering her phone or the door at her home address, and we do need to talk to her. Do you have any idea where she might be?'

'Oh,' she gasped. 'That's a relief, then. It would be hard for me to get back now. Anyway, the reason Nikki isn't answering her door at home is because she's staying in the little apartment above my office. I keep it for actors from interstate – you know, sometimes it's handy for them not to have those big hotel bills.'

'And why would Ms Cardone be staying there?' Bec asked.

'Well, I don't know that I should be discussing Nikki's private business, but it seems she's been in a spot of bother.'

'What kind of bother?'

'Loaned money to a male friend of hers who disappeared, leaving poor Nikki not quite able to pay her rent. That is, until I can get her cast into a regular soap again. She'll be fine. But these things take time, you know. So, I said she could stay for a few days. Is Nikki in trouble with the police?'

'No,' Bec said. 'It's just that there was an incident at her address last week, and we'd like to ask her if she remembers anything about it, that's all. We're speaking to all the neighbours, too. Just routine checks.'

'Alright. Nikki takes everything to heart, you know, so don't be too brusque with her. This boyfriend who nicked off with her savings has shaken her. I can tell. She's not herself. She'd been planning to go to Los Angeles to break into Hollywood for years – Lord knows she has the looks and the talent – but you see, now the poor girl can't even pay her rent. Her confidence is at rock bottom.'

'I see. So, Ms Duval, if we were to go to your offices in South Melbourne, we would find Nikki Cardone?'

'Should do, yes. Can't see she'd be going anywhere much without any money. I gave her a small advance, but … Would you like me to call her?'

'Thanks for the offer, but that won't be necessary. If we don't find her at your office today or tomorrow, you'll be back from Sydney …'

'I'm back on Friday.'

'Good, so if it comes to it, we can speak to you on Friday. Thanks for your time, Cammy. Tell me, how's the weather in Sydney?'

'Oh, sunny like always, Sergeant,' she said, and ended the call.

Shaun and Wendy were on their feet, ready to move, when Bec said, 'And while I think of it, Carolyn Moorhouse did give us something.'

'And what was that?' Shaun asked.

'She gave us a line of enquiry for what the intruder may have been looking for.' Shaun and Wendy waited to hear what it was. 'A case file about Bitcoin. Sounds more like fraud to me, but I'll make the call. You two just bring Cardone in.'

*

It was tenuous, Bec knew. A theft from a Sydney law firm, one missing file and a break-in at Carolyn's chambers. Just the same, it was a link that deserved following up. It wasn't every day that law firms were broken into, and their files stolen. It wasn't like theft of drug money or bank robbery.

She remembered Josh patiently trying to explain Cryptocurrency to her over dinner one night, and her absolute lack of comprehension. 'You give someone you don't know a pile of money in return for a passcode, and then somehow, a week later it's worth a lot more money but you don't know why?' He had been amused at her question.

'I didn't say it makes sense, babe. I run an upmarket place, remember. Lots of rich guys telling me how much they have made with it.'

'So, have you put money into it?' Bec had asked him, shocked.

'Not a chance in this lifetime. I work too hard to earn my pay packet to risk it on something I don't comprehend.'

*

Bec had a Zoom call set up with Aaron Petersen, the instructing solicitor who first briefed Carolyn.

His PA told Bec that Petersen was on his way.

Bec didn't mind waiting. Through her camera, she could see that the lawyer's desk was set up in a way that highlighted stunning water views behind it. Bec thought he had to be on the hundredth floor, or higher. She was staring at the brilliant blue sky and the harbour views when Petersen suddenly appeared on-screen and sat down.

'How can I help you, Detective Sergeant Harpin,' he said. 'I don't often talk to police in my practice.'

'Thank you for taking the call, Mr Petersen. I was admiring the view. That's quite a vista. I'd find it hard to leave the office if I had harbour views like that all day.' She smiled charmingly.

'Yes, we never tire of it.' He glanced around quickly.

Petersen had to be around the forty-year-old mark, tanned skin and teeth that flashed when he smiled. Expensive cut of suit. He was doing well.

Bec quickly explained the purpose of her call. 'I'm sure Ms Moorhouse has updated you about her chambers being broken into and the tragic consequences. When she informed me that the original file was stolen from your office in similar circumstances, alarm bells started ringing for me. This call is to find any links between the two break-ins.'

The solicitor coughed uncomfortably.

'So, my first question, Mr Petersen, is why brief Carolyn Moorhouse in Melbourne when you must have a thousand high-powered silks up there?'

'Please, call me Aaron. Yes, the similarity is concerning, I agree. I hope there's nothing to it, but I'm glad you're looking into it. As far as briefing Carolyn, all the evidence on our missing file is about a man who comes from Melbourne, where he perpetrated an alleged fraud. He met my guy in Melbourne, too, so that's why I thought the most appropriate jurisdiction for the case would be down there. And I've always found Carolyn to be excellent for these kinds of matters, where criminal and commercial issues intertwine. She was the ideal counsel for us.'

'I understand. But why, then, would this client use your firm rather than a local firm down here?'

He smiled. 'Sometimes I wish he would, but …' He became serious. 'My client, who I won't be naming, is high profile in business – his photo or name is in the media most days. He's used my services in all his commercial matters for a very long time. So, it was natural for him to call me when he had a "personal" legal issue,' Aaron explained, giving Bec no feeling that he was boasting but rather stating facts.

'Ms Moorhouse indicated you represented two clients, the other one also high profile.'

Petersen nodded. 'Yes, the other unnamed client is a well-known politician. A close mate of my guy.'

The secrecy by both Carolyn and Petersen was starting to make sense, Bec thought. 'Okay, I understand we are on touchy ground here. But it would be helpful if you could tell me about the case – off the record, of course.'

Petersen considered for a moment. 'Off the record, it was fraud,' he said, and launched into the details with gusto. 'My blokes were drinking in some private members-only bar. Too many drinks, too many cigars, but at some point, they were introduced to this other bloke, who was meant to be a financial wizard. Cryptocurrencies, getting incredible returns for his investors. He dropped lots of names as clients. Had a big deal coming up, he told them, and if they acted fast, he might be able to squeeze them in with a small part of the action.'

'What kind of deal?'

'The kind you just tap your nose and smile,' the solicitor said. 'Then he gave them the kicker. A guaranteed ten per cent return on their money per month for twelve months, then their original investment back with an extra fifty per cent for their trouble.' Bec could see the resignation in the lawyer's face.

'And they fell for it?'

'Not straightaway. Next day, lots of serious documents were sent to them. References, big firm letterheads, contracts, investment agreements – all fake, they found out later. Had to make a call within twenty-four hours. This bloke had a line of people waiting to take their place. So, they dipped their toes in, fifty thousand dollars each. End of month, five thousand into each account. After the second five thousand hit their accounts, the bloke rang and said someone had pulled out. He had two extra shares left to sell at four hundred and fifty thousand each, and my guys were faster than Cathy Freeman at the Olympics. Transferred the money within the hour.'

'And then?'

'Last they ever heard of the bloke or their money – a cool million bucks.'

'So, they hired you?'

'They had some investigators try to find him. Uncovered the name the bloke used was fake. The company was fake. The references were fake. Contracts were fake. Straight from Scamcraft, Lesson One.'

'Are you suing someone?' Bec asked, putting the picture together in her mind.

'Yes and no. Yes, they want this bloke buried. No, they don't want their stupidity to be made public. We have a file and we briefed Carolyn, but our clients have ranged between gung-ho and don't do a thing.'

'And now?'

'The file sits dormant,' Peterson said.

Bec remembered Carolyn saying it was on-again off-again, and how she'd been so annoyed that she hadn't read the file in any detail.

'Was that the only reason they changed their minds, do you think?'

'I think so, yes. You know better than me once a matter like that gets into the public realm, that's what it is, public. And these men don't want to look like fools. I mean, no-one's going to invest in my guy's company or vote for a pollie whose greed makes them take risks with that much money, are they?'

'So, the file goes into Carolyn Moorhouse's "maybe" cabinet,' Bec said.

The conversation paused while she scribbled in her notebook.

'That's all very helpful, Aaron,' she said, looking up. 'Who else knew your clients were planning to take legal action against this wizard broker?'

'Apart from my client, his politician buddy and Carolyn, no-one else that I'm aware of. Of course, I don't know anything about the investigators who were looking for the scammer. They may have let something slip, trying to get some information.'

'And what can you tell me about the break-in to your office?'

'To be honest, not much. I'd been only too happy to pass the matter over entirely to Carolyn. So, I hadn't looked at it for a while. My PA was doing a review of files. And when that file wasn't where it should be, she did all the normal checks and then notified security.' Petersen frowned. 'Until they saw the footage of a bloke entering and leaving with a file, we didn't even know he'd been here.'

'And how do you imagine that was possible, with you being so far up in the sky? I imagine security's tight.'

'That's a good question, Detective Sergeant. And it's something I and my partners addressed by changing all our service companies.'

Listening to the solicitor's explanation, Bec wondered about the depth of security in high-rise buildings and barristers' chambers like Carolyn's. How a high-profile politician, and the CEO of a public company, could have been so stupid as to hand their money over with so little information. That crypto salesman must have been some talker.

'One more question, Aaron, and I'll let you get back. The man on your CCTV who took the file. Were the police involved? Was there an ID?'

'The firm called the police in, but to be honest, I'm not sure they took it too seriously. One file? I watched the footage together with the police officers. The bloke knew what he was doing. In and out, no fuss, cap on, knew where the cameras were. No clear image of his face.'

'What was your impression of the man?'

'All I could see was that he was tall, dark hair, maybe a beard, that was about it.'

Not Aniken Smith, then, Bec thought, scribbling a line through the question mark next to his name.

'Appreciate your time today, Aaron. Would I be right in thinking that if the intruder in Melbourne was after this file and had gotten away with Carolyn Moorhouse's copy, given yours was stolen, that this could be a near-perfect crime? No record of a big sum of money stolen, no-one to press charges and no-one to hold to account?'

'That thought crossed my mind, too, Sergeant, the moment I heard what happened in Melbourne. We have some documents in electronic copy, but the actual incriminating originals were in our hardcopy file, and the only copies of those originals are with Carolyn. She hadn't sent a copy back yet, so yes, it would take a bit of scouring the clouds to find all the details, and the case certainly would have been hindered if Carolyn's file had gone missing.'

*

Bec was still scribbling her notes when she heard voices.

'What a wild goose chase,' Wendy sighed and fell into her chair.

'No answer. We rang the doorbell. We called the landline. We walked around the building. We asked local store holders. Nothing. Nobody has seen anything. Nikki Cardone wasn't there. Either she's deliberately not answering the door or her phone, or the agent got it wrong.'

Bec sighed. 'Alright, keep going. My guess is, for whatever reason, she's deliberately staying out of the way. Something will show up. She's gotta be somewhere. Keep trying her unit. Duval will be back in Melbourne on Friday. If we haven't found her by then, we'll pay her a visit.'

Chapter 28

It wasn't the best start to the day reading a note from Griffiths about wanting an update. *We need results, Rebecca. Come and see me.* This type of command would normally not bother her too much. She could always find a way through reporting to her superiors in situations when there wasn't a lot to go on – especially now they had a name for the dead cleaner. But today, she would have to be careful when she spoke to Griffiths. Not to show her frustration and to hold the line.

Without any further report from forensics, Bec hadn't been able to put any approach together that looked likely to progress the investigation. Her situation with the DI was fraught, and she knew it. He would act if she didn't have something soon. With a thousand thoughts running through her mind, none particularly helpful, she opened her takeaway double-shot coffee and took a sip.

Shaun calling out broke into her thoughts. 'Sarge, you're gonna want to see what I've just found,' he yelled, not even trying to mask his excitement. Bec got up and moved quickly to his desk, where she found Wendy already staring at the image fixed on his screen.

'From the second round of security footage at the units. This shot,' he pointed, 'from one month before Doreen died. And there's another picture with the same man one week before that. From how they behave, I'd say Ms Cardone had a boyfriend.'

'Oh, she's taken,' Wendy said, feigning sadness and nudging Shaun. He chose to ignore her. 'Watch this,' he said, clicking his mouse.

'If I run it on, you'll see that they stop at Doreen's unit, too.' The three of them watched Doreen opening her door and greeting them, the same warm way she'd greeted the other man with Nikki.

'What's going on there?' Bec leaned in for a closer look.

'It certainly looks like Ms Cardone has a mystery boyfriend,' Wendy said. 'And from the pics here, it was one big happy family. Doreen, Kenny, Miss "I didn't really know them", and now this mystery man.'

'Good work, Shaun,' Bec said. 'Run off some copies of those pictures. Might be worth taking them out to show the neighbours, see if they recognise him.' She paused. 'Wendy, can you get these images to the appropriate people to see if we can get a face match? I know the image isn't very clear, but you never know. With forensics lagging, it might give us a starting point.' She glanced between them. 'I guess Ms Cardone is still ignoring your calls?'

Shaun shrugged. 'I've left messages everywhere with the neighbours asking them to call when she shows up. Don't know if they will or not.'

'Wendy?'

She also shrugged. 'I say go and try the agent's flat again.'

'My question is why is she hiding? Bec said. 'She knew our dead woman very well, from this footage, but denied it. She's there with two different blokes, one who we think is the missing Kenny, so going into hiding certainly concerns me. But is she hiding from Kenny or from us? Either way, she knows more than she'd told us so far.'

'She's up to her armpits, Sarge, that's my call from watching the video,' Wendy said, scrutinising the image again up close.

'Looks that way,' Bec responded, studying the still frame on the screen. 'Now, we have to find out if she's part of Doreen's death or a patsy caught in something. The agent said she lost all her money and couldn't pay her rent.'

'Good excuse to hide out in the agent's flat,' Wendy countered. 'Doesn't mean it's true.'

'Nice to hear you're keeping an open mind, Detective.' Shaun laughed, making Wendy blush a little.

'Devil's advocate, Shaun. Just putting another point of view.'

Bec straightened. 'Let's keep both in mind, then.'

The three of them watched the footage again, positive by the end that Cardone, the two blokes and Doreen all appeared to know each other quite well.

'She could be dead,' Wendy said, voicing a concern that had been building in Bec's mind.

'Maybe Kenny and Nikki were caught up in something that led to all three being killed.'

*

From the outer office, Bec saw her desktop phone flashing. She rushed in to pick up and seeing who it was, pressed speaker phone. 'Avi.'she said, waving for Wendy and Shaun to join her.

'Good day, my dear. How are you?'

'All the better for hearing from you. Better still if you have something for us.'

'Yes, my dear, I have news. Not the whole kit and caboodle just yet, but something very interesting about your Buddha man.'

'Good news, then.'

'Yes, well, you remember when he first came to us, we ran his DNA through the system and found no match.'

The detectives exchanged a glance.

'You haven't mentioned that to us before, Avi,' Bec said. 'But we have the fingerprint ID, don't we?'

'Patience, my dear, I'm just building the dramatic tension. Anyway, here's the thing. We ran the DNA through again today by accident, without realising it had already been done. And guess what?'

'Same result, I guess.'

'Aha, that's the reason I was building the tension. No, my dear, in fact this time we got a match.'

His voice was so level, Bec thought she'd misunderstood.

'How does that work?'

'Because there was new DNA registered on the system since our first check. And now, I move on to the crux of the call.' He paused. 'We found something else.'

Bec tried to hold herself in but couldn't. 'Avi, come on, what have you got?' she said urgently.

'Alright, but hang on tight, my dear. We have Buddha man on the one hand, and our poor Thornbury soul on the other. And the DNA tells us they are a direct close familial match.'

'What? The two bodies are related?'

'They are. When we took DNA from the woman in Thornbury, it fed into the system. Wasn't there the first time we tested. But when we did the second search, bingo bango – all the indicators were present, same family. I'm sending a report now,' the pathologist said, sounding pleased with himself. 'Might have taken a little longer, but worth the wait, wouldn't you say?' He chuckled. 'Not what you were expecting, I'll bet. Enjoy!'

And before she could a say another word, the phone went dead.

Bec shook her head and couldn't resist smiling when Avi's email pinged, leaving Shaun and Wendy huddled behind Bec's chair, reading from the screen.

'That's a stunner,' Shaun said.

'Amazing,' Wendy echoed.

'So,' Bec said, agitated still, but in a good way. 'We've got two people killed on the same night. One, a man in a cleaning uniform who nobody at the cleaning company will admit to knowing, and we now know is Aniken Smith. Two, Doreen Madden, cause of death still to be determined. But DNA tests tell us she is directly related to Smith, although the two have different names. And three, Aniken could be shortened to Kenny, which means we now have a good reason why Doreen's son, Kenny, hasn't been in touch.'

'Because he's dead,' Shaun said. 'The cleaner was Doreen's long-lost son.'

'And we had no way to connect them until forensics provided their link,' Wendy finished, shaking her head. 'Did not see that coming.'

'Who could?' Bec paused, processing the information.

Shaun rubbed his forehead. 'Could Kenny have tied his mother up, then gone to rob the Moorhouse Chambers?'

'We have to consider that as a possibility,' Bec said. 'But it goes against what we've heard about Kenny and his mother, doesn't it? We're going to need some time to process this. So, why don't you two carry on, and we'll meet back here after I relay the news to DI Griffiths.'

*

'You still don't want the extra manpower?' Griffiths seemed surprised when Bec filled him in.

'With this from pathology, sir, we're getting somewhere at last. And as you mentioned a shortage of feet on the ground, I think we can crack this as we are. It's a good team and they are putting in, sir.'

Griffiths stared at her. 'Alright, as you wish, but don't say I didn't offer. Where to from here?'

'We keep working on it and tick every box we find. We will get there, sir.'

'Keep me up to date, then, Rebecca, and if you change your mind about Green and his cohorts you have only to flag it. I know he's old school, but he's a good copper. Could assist.'

'Yes, I know, sir. I'll let you know if I do need his help.'

'Alright. Let us try to make some sense of all this and solve it.' Bec smiled at his use of 'us' and how he said 'we' would solve it. *Bet I'll be on my own if I can't*, she thought in the lift back to her floor.

*

Shauna and Wendy were waiting for her.

'Where to, Sarge?'

It would have been good to have some pat response. Avi's results had come as startling new information. But the reality was, how to proceed wasn't so straightforward.

'Look, forensics was helpful, don't get me wrong, but it doesn't actually give us all we need. If anything, it makes our job more complicated than it already was.' She went to the whiteboard and wrote the name *Aniken Smith* under Kenny's photo. Then a line from him to Doreen. 'But we do have a fine jumping-off point that might help us solve both investigations.'

'And wouldn't the DI love that,' Wendy said.

'Wouldn't we, you mean,' Shaun replied firmly.

Bec smiled faintly. 'It seems to me that finding Nikki Cardone is our central task.'

Chapter 29

The drive home was routine, not too much traffic, plenty of thinking time to process the information they'd gathered so far. Bec knew she'd sidestepped a bullet by refusing the DI's offer for Green to help. Nothing against the man, but she knew she would struggle having Green contradicting her or second-guessing each step. Yet, no matter how good the day had been, none of it got her any closer to knowing why Doreen was dead. Or why Nikki Cardone had disappeared. Elated and weary in the same wave of emotion, she fixed her eyes on the road ahead.

As she made her way slowly up the mountain road, she wondered if she was in time to get to the local pub for a bite to eat. Absently weighing up the pros and cons of what was in her fridge, she was almost home when the sight of a vehicle parked right outside her house caused her brain to leap back into protective mode. Then the shock of familiar number plates on the black jeep set her heart violently thumping.

After the long silence and a couple of text exchanges between them, Bec could hardly believe he was right there outside her house. The light inside his car flicked on. She could see his outline. Her heart was banging with anticipation.

She pulled alongside as the window of the jeep wound down.

'What's a bloke gotta do to get you to call him up like you promised?'

'Hard to say, maybe drive up a mountain in the dark and wait hours for me to come home,' she said, ridiculously pleased to see him.

'Well, I may have been here a while, Detective Sergeant. Are you now going to invite me in, given the dedication and patience I've shown?'

Bec paused, and couldn't stop herself from saying, 'Since you've come all this way, I guess you could come in just to confirm there's nothing to eat in my fridge.'

Josh held up a shopping bag from the passenger seat. 'I already knew that.'

Chapter 30

Birds singing full throttle and a crack in the curtains revealed bolts of early light knifing through the trees. Bec stumbled out of bed to make coffee, while Josh stayed put, body stretched out with hands tucked behind his head. When she appeared barefoot with a mug of instant and placed it on his bedside table, Josh took one mouthful and stuck his tongue out. 'Ah, is this punishment?'

'Could be,' Bec said. 'Seriously, don't you ever get sick of that premium grade you drink all day long?' Josh claimed his establishment served the best coffee in Melbourne, and it was good. She just couldn't help revving him up. 'Come on, admit it, sometimes you're just yearning for a hit of the old instant.' She flipped his hair with her hand, and he lunged to grab her and missed.

'In a word, no!' he called after her.

Bec came back with a plate of Vegemite toast and placed that down on his bedside table, too.

'Breakfast in bed, that good, was I?' he said cheekily. She picked up a pillow and threw it at him.

'You know it wasn't what you think … at the bar …' he said as he defended himself from the pillow attack.

'We never said it was exclusive, remember?'

'Well, it is for me.'

She tilted her head sideways.

'Nothing happened in the bar or at any time. Until you tell me we're over, it's exclusive.'

Bec was suddenly tongue-tied. Was this what she wanted to hear?

'I understand it's tough for you to let your guard down. I mean, you're dealing with terrible situations every day, and when I put myself in your position, I would struggle to trust anyone, much less let them into my life. But Bec, we work. We probably shouldn't but we do. I know you love your job. I know it's demanding. But I want to be with you.' He smiled at her. 'Really want to be with you.'

'What if I only have instant coffee?'

'That might have to change, but you do make a mean Vegemite toast.'

Bec reached over and took a slice from his plate. 'High praise indeed.'

'Only for the toast, though.' Josh smiled as he took another mouthful of his coffee and rolled his eyes.

'Okay, it is bad, isn't it?' Bec put her coffee mug down and slipped back under the covers. 'Maybe we could go shopping for a proper coffee machine. Later ...'

'Later, as in you and me shopping,' he said softly. 'Does that mean you missed me, Detective?'

'What do you think?'

'I think maybe it does.'

'Maybe you're right,' she said quietly, and rolled over into his arms.

They lay together for a while. She heard his breathing slow. It felt wonderful to have Josh back in her life. His feel-good company and good sex were better than any tonic. But as relaxed as Bec felt, she couldn't stop her thoughts returning to what her next step was going to be.

She gently kissed Josh's head and slipped out of bed.

Chapter 31

The unmarked police car pulled up outside a standalone renovated period house close to the beach.

'Well-heeled for actors, I'd say,' Wendy said, 'living in a suburb like this.'

'It's been a while since I was here,' Bec said.

'It didn't look like this last time I was here either,' Shaun said, glancing around, taking in the leafy street in Elwood, the village feel of the suburb in the heart of Melbourne's seaside chic: a short walk to the ocean, trendy cafés, organic groceries, and more bikes than cars.

The house next door to where they were going had a 'Mindfulness Therapy' sign displayed at the front. 'I'd like to do that one day,' Wendy said, walking up the path to number five. 'Not sure it would help with this job, though.'

Shaun snorted.

Bec pushed the buzzer and heard an echo from behind the front door.

Cammy Duval had been more than tense when they had showed up at her door in South Melbourne without warning. But then she'd been cooperative, despite not liking police interest in 'her' people.

On their behalf, she made calls to two of Nikki's friends, and without giving any details managed to locate exactly where Nikki was staying.

'Nikki is a lovely girl,' Duval told Bec. 'Had a difficult family life, but she brings it all home when she's in front of a camera,' the agent said, handing over the friend's address and phone number. 'Nikki will be alright, won't she?'

Bec pushed the buzzer again, and this time the door opened suddenly. A pretty brunette, thickly made up and holding a bathrobe tightly around her chest, stared out at them. 'Yes?'

Bec showed her ID.

'What do you want?'

'What's your name?'

'I'm Jenny.'

'Okay, just Jenny, we're looking for Nikki Cardone. We believe she's staying here with you?'

'Who gave you this address?'

'We just need to talk to her.'

'What about?'

'That's for her ears only, I'm afraid. Please, if you could let her know that we're here and we'd like to come in.'

'Just a minute.' The woman disappeared, pushing the door closed.

'Not happy, is she?' Wendy whispered.

'It would seem not,' Bec said.

When Nikki appeared, she was visibly shocked. 'We're expecting friends over,' she said, instantly recognising Wendy and Shaun. 'Can we do whatever this is another time?'

'I'm afraid not, Miss Cardone,' Shaun said.

'How did you find me here?'

'Your agent told us,' Wendy said.

'You've spoken to Cammy?' the actor said, horrified.

'I'm Detective Sergeant Rebecca Harpin, Miss Cardone. May we come in?'

'Why did you have to speak to Cammy? Are you trying to ruin my career?'

'We've left a number of messages at your home and on your mobile, Miss Cardone,' Bec said. 'We don't need long, but we do need to ask you a few questions.'

'If it's about Doreen, I've told you all I know, which is nothing,' the actor said, not moving.

'Now that just isn't true, is it, Ms Cardone?' Bec said, taking a step forward.

Nikki turned and called out down the hallway, 'Rug up, everyone, visitors.' Then, shaking her head in disbelief, she moved back and allowed them in.

'Nice place,' Wendy said, strolling down the main passage with bedrooms running off both sides. But it wasn't until they reached the add-on at the back, a big open-plan family living area, that Nikki responded.

'Yes, a few friends of mine are sharing.'

'We'd like to show you some photographs, Ms Cardone, if you don't mind,' Bec said, taking in the camera set-up focused on a couch and surrounded by lights. Jenny and two others in matching pastel-coloured bathrobes were huddled together right next to it.

'Jen, do you mind giving us some space?' Nikki asked her friend, sweetly.

The three seemed relieved and quietly scuttled past, clutching their robes around them as they disappeared.

'I'm hoping you can provide us with names for the faces in these photos,' Bec continued. 'Can we sit here?' She pointed to the circle of chairs and side-table stacked with magazines.

'Yes,' Nikki said, 'sit wherever you like. And call me Nikki. Ms Cardone sounds like I've done something wrong, and I haven't.'

'Alright, Nikki, you're staying here now?' Bec said.

'No, I've been staying at Cammy's.'

Bec glanced over again at the camera and lights, and without her having to ask, Nikki said, not even slightly embarrassed, 'My friends are on OnlyFans, making a fortune every month. Cammy says she can get me a gig, but I've got to have a fall-back position. I've got bills.' She shrugged. 'They're going to help me set it up.'

'Alright, we won't hold you up for too long, Nikki. Can I ask you to look at these photos? They were taken from security footage at your place in Thornbury,' Bec said, pushing magazines aside to make room for the photos. She lined them up and pointed to the first. 'Is this you?'

Nikki sat down, leaned over, and sighed. 'Of course, it is.'

'Right. Can you tell me who this is, then?'

She sat back, closed her eyes, and sighed. 'That's Kenny.'

'And who, for the record, is Kenny?' Bec said.

'Kenny Smith, Doreen's son.'

'It was my understanding, Nikki, when you spoke to Constable Hanley and Senior Constable Santos, that you told them you didn't know Doreen's son. And you said you didn't know Doreen very well, either.'

Bec kept showing different shots of Nikki and Kenny at Doreen's door, Doreen hugging them. 'It appears from these that you knew both quite well. I take it you'd like to amend your original statement?'

'Okay, what I should have said is that I haven't known them for very long.'

'Why did you deny knowing them?'

'Probably 'cause you got me on a bad day, and I didn't want to go into it,' she said, looking away.

'Alright, what was your relationship with Kenny? From these photos, it seems that you and he were quite friendly.'

'I guess yes, but not for very long. I met Doreen a year ago, when I moved in here, and I met Kenny soon after.'

'And what do you know about Kenny?'

'Not much. I knew Kenny was doing time. Doreen talked about him a lot and told me she visited regularly. She asked me not to mention to anyone that Kenny was in prison. Once people know that about you, Doreen said, it's hard to make friends.'

'And you met him after he was released?'

'I was at her place one day having a cup of tea when he just walked in.'

'To the best of your knowledge, did Kenny stay with his mother?'

'Originally he did, then he got his own place. Sharing with another ex-prisoner near Doreen's place. He said it was temporary. I didn't ask where it was.'

'And how old is Kenny, would you estimate?'

'In his fifties, I'd say.'

'What did you think of him?'

'Kenny is fun to be around. He's always ready with a joke. Doreen told me he was good at his job.'

'And what was Kenny's job after he got out of jail?'

'Not sure. He mentioned once that he was exhausted from moving furniture, but I didn't know where.' She flicked her hair.

'But you became friends then, is that a fair thing to say, Nikki, you, Doreen, and Kenny?'

'Yes, we got on.'

'When did you last see Kenny, do you recall?'

'Yes, I remember when that was. The day before I heard about Doreen. He hasn't been around since, and I don't know why. He's not answering his phone. I called to tell him about Doreen, but I couldn't think of what to say. He'll be devastated. He doted on his mother.'

This was not the time for Bec to inform Nikki that Kenny was dead.

'Thank you, Nikki. Now, I just have one more photo I'd like to show you.' Bec spread the shots across the table. It was the photo of Nikki and the other man who was not Kenny. 'Can you tell us who this man is?'

Nikki jumped back and gasped. 'Ah, that's Mark.'

'And who is Mark?'

'My ex, that's who,' she said, turning away.

Wendy and Shaun exchanged glances.

'And where does he fit into the picture here with you and Doreen?' Bec asked. 'This was ten days earlier. You're all quite friendly.'

'I can't bear to look at him. This is the man,' she said, covering her eyes and pointing blindly, 'who stole my money and lied to me.'

'And your ex, Mark, was he a fellow actor like yourself?' Bec asked, thinking she might already know the answer.

'No, he was an investment broker. He specialised in selling cryptocurrency.'

'And could you give me his full name, Nikki, please?'

'His name is Mark Brereton.'

'Do you know where we might find Mr Brereton, Nikki.'

'If I knew the answer to that I'd come with you to arrest him, wouldn't I?' the actress said in a fiery voice.

'When you say he stole your money, can you elaborate on exactly how Mr Brereton did that?' Wendy asked.

Slowly, Nikki told the three officers how she'd met Mark in a nightclub, and how they'd fallen in love. She described how she'd thought that part of her life had finally turned around. She was so happy after a hard home life. Until one day she woke up, he was gone, and her bank account was empty.

'The worst thing is, I have no idea how he did it. I'd never mentioned my savings. I'd been stashing money for years to fund myself to try out in Hollywood. Now it's gone.' Nikki shook her head so sharply, her hair whirled wildly around her face. 'That's why my friends are helping me,' she said, suddenly emotional and rubbing her eyes so it smeared her mascara. 'Sorry,' she said, and pulled out a hanky to dry her eyes.

'You mentioned he was involved in cryptocurrencies. Did you invest yourself? Help Mark convince people to invest?' A connection was forming in Bec's mind.

'I chatted with some people because Mark asked me to keep them entertained,' she said. 'But no, he asked, and I refused because I was saving to go to LA. I didn't want to risk my money. My occupation is risky enough.' She shook her head again. 'Plenty of others did though. He said he always had a queue of people waiting to sign up.'

'So, he talked about his business?'

'He talked about selling crypto all the time. He told me he was making a lot of money and he always seemed to have plenty. Now, I think he was just a crook.' Her eyes filled again, and she dabbed them with her hanky.

Internally, Bec was excited. Strands of the cases coming together was lifting her energy. If Carolyn could confirm the name of her conman in the case of the missing file, and it turned out to be Nikki's ex, then she had her link.

A bloke cruising the nightclubs and bars conning people into Bitcoin investments. Nikki and Kenny, Kenny and Doreen, Nikki and the conman. It wasn't there yet, but they had a link and a strong line of enquiry to investigate.

'We're going to need you to come with us to the station to make a statement,' Bec said, gathering up the photos.

'But I told you, I can't, my friends,' Nikki said anxiously. 'We're filming.'

'I'm afraid you'll have to tell them you've had a change of plan.'

The actress jumped to her feet. 'But I'm the victim here. How can me being ripped off by Mark help you with poor Doreen?'

'We need you to make another statement, Nikki. That's all.'

She stared at them, silently weighing the situation. 'Just a minute.'

She left the room and Bec heard raised voices. 'What?' 'You don't have to.' 'What about us?' A minute or so later, Nikki emerged wearing jeans and a shirt, and was pulling on a jacket.

'Alright,' she said, 'let's go. But please, don't tell Cammy any of this. You have to promise. If she finds out, she'll never help me get another part as long as I live.'

'She already knows you've lost the money, Nikki,' Bec said, 'you told her yourself.'

Wendy and Shaun got to their feet.

'Yes, but I didn't tell her who it was who stole it. Cammy met Mark and she warned me to stay away from him. He hit on her, too, to invest. She said no. She didn't like him and didn't want him near any of her people. If she knows I went against her wishes, she'll let me go. Say I'm not her type of client. Please,' she implored. 'I'll give any statement you want, but please don't tell her about Mark.'

Chapter 32

Nikki gave her statement reluctantly, answering more questions about Mark Brereton and her relationship with him, then a police car returned her to Elwood.

Before she left the station, Bec spoke quietly to her. 'I have to ask you to stay in touch and answer your phone when we ring.'

The actress frowned. 'Okay, but why? I've told you everything I know.'

'Yes, but we have to get to the bottom of this, and whether you think so or not, you may be able to assist further with our investigations,' Bec said.

'But I really don't know anything else,' the actress argued.

'You need to trust me on this. We have another investigation that may involve Mark Brereton, and, as you knew him quite well, we may need to speak to you again. Okay?'

Nikki returned a question of her own. 'Will you call me when you find Kenny? I'd like to be there to help him when he finds out about Doreen.'

Bec could only nod.

*

From her office, Bec heard Wendy taunting Shaun.

'Cleared your credit card for OnlyFans yet?'

Unmoved, Shaun sat glued to his computer screen.

'I still think she knows more than she's telling,' Wendy said, catching sight of Bec heading towards them.

'She's given a statement and seemed pretty genuine to me,' Shaun said without moving his gaze from the screen.

'All that "poor me" story about being raised by a single mother, then when her mother remarried and started another family, them all ignoring her. I don't know how that comes into anything, Sarge.'

Bec dragged a chair over and sat down. 'It seemed important for her to tell us, so we'll see if it plays any role in the case,' she said, 'But the most important thing here is Nikki's link to this Brereton character, and how that relates to Kenny and Doreen. I've spoken to the lawyer in Sydney who sent a brief to Carolyn Moorhouse. It's a fraud case, where two unnamed high-profile men lost one million dollars in a cryptocurrency scam. Moorhouse was meant to be drafting documents to get the money back, but the victims got cold feet, plus they couldn't find the scammer.'

Shaun whistled, 'A million bucks, and they got cold feet.'

Bec nodded, 'Long story. Now we have Nikki Cardone, who was a friend of both of our victims. She had a boyfriend, Mark Brereton, who also knew our victims – and he just happens to be a specialist in cryptocurrencies. Are you seeing a connection?'

'No matter which way you look at it, Cardone is involved,' Wendy said.

Bec nodded in agreement. 'The Sydney lawyer didn't give me a name for the perp in his case, but I'm going to chase that now,' she said. 'He also told me that they had a break-in up there, too, same MO, pro guy, in and out fast, knew what he was looking for. The description doesn't match Kenny, but one guess as to what went missing?'

'Crypto guy's file?' Wendy said.

'Yes, all the original documents for the brief his firm sent to Carolyn Moorhouse – meaning her file is the only complete copy.'

'So, we think that's why Kenny was there? To steal one file. Doesn't fit his profile, does it?' Shaun shook his head.

'I agree, Shaun. Big jump from house breaking to this. But the link is there, and we must treat it as our focus. I just have to find out if Nikki's Mark Brereton is our Sydney lawyer's scammer. If it's a match for the name, we'll have someone in our sights.

'While I do that, can you both … on second thoughts, I'm going to make a call and if that pans out you come with me, Shaun. And, Wendy, can you find everything you can about both Nikki Cardone and Mark Brereton?'

'Shouldn't we just hand it over to the fraud squad, Sarge?' Wendy asked.

'After we find out who killed two people, maybe,' Bec said, thinking she wouldn't be talking to fraud just now. Or even to the DI. 'Let's focus on our part for now and leave the crypto side for later.'

Chapter 33

The afternoon sun cast long shadows over the city streets as Bec and Shaun pushed through the entrance to one of the tallest buildings on this end of town. They took the lift and rang the buzzer.

'I'm not sure what's worse, meeting you here or at my home. Either way, I'd rather not be meeting you at all.' The man stepped back to allow them entry. 'My lawyer says I should, and my PA is out, so some privacy. Come in.'

Bec had called Aaron Petersen to ask him for a name for either or both investors who had lost their money. She'd thought it would be faster than trying to squeeze a name out of Carolyn, whom she would ask later, depending on what happened. It turned out to be the right move. Petersen had been cooperative and said he would persuade his client to cooperate if the specifics of the crime and his name stayed confidential. Bec had given him her guarantee, and the lawyer had been as good as his word, calling back a few minutes later.

'Thank you for your time, Mr Wilson,' she said. 'This won't take long.' Bec had already spoken to the man on the phone, so she didn't need to show her ID. 'This is Detective Constable Shaun Hanley.'

'Alright,' Wilson said, not offering a handshake.

Businessman Ian Wilson's personal office was in a discreet building in Collins Street. He had refused to meet at his main office at the public company he ran as CEO. Nonetheless, there was nothing down market about these offices. Surround views over the city, thick carpet your feet sank into, subtle colours and expensive-looking paintings on every wall. Bec didn't know any of the artists' names as she walked by, but from the way they'd been hung, with special downlights, she just knew they were there to impress.

He led them into the inner office and gestured for them to take a seat.

'We appreciate your time.' Bec sat down and Shaun followed her lead. 'We've asked to speak to you because we're investigating a break-in at the chambers of the barrister who is representing you in your cryptocurrency matter. We think it may be related to a break-in at your Sydney lawyer's office.'

'I know that, Detective. Spare me the summary. Petersen has done all of that. I gather your actual interest is the name of the cockroach who stole my money,' Wilson said, straight to the point.

'Thank you, Mr Wilson. That will certainly save time. A name has come up in relation to the Melbourne break-in. This person has been identified as someone who sources investors for cryptocurrency schemes and who is not who he says he is.'

'The name you want, Detective, is Mark Brereton,' Wilson volunteered imperiously. And Bec watched as the man tried to control his anger. 'That's the name this cockroach used. But it's not actually his name. That much I do know.'

'You know his real name?' Shaun asked.

'Not yet … but after I find it, and I will, my people will have a quick chat with him and then I will happily hand over his details to you.'

'I certainly hope you're not considering any type of violence against the man, Mr Wilson,' Bec said, thinking from the man's facial expression that he might be thinking about exactly that.

'As long as I, and my colleagues, get our money back, Detective, there is no such risk. I've confirmed the name now, so I think our meeting is at an end.' He stood.

'Almost, Mr Wilson,' Bec said, remaining seated. 'We understand initial contact with a man calling himself Mark Brereton was in a private club. Did you at any stage see if anyone was working with him?'

Wilson resumed his chair. 'Anyone else? Do you suspect he had partners or something?'

'Just making sure we can focus on Brereton. You didn't see him with anyone else?'

Wilson paused, a frown of irritation on his forehead. 'We were in a private club, of course there were people around – a bit of the eye candy that the club seems to attract. But I didn't see anyone with Brereton.'

Shaun leaned forward. 'So, did he approach you himself, sir, or did one of these glamorous "bits of eye candy" make the introduction?'

Bec, surprised by the directness of Shaun's question, waited.

Wilson didn't seem bothered. 'No, Brereton was introduced to me by a mutual friend, who, as Petersen has told you, I won't be naming. They had struck up a conversation in the cigar room. My colleague thought I'd be interested in some of this bloke's ideas on investing, so brought him to my table.'

'No intermediary at any point?' Bec said.

'Not that I saw.'

'And I understand, Mr Wilson, that you've undertaken extensive searches to locate this Brereton man. But from your comments, you haven't yet been successful in locating him, finding his real name, or locating anyone who even knew him. Is that right?'

'So far, that's true, yes, but as I said, I will find him. And once I have, I will provide that information to you through my lawyer. Now, I think we are done.'

'Just one more question.'

He sighed.

'Amongst the "eye candy" you referred to earlier, did you ever come across a Nikki Cardone, Mr Wilson?'

'No, never heard that name before. I don't speak to those women, Detective. Other members might, but that's not why I'm a member.' He paused. 'Is she Brereton's offsider?'

'No, just another one of his victims, unfortunately. That's all, Mr Wilson. Of course, should you come across any more information about Mr Brereton, you will let us know,' Bec waited a beat, 'immediately.'

'Yes, of course I will, Detective.'

Once they were in the lift on the way down, Shaun looked at Bec. 'Who knew there was a part of the world where "eye candy" is still a real phrase.'

'Welcome to Jurassic Park, Detective, where the dinosaurs still roam. But it does seem that the lovely Nikki was telling the truth about her involvement. That she too was scammed by an expert.'

'Mark Brereton,' Shaun said. 'I think the bloke's got quite a few headaches with us and Wilson's guys looking for him.'

*

The parole officer was playing hard to get. Wendy had left two messages. She was checking security pictures from Thornbury when her phone rang.

'Senior Constable Santos.'

'Is that Wendy?' said a voice with a smoker's croak.

'Yes, who is this?'

'It's Reginald, Reg, you know, Doreen's friend. You left your card.'

'Of course, hello, Reg.'

'You told me to call if I thought of anything. Well, after you and your mate left those photos with me the other day, I had a good look, and

I do reckon I've seen the bloke in the hat and the other one, too. I saw 'em together a few times, before Doreen ... you know.'

'Together? As in just the two of them?'

'Yeah, I saw 'em walking up the street, and once going into Doreen's place. I didn't pay that much attention, thought Doreen was just having a few friends over. But she hadn't invited me, you see, so I was little bit interested. Didn't even cross my mind that it might have been her son and this other bloke, whoever he is. Like I said, I saw 'em together a few times.'

'And there was no-one else with them?'

'No, no, just them. And the younger one was doing all the talking, now I think about it.'

'You didn't mention anything when we asked you about Doreen's son.'

'No, because I didn't know what her son looked like. Then after you showed me these photos, the old memory slowly cranked into gear. Takes a little while at my age, Wendy. Actually, everything does, but that's another story.'

'Well, you've remembered, that's the main thing. Excellent, Reg. We might have to get you to make another statement. Would that be okay?'

'Righto.'

'Alright, I'll call when we're going to come out and see you.'

'No worries. If it helps you find who did that to Doreen. Did I tell you she was a lovely woman?'

'Yes, Reg, you did. We're doing all we can to find out what happened, okay?'

'Alright, then.'

'I'll be in touch. Thanks, Reg.'

Wendy rang off, now feeling pleased that she'd been left out of the investor interview. This was big. The mysterious Mark Brereton seen with Kenny on several occasions. She grabbed her phone and pushed Bec's number.

'DS Harpin, you're going to love what I'm about to tell you.'

*

'Good work, Wendy. You certainly got to that old bloke, Reg. That's another piece of the puzzle.'

'Must have been you making his tea for him,' Shaun said.

Bec was thinking aloud. 'What was some high-flier like Brereton doing with Kenny, a known housebreaker, and where does Doreen fit into the picture? If Kenny got paid to steal the file, that makes sense, but what about Doreen?'

'You think Brereton paid him to steal the file?' Wendy asked.

'That's what we're going to ask him. That's why locating this Brereton just became our highest priority.'

Chapter 34

Bec was gathering up her car keys and jacket, preparing to leave, when Wendy burst in, out of breath, a huge grin on her face.

'Kenny's parole officer, Ray Collier, has just moved and set up a private practice,' she said brightly. 'Won't be too keen to hear from us, according to his former office, but at least we know where to find him, in Castlemaine, got his number.' She waved her note, triumphantly.

'Good work, Wendy. Speak to him on the phone first. Make sure he understands that we could be in his driveway in about forty minutes with some blue lights if he's reluctant. You two feel like a little trip?'

'That possibility depends on dragging Shaun away from his security pictures,' Wendy said in a voice loud enough for Shaun to hear.

'We'll see how it works with the parole officer after you've spoken to him. If he's happy to talk, we can do it by phone.'

'One more thing, Sarge. Just so you know,' Wendy said. 'Ray Collier is a psychologist as well as a parole officer. He's taking private patients in Castlemaine now, too.'

'Good, he might have a spin on Kenny's character,' Bec said.

Wendy grinned. 'Okay, I'll see if I can "psych" him into talking to us.'

*

Bec had left a message on Carolyn's voicemail and had received only a short text back confirming their meeting, informing her that Juan would also be in her office. It shouldn't have come as a surprise, but it did. In the lift on the way up, Bec weighed her approach to the interview.

When she presented her ID to reception on the ninth floor, the young receptionist took one look at Bec's bona fides and said, 'Are you here to investigate the death in Ms Moorhouse's rooms?'

Surprised by the blatant nature of the question, Bec didn't respond.

Undeterred, the receptionist continued, 'I've heard around that Juan Zamora, Moorhouse's student barrister, might be implicated. Is that correct?'

'I'm sorry ... what's your name?'

'Claire. I'm a temp.'

'I'm sorry, Claire, you'll understand that I'm not at liberty to discuss details of an ongoing investigation.'

'That's alright. It's just that ... do you have a minute? I might have something to tell you?'

Bec glanced at her watch.

'It won't take long. We can duck in over there,' Claire whispered, and before Bec could reply or stop her, the receptionist was heading for the same empty room that Bec had waited in with Carolyn and Juan on that first night. Bec remained where she was but when the woman kept glancing back looking for her to follow, she strolled over.

'Look, this is probably nothing,' Claire said, speaking softly, when Bec came in behind her, 'but it might be something. I watch a lot of crime shows, and I know that sometimes it can be the tiniest clue that ends up solving a whole investigation.'

Bec supressed a smile. She really needed another amateur sleuth offering advice.

'Juan seems like a nice man, but sometimes, well, you just don't know, do you?' Claire stared wide-eyed at Bec.

'No, you don't. Anyway, what is it you'd like to tell me, Claire?'

'As I said, it may not be important, but I saw him arguing with someone in the foyer on the day that man died. He was shouting and he looked angry. Then when he came up, I could hear doors slamming. Ms Moorhouse was out you see, and he, being the student barrister, was meant to be manning the fort. But with all the racket and door-slamming behaviour going on, it caused a bit of a commotion. Even the senior KC poked his head out. Anyway, it wasn't appropriate if you know what I mean. Not here. He was in a right mood.'

'Are you positive that the argument you witnessed occurred on the same day the man died in chambers?'

'Yes, positive.'

'And do you know who Juan was arguing with?'

'A woman.'

'Did you happen to hear what it was about?'

'No, sorry.'

'What did the woman look like?'

'She was really pretty. She was giving it to him.'

'Do you remember what time that was?'

'My lunchbreak finishes at one forty-five. I'm always cutting it fine, so I think right on one forty-five.'

'Thanks, Claire.'

'Is it helpful?'

'I don't know, but I'll follow it up. Now, if you'll excuse me, I don't want to be late for my appointment.'

'Of course, sorry,' she said. 'If I see anything else …'

Bec produced her card. 'You can reach me on this number.'

Claire stared down at the details and began reading aloud. 'Detective Sergeant Rebecca Harpin, homicide. Oh, this is giving me goosebumps. You know, you're the only real-life homicide policewoman I've ever met.'

'Thank you for your information, Claire,' Bec said, using her polite PR voice.

*

Bec walked away thinking the argument the secretary had described was far more aggressive than the description Juan Zamora had given about the break-up with his fiancée. If Juan was having a shitty day, he could have lost his temper, thrown a punch and killed the cleaner. The biggest percentage of blunt-trauma deaths happened that way; no prior intent to kill but misplaced aggression.

Carolyn's pupil was most definitely still in the hot seat; waiting for his name to be cleared or for charges to be laid. The fact that he'd come back to chambers prepared to face everyone – what did that say about him? A clear conscience or just plenty of nerve? Remained to be seen. He, of course, would have had Carolyn and the Bar Association on the front foot arguing for his right to remain in chambers until such time as the investigation was completed.

Bec decided to change her approach to the meeting with Carolyn, now that Juan Zamora's actions on the night were back in the frame.

Chapter 35

'What's this, a welcoming party?' Bec said light-heartedly, seeing Carolyn and Juan Zamora hovering in the doorway of her chambers.

'Detective Sergeant.' Juan acknowledged Bec with a nod. Carolyn stood by until Bec was close enough to receive two proffered air cheeks.

'Come in,' she said, ushering Bec in as if she were a client. Was this her old friend, this cool, impersonal woman whom she once would have trusted with her life? Before she closed the door, Bec, in her best professional voice, said, 'Carolyn, could I ask you to step outside for a moment? I need to have a private word with Juan.'

'Don't be ridiculous, Rebecca. This matter is pending investigation and I thought your message said you needed to talk to me?'

'I do. Something just came up. Won't take long,' Bec said evenly, choosing to ignore Carolyn's attempt to override her request.

Carolyn sighed, picked up her phone and said, 'Call me when you're done.' Then proceeded to pull the door closed too firmly.

Juan panicked. 'Can you explain to me, Detective Sergeant, what has happened to the legal dictum *innocent until proved guilty*?' The intensity of his voice was perfectly pitched to the expression on his face.

'That's a good question, Juan,' Bec said. 'Can you just sit down for a moment.' Juan looked around to find a chair. 'Far as I am aware, innocent until proven guilty is how the police and the courts still operate, which explains why we're here and not back in Spencer Street.' Bec pulled out her own chair and sat opposite. 'Of course, parts of the media seem to have a very different view these days,' she said. 'Luckily, now it's only your colleagues at the Bar who know your identity. The media hasn't managed to get any details yet. And I hope we can finish our investigation before they do.'

He nodded, still clearly unhappy.

Bec hadn't been surprised by her background checks on Juan. He still lived under the same roof as his family, emigrants from the south of Spain, who had arrived here when Juan was barely into his education. No obvious reason for them to make such a move, except maybe Juan's engineer father, Carlos, might have been looking for opportunity. His mother, Victoria, was an academic, and Marita, his sister, was a student a few years younger than him. From the outside, at least, Juan's story replicated the pattern of any hard-working immigrant family. Bec figured the ramifications of Juan's involvement in the death of a man at his employer's chambers would be playing out big time at home. She also knew that a stable or unstable home life was not always an indicator of a person's propensity to violence. Carolyn's pupil wouldn't be the first person from a steady family to commit a serious crime. He was looking expectantly at her, like a boxer waiting to parry the first punch; guarded.

'Okay, Juan, a witness has come forward to say that on the day of the assault, the argument you told me about, with your ex, was far more serious than you recounted. And that it took place only a few hours before Mr Smith died. You were "in a mood", was the term used to describe your behaviour, banging doors and so on afterwards. I need you to tell me what happened.'

'Mother of God, can't I even have a personal argument without someone talking behind my back? It was hours before the break-in and had absolutely nothing to do with what happened later in chambers.'

'Well, in that case, you can explain why I should disregard it,' Bec said calmly. 'Could you just answer my question, please.'

'I've already told you I fought with my girlfriend.'

'So, just to clarify, the woman you were arguing with downstairs was your girlfriend. And this was the argument you told me about?'

'Yes, my fiancée, my ex-fiancée,' he corrected.

'From what the eyewitness said, you were angry, really angry. What was it about?'

'The argument?' He ran his hands through his hair.

'It's a simple enough question,' Bec said.

'If you must know, my fiancée showed up to confront me about something she believed.'

'Something she believed about you, obviously?'

'She thinks I'm seeing someone … at work.'

'And are you?' Bec said.

'She threatened to write to the Bar Association,' he said, leaving Bec's question unanswered. 'Was I pissed off? Yes, I was.' His eyes darkened. 'Yes, Detective Sergeant, she accused me of having an affair. I denied it, and she told me it was over. She handed her engagement ring back. I broke up with my girlfriend, alright? Yes, I may have played down how angry I was, but that had nothing to do with the man's death. Is there still no result from the forensic tests?'

'Not yet, unfortunately. As I've said, blunt-trauma results can take a while to process. I'll need to get your ex's details to corroborate your story, but we can leave that there. Thank you.'

*

Bec texted Carolyn to rejoin them. When the barrister came back in, her eyes glanced back and forth, trying to divine what had transpired in her absence. She seemed to be worried about the unexpected chat with Juan. If they had concocted a story about that night, Carolyn could be worried that Juan had gone off script.

'It's your turn now, Juan, if you wouldn't mind. Could you leave us while I talk to Carolyn?'

Juan stood up and left the room without looking sideways at either of them. 'I'll be in the meeting room,' he muttered.

The minute the door closed, Carolyn was on the front foot. 'You said you wanted to go through my statement. Was there something that needed to be clarified?' Carolyn sat down.

'I'm here to inform you that the man who died on the floor of your chambers is connected to another case we are investigating.'

'Unusual, but alright,' Carolyn said, alert, waiting to hear more.

'The man who died here, Aniken Smith, was the son of a woman who lived in Thornbury, and her name was Doreen Madden. She died on the same night as her son. As your break-in and the circumstances of her death are suspicious, we have reason to believe that the two deaths maybe connected.'

'How so?'

'That's what we're looking into.'

'What does that have to do with me?'

'Aniken Smith was a client of yours.'

'I explained that I represented him once a long time ago.'

'Did you at any stage meet any of his family?'

'How would I know. There may have been a family member sitting in the courtroom. I wouldn't have a clue. What is this, Rebecca?'

'Have you told Juan that Aniken Smith was a client of yours?'

'No, I haven't.'

'And do you intend to?'

'It has no bearing on his or my involvement in the death of the man.'

'Okay, one more thing. Do you have a name for the person you were looking to sue in relation to the cryptocurrency scam we spoke about?' Bec wanted to see if Carolyn would cooperate, given the name Mark Brereton had been confirmed by Carolyn's client as the scammer.

Carolyn stared at Bec. 'Why do you need to know that?'

'You must have the name on file somewhere.'

'Yes.'

'So, could you give me that name, please.'

Carolyn didn't move.

'Let's try this another way, Caro. The name of the man you were about to prosecute for fraud and theft, was it Mark Brereton?'

*

Bec walked away feeling sick. She knew she was testing her friend, but Carolyn had refused to give a name on the grounds of client confidentiality, even after Bec had explained how she had got the name. Carolyn had said formally, 'If that's all,' and shown her the door.

Across the street and still sitting in her car, Bec phoned Shaun. 'Can you leave what you're doing and chase up all phone records for Carolyn Moorhouse for a few weeks before and after Smith's death?'

'Carolyn Moorhouse?'

'Yes. We need to check who she's been talking to.'

'Okay.' He sounded surprised but didn't question her request. 'Consider it done.'

Bec sat for a moment considering what had just taken place. There was something serious going on with Carolyn Moorhouse. Her behaviour had been out of character since the night she called Bec asking her to come to her chambers. Her phone records might reveal something. She pushed the ignition, flicked her indicators on and waited for a break in the traffic.

*

Whenever she could, Bec chose to circumvent the city. Today, she had no other option. Traffic was stop-start on all roads leading to and from the city centre: trucks, bikes, roadblocks, and detours from one building site to another. The transformation had taken place in only a handful of years. The city skyline she remembered from her youth was barely recognisable these days. In twenty years' when new designs and city rhythms settled, maybe the reinvention might be fine. But right now, what was once a simple, easy-to-navigate grid of street had become unrecognisable, like her friendship with Carolyn Moorhouse.

Turning into the basement carpark, Bec's phone pinged a message. She parked her car and looked down. Josh.

Missing you.

A spontaneous smile spread over her face.

She texted back. *Same.* Easier to say the second time.

This is good.

Her mood brightened.

Chapter 36

The lift doors opened and Bec walked towards what appeared to be a sea of pink balloons. Pink balls and hearts fluttering above desks and streamers waving in the air said it all. *Onya Sally* and *Congratulations*. Sergeant Sally Gibson, whose job Bec was covering, had delivered a daughter. Delight from the team and everyone on their floor was obvious.

'I've got cake,' Wendy called out, holding up a tray of pink-and-white cupcakes with silver balls.

'Come on, Sarge, DI's treat. Grab one now. Don't know if he'll shout us again,' Shaun said, grinning and speaking with his mouth half full.

Bec wandered over and picked up a cupcake, took a bite and savoured the sweetness. It wasn't often her team got in earlier than her, but looking around the room, she was pleased she'd chosen to run hard before the drive in. She might have arrived late, but she felt good and didn't have to feel guilty as she bit into the cake.

While concentrating on the taste of vanilla and sugar, it crossed her mind that she'd have to ask Lyn for help if she was to buy Sally a gift she might appreciate. A picture of herself in a baby shop scanning rows of booties and soft toys wasn't coming easily.

'I'm so pleased for her, aren't you, Shaun?' Wendy said, following Bec to her office.

Walking carefully, cake in one hand and balancing a coffee cup in the other, he nodded.

'She wanted this so much.' Wendy turned to Bec. 'My bet is she won't be back.'

Bec had never met Sally, so she had no way of offering an opinion either way. What she did know was that babies and young children needed attention, and that oftentimes a dangerous job and motherhood would be hard to manage.

'What if we pool our money and buy Sally something decent?' Wendy said excitedly.

'Such as?' Shaun said.

'What about one of those little walker things. I'll organise it,' she volunteered.

'Fine,' Shaun said. 'What's the damage?'

'Not sure. I'll tell you when I've done it, okay?'

'Yeah fine, long as you don't break my bank account.'

'You alright with that, Sarge?'

''Course,' Bec said, booting up her computer.

'Good, I'm going to love doing this.' From the way Wendy was rubbing her hands together, she looked as if she might run off immediately to buy Sally's gift.

'Can I have a minute?' Bec said. 'We've got some new information on Moorhouse that I want to walk you both through.'

She explained the new information about Juan's argument.

'So, he may have been all pumped up and hit out?' Wendy said.

'Have to consider it.'

'Wouldn't he have to have a better reason than that for clouting the cleaner?' Shaun was unconvinced.

'I don't know. We probably need to check any possible link between the victim and Juan Zamora's girlfriend.'

'See if Aniken Smith is related to Zamora's girlfriend and Doreen?' Wendy asked, unconvinced.

'Unlikely, I know, but we need to track it just the same. Even if it's just to rule that out. The girlfriend thought Juan was having an affair with someone and broke off their engagement. We need to hear her version and how steamed up Zamora really was. He gave me her details. I'll send them through now.'

Bec doubted that Zamora had any intention to kill the cleaner. But he was obviously a hot head, so it could have been a furious shove gone wrong, and that could move from accidental to manslaughter.

'Alright, Shaun, how did you go with the phone records?'

'Request in.'

'Okay, and Wendy, what about Kenny's parole officer?'

'Waiting to hear back, Sarge.'

Chapter 37

The burglaries had to be connected. Bec was brainstorming a million miles an hour. The Sydney break-in guy Aaron Peterson had described was a pro. So was Kenny. But why would Kenny, just out of jail for housebreaking, get involved in something like that? Bec was about to go for a water refill when Wendy walked through the door.

'Ray Collier, the parole officer, finally got him,' she said.

'And?'

'Not much.' She sat down. 'Couldn't wait to get me off the phone. Said he looked the name up after I left a message. Aniken Smith, who he referred to as Kenny by the way, was an unsupervised parolee. Someone he only met on the inside. Since his release, he said that Kenny was golden, meaning no additional trouble with the law since he got out.'

'Thank you, Senior Constable Santos, I'm aware how the parole system operates.'

'Sorry. Anyway, he thought I was calling to tell him Kenny was in trouble again. Put the phone down in my ear. Said he wasn't a parole officer anymore.'

'Kenny certainly lived under the radar,' Bec said softly.

'Too busy with his mum and her friends to get into trouble, you mean?' Wendy joked.

'Maybe that's it. Oh, and Pepita Mendez, Juan Zamora's girlfriend, according to her neighbours, is away on an overseas holiday,' Bec said.

'I left a phone message and a text asking her to call. The neighbour said she should be back this week.'

'It'll be interesting to hear her side of the argument. Something serious to break off an engagement,' Wendy said, no longer joking. 'And it's looking like a trip to Castlemaine to visit Ray Collier,' she added, before getting up to return to her own desk.

Bec was still thinking about Juan and his girlfriend when her phone rang. A number she didn't recognise, so she let it go. Then a message beeped. Curious, but with a familiar feeling of apprehension after years of threats over the Rigby case, she pushed 'playback'.

'*This is Ray Collier,*' a slow-drawl voice said. '*I believe you're in charge of an investigation involving Aniken Smith. Not sure if I can be of any help to you, but you have my number, so call me. Anytime will do.*'

Bec called the man back and was surprised at the parole officer's response when she introduced herself and said, 'I believe Senior Constable Santos is waiting to hear from you.'

'No offence, Sergeant, but I've still got friends in the force,' Collier said. 'I was told you're the one running this investigation. I'm trying to minimise my time talking about former parolees, you understand, especially now I'm in private practice again. What's happened?'

Bec thought from the pace of his speech that she might be there all day. Wendy was not going to be happy, either, at being passed over. But Bec supposed men of a certain generation only ever wanted to speak to 'the boss', which technically was Griffiths, but he'd called her, and she needed his cooperation.

'Thanks for getting back to us, Ray. It's early days and we still don't have much to go on. We don't know what happened exactly, or even why. But Kenny was found dead from a significant bash to his head. I'm hoping that knowing a bit more about him might help us understand what went on.'

'Kenny wasn't a violent type, that much I can tell you. I met him when he was coming up for release,' Collier said.

'When was that? And how long did you know Kenny?'

'Met him about a year ago. Helped him get ready for the outside.'

'How would you describe him?'

'A quiet type, like I said. Unlucky to be in prison. Mixed with the wrong crowd when he was young. Never stopped. This was his third stay. But I do remember one thing. Kenny was looking forward to his life outside this time. He thought somewhere in the universe his lucky star had risen.'

'And why was that?'

'He'd found his mother. From not knowing anything about who he was – he'd been adopted at birth, you see – he'd found his real mother, the one who gave birth to him.'

'And gave him up,' Bec added.

'That's right and gave him up for adoption. She was very young, no means,' he said by way of explanation. 'Some people value that biological connection more, don't they?' he added, as if he didn't necessarily agree. 'Meant everything to Kenny. Meant a lot to her, too, the unexpected reunion with her long-lost son, if what Kenny said is anything to go by. Apparently, she'd been working in a dress shop in the city all those years. Never married, only had the one child, him. Kenny was cut up about that. Could have known her his whole life. Anyway, once they reconnected, they were devoted to each other. She came to see him regular as clockwork, never missed a week. Kenny used to tell me that whenever I spoke to him. He was so proud. There's information on the file about how he found her, if you're interested.'

'And the adoptive parents, what happened to them?' Bec was thinking about the family that had raised him and that talking to them might put into place more about who he was.

'Kenny had no hard feelings about them. Just not around anymore. I think he felt at a loose end after they died. You know, wanted to find out who he really was. It pleased him to find that his biological mother was a nice woman who had never forgotten him.'

After some more explanation from the parole officer, Bec tried to summarise. 'So, the Kenny you knew wasn't a violent, hardened criminal?'

'As far from it as you could get, Detective Sergeant. What if I make a copy of my file and send it to you? Not that there's much more on it, but at least you can look through and see for yourself.'

'Excellent, thanks, Ray, that would be really helpful.'

Chapter 38

Bec used the drive to the forensics lab to try to fit all the new evidence together. It was frustrating that every time she got a new piece, it slotted into one picture but shed no light on why Kenny and Doreen had died on the same night.

They knew that Nikki Cardone's ex was the conman in Carolyn's crypto case. And thanks to Reg, Doreen's neighbour, they could place Mark Brereton and Kenny together. Wendy's phrase 'Kenny and the conman' sounded like the name of a TV series, but this was no comedy. Kenny was dead, obviously trying to steal Brereton's file from Carolyn's office, but Kenny's parole officer had been positive that Kenny had retired for good.

Had Brereton offered Kenny a large enough payment to get him to do one last break-and-enter? Wouldn't be the first ex-con to find life on the outside more expensive than he could afford.

Finding Brereton was the key now. And Nikki was the ticket to that. She knew every one of the players, and Bec was sure there was something the woman wasn't telling them. There was a link missing, and Bec now believed Nikki Cardone was that link.

*

'Ready?' Bec asked, pulling up out the front of the facility.

'I guess,' Wendy answered.

Shaun just nodded.

The exuberant message from Avi confirming that crime scene investigators and forensics had found a match for the rope used to tie up Doreen was a huge plus. It raised Bec's hopes of progressing the investigation, despite having to attend the autopsy, which was, she had to admit, one part of the job she hated. Autopsies were just sad. Hard enough to watch the physical side, to see the harm done, and to witness evidence of the cutting and slicing that determined the cause of death. But the combination of all that, coupled with the emotional human side of how the person ended up there, that was the worst. Externally, Bec knew she would do what she had to as the senior investigating officer, but it never got easier.

Shaun and Wendy weren't exactly jumping out of their skin with anticipation, either.

'How many PMs have you been to, Sarge?' Shaun asked as they approached the entrance.

'Too many,' Bec said.

'This is my first.'

'You'll be fine. Just remember why we're here. Focus on the investigation and whether Avi can shed any extra light on why Doreen is here.'

Once inside, they fell silent, trying to ignore the chemical smell in the air. They found Avi and Pip seated in the office opposite the examination room glued to a computer screen, oblivious to everything except what had gripped their attention.

Bec knocked. 'Avi.'

He leaped to his feet.

'My dear, lovely to see you in our part of the world. DS Rebecca Harpin, meet Pip, our newest team member.' He gestured to an average-height young woman, roughly late twenties, with a solid build, like she might play a contact sport.

Bec nodded. 'We've spoken on the phone.' Pip had red hair like Avi, Bec observed, and for some reason she found that fact mildly comical. She'd read once that only two per cent of the world's population was born with bright-red hair. She didn't know if that was correct, but if it was, there was a fair representation right here in the mortuary.

'You remember Constables Hanley and Santos?'

Avi nodded. 'Hope you have more of a stomach for our work than your boss does.' He glanced at Bec to see if she was rising to his bait. The constables exchanged a glance, mildly anxious when Bec didn't react.

'So, what have you got to show us? Pip mentioned you had a cause of death for Doreen?' Bec said, wanting to get the visit over and done with in the best possible time.

'I have my thoughts, but I'll be sure once we finish the PM,' Avi said, all business. 'That's next, but let's first take you through this,' he picked up a piece of black rope that was lying on the desk and held it in the air, 'which you should find fascinating.'

It looked identical to the rope used to tie Doreen's hands and feet. Bec had noticed it at the scene: not too thick, synthetic.

'The rope used to restrict our body is one typically used by boat owners,' Avi said, his face alive and in his element. 'Found mostly where marine equipment is sold, and we are told is suitable for small lashing jobs. VB Cor, it's called, and comes in different widths up to six millimetres. This one is two millimetres. Big range of colours, too, not just black.'

'It's high strength with good UV resistance,' Pip joined in. 'Hence its use in the maritime industry, but it was originally designed for pulling venetian blinds. And interestingly, is still used for decorative plaiting and macrame applications.'

'So, it could be Doreen's hobby?' Bec asked.

'Perhaps, my dear, but only if she had for some reason soaked the rope regularly with sea water,' Avi said, glancing between the three detectives. 'But here is the other interesting thing about the restraint. Your perpetrator used bowline knots to restrain the victim.' He held two ends of rope together and deftly tied a knot, pulling it tight to demonstrate the holding security of it. 'This knot has many useful applications, but it is the one-o-one of knot tying for sailors, with the high content of sea water residue, are you hearing the nautical theme here?'

'I am, but that's not ringing any bells with anything we have so far,' Bec said.

'Alright, then. Now, finally we found a fibre in the victim's mouth consistent with a type of material used for men's handkerchiefs.'

'She was gagged?' Wendy asked.

'Yes, at some point she was gagged as well as tied up. Highly frightening for anyone, but,' he held up an evidence bag containing an asthma spray, 'for someone whose asthma meant she used a puffer, it was likely her inability to breathe properly brought on an asthma attack, which in turn led to her having a massive heart attack. That's clearly the external evidence that I'm looking to corroborate in the PM.'

'So, cause of death?'

'At the moment, I'm thinking heart attack, most probably brought on by stress,' Avi said.

'Any DNA on the handkerchief?' Shaun asked.

'Not found at the scene, unfortunately.'

'What about prints?' Bec said, still staring at Doreen's puffer.

'Plenty of prints at the scene we couldn't identify. But the only other useful thing we found was a hair that was caught on one part of the rope. It was no match for the victim, or her deceased male relative, Aniken Smith. So ...'

'So, all we need is a suspect and a sample of their DNA,' Bec finished the sentence.

'DNA would be most helpful, yes,' Avi said, raising an amused eyebrow.

'Are you closer to a time of death?' Bec said.

'Best estimate is Doreen left us between 8.30 and 9 pm that evening.'

Bec paused. 'Can you say, Avi, how long Doreen had been tied up before she died?'

He considered the question for a moment. 'Alas, I'm afraid not. I can't think of any way to pinpoint that. Bruising around her wrists just confirms she was tied up when she died, but not how long before she died.'

'Okay, thanks. And the Aniken Smith results, still in the pipeline, I presume?'

'Yes, it shouldn't be too much longer, but there are all sorts of tests to determine the cause of death for that type of head injury with any certainty. Unless "bump on the head" will suffice.'

'I probably wouldn't put that in front of a judge, no. We'll wait for you to confirm his time of death, too, soon as you can,' Bec said.

'Yes, of course. I'll follow up and send it to you. I just don't have it yet, sorry.'

Pip's colour heightened as she glanced across at her boss.

'If we are all ready, come on, then, this way,' Avi said. Taking the initiative, the pathologist started for the door leading to the cool rooms on the other side of the corridor.

'Avi, before you go,' Bec said as the others left the room. 'Is it necessary for all of us to attend?'

'My dear,' his eyes sparkled again, 'not up to it today?'

'I don't think either of them have gone through an autopsy before, so if it's not imperative, I might let them head back and just stay myself.'

'We can save their first time for another occasion, DS Harpin, certainly. Alright, let's get on our way and leave the less experienced to see themselves out.'

Wendy seemed relieved, but Shaun said he would prefer to stay, having steeled himself in advance. Wendy would continue with follow-up calls from Avi's office until they were finished.

*

'Thanks, Sarge, I wasn't looking forward to that,' Wendy said, on their way back to the city.

After a prolonged silence, Shaun, who'd been subdued in the back seat, piped up, 'Why did you ask how long Doreen had been tied up, Sarge?'

'Just a thought. If it was a while, then Kenny could have tied her up before he left, expecting to be back in an hour, but then couldn't come back to untie her. Like I said, just a thought. Doesn't really make sense. I mean, why tie up your own mother?' Bec shook her head.

'Because she didn't want him going back to jail and threatened to call someone to stop his robbery plan?' Wendy suggested.

'Doesn't really feel right, does it?' Bec said. 'Just the same, stranger things have happened. Anyway, I think our next step is to check Doreen's finances. See if she had any other money – a bank account with savings, for instance – and check the status of her unit. Should have done this before. Did she own it outright, or is money still owing?'

'What are we looking for, exactly?' Wendy asked.

'Well, we have Kenny getting friendly with crypto guy. And crypto guy steals money. Maybe Brereton was trying to get his hands on Doreen's money.'

'Like mortgage her flat or something?' Shaun said.

'Yeah, any of that. Did she loan Kenny money, and did he put it into crypto guy's schemes and was desperate he'd lost it. Didn't want his mum to find out?' Bec said. 'Whatever we can find to help pin down who exactly tied up the poor soul and scared her literally to death.'

*

'I'm still waiting to hear back from Ray Collier's office.' Wendy appeared in Bec's doorway on her way home. 'I'll follow up tomorrow.'

'Sorry, with everything, I forgot to mention it. I took a call from Kenny's parole officer.'

'He rang you instead of me?' Wendy's face fell.

'He did, don't worry about it. Some blokes are like that. Only want to talk to the person in charge.' Bec ploughed on, saying what she could to mollify her senior constable. 'He certainly believed Kenny was going straight. He told Collier that he'd seen blokes who couldn't even attend their parents' funerals because they were locked up, and he didn't want to be one of them.'

'Looks like he lost on both counts, then,' Wendy said. 'Died break-and-entering and won't be at his mum's funeral.'

'He wouldn't be the first to go back to it, but the question for me is why now, and why an office instead of a private home? Bucketloads more risk, I would think, with CCTV and corporate security everywhere.'

'Righto, I'm off,' Wendy said as Shaun wandered in with printouts of Carolyn's phone records and dropped them on Bec's desk.

'Is that all barristers do, talk on the phone all day?' he said.

'Anything interesting?'

'Maybe. Quite a few days just before the break-in, there are a lot of calls to two numbers in South Australia, and a few at odd times from a phone number that looks like a burner. I wouldn't imagine Moorhouse's customers use that to communicate with her. Although, I guess she is dealing with criminals for the most part.'

'Do you have a name for the South Australian numbers? I do have an idea who that might be.'

'Who?'

'Carolyn's ex-husband, Ian Baxter, lives in South Australia.'

'Right, so it's nothing, then.'

'I wouldn't say that. Burner phones and late-night calls could easily be something. I'll follow that up.'

Before she changed her clothes in readiness for her date tonight, a message from upstairs popped on her screen asking her to make a time. Bec wasn't sure this time she could stop Griffiths insisting that she take on Green or someone more senior than her. She pushed the thought aside and allowed herself to wonder about meeting up with Josh.

She gathered her keys and left for the day.

Chapter 39

Their old chemistry and togetherness had come alive again the minute Bec had seen him waiting for her outside her mountain home. Back to the way it had been. His company washing away the cares of a long day.

'You happy to eat out?'

She waited for him to grab a jacket and brief his people. 'You look gorgeous,' he said, placing his arm on her back.

Changing for an actual date like a teenager was new territory for Bec, and she felt slightly uncomfortable. But Josh's appreciative smile relaxed her.

'I've missed this,' he said, taking her hand as they sauntered along laneways that were wall-to-wall restaurants.

Out on the street, Bec still found it hard to switch off, to not notice, to not stay super alert. Out here, the world could eat you alive, and it acted like a vice, stopping her tongue from speaking easily. Her own deep reticence at expressing private emotions was one thing. But the street always affected her this way. It was not conducive to romance. Josh was chatting away. And Bec was trying to relax, to give her full attention to what he was saying. One of the shrinks had told her that cops who'd been shot at often had repercussions like this. She'd been in two firearm incidents, both of which had come close to ending badly. She was dealing with it in her own way. It wasn't perfect, but no calls to her 'Safety Net' number so far. That would mean having to admit her mental load was rising. The too-high zone would mean contacting human resources, a note on her file forever and a question mark over her abilities. She wasn't about to say 'I need help' to anyone. Not yet, if she had her way. *Not ever*, her brain chipped in.

'I've missed you, too,' she whispered in his ear and laughed. 'But I think I'm not used to crowds anymore.'

'Too long on that mountain,' Josh responded. 'And now, you say out loud that you missed me.' Josh stopped and turned her around to face him. 'Whoever has taken over Detective Sergeant Rebecca Harpin's body, I demand you leave now.' His face was deadpan, but his eyes were filled with laughter. 'Then again, maybe I can live with this alien controlling your behaviour.'

Bec grinned; he did seem to understand her. Laughing with Josh was an antidote to the world, and even to DI Griffiths. She grabbed his arm tighter. Happily walking this way for one more block, Josh suddenly waived out to the spruiker and asked for a table. To her, he said, 'Here we are. Best Korean street food going.'

When it came to eating out and deciding where to go, Bec usually deferred to Josh. His culinary choices were impeccable. What did she know about such things? Her working life seemed to exist in a parallel universe to Josh's. Hers was which food she could find to swallow quickly and get on with her day. His was all about fine-tuning food for his business and making interesting choices.

The place was packed, the ambience lively. They had to shout over the noise to talk. Bec didn't care because seeing Josh's face on the other side of the table was reward enough.

Afterwards, strolling the laneways back to the apartment above the bar where Josh lived, his arm clamped firmly around her shoulder and holding her close, Bec couldn't remember a happier time, and in those brief moments she gave herself up to it.

'Coffee or Riesling,' he said, appearing from the kitchenette, a bottle of wine in one hand and two wineglasses in the other.

'I'm always surprised how quiet it is up here,' she said, pointing to the wine bottle. 'It's so lovely.'

Josh's talents extended to a definite flair for fitting out interiors. His space was comfortable and organised, which also meant it was calm and comforting. Surprising, considering it sat above a busy city café. Oftentimes, she'd wondered how he managed to keep the business noise downstairs from infiltrating his private living upstairs. 'Easy,' he'd grinned, 'only certain people are allowed up here and a heavy door helps.'

Pouring a finger of wine in both glasses, he sat on the couch next to her. She leaned against him and he lifted his arm around her.

'We are a good fit you know, Rebecca.'

'Well, this does feel nice,' she said, putting her head on his shoulder and feeling his warmth and energy.

'I mean, more than how we fit physically. I mean, in every way.'

Bec realised that she hadn't been so chilled since the last time they were together. 'I like the way you let me just be with you, Josh. I don't underestimate what that means.' She extended her glass to touch his.

Then, with the strongest will, she pushed all thoughts of the job away. This was something she'd discovered the shrinks had been right about. 'When you are close to someone, Rebecca, and we know it's especially difficult for police officers, but when you spend time with your special people, you must be with them. Give them your attention. You must actively try not to let your mind always wander off on details of an investigation.' This was something Bec was actively working at, even now. She didn't want to ever hear Josh say that he felt as if he was sleeping with a whole police investigation.

'I've never been able to just be with someone before, either, Bec. Feel comfortable enough not to have to talk but still know everything's okay. I don't know how you turn your brain off. Christ, if I had to deal with just some of what you see every day … I struggle with clients saying, "Are you sure this is almond milk." But it's okay. I met a cop, I fell for a cop, and I'm gonna be the last person who wants to change that, even if I'm the one having to do all the talking … like right now …'

She took his wineglass and put it on the coffee table with hers, then kissed him. 'Sometimes talking is …'

'And sometimes not …' Josh flicked off the lamp.

'Yes,' Bec said softly, and they fell against each other, urgently.

Chapter 40

Rebecca, it's Carolyn, can we meet, preferably somewhere private?

Bec replayed the message on her phone. She was dressed and about to leave. Josh's establishment was barely one block from Carolyn's chambers, and only a few large blocks further to her office. *I'm in the area*, she texted back, *we could meet in fifteen.*

Carolyn responded lightning fast, and they agreed on where to meet.

Josh had made breakfast, gone to the carpark to retrieve Bec's change of clothes and was downstairs in full flight attending to a packed café, when Bec, bag over one shoulder, slipped down the stairs. She waited for a second to catch his eye. He blew her a kiss, held his hand to his ear like a phone, and she was on the street, her heart lighter than it had felt in a long time.

Carolyn was waiting at a corner table. 'Rebecca, thank you for coming at short notice. Are you on your way somewhere?' she said, glancing at Bec's bag. 'Coffee?'

'Thanks, your message sounded urgent,' Bec said, and sat down, not knowing what to expect. She'd learned not to bother too much over Carolyn's mood these days, which could range from rude to polite, cold to friendly, angry to focused, in a split second. Bec acknowledged that her friendship with Carolyn was in a strange place. The easy going warmth that had existed between them had plummeted to depths it would have once been hard to imagine. Carolyn was even doing simple things like ordering coffee differently.

The Carolyn Moorhouse Bec had known never ordered from the bench. She always waited for table service. Observing the barrister's long frame – the hint of round shoulders as she sat back down – Bec tried to anticipate what was coming.

'Yes, it is urgent because I should have told you this sooner.'

'You have my full attention,' Bec said, trying to make light, feeling she was suspended in air not knowing where the landing place might be, which meant she was not relaxed around Carolyn Moorhouse anymore; on guard.

'Where to start?' Carolyn said seriously, pushing long strands of hair away from her face. 'We've known each a long time, Bec, and by now you know that divulging personal details is not my strong point, which if I may say is a trait shared by both of us.'

'That might be true, Carolyn, but I didn't drag you into a shitshow with no warning,' Bec said, and instantly regretted her sharp response. She'd spoken like a wounded friend looking for an explanation. Not a detective sergeant in the throes of an investigation. 'Sorry, this isn't the place …'

'Look, I'm the one who's sorry and I apologise.' Carolyn's eyes flicked away, unable to meet Bec's.

'Seeing as we are here, I think some explanation is warranted, don't you?' Bec said, hoping that this time some truth might prevail.

Carolyn faced her. 'Yes, I suppose, but honestly, when Juan called that night, I had already had two glasses of champagne and hadn't eaten, so I really wasn't thinking straight.'

'You couldn't tell me there was a dead body in your room?'

'Let me explain. When I got back to chambers, and there really was a dead man on the floor, the alcohol hit me hard. I think I had a panic attack. The only person I could think of to call, Bec, was you. It didn't occur to me the position I'd put you in until you were there, when my brain seemed to clear. By then, you had called your colleagues and it was too late to explain.'

Hard to believe, Bec thought, *given barristers consider every word that passed their lips*. 'So, you stayed silent – even to me. For goodness sake, Caro. Why? So, you were drunk. Big deal. You weren't even there when it happened. I mean, no-one could sheet any blame back to you. Your reputation is as a highly respected barrister. No-one is—'

'Stop there,' Carolyn interrupted, her voice charged with emotion. 'My reputation, Rebecca, is a sham.' She lowered her voice. 'I'm not the person everyone thinks. And that's the problem here. That's what I want to speak to you about. I need to tell you something, even if it alters your thinking about me forever.'

Bec thought she saw moisture forming in the barrister's eyes, as she waited to hear what Carolyn was going to say next.

'The worst part is that I wasn't thinking about you. I wasn't even thinking about the poor dead soul lying on the carpet in front of me. I was thinking only about my reputation.' Carolyn paused, composing herself. 'And I knew that any investigation would involve the police finding out that I've been having a liason with my student, Juan.' She shook her head. 'Well, if I'm honest, not just Juan. There have been others over the years …' She glanced at Bec, trying to gauge her reaction.

Bec tried not to let the shock of what she'd heard show on her face. Whatever she had been expecting Carolyn to tell her, it wasn't this.

'Is this … affair with Juan ongoing?'

'Polite of you to call it an affair. But honestly, Rebecca, it was just sex, nothing romantic about it. Physical lust, over-the-desk stuff.' She shook her head again. 'Sorry to burst your belief in me.'

'Why are you telling me this, and more to the point, why involve me in the first place?' Bec shifted in her chair, unable to fathom what was going on with someone she thought she'd known for years.

Carolyn examined Bec's face. 'I think I called you because somewhere in my drunken brain I needed to know that if this came out, which I feared it might, that I had someone in my corner. I've seen it all before in similar situations: the photos, stories leaked to the gossip columns showing up on the internet and ending of careers. Pathetic, in retrospect.'

Bec was stunned, even though what Lyn had told her fitted perfectly with what Carolyn was confessing to her now. Carolyn was saying that her behaviour had been outside the 'woman who couldn't put a foot wrong' persona that Bec had always believed of her. Had she even known this woman at all? Frantically gathering her thoughts about what it all might mean, Bec saw anxiety playing out on Carolyn's face. 'What you've told me doesn't change the outcome, Carolyn. Aniken Smith still died, and he has nothing to do with your private life. But I have questions.'

Bec saw Carolyn gear up. 'Of course.'

'We know that Juan had an argument with his girlfriend on the same afternoon Smith entered your chambers. Was their argument over his affair with you?'

Carolyn didn't hesitate. 'Yes, it was. I was furious that she'd found out. He said he didn't know how she had. I stormed out after he told me. Next thing I hear, there's a body in my office.'

'Was Juan angry when you left?'

'Angry enough to murder someone, you mean? No, of course not. He's a lover, that one. Was he angry? Yes. But I think the incident happened the way he said. The bloke didn't know Juan was there, Juan surprised him and he fell. I don't think our argument, or the girlfriend caused him to use excessive force. Simply a case of wrong place, wrong time for the intruder.'

'For Aniken Smith, you mean.'

'Yes.'

'I hope that's right for his sake and yours, Carolyn,' Bec said evenly. 'If forensics confirm that the blow was accidental, then none of what went on between you and Juan need ever come out. But if their verdict says it was something else, then I won't be able to keep a lid on it. You know that?'

'It may not feel it to you now, Bec, but I really value our friendship. I admire the person you are, and I know that of all the police I've known over the years, you're the one who won't let anything cloud finding the truth. That's why my drunken, panicked brain told me to reach out to you. I understand, I'm just sorry that I compromised you.'

'Let's see what happens.' Bec saw that Carolyn meant her apology. 'But you need to take stock. Sleeping with your pupils, Caro, really?'

'I know, I know. Pathetic, isn't it? God, imagine I've become one of "those" people, she said, and glanced away. 'Usually it's men, who behave like this, in positions of power?'

Bec didn't respond.

Welcome as it was, one forced apology from Carolyn long after the incident could not stop whatever was going to happen to Juan Zamora or Carolyn. Bec's investigation had to continue. She took a deep breath. 'In the week leading up to the break-in, Caro, you made several calls to South Australia, and there were three calls made to you from burner phones. What was that?'

'You've checked my phone records?'

'Normal procedure in an investigation of this nature.'

Carolyn looked stricken. 'I didn't think … I thought you … you checked my phone records?' she repeated.

'Yes, can you tell me what those calls were about?'

Her face drained, Carolyn's body seemed to collapse as she said, 'Calls to my husband. About our daughter. I haven't spoken to you about that part of my life, Rebecca. There was a family matter to work through. And the others, I have no idea. Any number of the clients I see could use burner phones.'

'Okay.'

*

Bec stepped onto the street, thinking it paid not to be surprised. But the thought of Carolyn and Juan together blew her mind. Carolyn Moorhouse, whom Bec had always thought of as a pinnacle of propriety, sleeping with her students? This case, with its missing boyfriends, affairs, and adoption, sounded more like the plot from a soapy TV crime drama than a matter for homicide, but there it was. *Stranger than any fiction*, her old boss used to say.

On the walk back to her office, Bec's shock faded, and her instincts took over. Carolyn was single, and so was Juan, and they were both adults. The strict rules of engagement aside, between how a student barrister and a mentor were meant to conduct themselves, the terror of it coming out didn't seem to be enough to explain Carolyn's behaviour. Or maybe it was. Just not enough for Bec to feel comfortable about it.

*

'Not like you to be last in, Sarge,' Wendy said, when Bec came through the door.

'Bad run with the lights,' she said, which caused Shaun to raise his head and glance briefly at Wendy, a sign that they'd been discussing her late arrival and the possible reasons.

Bec went to the door of her office.

'Any luck with the burner phone,' Shaun called after her.

'Not yet. I did catch up with Carolyn Moorhouse just now. There's something I need to follow up first before we take any action.'

'Sarge,' Wendy said, following Bec into her office.

'What is it?'

'I've been thinking about what we've seen on the footage outside Doreen's unit, Kenny and Mark together, and Reg's statement that he saw them together more than once out on the street.'

'What about it?'

'Well, how did Brereton travel? If he was this cool, rich guy, how come no-one has mentioned his car? He didn't live there. So, how did he go back and forth?'

'Good point, Wendy, he must have a car.'

'We can ask Miss Dishy again,' Wendy said. 'I really don't think she does know where he is. But she might know what kind of car he drove. If not, what if we try further afield for some more footage, see if we can find it that way. You know that strip of shops near the flats, for instance. Some of those store holders might have security cameras directed at their front doors, which would take in cars passing or parking on the street. We might get a shot of him and his car. What do you think? A month of footage will take time to look at but might give us a rego number.'

'Worth a shot,' Bec agreed. 'Go for it. Let's leave Ms Cardone out of that part of the investigation for now. If we find anything, we can run it past her then.'

Bec sank into her seat and booted up her computer to record details of the interview with Carolyn. As she did, a flash from last night's dinner brought a smile to her lips. The dynamic between her and Josh had definitely changed. And she definitely liked it. A few short weeks ago, she'd never wanted to see him again. This morning, her mood, after spending time with him, was optimistic. *Who said police officers couldn't have successful relationships?* she asked herself before her brain started thinking about carts before horses.

Chapter 41

They found the actress back at home in Thornbury.

'Can you tell us again, Nikki, about your movements on the day Doreen was attacked?' Bec opened the conversation feeling, for an instant, like she was visiting a parallel universe. One minute happily ensconced with Josh, the next stepping into Nikki Cardone's small unit.

'I told you before, I was in bed sobbing my eyes out,' Nikki said, staring back at the three detectives who were seated around the table in her small unit. 'I missed out on getting a part I really needed, and I was upset. Being a jobbing actor has its highs and lows, but when someone steals your money and you're broke, it's even worse.' She raised her voice in frustration.

'Okay, so can we talk about Mark and your relationship with him. How would you describe it?'

'Describe it? Sure, at school they would have yelled, "sucked in" at me. Oh, Mark was perfect,' she swirled her arm in the air, 'soulmates for ever and all that crap, and I fell for it. He said he loved me, and I was in love with him. I trusted him. When he said he wanted to know all about me, I didn't think that meant how can I steal your money.'

'What kind of things did you tell him about yourself?' Shaun asked.

'The same things I've already told you, about me being an only child, single mother growing up, till she got married and ignored me, who my friends were. That kind of thing.'

'He spent a bit of time here, then, did he?'

'Yeah, said it wasn't his style, you know, but said he could slum it here because of me. He was so nice to everyone.'

'And you have no idea where he is now?'

Nikki flushed with annoyance. 'I told you I don't know.'

'And when he met Kenny and Doreen, he got along well with them, too?'

'Doreen was a very trusting woman and Mark is a conman. At the time, I wasn't surprised when she opened up and told him all about Kenny. I just thought it was so nice of him to be interested. Doreen told him about Kenny being in prison and the reasons behind it, how he just got mixed up with bad company. Doreen was happy when Mark told her that in his opinion, that kind of thing can happen to anyone. He gave her some story about how he'd almost gone off the rails himself.' She shook her head. 'It's embarrassing the BS I swallowed.'

'And had Mark met Kenny at this stage?'

'Not then, but Kenny showed up not long after. He got along with Mark, too.'

'So, you sometimes hung out together in Doreen's flat, the three of you. Mark, Kenny, and you?' Bec wanted to confirm their thoughts about the photos on the security cameras.

'A few times, yeah, we did. Mark would pick up Doreen's favourite cakes. He knew all the scams, didn't he?'

'Didn't that strike you as odd, bringing cakes to your next-door neighbour, given Brereton was, as you said, so wealthy and moved in a different circle?'

'Not at the time – he was my boyfriend. But now … of course it does. Mark said he wanted to know all my friends. He said that's part of why he loved me, I had so many. He said he had worked so hard, he never had time to make his own, so he loved meeting mine.'

'Okay, let's leave that. Can you remember anything else about yourself that you might have mentioned to him?'

'Like what?'

'Like your financial details?'

'Well, I did tell him I'd been saving to go to Hollywood, but as if I would say oh and here's my password in case you ever need to steal my money.' The actress was looking really flustered, the pink in her cheeks almost red. Bec saw she had no more to give them.

They were on their feet and about to leave, when Bec said, 'You wouldn't happen to have anything belonging to Mark still here, by any chance?' She'd been thinking about her comment to Avi, about how all they needed was a fingerprint or a DNA sample to know who Brereton was.

'You mean after he cleaned out my bank account, he might have left something behind for me to remember him by?'

'By accident, yes, maybe,' Bec said, knowing it was a long shot but worth asking.

The three detectives swapped a glance as Nikki got up and disappeared into the other room. But when she came back holding a black cosmetic bag in her hand, it was Wendy who said, 'And this belongs to Mark?'

The actress nodded and set it down on the bench. 'Take it. I don't want it in my flat anymore, that's for sure.'

*

'His only mistake so far, an overnight bag he forgot,' Bec said, getting into the back seat, leaving Shaun to drive.

'How did you know, Sarge?'

'Just like that. Incredible,' Wendy said, sliding into the passenger seat.

'He's good at covering his tracks, but his mistake can give us a shot at finding him.' Bec placed the cosmetic bag, wrapped in a large evidence bag to avoid further contamination, on her lap.

'If any hair on the brush in the bag matches anything on the forensic database, we are on this bloke's trail,' Shaun said over his shoulder.

'He sounds like a smooth talker, though, doesn't he? What's the old saying, if it seems too good to be true …?' Wendy said, turning her head to look out of the side window. 'I'm starting to feel a little bit sorry for Nikki.'

'Easy target for a conman like Brereton, rather than the murdering assassin you thought she was?' Shaun said with a quick grin.

'She might have been gullible,' Bec said, 'and I do think she's been taken advantage of. Question is, how did this bloke convince Kenny to break into the barrister's offices to steal a lawyer's file? Hopefully, the DNA from the bag can give us a name, and once we locate him, we can find that out.'

*

The drive back was quick, and the cosmetic bag dispatched to forensics in record time with a special request for a twenty-four-hour turnaround.

The mood between Bec and her team was bright. They set to work like a fireball scorching all before them – working the phones, cajoling, and persuading to obtain the results they needed for a full picture of Doreen's circumstances, chasing everything they could about Kenny and Brereton.

Wendy finally said, 'Are you sure about that? Can I have her number?' Wendy was especially good at extracting facts from stubborn government bodies. 'Doreen isn't holding any secret stash anywhere,' she told Bec. 'She was a pensioner. Centrelink has confirmed it.'

Bec looked up. 'Doesn't surprise me, from the way she lived. I wasn't expecting her to be running off to a tax-free haven anytime soon.'

Shaun wandered into Bec's office grumbling with frustration. 'This privacy business is out of control, even for us. Body corporate wouldn't admit that Doreen owned the unit, even when I told them I already had a title search confirming it. Some twelve-year-old saying privacy laws prevented him from disclosing a client's financial details. Sarge, do you reckon Kenny could have been trying to force his mother to move out, sell the unit, so he could pocket the proceeds?'

Bec had considered this. The unit would be worth a bit of money – the area had gone up a lot in value in the past few years, and Doreen's flat was in a good location. Kenny might have figured she could sell and move to a much cheaper place, and he could take the balance. But tying up his mother? 'Let's keep that on the table, Shaun. I'm not sure it's a possibility, but money does strange things to people.'

Bec heard her computer ping an incoming email. Quickly scanning the contents, she read out loud to the team.

'Kenny's time of death was noted as 6.45 pm. Doreen's was 8.33 pm on the same day. Which means Kenny had already been dead for almost two hours when Doreen died.'

Bec stood and went to her whiteboard and wrote Kenny's time of death, and Doreen's next to it. 'So, Doreen dies of fright at 8.33 pm. Let's just say for a second that Kenny did tie her up before he went to the office building, planning to untie her when he gets back. But thanks to Mr Zamora, he never makes it back. Doreen panics and her heart gives out when he doesn't return.'

She tapped the whiteboard. 'But why would he tie his mother up? The mother his parole officer says Kenny adored.'

Shaun spoke first. 'He wanted her scared enough to sell the flat?'

'Still doesn't feel right, does it?' Bec stared hard at the times on the board.

Wendy joined in, hesitantly. 'What if Doreen had found out that Kenny was going back to his old profession, and had threatened to call the local cops to stop him …?'

'That's got more legs, I think, Wendy.' Bec considered for a minute. 'He gets an offer from Brereton, Doreen finds out, begs him not to, tries to stop him, threatens him with going back inside, he panics, ties her up thinking it's a quick job, but doesn't get back to untie her and Doreen has a panic attack.'

'Makes sense,' Shaun said.

'Yeah, it fits,' Wendy agreed.

*

Bec was back at her desk scribbling notes as fast as she could. She'd never changed that habit of writing down the key points of an investigation, allowing those facts to mull around until a solution emerged.

'Who was it that said some days are better than others?' Wendy asked.

'Some country and western singer, I think,' Shaun responded. 'Didn't know you were into that music, Senior Constable.'

'Shania Twain's good,' Wendy replied.

'She is,' Shaun said enthusiastically. 'What about you, Sarge? You into Shania?'

Without thinking, Bec said, 'Yeah, I am.'

'Let me guess your favourite song, then,' Wendy said, 'I'd say, "That Don't Impress Me Much," right?'

Bec glanced up this time, and couldn't help but grin at the accuracy.

'Okay, Miss Pick That Tune, you're on my team at the pub,' Shaun said.

'I don't drink, remember?'

'Couldn't you make an exception just once for me to win the quiz?'

'If you are nice to me, I'll think about it.'

'I'm always nice to you.'

The banter stopped when Bec dropped her pen and swore. 'Shit.'

Both officers were shocked to hear the boss swear for the first time, and they waited as she looked up.

'If Kenny tied her up, who removed the hanky from Doreen's mouth?'

Chapter 42

Wendy stuck her head through the doorway to Bec's office. 'Pepita Mendez is asking to speak to you. Said she got your message to call. Won't speak to me or Shaun. Are you available?'

'She's here?'

'Yes. Asked for you at reception.'

Bec took the lift down, full of anticipation about what Juan Zamora's fiancée might have to say. And why she would feel the need to come to them in person to say it. Once she was on the ground floor, she found the young woman sitting by herself in the vast hallway and looking anxious. Bec walked towards her.

'Pepita?'

The woman, who was small in stature but striking looking, jumped to her feet. 'Yes, Detective Sergeant Harpin?'

'Please, call me Rebecca,' Bec said, and sat next to her on the long leather bench. Up close, Pepita was young, probably mid-twenties. Jet-black hair pulled off her face, a cropped jacket, tight denim jeans with a small black bag strung across her chest. She wasn't at all the kind of woman Bec had imagined for Juan Zamora. Nothing corporate about Pepita Mendez.

Bec smiled. 'Pepita, I've been trying to contact you to confirm some information about your fiancé, Juan Zamora.'

'Ex-fiancé,' she said steadily, studying Bec's face. 'I got your message, but I had to do a lot of thinking before I could consider talking to you.'

'Would you like to come upstairs to a meeting room, or are you happy to tell me what you have here?'

'A meeting room, please. I wouldn't want anyone else,' she turned left and right, 'seeing what I have to show you.'

'Alright, this way,' Bec said, getting to her feet.

Mendez did the same. Bec towered over the young woman as she signed her in, and walked to the lifts.

Seeing the approving way Mendez was inspecting the décor of the meeting room, Bec commented, 'It's a new building. Please, take a seat.'

'Thanks. Compared to the bland office building I work in, this is like a hotel,' the young woman replied, nestling into the chair.

'And where do you work, Pepita?'

'Heidelberg. I work for an accountant. I'm studying to be one, too.'

The girl certainly didn't dress like any accountant Bec had met, but she continued, 'Now, what is it you want to share?'

Pepita pulled her bag around and dived in to retrieve her phone. She fiddled for a minute, then turned the phone around and gave it to Bec. 'It's Juan, look at this.'

Bec recognised instantly that she was watching a recording from within Carolyn's chambers. The sound was poor, but she heard the door open and saw Aniken Smith come in dressed in his cleaner's uniform, medical mask partially covering his face and heading straight to the filing cabinet. Bec didn't know what she was expecting from here on, but what followed was exactly as Juan had described in his statement almost to the letter. There was the struggle as Smith tried to get past Juan, then the two of them wrestling and the Buddha flying to the ground. Finally, Juan's strenuous push that knocked Smith to the ground exactly where the Buddha had fallen. The terror evident on his face as Juan tried to revive the fallen cleaner.

Bec sat transfixed and glanced up at Pepita only after she'd witnessed Juan's frantic call to Carolyn. 'Where did you get this?' she said.

'I hate him, but I don't want him to go to jail,' Pepita said. 'I want to show you something else, please, if I could just …'

Bec handed her the phone back.

Pepita sat flicking through it for a second, handed it back to Bec and said, 'He was having sex with his boss. This is the video of that. There are a few of those.'

'This is irrelevant,' Bec said, and muted the phone but held onto it. 'Pepita, how did you get a hold of this?' The video was a bomb that could save Juan's career, as it clearly showed how Smith had fallen. But it could also end Carolyn's. Her obligations as a mentor demanded strict integrity; a regulation that was strictly enforced by the Bar Association. Both of their futures lay in the hands of this young woman, who'd been cheated on and probably had her heart broken.

'I know I shouldn't have, but I put a camera in his room,' Pepita said, and burst into tears.

Bec waited for a minute while she scrambled around in her purse for a tissue. 'Could you explain to me, Pepita, how you did that?'

Sniffling and blowing her nose, she said, 'I knew something was going on with his boss. You know, the way you do?'

'Go on,' Bec said.

'I knew it had to be her. The way he spoke about her. How when she called Juan got all weird. Changing our arrangements constantly, always working late. At first, I wasn't worried. I mean, she's old. But it got worse. He didn't seem so interested in our wedding plans, either, for a while. So, rather than keep suffering in silence, I thought I would see what I could do. It wasn't hard,' she said, her eyes full of tears. 'I found this clock online. It's a model that has a hidden camera in the mechanism. I told

Juan it was for his desk. I said it was so he wouldn't always be late for our dates. The way the office is set up, I knew I'd be able to see everything. He was thrilled when I went into chambers one day to position the clock for him. There was even an app for it. I've had live streaming from Juan's office direct to my phone since then.' Pepita had stopped crying and was just bereft, glancing at Bec like she expected punishment.

'It's a terrible thing to do, I know. I googled it, and I think what I did is illegal. But then I thought maybe this recording might show it was an accident, you know, and save him from prison? I might be in trouble for the camera, but I couldn't face the priest if I didn't try to help Juan. Despite what he did to me.'

'You've done the right thing coming forward, Pepita.'

'Anyway, I loved him, now I hate him, but like I said, that doesn't mean I want him to go to prison. I thought I better show it to you in person. This proves it was an accident, right?'

Bec nodded. 'It does, Pepita. The recording confirms everything Juan has told us. We won't be looking at the legal aspects of you putting the camera in the office, although Ms Moorhouse would have the final say on that. But what about the part of the recording showing Juan and Ms Moorhouse? What are you thinking there?'

'Nothing, she's old enough to be his mother,' the young woman said scathingly. 'I wasn't worried about her. It was Juan. I just wanted proof. My friends told me he had behaved that way before. I didn't believe them till I saw this. So, now I know, I broke off our engagement for good,' she said, a definitive tone to her voice.

Bec thought about seeing Josh with his arm around someone else. It hurt. And it was far less graphic than this. What did it say about her? That she'd believed him when he said it wasn't what she thought. She hadn't tried to get proof. How desperate must this young woman have been to take the steps she had.

'Pepita,' Bec said seriously. 'I'm sure that if you're happy to give a statement regarding the installation of the camera and how you got this recording, without the other footage being mentioned,' she paused, 'then Ms Moorhouse would show her gratitude by not taking it any further.'

'I never want to see that recording again, to be honest, Detective. It makes my skin crawl.'

'Alright, leave it with me, I'll sort it out with Ms Moorhouse. In the meantime, I will have to hold onto your phone, please. I'll need to send it to our forensics team, who can lift the film, and it will become part of our evidence. If you give me your details, I'll make sure it's back within twenty-four hours.'

'If I have to. I can't be without my phone for too long, you—'

'Yes, I understand. We'll be as quick as possible. And we'll need to remove and dismantle the clock, too. Alright?' Bec pushed a pad and pen towards her.

'Now, if you could give me all your details, address, home and office phone numbers. Also, I'll need you to come back in to sign a formal statement to the effect we discussed, okay?'

Pepita nodded.

Bec pulled out her phone and called Wendy to take the girl home.

'Senior Constable Santos will be with us shortly. I'll take your phone and she will organise a car to run you home, alright?'

Pepita nodded, dabbing her eyes. 'Are you sure nothing bad will happen to me?'

'You've done the right thing, Pepita. You've certainly helped Juan, coming forward like this. I'm just sorry that you had to find out about him that way.'

'Well, at least I found out before the wedding,' she said defiantly. 'You've met him, everyone thinks he's wonderful. A sweet family person. But he's not. My family thought because he worked as a lawyer, he was a special person. I used to think so, too. It was going to be such a beautiful wedding.'

'I'm sorry, Pepita, but it was certainly better to find out before the wedding than after.'

Then, before the young woman could respond again, Wendy walked in.

'Senior Constable Wendy Santos, this is Pepita Mendez.'

'Hello, Pepita,' Wendy said, beaming a smile.

'Wendy, Pepita has given me a statement about why and how she placed a camera into Juan Zamora's office. And a recording from that camera appears to corroborate his evidence that Mr Smith's death was a terrible accident. It's all here,' she said, holding up the phone. 'I'm going to draft it, and Pepita will come back in to sign, but for now, could you organise to get her home, please?'

'Sure,' Wendy said, surveying the scene.

'Pepita, can I ask you to find the appropriate footage for Senior Constable Santos? Please, show her specifically the incident between Juan and the intruder. Then we need to get this to forensics as soon as possible.'

Wendy watched the footage and turned to Bec, nodding her agreement with Bec's assessment.

Bec stood up. 'Pepita, we'll speak again. And thank you so much for coming in. Juan owes you a lot.'

The girl smiled weakly.

*

Bec always found that the ease with which our movements could be tracked unsettling. Yet, for Juan and Carolyn, the secret camera was the best news they could have. Pepita's illegal filming took Juan off the hook. And if Pepita did as she said and didn't report her ex-fiancé to the Bar Association for an inappropriate relationship with his mentor, then Carolyn would be off the hook, too. This meant part of the investigation would be over. But that still left Bec the two main questions. How did Brereton convince a retired housebreaker, who had only ever stolen petty cash and jewellery from private homes, to break into Carolyn Moorhouse's chambers to steal a file? And why on earth did Doreen end up dead in her own home?

She pressed speed dial for Avi to take him through what she needed him to do with Pepita's phone.

'Well, of course, my dear, I can see the sensitivity here. I'll handle the file transfer myself. You can relieve yourself of that concern. Consider the rest of the recording gone. It will never be on our system. Imagine that you found the recording device when the scene-of-crime team missed it. Chalk it up, I say, there's a first time for everything,' the pathologist said cheerily.

'Not sure how anyone would have found it if the woman hadn't come forward. It's just one of those unusual bits of evidence that can show up at any time – a lucky break, I'd say.'

'And I would have to agree, my dear. Still, we backroom dwellers don't like to be bettered by you lot, do we? By the sounds, it's good news for Zamora.'

'Yes,' Bec said. *And Moorhouse.*

'All of our indications so far have been on that page,' the pathologist said. 'It does appear the deceased died from a blow sustained from falling onto a solid object rather than being struck forcibly with a blunt instrument. I was waiting for some more results to come in, just to be on the safe side. So, what shall we do, continue with the final tests?'

'Have a look at this first, Avi, would you? I'm thinking it will be sufficient to exonerate our young barrister. But I'd like you to confirm that before I take it upstairs. Talk tomorrow?'

'If not sooner, my dear,' and the line went dead.

Chapter 43

Wendy was triumphant. The security footage outside the strip of shops in Thornbury had paid off.

'He was right there,' she said, leaning into the screen and pointing to the curb outside the florist shop. 'I reckon he's parked just out of range, but there's Kenny, and the other guy. Damn, he's wearing a hat again. Come on, just move back a bit, will you, so I can see your face?' she said impatiently as the two men moved away. 'Then, I found this one …'

Shaun read from the grainy photo of a silver BMW with a partial registration number in view, 'Two-M-J … could be a one, then something, something.'

'Just shows you, doesn't it, always gotta try the long shot. I thought it was worth a look.'

'Good one, Wendy,' Shaun said. 'Let's get onto this before the sarge gets here. We need a list of Beemers that match that partial, and to find their owners.'

'You gonna help? It's tedious.'

'I am.'

She laughed. 'Just for that, I just might share my coconut custard bun with you.'

The pair set to work, and were busy on the phones when Bec arrived. 'Time for a briefing,' she said, calling them to her office.

'The A team has been busy in your absence,' Shaun said, keen to inform Bec of Wendy's success. 'He's one smart cookie, that guy. He's always got a hat on to obscure his face. Aware of cameras.'

'He can't hide the rego, though, and we've at least got part of it,' Wendy said, clearly pleased.

'Nice work, both of you.'

They all took their seats.

'Now, the statement from the Mendez woman, Shaun, I presume Wendy has filled you in. Pathology is getting back to us today. But Avi seems convinced that between the result of their testing so far and the footage from Mendez, it puts Juan Zamora in the clear. So, here's our working theory. Kenny was in Carolyn Moorhouse's chambers to retrieve the last hardcopy of a file that implicates the man who called himself Mark Brereton. Kenny wasn't expecting anyone to be in that office, and certainly not a fit young bloke like Juan. Kenny fired up, probably in fright, and ended up falling onto the Buddha statue that killed him.'

'I've always thought the Buddha brings good luck, Sarge,' Wendy said.

'Not for our friend Kenny, unfortunately,' Bec said. 'The two big gaps for us are how did Brereton convince Kenny to come out of retirement, and where does Doreen fit into it. We have to find the man calling himself Mark Brereton. Let's continue to focus on that.'

'We're not too far away, Sarge. We'll chase the car. We've got the model and part rego. Just got to eliminate all the possible owners till we find him.'

'Alright, I'm going over now to share a few happy facts with Carolyn Moorhouse. I'll be gone a while. You two keep going. We'll meet back here later.'

*

It felt odd to be so close to Josh and not stop by for a quick hello. Just thinking of him was enough to make Bec smile.

She crossed the street and walked into the building, thinking that not so long ago, Kenny had walked through these same doors expecting to be out again soon.

Carolyn would be more than relieved to hear what Bec had to tell her about the case against Juan. But in return, Bec wanted a more in-depth conversation about the cryptocurrency file that went missing in Sydney, and the copy Carolyn had been holding in her rooms. For that, Bec was prepared to give away a little information.

However, it didn't start well.

'Forensics were just here, again,' Carolyn said accusingly when Bec appeared at her door. 'They removed the clock on Juan's desk and refused to tell me why. Do you know what's going on?'

'Good morning to you, too, Carolyn,' Bec said, and closed the door behind her. 'Is Juan about?'

'No, he's searching a file for me at the County Court, why?'

'May I sit down? I have some news on the case that you need to hear.'

'Sorry, these forensic people showing up has put me on edge. Come in.'

Bec followed Carolyn into the offices.

'I'd like to ask you about the crypto files.'

Carolyn tilted her head.

'But first, I need to tell you that Juan's ex-girlfriend, Pepita Mendez, came to see me.'

By the time Bec had explained about the clock, Carolyn's face was drained of colour. She sat perfectly still and said nothing, allowing Bec to keep talking.

'We have footage of our cleaner, Aniken Smith, coming to your door, and you'll be pleased to learn that the sequence of how he died is in sync with Juan's statement. So, from that point of view, Pepita coming forward will no doubt exonerate Juan from more serious charges.'

Carolyn was staring at Bec like someone sitting in the dock expecting a conviction.

'In addition, pathology has come back to us with their results, which align with the fact that Smith fell onto a metal object, rather than him being struck by one. I tell you this in strictest confidence, Caro.' She leaned forward, lowering her voice. 'The case for Juan is looking much brighter.'

'But not so for his mentor,' Carolyn added dolefully. They stared silently at each other until Bec spoke.

'It's not often I'm surprised in this job,' Bec said quietly. 'And you had told me about you and Juan. But when Pepita came in to share the recording, honestly, Caro, I must admit I was shocked.'

The barrister leaped to her feet, agitated. 'So, what now? I'm to be ridiculed. Your entire department has the film. They'll be snickering over this sad middle-aged woman getting her rocks off, it'll be leaked to the press, I'll be a laughingstock … ruined. Won't Ian's family have a field day with this,' she cried. 'They already think I'm a trollop for not giving up my career to devote myself to full-time mothering. And, Merrily, my God, what have I done to her? Hearing this about your mother, oh God, even worse that she sees it.' She looked pleadingly at Bec. 'Is it clearly me? I mean, would anyone else know it was me?' She waited for Bec hopefully, but fell back into her chair when Bec, said, 'I believe so.'

'I'll sue that cow who put the camera in here, illegally. She has broken every law she could break …'

Bec waited for the storm to pass, then said calmly, 'Before you crucify anyone, the clock has been picked up and is safe. Pepita's phone is with pathology. They've been asked to look only at the incident with the cleaner. The rest of the footage I've asked to be returned to me alone, and all record of it erased from the phone. And Pepita herself was at pains to say that you weren't the issue. It was Juan's other dalliances and his suitability as a marriage partner that was her main concern. She has no intention of using it publicly. And you know I'm not about to let it out of my possession. These are things I can do,' she finished.

Carolyn said quietly, 'You know what I can't believe about you, Rebecca?'

'That list could be pretty long, I think.' Bec steeled herself.

'Well, despite the job you do, you still have faith that people are basically good, that people will do the right thing, that this Mendez woman will say nothing.'

Bec had never thought of herself that way. 'Not all of the people all the time,' she said. 'Some of the people some of the time, I'll accept. Can't remember who it was said it,' she added and shrugged. 'Truth is, Carolyn, if I didn't have that view, I wouldn't be able to get out of bed to face this job ... or any other.'

'I wish I shared your world view,' Carolyn said seriously, her face devoid of expression.

'How can you say that? You've fought for right every single day for a long time.' Bec could never forget the prosecutions Carolyn had led, which she had witnessed as a young officer. Not only Lyn's family case, but countless others, as well. The help Carolyn had given pro bono in her practice would have impacted thousands of people over the years. Bec used to think of her as something of a legal gladiator fighting to the death to uphold the law. That view might have been skewed by recent events with Caro involving Bec, as she had in Kenny's death, but the good work was there, no matter what else she'd done, whatever other flaws she might have.

Carolyn smiled wanly. 'Nice of you to say. Maybe underneath this calcified exterior, my original belief system is still intact.'

'Listen, I think this can be worked through,' Bec said encouragingly. 'But you must be more careful, Caro. I'm not going to tell you how to live your life. But pay attention to who and what people bring into your office, for a start. Something as harmless as a desk clock can be a recording device these days. The technology is sophisticated. It works for good but equally well for a total invasion of your privacy and confidentiality.'

'I've been a fool,' Carolyn said in a low voice. 'And I know it. I have a lot of thinking to do.'

Bec wondered whether Carolyn would change or even if she could. But Bec had done what she could for her, without compromising the case or her own principles. Whether even a semblance of their former friendship could prevail was another question. Friendship was a journey. No guarantees of the outcome.

'Just before I go, I need to ask you about the crypto files,' she said. 'Do you have anything that might help us find out what was so important that someone got Smith to try to steal them? I mean, he was a petty house thief. It doesn't fit that he was suddenly breaking into legal offices without some clear reason.'

'I've read the file from cover to cover,' Carolyn said slowly. 'Aaron has set out everything very clearly, as I would expect. There's nothing in there you don't know. Same old story: smart guys with money meet a smarter guy. Smarter guy ends up with the money.' Carolyn shook her head.

'So, the file didn't tell you anything else?'

'The only thing that I can see is, it sets out the man's modus pretty clearly.'

'Modus … as in how he conned these blokes?'

'Yes, exactly. Maybe he wanted to use it again with some other bunny. It's a tempting scam, to be honest. Convinced my clients, who are highly experienced operators.'

Bec thought for a moment, working it out. 'So, if no-one has the documents, Mark Brereton gets a new name ...'

'And a whole new raft of potential victims opens for him. A lot of people still seem to think crypto is a road to quick money,' Carolyn finished.

'So, worth paying someone like Smith to break in and retrieve his documents.'

'Yes, I think so,' Carolyn said.

'Makes sense once the file in Sydney was taken,' Bec said. 'Okay, thanks, Caro, that gives me more to go on.' She stood to leave.

Carolyn got to her feet, as well.

'Bec?' she said as Bec got to the door, the desolation in Carolyn's voice forcing her to turn around. 'Thank you for trying to contain this. I'm just not sure you can.'

Chapter 44

When Nikki woke, her mouth was dry, her eyes swollen and sore. She'd cried her eyes out yesterday afternoon after the police called to say they needed to speak to her again as a matter of urgency. Why did they need to keep coming back? So far, they had asked enough questions to fill an encyclopedia, and she'd answered every single one. Told them everything – well, almost everything. But then, they didn't need to know 'all that'. It made no difference. Kenny was missing and Doreen was dead. She had lost her life savings. Did they really think she had anything else to tell them? She wanted so much to talk to Kenny, but there was no sign of him. Everything had been so wonderful, she'd thought in her silly romantic bubble: meeting Doreen, getting to know Kenny, Mark being perfect and Hollywood beckoning. Now, she was back to the chaos her life seemed destined to be.

Her head was fuzzy. No counting sheep made the slightest difference when her mind ran away with crazy scenarios in the middle of the night. Emotional and exhausted, she was especially angry with Kenny for not getting in touch. He must have found out about his mother by now, and would know how devastated Nikki would be. Why would he treat her this way?

And Mark, her other nightmare. Why had he been so cruel? For the briefest moment, Nikki experienced a desperation and fury she had never felt before.

She heard the tap on her door and knew it was them. She walked straight to the television set and turned it off, her desperation on hold for now. After they'd left the last time, she'd felt like a complete fool. Broke, no job, Cammy Duval propping her up, living hand to mouth, and waiting for call-backs for reality TV. This wasn't where she was meant to be. Quashing all these thoughts, she swung the door open.

'Nikki,' the detective sergeant said, 'may we come in?'

Drawing on her training as an actor to hold her poise and not let them see the anger burning inside her, she replied calmly, 'Of course, Sergeant,' and stepped back to allow them past.

*

Nikki waited for the detectives to find a seat before sitting down herself.

'We're here to bother you again. I'm sorry, Nikki, but if you don't mind, we'd like to ask you a few more questions.'

'I don't know what else I can possibly tell you.'

'You see, we're struggling to find a motive for Doreen's death. There were no signs of a break-in. Nothing in her unit was stolen, which suggests we can rule out burglary. As there were no signs of any sort of assault other than being restrained, we're ruling out violence. So, we're trying to see if you had any ideas.'

'Me? How on earth would I know more than you?' Nikki said angrily, her eyes darting between them.

'I'm not sure,' the sergeant said. 'We thought after seeing those pictures from the security cameras of you and Kenny going into Doreen's unit – you all seemed so friendly – I thought you could shed some light on how things were between you.'

'What do you mean between us?'

'My question Nikki is to see if you know more than you realise.'

'What do you mean?'

'I mean maybe you heard Doreen or Kenny say something? An exchange between them or with Mark, a throwaway comment ...'

'About what?'

'I don't know, a small detail, something that didn't seem important at the time. A mention of someone, a place, anything you recall that might help our investigation.'

'I don't know anything else.' Her anger was growing.

An uncomfortable pause descended.

Bec spoke more quietly. 'Okay, Nikki, let's leave that for now. We have a different investigation that we're working on. An investigation we had no idea would turn out to be related to Doreen's death, but it is.' She paused. 'A man called Aniken Smith was found breaking and entering a barrister's chambers in the city. Mr Smith fell during a struggle, which caused a fatal blow to the head. And this took place a couple of hours before Doreen died.'

The detectives watched Nikki's face turn pale.

'This is a mistake,' she said, breathing heavily. 'It has to be.'

'Turns out this man, Aniken Smith, known to his friends as Kenny, has been identified from fingerprint analysis as your friend Kenny, Doreen's son,' Bec finished.

Nikki's eyes filled with tears.

'I'm very sorry to be the one to tell you, Nikki, but Doreen and her son have both died. So, now you can understand the reason for our questions. We're looking for clues as to why. Some connection. A mother and son are miles away in different parts of the city and die within hours of each other on the same night.'

Nikki burst forth like a dam breaking. 'You said Kenny was breaking and entering, that's a lie. He wouldn't be doing that. He was going straight,' she cried as a loud sob racked her body.

The detectives stayed silent, waiting for this storm to pass.

'Other people have told us Kenny was going straight, as well,' Bec began, 'but in the end, that was what he did most of his life.'

'But this was different,' Nikki wailed. 'He promised me. He promised Doreen. He asked me not to tell anyone he'd been in prison. He'd even found a job at some charity, and he said he was never going back.' She wiped away the cascading tears running down her cheeks with the back of her hand.

'And he may have meant it, Nikki, but sometimes life gets hard. Kenny was a career criminal. He hadn't just been in jail once, and finding a life outside is tough. Maybe he meant for this to be one last way to get some money.'

'You don't understand,' Nikki sobbed. 'He promised that he would never go back. He said he had missed too much already, and he wanted to spend as much time with Doreen and me as he could.'

'People say these things, Nikki, but you had just met him. You couldn't know him ...'

Nikki mopped up her tears with her right sleeve and stopped crying. 'No, you're right, I didn't know him and he didn't know me, but ...' She paused, looking directly at Bec. 'What we did both know is that he was my father.'

Her words exploded into the air.

'Kenny Smith is your father?' Bec looked at Nikki as if she had taken leave of her senses.

'That's why I knew he meant it. We had a lifetime we had missed, and we were going to spend as much time as we could making up for that.'

'And are you sure about this, Nikki? You told us before that your mother was a single woman.'

'Yes, she was, and Kenny is my father. I tracked him.'

'What do you mean you tracked him?'

'My mother gave me a few facts a long time ago. My father was the sperm donor. I followed up on that.'

Bec got to her feet. 'I am sorry, Nikki, but this could affect everything. We're going to need you to get this into a formal statement.'

Chapter 45

There was no conversation on the drive. Nikki sat in the rear seat with Bec without saying a word. She just stared out of the car window.

All the way back to the station and while setting up in the interview room, Bec was trying to figure out what this information meant for their investigation. She was used to surprises during the course of an investigation, and this was up there with the best. Her first reaction was that it changed things, but now she couldn't clearly see how. After settling her down, she asked Nikki to explain her comments about Kenny.

'Kenny is my father. I found him. He found Doreen again too after being adopted, so she is my grandmother. That's what I can tell you.' She took a sip of water from the glass on the table.

'Could you explain how you found Kenny. Why do you believe he's your father?'

'My mother was single, but she wanted to have a child. Kenny donated the sperm. And here I am.'

'How did you find out who he was?' Bec said.

'I've always known my mother made a private arrangement with a man. She told me that when I was young. She told me I didn't need to know his name, but he was her best friend's boyfriend at the time. A public service, she said he called it, creating a child as a public service.' Nikki stared away like she was imagining how it might have happened. She carried on, her voice flat and expressionless. 'She told me he'd done this for other women. They'd pay him, no strings. It wasn't documented, so you see, in a way, I'm invisible.' She brightened. 'But if it's true he did help other women get pregnant, then I might have brothers and sisters floating around all over the place. So, that's kind of intriguing. But now he's dead, and so is my grandmother.' Her eyes filled again as she stared blankly at the other police officers silently listening.

Shaun's expression was hard to read, but Bec could see from the knot in his brow that the situation with Nikki's background was shocking him. Wendy too was unusually subdued.

'When you said you tracked him down, Nikki, how did you link up with Kenny?'

'Like I said, my mother's old grapevine. I got in touch with her old friend, the one who had gone out with Kenny. She knew all about him and knew he was in prison.'

'And what did you do then?'

'I was shocked that he was in jail. It scared me at first. I mean, I'd always thought from how Mum had spoken about him that he would be some successful businessman or something. Anyway, after a bit of thinking, I decided to write to him.'

'And how did he react to getting a letter out of the blue like that from you?'

'It took a while to get a response. I'd given up, but then a letter arrived. He was lovely. Said he had always wondered about me and wanted to know all about me and my job, my life. Asked me to send a photo.'

'And you did?' Bec groaned inwardly, imagining this beautiful young woman's publicity photo pinned up on prison walls.

'He's my father, of course I did. Sent him a photo and told him all the things I'd done.'

'And how did he react to that?'

'He was over the moon. Said he couldn't believe that "his little girl" was the one on TV in the peanut-butter ads. He even apologised that he didn't like to watch TV serials, but he would if I was in them. He told me he became a mini celebrity because of me, when the other prisoners found out he was my father.'

'And what did your mother think about all this?'

'My mother? I didn't tell her. She's so busy with her "other" family, the one she had later, she doesn't bother too much about me. I've never been a part of that, you see. Except for when I got the part in *Home Away from Home*, then she started calling, didn't she? Her children wanted signed photos of the cast.' Nikki pulled a face. 'Anyway, Kenny said he didn't want me to meet him in prison. He said he was coming up for parole and wanted to meet me after he got out.'

'So, how did you end up living upstairs from Doreen?' Bec asked, genuinely intrigued at the way this story was unfolding.

'Kenny said that he had only found his birth mother late in life, too. He was adopted out as a baby. Doreen was too young and too poor to raise him. Said it broke her heart, but ...' Bec nodded, and Nikki went on. 'Anyway, he told me all about Doreen in his letters, and I kind of stalked her. Nothing dangerous. Found her address and came past a few times. But I didn't ever talk to her. Just, I guess, wanting to feel close or something. We agreed, Kenny and I, that we'd tell her together once he was out. Anyway, my lease was coming up, I was looking for a new place and there was a "For Rent" sign out the front of Doreen's building, so I applied and got it.'

'And when did you finally tell her?' Bec asked.

'I started chatting to her whenever I saw her. She was so nice. But I'd promised Kenny that we'd tell her together after he got out. So, we told her together. She was a bit in shock. I mean, she had only reconnected with Kenny a few years ago, and now she found out that she had a granddaughter, as well.'

'And she was okay with it?'

'Oh yes, she was very okay with it, once the shock wore off. She hugged me and said I'd made her very happy. She'd always wanted to be a grandmother. We went out for a meal together to celebrate. It was lovely. I felt a special connection to Kenny and Doreen right away. We were family, blood, you know?' She glanced imploringly at Bec and the other two detectives. 'Only we didn't have any time to do much because …'

She paused, and so did Bec. The atmosphere in the room had become unusually still.

'Before I call a car to drop you back home, Nikki, just a couple more questions, please, if you can.'

Nikki gave a resigned nod.

'Can I ask if this was a part of your life that you shared with Mark Brereton?'

'Not right away, no. I was afraid he might have thought I was weird. I mean, sperm donors, jailbird father, it even sounds crazy to me. I just told him I really liked Doreen and Kenny. Told him Doreen was like the grandmother I never had, which I guess was true.'

'But you confided in Mark later?'

'Well, yes, of course, but not until I thought he loved me enough that it wouldn't change his mind to know the truth about my background.'

Bec leaned forward. 'If it's any comfort, Nikki, it seems he convinced a lot of people that he was a man to be trusted. Businessmen, politicians, he seems to have swindled them all.'

'And that's meant to make me feel better, is it? That I'm just one in a long line of suckers he's conned.'

'No, I'm just saying he's a high-level scammer. We think it may have been Mark Brereton who convinced Kenny to go back to his old ways. That's why we need to find him and that's how you can help. You knew him better than all of them. You saw him in his unguarded moments and you can help us track him down. You know something that we can use. I need you to go through everything the man ever said, did, wrote, text messages you may have seen, overheard … anything.'

Bec realised that Nikki had started to cry as she was talking.

'I'm sorry, Nikki, I've overloaded you. We can call it a day. Is there someone I can call to be with you tonight?'

She cried harder. 'No, there's no-one. Please, can I just go home.'

'Of course,' Bec said, and nodded at Wendy to organise it.

Chapter 46

The lift doors opened, and as soon as Nikki and her driver disappeared inside, Wendy burst forth.

'A new father and grandmother, how would that feel? Wow, there's no map to navigate that kind of outcome in the real world.'

'Yeah, and the lack of regulation bothers me, too. Pretty scary. You might fancy someone without knowing she's your half-sister,' Shaun said.

'Shouldn't be too difficult these days with social media to find people who share the same donor. I reckon there'd have to be an online sibling registry. I'm gonna check it out.'

'Didn't you hear what she said? Her situation was unrecorded.' Shaun shook his head, genuinely perplexed.

'Yeah, I know, but I'm gonna check it anyway. It's interesting.'

'It certainly puts a weird new spin on our investigation. I don't know if it changes much for us. We still need Brereton to piece it together,' Bec said, looking up from her notes. 'And we will have to get DNA support for Nikki's statement. Another job for Avi.'

After the team had gone, Bec sat by herself for a long time to reflect on everything that had happened to Nikki Cardone. The fact that, after everything the woman had been through, for all her glamour and recognition, she had no-one to call when everything went wrong. Her answer to the question, 'No, there's no-one,' was of the saddest phrases Bec had ever heard.

Bec thought her family might not agree with her career choices, but she liked to think there would be some support if things went that seriously wrong for her.

She reached over and picked up her phone to call Josh. Something deep inside her needed to hear his voice. At this time of the day, the café would be busy.

'And to what do I owe this pleasure?'

'Just your good luck, I suppose.' Bec laughed.

'What, no bad guys on the loose?'

'Do you have anything on tonight?'

'Seeing you, I hope.'

'Not sure what time, got a few things to finish here.'

'No problem. Come here whenever you can. Eat in or out. Decide then.'

Suddenly, she heard a commotion in the background and a voice calling his name.

'Gotta go, see you tonight,' he said, and the line went dead.

Bec was still smiling at the thought of spending more time with Josh as she finished her tasks for the day. Her desk phone buzzed. Juan Zamora's number came up. *What does he want?* she thought and picked up.

Chapter 47

Trying to sneak into her unit, she heard a door open, and suddenly her neighbour was right there beside her.

'Nikki, is everything alright? I saw the police here again.'

Nikki hurriedly turned the key to her unit. 'Yes, everything's fine, thanks. Police were just doing some routine checking.'

'Did they give you any news on what happened to poor Doreen? Someone downstairs told me earlier that her son, Kenny, is dead, too. Said she saw it in the paper. What a shock. I'm thinking of moving.'

'Me, too,' Nikki said, which was true. She couldn't bear the thought of living here without Kenny and Doreen.

'One minute this was a quiet little block of flats, and now it's murder central. It's so nerve racking, don't you find?'

'Yes, I do. Sorry,' she said, nodding to the inside of her flat. 'I've got an important phone appointment.' Nikki gave her publicity smile.

'Of course, a showbiz thing, I understand. I won't keep you. But do come in for a cup of tea sometime, anytime …'

'I will,' Nikki said with a wave as she entered her unit, and collapsed against the locked door. 'Oh, Kenny. Why? Why now? We had years to catch up on.'

Her brain was spinning with dark thoughts. Her mother didn't want to know her. Her father was dead. Her newly beloved grandmother was dead and her career reduced to considering stripping for an OnlyFans site.

It was only when she couldn't cry anymore that she noticed the red light flashing on her landline answering machine and five missed calls on her mobile.

Seeing they were from her OnlyFans contacts, she furiously deleted all the messages and was about to delete the last message when she saw it was Cammy's number. *What now*, she thought. Bad news from her last audition would be too much.

Nikki collapsed onto the couch and dropped her phone. That was the last thing she needed now.

Her thoughts turned even darker. No money, no job, no family. The police seemed to think that she knew something about Kenny and Doreen being murdered. If only they knew how important Doreen's kindness and her new dad had become. For Nikki, they'd come along just at the right time. There came a time in any performer's life when the darkness could outweigh the light. Mark, with all his promises, she'd thought was going to turn her world around completely. Now this. She was out of tears. All she had left were questions to help her figure out the tsunami that had just swept through her life.

Could the police be right? Mark somehow had enticed Kenny to start breaking and entering again? But how? Nikki remembered Kenny putting his hand on his heart when he'd told her that his 'light finger' days were over. Nikki had believed him. She believed in her bones that Kenny had lost heart for a life of petty crime and jail time, and that he would not have gone back on his word. Unless he had some very good reason.

She searched her memory. Had she told Kenny that Mark had stolen her savings? Could he have agreed so Mark would return it? That sounded like Kenny, but had she told him? She didn't think so but couldn't clearly remember. What she did know was that Mark was someone who knew how to find people's hot buttons. Or maybe Kenny wanted extra money for some reason. Mark would have promised him the world. He'd done the same thing to her, found out her deepest wishes: love, money, marriage, security, even family. Everything Nikki dreamed of – all lies.

One persistent thought would not go away. It kept tapping at her brain. That Mark was to blame for everything. If she'd never met him, none of this would be happening. If she hadn't introduced him to Kenny and Doreen, they would still be here. The more she thought about it, the more nothing else made sense.

Nikki was close to exploding with possibilities and scenarios that kept ending with a picture of Kenny and Doreen smiling. It was too much. As a final act of self-harm, she decided to listen to Cammy's message. Then it would all be over.

'*Nikki darling. Where are you? I've been trying and trying. The producers from last week ...*' Nikki steeled herself. '*They love you! They want you back to read with the rest of the cast. This is it, Nikki. Ring me, will you!*' Cammy was shouting as she finished the call.

After ringing Cammy, hands still shaking, Nikki sat on her couch nursing her phone. Suddenly, she realised she was smiling, and with that came the feeling of something else creeping through her body. A feeling she thought the last weeks had destroyed forever. She was going to survive this. She was going to get that role. Everything was going to fall into place if she took control. No more victim. She had never been one, and she wasn't going to let anyone, much less a piece of work like Mark the liar, turn her into one. If the police couldn't find where he was, then she was going to track Brereton down herself and get her money back.

She got up and dialled the number from the card Detective Sergeant Harpin had left on her benchtop. Just maybe, there was some information she had to trade, and that would set her plan into motion.

Chapter 48

Juan Zamora was standing by the entrance to emergency at the Royal Melbourne Hospital, waiting for her.

'I didn't know who else to call,' he said anxiously.

'It's alright, Juan, you did the right thing,' Bec said.

'We can't see her yet, but the doctor said she's stable and in a little while we can visit.' His face was drawn, and he looked thinner than the last time she'd seen him.

'Follow me, we can wait nearby,' he said, leading the way.

'What happened?' she asked, matching his stride along the corridors.

'I needed to speak to Carolyn, but I couldn't find her. She wasn't in chambers. No-one had seen her. I rang all the usual places. I left messages on her phone. No response. It's not like her. Here, we can wait here.' He sat in one of the plastic chairs in the corridor outside the emergency ward and pointed to the second curtained partition closest to the door. 'She's in there.'

Her stomach tight with tension, Bec took the seat beside him, checking out the surrounds while he kept talking.

'So, like I said, no-one had seen her. I don't know why, but I thought that something was wrong. So, I went to her place. I still have a key,' he said, eyes downcast.

Bec had never been to Carolyn's place. An apartment on the seventeenth floor in a Collins Street building, was all she knew about it.

'I found her. She was on the floor in the bedroom.'

'What did you do?'

'I didn't know what to do. I thought she was … There were bottles, pills. I checked she was breathing. It was faint. I rang for an ambulance. They told me what to do till they got there.' Bec saw that Juan's hands were trembling. 'The ambulance said it wasn't an accident. Caro had tried to take her own life.' A sob racked his body. Bec placed her hand on his arm and waited silently for him to recover.

'Okay, you wait here. I'm going to speak to one of the doctors.'

The thought of anyone talking about Carolyn Moorhouse, the woman Bec knew, wanting to take her own life, was like some terrible nightmare.

Bec showed her ID to the young doctor approaching, who barely looked old enough to drive, and said, 'I'm a friend of Carolyn Moorhouse.' She gestured to Carolyn's curtain. 'Can you tell me how she is?'

'I wasn't here when she came in, but she's doing better now, with the drugs pumped from her stomach.' The doctor spoke matter-of-factly. 'I checked on her a while ago, her vitals are rising.'

'Is there anything else you can tell me?'

The young woman scrutinised Bec's face. 'My colleague who was on duty when your friend was admitted has recommended a full psychological assessment when the patient is well enough to talk.'

'Right and that …'

'It's good you're here. She'll need a friend when she comes to.' The doctor smiled.

'How long do you think that might be?'

'Not sure. Tonight probably.'

Juan looked like a ghost when Bec sat down again.

'She's doing better, they said.'

Bec pulled out her phone texted Josh and saw three missed calls from Nikki Cardone. She played the message back, stood up and moved away to return the call.

Chapter 49

Bec and Juan had finally been allowed to sit with Carolyn. At one stage, Carolyn had opened her eyes long enough to see them both and to squeeze Bec's hand, whispering that she needed to talk to her. To Juan, she wanted him to contact her daughter and her ex-husband, Ian. 'Ask them if they could come,' she murmured before drifting back to sleep. From his nod, Bec realised that Juan must have known about Carolyn's family, whereas she never had.

'I have to go. Will you be alright?' he asked Bec, his voice tight with emotion.

Bec nodded. 'Yeah, I'll wait to see what the doctors say.'

'If she wakes, could you tell her I will notify her clerk to find some assistance for myself so none of her matters hit the wall? I'll just tell them she's not well.'

'Okay,' Bec said.

Casting one lingering glance at Carolyn, Juan was gone. And as soon as the door closed, Bec moved her chair closer to the bed. The time passed slowly, the clock ticking past one. With just the sound of Carolyn breathing, the machine noises and nurses coming and going, finally Carolyn's eyes flicked open. Recognising Bec, a fleeting smile crossed her face.

'He threatened Merrily. What else could I do, Bec?' she whispered.

Bec leaned in. 'What do you mean, Caro? Who threatened you, when?'

'I wanted to tell you, but I couldn't.'

'Tell me what?'

'He wanted the file and the code to erase it from the cloud.'

'Who wanted the file?'

'I don't know. But a man called me and said if I didn't follow his instructions, he would harm Merrily. He knew where she was living, he knew about me, and Ian – he knew everything.'

Bec was trying to understand what Carolyn was saying, to put together the scenario that had brought her to this.

'I couldn't let anything happen to Merrily.' Tears squeezed through her eyes and ran down her cheeks onto the pillow. She grasped Bec's hand.

'I told him which night. I organised to be with friends. It was meant to be simple. Empty office, after hours, Juan off on holiday. I told him it was all set, then Juan was there. I didn't know what to do. I had no-one to call to cancel. I told Juan to go home. I said he was too angry to do any work. I thought he would leave with me and it would be okay.'

'How was I to know he would still be in chambers? I'd left the file cabinet open and told them to make it look like a break-in. Now, a man is dead and it's my fault. Don't you see, Bec, it's my fault. Everything is my fault. I didn't have a choice. Couldn't let anything happen to my daughter,' Carolyn said, agitated and trying wedge herself up onto her elbow.

A nurse breezed into the room. 'I'm sorry, Sergeant, you'll need to go now. Carolyn must remain calm. There's a doctor coming to speak to her,' she said firmly, laying Carolyn back down.

'Bec …' Carolyn pleaded, 'don't go.'

Bec got to her feet, and to the nurse said, 'Okay, call me if anything changes.' And to Carolyn, she said softly, 'You need to rest. I'll be back soon. You're in good hands.'

By the time she got to Josh's, it was late. Overwrought and exhausted, she slipped onto the couch and kicked off her shoes. Josh made her a hot chocolate and they talked for ages. She told him about Carolyn and about what had happened, sharing all her feelings about it, and he just listened. It was something she had never done before – revealed anything about her cases. Yet, falling asleep against his shoulder, she had no regrets. Not one.

Chapter 50

Heads turned as Nikki Cardone approached the corner table, either from face recognition or simply that Cardone, long hair flowing fetchingly, with full TV glamour makeup in place, would create a stir wherever she went.

Bec was ready. She liked meeting witnesses in places they felt comfortable, away from the pressure of an interview room. A familiar setting increased the likelihood of getting them to divulge more. This little café belonged to the strip of shops that was an easy walking distance from Nikki's unit. It was cosy and smelled of toast and coffee.

Nikki's call the night before had come as a surprise. 'I'll tell you everything I can remember if I can pick your brain about Mark and Kenny,' the actress had boldly stated.

'It doesn't work like that, Nikki. That's not how the police operate – bartering for information.'

'Not bartering. Fair exchange. Like you said, I know Mark better than anyone. You need me. I want you to tell me about few things in return.' Bec heard a much different firmness in the woman's voice.

'It's not that simple,' Bec said. 'But I'm more than willing to meet up for a chat, and we can see if we can help each other.'

'You've heard my terms. It's not a negotiation, Detective.'

Surprised by the change in the woman, Bec had arranged to meet the actress the next morning for an off-the-record conversation.

'Hello again, Detective Sergeant Harpin.' The actress sat down. When Bec had seen her out the day before after her interview, the woman was destroyed. But now, not eighteen hours later, there was no sign of that person.

'Morning, Nikki.' Bec smiled and raised her cup. 'Coffee?'

'Yes, please, a mochaccino,' Nikki said, spinning around to face the young woman wrapped in a long black apron who'd followed her to the table, clearly a fan. While Nikki played the part, blazing a smile, and elaborating on how hot she liked her coffee and how much chocolate she desired, Bec thought about what they had so far.

Yesterday, she had crawled over all the statements, the information they'd gathered about the parties involved. She'd called the businessman back to see if his private search for Mark had yielded any results.

'Nothing, I wish I could tell you differently, Detective, but this toad seems to have disappeared into thin air.'

The Brereton character was the key to their investigations but locating the man had so far eluded everyone. The actress might at least have some clue of where to start looking. With forensics still pending on the cosmetic bag, Bec's best shot was sitting right in front of her.

'Thanks for agreeing to this informal chat,' Bec said.

'And thank you in return.' The actress batted her eyelids. Bec wasn't sure if it was for effect, or it just appeared that way because of her long fake lashes.

'We have a common goal, Nikki,' Bec said, wishing to convey to the actress how more information could only assist them in solving these crimes. 'Finding out what happened to Kenny and Doreen is paramount. And we need to know all we can about the man you knew as Mark Brereton. You mentioned you had some information to trade.'

'Well, to start,' Nikki said, without hesitating. 'One thing I can tell you is the last few weeks, Mark was preoccupied, seemed worried about something, then he disappeared.'

'Before Doreen died?'

'No, he disappeared just before that. I got home late and he was gone. No note, nothing. I expected a call, you know, "sorry babe, business," something like that, then my credit card bounced and I found out about the money. I wish it was him dead and not Kenny,' she said suddenly, savagely, spitting out the words.

'In your situation, I would say the same thing, that's for sure. Do you have any idea what he was worried about?'

'Maybe the fact that he was about to steal money from the woman he said he loved. Maybe he was worried I'd find out before he left.'

'We checked your bank statements Nikki, and the money was transferred from your account to an offshore one. We're trying to trace it for you.'

'You can check my account easily enough, but you can't find Mark or my money.' Nikki shook her head.

'That's what I need from you, Nikki. Where he might run to.'

'Like I said before, if I knew the answer to that I'd beat you to him.'

Bec believed what Nikki said was true. From the determined expression flashing over her face, she probably would have gone after him. 'You said you noticed a change. When did Mark first appear worried to you?'

'It started a couple of months ago,' she said, frowning.

'So, not to do with him stealing from you,' Bec said.

'Suppose not.' The actress picked up her tall mocha and sipped it without smearing her lipstick.

'Alright. Can you tell me what kind of car Mark drove?'

'He loved his Maserati,' Nikki said, 'But the silver BMW – that's the one he mostly drove here.'

'Parked it on the street out front of the units, did he?'

'I gave him my passkey so he could use my spot underneath,' she said. 'I don't own a car.'

'Wouldn't remember the rego, would you?' Bec asked hopefully.

'Wouldn't have a clue.'

'What about his home? We haven't located any property in the name of Mark Brereton,' Bec asked.

'Yeah well, if that's not his real name you wouldn't, would you? Murphy Street, South Yarra, seven-one-four, but he's not there,' the actress responded, quick as lightning. 'I've checked. Long gone. No forwarding address. Trust me, you won't find him there.'

'Is that the only place you knew?'

'Yes. I only went a couple of times and not for the last few months. Mark came here or we went out.'

Bec heard a text land on her phone. 'Excuse me, I have to look at this,' she said, and glanced down.

Sarge, forensics have a match for the DNA on the rope and the hair taken from the cosmetic bag. Should I call to confirm?

Bec contained her reaction and texted back. *Wait till I'm back.*

Her mind was swirling. The DNA placed Mark Brereton in Doreen's unit and on the rope that was used to tie her up. She needed to get back. This actress was game-playing. Tucking her phone away, keys in hand, Bec was about to excuse herself, when Nikki, checking her makeup in a small mirror and not looking directly at Bec, started talking. 'I don't know if this will help matters, but we were on the Gold Coast last year when a bloke came over and greeted Mark like a long-lost friend. Called him Andrew.'

Bec placed her keys down. 'Andrew? And what was Brereton's reaction?'

'Oh, he said, "Don't know what you're talking about, pal, you're mistaking me for someone else," all that stuff.' Nikki clicked the mirror shut and popped it back into a handbag large enough for an overnight stay.

'But as soon as the bloke was gone, Mark dismissed it to me. Whisked me straight back to the hotel, then some business thing came up and we had to fly back the next day. I remembered it last night.'

'And Mark, did he give any indication that he knew this person?'

'Not at all. But he certainly didn't want to talk to him. Not even to have a laugh about being mistaken for someone else. Mark was always good for a one-liner, but not to this guy. I mean, people get wrongly identified, don't they? No big deal. Even Dolly Parton lost in a line-up of Parton lookalikes. Someone else looked more like Dolly than Dolly.' Nikki pulled a 'would you believe that' face, tightening her lips. 'But Mark, he seemed furious the guy had even spoken to him.'

'Did this bloke give a name?'

'This is what I wanted to tell you when I rang up. He did say his name, and I remembered it because it was Tony Packer. He said he and Mark had gone to Manly High School together.' The actress was watching to see if Bec had made any connection. And when she hadn't, Nikki continued. 'I remembered that James Packer used to live in Manly.'

'Of course,' Bec said, slightly embarrassed that she hadn't made the connection. *Which Australian wouldn't know that name?* 'Is that how you remember things – by association?'

'Yes, mainly association, word games. Whatever gets things to stick in my mind.' Nikki shook her head. 'Anyway, it might be nothing, but when you said Mark Brereton wasn't his real name, I remembered that.'

'Alright, I'll check it out. Thanks, Nikki, we're going to find him.'

The actress stared at her. 'If you find Tony Packer, will you let me know if Mark the conman is Andrew the conman?'

'If I can, Nikki.'

'We have a deal, Detective,' Nikki countered.

'I'll do my best,' Bec said as she paid for the coffee and left.

*

From her car, Bec called the hospital, then spoke to her team.

'Shaun, I've just spoken to Nikki Cardone. Get all the information you can on a Tony Packer who attended Manly High School somewhere around the 1980s, and check before and after, too. Also, look for anyone enrolled at the same school at the same time, with the Christian name of Andrew. I'll fill you in on the rest when I get back, okay?'

Shaun repeated the names. 'Who is it?'

'Not sure, but Andrew could be our guy's real name. Won't be long. I need to stop by somewhere first.'

'Righto.'

The phone clicked in her ear, and Bec sat for a moment, gathering herself. The next step would not be easy.

Chapter 51

Carolyn was seated by the window, a cup of tea sitting on the table in front of her. Bec gently closed the door behind her. Tousled, pale arms poking through the hospital gown, Carolyn's lips widened in greeting.

'How are you feeling?' Bec said softly and sat down.

'Stupid, embarrassed. Pathetic. Is that enough?'

'Aren't you being too harsh on yourself?'

'I don't think so. I plunged headlong into a pit, Bec. It was so dark that for a time, I couldn't see any way out. And what did I do? I just kept drinking and popping pills.' She shook her head. 'From what I know in my life, that wasn't the answer.'

Bec sat quietly listening.

'I can't remember what I said exactly, but I do remember telling you that I'm to blame for the death of that poor man in chambers.'

'You don't have to talk about that now, I just came to see—'

'But I need to tell you.'

'Alright, if you're up to it.'

'You probably haven't had an experience like the one I've just been through, and I hope you never do.' Caro's eyes met Bec's. 'But in the moments when I thought I might be departing the world, let me say that a few things suddenly became very clear to me.'

Bec let her talk.

'I know now that if I'd handled things differently throughout my life, I might not have become a part of what I call the aging equation. And this would never have happened.'

'I'm not sure I'm understanding here,' Bec said.

'You know that time when a woman sees her horizon of potential receding day by day and behaves outlandishly to try to avoid it? Maybe you haven't encountered that yet.'

Bec thought most days for her felt that one wrong step and her horizon of potential could disappear. She didn't know about the outlandish behaviour part, that didn't fit. But she understood how hard she was prepared to fight for the job she cared about.

'Well, that was me. I did that. My whole career. Ambition, Bec. I was consumed, one case after another. Coming home in the small hours, celebrating wins and losses in bars, long hours, never home for meals, no time – or interest, I might add – in running a household. I loved Merrily, of course, but generally I didn't behave like a mother. And I was barely a wife. If I hadn't done that, I wouldn't have made myself vulnerable for the sleaze who threatened me and my daughter. He said terrible things to me.'

'Crimes can happen to anyone. You shouldn't take the blame for what this guy did, you were just living your life.' Bec said carefully, trying to reassure Carolyn that no matter how she'd conducted her personal life, she wasn't to blame for a man's criminal behaviour.

'But I do take it personally, Bec. He researched my life. He knew that I had a daughter living in the UK who had recently arrived back in Australia. He must have been watching me when I went out amongst the nightlife. He knew where to find me, where my favourite bars were, even who I'd gone home with. Worst of all, he picked that I was not the in-charge person I saw in the mirror, but a vulnerable aging woman. Somehow, he saw that I was not dealing with the changing circumstances in my life. He picked it, Bec. Was I so easy to read? Just another older professional woman losing her power?'

'Do you remember what he said? Did you recognise the voice?'

'I didn't know the voice, but every word he said is burned into my brain.' She paused. 'Do not call the police. Do not lift a finger until I call you again in one hour's time. Pick up when I call. Tell me you will give me the file. If you contact the police, you will regret it for the rest of your life.' She glanced at Bec, checking her reaction.

'Serious threats,' Bec commented.

Carolyn grabbed her by the wrist. 'It got worse. "Let this be something you do for your daughter," he said, "because from what I can see, you haven't done much else. You haven't even been over to England in three years. What kind of mother makes her daughter come to her all the time. You've been lucky to have Ian because he's done it all. Your luck has just run out."' She stared at Bec. 'He said that to me.'

'I understand, Caro. These are not idle threats.'

'That's why, when he called, I gave him a plan. I told him the office would be empty, and I would leave the file clearly marked in the first drawer of an open cabinet. I said he had to arrange the rest, to make it look like a burglary. I was terrified. He threatened to ruin me even if I did what he said. "Not exactly a cleanskin yourself, if I may say, Ms Moorhouse, putting yourself about like that. Won't that make a nice little story in the gossip columns." I couldn't risk any of it. I was forced to become complicit.' Bec saw genuine horror in Carolyn's eyes. 'I've been frozen with fear and self-recrimination since.' Her shoulders caved. 'How I wanted to tell you, Bec.'

'So, you thought Juan would be away?' Bec needed to be clear on the sequence. Never mind that Carolyn thought reaching out to her, or the police, would not have helped her.

'Yes, but when he stormed back in that afternoon and told me what had happened with his fiancée, he said he wasn't going on holiday. I couldn't believe it. I ordered him to go home. I thought he would.' Then in a voice devoid of emotion, she said, 'The instant he called to tell me he'd tried to stop a burglary, I knew I was finished.' There were no tears in the eyes that found Bec's again. Neither spoke.

Bec rose to her feet. 'I'm sorry you felt you had to deal with all of this by yourself, Caro, I really am, but you've filled in some of the gaps about what happened. I just wish you'd called me when it started, not afterwards. I'll leave you to rest now, okay? I'll be in touch.' She squeezed Carolyn's hand. Carolyn reciprocated but didn't say another word.

Bec was a couple of metres along the corridor when she saw a young woman, straight long hair and tallish, walking briskly alongside an older man in an expensive suit. From the concern etched on their faces, she figured they had to be Merrily and Ian. She turned to observe their progress and watched them turn into Carolyn's room.

*

On the drive back to the office, Bec couldn't stop thinking that Carolyn had a light and darker side, like most people did. Two parts of the same coin. On the professional side, Carolyn had done all she could to help clients. Yet on the other, private side: a broken marriage, a problem with alcohol, a 'consent order' from her husband, who'd won custody of their daughter and moved to Adelaide. Carolyn had been so hellbent on becoming one of the highest achieving lawyers, she hadn't even told most people, including Bec, that she had a family. Now, she was someone coming to terms with what her life had been and what it was about to become.

One thing Bec did understand was Carolyn's need to escape the dark thoughts they both constantly had to deal with in their professions.

Running was what Bec used to combat those overwhelming times. Carolyn had chosen alcohol, nightlife and dangerous thrills like random hook-ups, all of which involved massive highs and lows, even without the risks involved. There was a daredevil side to Carolyn Moorhouse. It flashed through Bec's mind now, how once, a few years ago, Carolyn had sung the praises of paragliding to her. She'd even suggested that Bec try it. Extolling the 'mind-clearing benefits of a bird's-eye view of the world' trying to persuade her, Carolyn had said there was nothing like 'getting away from it all in the sky'. Bec clearly remembered her response. She'd said she needed any mind-clearing exercise to be firmly on solid ground. And that was still the case.

She made a note to go through the officers' report of the incident where Juan had discovered Carolyn in her darkest hour.

Offering the briefest summary to her team about Carolyn Moorhouse and the impact of the events that overtook her on the night Aniken Smith died, no-one spoke for a moment. Then Wendy said, 'Wow, explains a few things.'

There was nothing to add. Bec knew Griffiths would have plenty to say when she reported this latest development, but she felt only a solid knot of regret in the pit of her stomach. Not just because of what had happened to a friend, someone she never imagined could ever find herself in this situation, but because Carolyn had believed no-one could help her. Yes, she'd called Bec to the scene of the crime, but only in desperation. It reminded Bec of why she'd become a cop in the first place. The world was a dangerous place, and everybody needed to know there was someone trying to make it that little bit safer. Something Carolyn, for all her professional achievements, seemed to have forgotten.

Chapter 52

By the time Bec had read the email from forensics, Shaun appeared with search results for Tony Packer at Manly High School. He'd also found an Andrew Johns, shortened from Johannsen, in the same year, 1990.

'Too easy,' he said, grinning. 'Pity you weren't here earlier when DI Griffiths came in. He was chuffed when I showed him the DNA result from forensics.'

'Good,' she said, 'this lead may have given us a real name for Mark Brereton. Did DI Griffiths say if he wanted anything in particular?'

'No, just a walk by,' he said.

Unlikely, Bec thought.

Shaun seemed empowered by his positive one-on-one with the DI. 'Nikki is delivering in spades for us now, Sarge.'

Bec looked at the young constable. 'She has given us this name, but let's not get too ahead of ourselves on her reasons for doing so. She held back a fair whack of information that could have saved time if she'd given it to us earlier. If she's talking now, we need to think about why that is. Why now and not before.'

'Harsh, Sarge. You reckon she's that contrived?'

'I reckon she just could be like every person I've ever interviewed,' Bec said. 'People always have a reason for what they tell us and when. Best to keep that in mind, even if that person is a beautiful woman like Nikki.'

'Shall I tell you my other good news?' he asked.

'What have you got?'

'I've got an address and a phone number for Tony Packer. Would you like to try it, or shall I?' He grinned again, knowing he'd impressed her.

'Excellent work, Shaun. Why don't you give it a go?'

'Yes, ma'am.' His smile said it all.

'Where's Wendy?'

'In there, watching the footage again.'

'Alright, I need to speak to the forensics team now. We'll get together when you're done to debrief.'

Bec pushed Avi's number. When she spoke to Griffiths later, she would need to give him chapter and verse on the DNA match, the rope, the hairbrush, and fingerprints. And Carolyn's admissions.

*

New evidence fuelled any investigation. The mood within her team was upbeat when Shaun went through his phone call with Tony Packer. And now that things were moving, Carolyn's confession changed things even more. Bec's strong feeling was that it was Brereton who'd threatened her and hired Kenny to carry out the break-in. It still didn't give them a motive for Doreen's death. That would only come when they found Brereton.

Shaun was chipper reporting on his call to Tony Packer. 'He seems like a nice bloke. Pretty amazed at what happened. Bumping into someone he thought was his old friend, who totally blanked him.' Shaun gave a slight nod to the back of the room. Bec turned and saw DI Griffiths listening from the doorway.

She turned back and said, 'So, Nikki's story stacked up.'

'Happened exactly like she said, Sarge. Packer recognised Andrew Johns the minute he saw him sitting in that coffee shop in Surfers

Paradise. First, he noticed the woman, couldn't take his eyes of her,' he said. 'He remembered he'd seen her on TV. But when he looked to see who the lucky guy was, he nearly fell over when he saw it was Andrew, his buddy from school. Looked just the same, hardly changed. Said he couldn't believe it when Andrew denied being Andrew and called himself Mark. Got stroppy with him. "Mate," he tried to explain, "it's me, Packs from Manly High." Anyway, he said that the woman had looked embarrassed when the Andrew/Mark character just got up and left him to it. Made him feel weird, he said.'

'No likelihood of a more recent update on the whereabouts of our friend Mark, by the sounds of that.'

'No. I did ask, but he didn't know.'

'Right. We have a name,' Bec said, writing *Andrew Johns* under the name of Mark Brereton on the whiteboard. 'We have a DNA profile, putting him in Doreen's unit, we have witnesses who can identify him, but we still don't know what name he's using now, or where to find him.'

Bec turned but the DI was gone.

Chapter 53

Nikki saw him hanging around the entrance when she got home. Leaning casually on the wall opposite the stairs – her stairs – studying his phone. He wasn't obviously looking at her. But Mark was still on the loose, so she'd been keeping a close eye on anything out of the ordinary. While she didn't think Mark would come looking for her – she had nothing more for him to take – but she couldn't be sure. He'd stolen her money, and the police seemed to believe that he was the one who'd convinced Kenny to go back to his old ways. *Possible*, she thought now. *Who knew how a mind like his worked?* Probably better not to, she decided.

On public transport, she was constantly on guard, checking her surroundings and fellow travellers. She went without makeup, wore aviator sunglasses, and kept her hair tucked under a baseball cap. Seeing this tall man loitering near the entrance of where she lived, made her instantly wary. Keeping her nerve, she passed by without making eye contact, and arrived at her front door without incident. Once inside, she leaned against her door and breathed out. Had to be nothing. It had been a very long twenty-four hours, what with reading the role for a second time and everything else.

'These new producers, they loved your audition and it looks promising,' Cammy had said. So, Nikki had agreed to meet with them again. She thought it had gone well, but the strain of all that smiling was exhausting. All she wanted to do was put her feet up, watch TV and try to relax. Plus, she had another job to consider, the promise she'd made to herself to find Mark Brereton. The interview with the sergeant hadn't gone the way Nikki had intended. Nikki had been the one giving up all the information when it was meant to be the other way around. What she needed right now was time to think. To reset.

She was resting quietly on the couch, when she heard a loud knock. Then another. She leaped up and raced to the door, double-checking that her security chain was in place.

'I know you're in there, Nikki, open up,' a man's voice Nikki didn't recognise said.

'I'm calling the police. Did Mark send you? Tell him he already took everything. There's nothing else.'

The muffled voice said, 'Mark didn't send me, I'll explain if you just open the door.'

'I'm calling the police,' Nikki said, bluffing. She was scared. It was that in-between time when there wasn't much activity around the units, people weren't home from work yet, and she couldn't hear her neighbour's TV through the wall, which meant she was out, too.

More loud thumping. 'Nikki, I just want to chat. You can either open up or I'll wait here and see you when you go out.'

She put on her best telephone manner, pretending to be calling. 'Detective Sergeant Harpin, please, tell her it's Nikki Cardone and it's extremely urgent.' She projected her voice to make sure the man could hear.

She heard footsteps retreating and broke into a cold sweat.

Hands shaking and drinking water to calm herself, she tried to work out what to do. Who was this man? What did he want with her? Had Mark sent someone to abduct her, or worse? *Don't be ridiculous.* No, this was something else. As her brain calmed, she realised he couldn't have been sent by Mark. He had a set of keys and she still hadn't changed the locks, so the man would have been waiting inside when she got home. Should she call Sergeant Harpin? Maybe. But then another idea started to form in her mind. She didn't want to be stuck inside forever. He wasn't here because of Mark, so maybe there was something she could do. She could go out in broad daylight and confront the man, if he was still there. If he wasn't, then she might call the police. She went quickly to her bedroom, changed into fitness track pants and top, tied her hair up and reinstated the cap, belted a pouch around her waist and placed a few bank notes and her credit card (not that that would be any help) in it. Last of all, she slipped into her trainers and picked up the can of pepper spray given to her by the TV station once when a fan had got a little too eager and followed her to the car after a shopping centre appearance. Spray and run, she'd been instructed then. She was ready now, and she'd always been a fast runner.

*

In one quick action, Nikki unlocked the front door and checked left and right. Then, right and left. No-one. Outside the units on her level, there wasn't anyone about. She jogged down the stairs and along the passageway, as if she was going to the street. Then she saw him. The tall man, jeans, cropped jacket and a black cap, was sitting on the seat just along from Doreen's front door. The only exit. He jumped to his feet when he saw her. Her heart was thumping, but Nikki kept going until she was as close as she dared.

'Who are you?' she demanded, her arm extending so she was aiming the spray directly at the man's eyes.

He stood still. 'Nikki, don't do that. You're too close. By the time I feel the spray, I could already have grabbed you. I'm not here to harm you. I've been hired to find Mark Brereton.'

'Well, welcome to the club. Let me know when you find him, won't you,' Nikki said, carefully stepping backwards in case the man was right about the distance.

'I'm a private investigator, Nikki. Brereton stole a lot of money from my clients and they want it back. The police paid my client a visit, and one of them mentioned your name in the same sentence as Brereton. My client had never heard of you. So, it was my job to find you.'

'And who is your client?'

'A group of businessmen, who, let's say, will not spare any expense to get their money back. In my top pocket is my card. Can I get it out and show you?'

Nikki nodded and moved the spray closer to his eyes, then grabbed the card he held out to her. She was shaking slightly but trying hard to mask it. She felt his eyes on her as she glanced down and saw his name and a mobile number. *Serge Batrouny, Private Investigator.*

'So, you're looking for Mark?'

'That's what I said.' His voice had relaxed a little and was lighter than she'd anticipated for such a big man.

'Well, Serge Batrouny, Private Investigator, you are way off track if you think I know where that toad is. But what I do share with your clients is that he stole my money, too. Of course, the money he stole from me is all the money I had in the world, but I doubt that's the case for your clients.' Nikki still held the spray on him.

'I think it's a "principle" thing for my guys, Nikki. Certainly, they're not broke. But we've got something in common. Maybe we have different reasons, but you and I both want to find this bloke.'

Nikki considered this for a moment. Another plan was forming, one that wasn't reliant on the police to drip-feed her information. She decided.

'Okay, Mr Batrouny. I do want to find him, so if I share information with you, I need you to share your information with me. Two heads and all that … you know?'

Batrouny put his hands in the air as a sign of surrender. 'That's okay if you have any information that helps.'

Nikki laughed. 'Well, so far, your incredible investigative skills have led you to a point where the TV peanut-butter girl is threatening you with pepper spray in a corridor in Thornbury. I'm not sure you're the one with much to share.'

Suddenly, he smiled. 'I knew I'd seen you before. The chick on the peanut-butter ad.'

'Yes, I am, my big claim to fame,' she said. 'Do we have a deal or not?'

'Yes, alright,' the big man said.

'In that case, Mr Batrouny,' Nikki lowered the pepper spray slowly, 'I think we have a few things to discuss.'

Chapter 54

Next morning, Bec knocked on Nikki's door with Shaun beside her.

'Nikki,' Bec said when the actress opened her door. 'A few more questions if you don't mind. Just in the area.'

Shaun stepped in behind her.

'Sometimes, I think you don't have anything better to do than interview me,' Nikki said, annoyed but with no trace of irritation on her face.

Shaun had called in advance to arrange their visit, and he said at first Nikki had been uncooperative. Told him she had to go somewhere. But he had persisted until the actress had agreed to change her arrangements. Not that he'd believed she had anywhere else to be. 'She sounds different, Sarge,' Shaun had said. 'Something is going on with her. Not sure how you recover from losing everything so fast.'

Bec agreed.

'Thank you again for your time.' Bec smiled.

'Tell me you're here because you've found Mark.'

'Not yet, unfortunately,' Bec said, glancing around the sparsely furnished unit.

'Didn't the information about Tony Packer help?' Nikki said, gesturing rather grandly for them to sit.

'Thanks, but we won't take long,' Bec said, still on her feet. 'That information was helpful, thank you. And yes, we did manage to locate Tony Packer.'

Nikki clapped her hands together. 'Hurray. What did he say?'

'He cooperated and confirmed your recollection of events.'

'I told you, didn't I?'

'Yes, but he had nothing else to add. That's why we're here today, Nikki.'

'What?'

'We now believe his name, at one stage, was Andrew Johns so now we need to be able to clearly identify him.'

'Haven't I already done that?'

'You did point him out in photos from the security footage we showed you, but we don't have a clear enough image of his face, so I'm wondering if you could help now.'

'How do you mean?'

'That lovely holiday you mentioned on the Gold Coast, surely you would have taken a keepsake photo of a trip like that?' Bec prompted.

Nikki thought for a second. 'No,' she said. 'We didn't. Come to think of it, Mark shied away from photos.' She shook her head. 'Didn't bother me. I spend my life in front of cameras. I wasn't looking for that when we were together. I was too busy being in love and enjoying myself,' she said, shrugging her shoulders.

'What about some other occasion – would you have a photo of the two of you in a group, perhaps?'

'No, nothing like that.'

'Not one photo?' Shaun repeated.

'I don't need photographing in my private life. And like I just told you, Mark wasn't into it.'

'Okay, that's all. And thanks again, Nikki,' Bec said. 'We'll be in touch.'

'I've given you facts, his washbag. Now, what have you got for me?' the actress said, stepping towards Bec. 'Have your scientists come up with what killed Kenny or Doreen yet? Fair's fair.'

'I can't tell you anything more, Nikki. It's all part of an ongoing investigation. As soon as we have something definite … I promise.'

'Miss Peanut Butter doesn't look so happy with us,' Shaun said as they walked back down the stairs.

'Worst comes to worst, we can see if we can get Manly High to send photos and have the computer age him to match it with what we have on the security footage,' Bec said. 'And her name is Nikki.'

'Yes, Sarge, just joking. Sorry.'

'I know a nice little coffee place down the street. Why don't we pick up Wendy and take a short break,' Bec said, changing topics, mildly surprised at herself for suggesting the coffee break. 'Could you call and find out where she is?' she said, getting into the driver's seat.

Earlier, they'd dropped Wendy at the strip of shops closest to the units. She was chasing up more CCTV to see if they could find a clearer photo of Brereton or his car.

'There she is,' Shaun said, pointing to Wendy standing outside a florist shop.

Bec pulled over.

'That went well, what an agreeable bunch,' Wendy said, jumping into the back seat. 'Just had to mention the two local murders and it was full cooperation. All signed off, the whole strip is in.'

'It's just up here a bit,' Bec said. 'We're gonna grab some coffee. Do you want to go in or do takeaway?'

'I'll go in if there're coconut custard buns.'

'I don't think it's that kind of shop,' Bec said. 'Not too many bakeries out this way do pastries from the Philippines.'

'Too bad. The yuppies around here don't know what they're missing,' Wendy said as they pulled up. 'Can I show them Brereton's photo, Sarge? Might ring a bell, and if not, maybe they'll have custard buns.'

Chapter 55

As soon as she was sure they'd gone, Nikki grabbed a chair to stand on, went straight to her wardrobe and reached up. She'd packed a few items away in a carry bag. An idea was forming in her mind, and when she found what she was looking for, she stepped down and went to her phone.

'*Serge Batrouny. Leave a message.*'

'Serge, it's Nikki, call me. I have a name for you.'

The phone rang immediately.

'What is it?'

'How are you going?' Nikki said. 'Have you found anything yet?'

'Since yesterday, sure I've solved it,' Batrouny said, his voice dripping sarcasm. Nikki knew he would be on a tight timetable with his employers. But they'd agreed to share information and work together, in what could only be called a 'we win and Mark Brereton loses,' arrangement. She would tell him everything she could remember, and he would let her know when and if he found Mark. She'd agreed to tell him how the police were progressing in their search, whenever she had any information from Harpin. But Nikki knew she was taking a chance. Even if Batrouny found Mark, he could end up stiffing her. So, she'd thought of a way to prevent that from happening.

'The police were just here,' she said.

'And?'

'They seem to believe that Mark was involved in Kenny's death, remember I told you about him?'

'Do they have anything?'

'Not yet. But I remembered something after talking to them.'

She heard the private detective grunt.

'I have a plan. I think if you do your part and I do mine, the situation I have in mind will work for us both. What do you say?'

'Depends on what the plan is.' Batrouny sounded sceptical but like he wanted to know what her idea was just the same.

Nikki reeled him in.

'All you have to do is find the woman whose name I'm going to give you and tell me where she's living. Once you've got that, I'll tell you the rest and how it can work for us to get what we want. Do you agree?'

She heard him sigh. 'Okay, it's better than what I've got right now,' he admitted.

*

Nikki's phone rang. Seeing that familiar number, she quickly accepted the call.

'How are you, darling?' Cammy Duval said. 'I've got some really, really good news for you.'

'Cammy, hello.' Nikki felt her heart leap. 'Good news?'

'Are you sitting down?'

'That good?' She laughed.

'It took longer than I expected, but we've done it this time,' Cammy said, her voice excited. 'They want you for the co-lead role, darling. I've done you a great deal. This will run for two series, minimum.'

Two series, co-lead ... Nikki could only blink to make sure she wasn't dreaming this.

'You're back!' her agent exclaimed.

'Thank you so much, Cam, for having faith in me,' Nikki said, tears of relief starting down her cheeks.

'There, there, didn't I tell you I'd do it?'

'You did, but it's still the most wonderful news I could ever hear.' Nikki grabbed a tissue from the box sitting on the benchtop.

'Day one of pre-production in three weeks. Okay?'

'Absolutely.' She blew her nose. 'Gives me time to tie up a few loose ends so I can focus everything on it.'

'Well, get on with it, darling. There'll be press announcements next week, then you'll have sixteen million interviews. Come in and we'll have a champagne lunch and go over the schedule. This is it, Nikki,' Cammy said happily.

Nikki clicked off, beaming on the inside. Itching to do something, she ran into the bathroom, rinsed her face with cold water and fluffed her hair. In the mirror above the basin, she smiled at her puffy red-eyed reflection. Things were finally starting to go her way.

Chapter 56

Back on the mountain gazing out at the dark night of the forest through her window, Bec imagined how it would feel to leave this sanctuary behind.

'Lyn, it's Bec.'

'Hello, lovely, what are you doing calling at this hour?'

Bec hadn't been home for more than three nights. She'd begun to worry that if she didn't go home soon, she might stay at Josh's for good. While she loved staying with Josh and being with him, the demons were never far away. There'd been instances, only brief, but still there, when she'd felt herself stepping back. And she couldn't put her finger on the reason for these little outbreaks of fear.

'Why don't you move in permanently? It makes perfect sense, we both want this,' Josh had said over breakfast. They were getting on famously and Josh was right. It made sense. But at the same time, she missed her morning runs through the trees and the peace of her mountain.

'What's stopping you?' he'd asked quietly, holding her close.

Bec didn't even know what it was, exactly. She just couldn't say yes, yet.

'I'll be here, gorgeous, whenever you're ready,' had been his last words to her this morning.

'Just touching base,' she said to Lyn, pleased to hear her friend's voice on the line.

'Come on, out with it. That's not why you called,' Lyn said. 'What's happening with Carolyn Moorhouse? Need help from your trusty assistant again, do you?' she teased.

'Can't talk about Carolyn Moorhouse right now. I really want to talk it through once this case is over. But if you're interested, I have a different update?'

'Go on.'

'I've been staying with Josh.'

'Well, hooray for that! What took you so long?'

'You're not surprised?'

'No, Bec, I'm not. I've seen you two together. I'm just surprised my extremely pigheaded best friend could do such a kind thing for herself. You're not softening up, are you?' Lyn laughed.

'Well … maybe a little. Anyway, I'm not that pigheaded, am I?'

'What's that saying in American TV shows … I plead the fifth on the grounds my answer may incriminate me?'

'Okay, I can admit to strongminded,' Bec said, thinking there was no friend like an old one to say it how it was.

'And thank goodness you are. There are a lot of people who depend on it, including me, remember?'

'I could say the same about you. Anyway, I didn't call to remind you of all that. I did want to talk about Josh. Hear that, I've said it?'

Lyn knew Bec well enough to stay silent.

'I mean, we've been seeing each other again for a week or so, and it's … well, it's great. He's great …'

'And?'

'I'm scared. I've had bad guys shoot at me, hit me over the head, and with all the adrenaline running, I've never been scared. But …'

'But Josh has got under your armour?'

'Yeah, he has.'

'And you think he'll hurt you?'

'Not on purpose, no. But seriously, Lyn, can he really be the one guy in the world who can put up with me?'

'I have no idea, Bec,' she said. 'The thing is, no-one does. All anyone can do is decide if the risk is worth it. If what you feel when you're with Josh is worth it.'

'What if I hurt him?'

'His choice whether he wants to take that risk, not yours.'

'He seems to be fine with it, to be honest. It's just me.'

'In that case, my beloved friend, the best advice I can give you is jump in and see what happens. Grab someone you love with both hands. I know that's not the way Rebecca Harpin does things, but we mere earthlings just have to risk it. And you know what? Sometimes it works. Not always and not everything is perfect. Look at me, haven't I learned to love camping trips to the Murray River?'

'You seem to have,' Bec teased, knowing how Lyn detested mosquitoes and flies, and how camping by a river was never going to be her perfect holiday.

'Actually I haven't, but see, if you care enough, you just do it. And that's my advice to my best friend. Stop worrying.'

'Thanks for always being there, listening to me and my neuroses. And sorry to call so late.'

'No worries, it's good to catch up.'

'I'll be out to see you soon. Like I said, I've got a few juicy topics to throw at you,' Bec said. 'When this investigation is done.'

'I'm ready. Any time. And just make sure you bring Josh with you one of these days, you hear me? Love you.' The phone clicked off.

Bec sat for a moment. She had rung the hospital earlier and been told that Carolyn had been discharged, was with her family and doing much better. She texted Carolyn and went to bed.

Bec woke to the sound of a message pinging on her phone.

I'm in East Melbourne with Merrily and Ian. Thank you, my friend. Call when you can. I'd love you all to meet.

Chapter 57

'What's this?' Bec said, throwing her bag down on her desk.

Wendy and Shaun were huddled over Shaun's screen when Bec walked in. Shaun, who was busy talking on the phone, looked up and waved.

'So, you own a silver BMW plate number starting two-M-J? Can you confirm your name and address, please?' He looked up at Bec and raised his eyebrows. 'And you don't remember being in Thornbury at any time in the past month?'

'Only four to go,' Wendy whispered, stepping away. 'The database gave us nine. No luck so far, but we are on it. One lives in Shepparton. That'll be a trek if it turns out to be the one.'

'Let's hope it's closer than that,' Bec said.

'Alright, thank you, Mr Henderson, appreciate that. We'll be in touch if we need any more.' Shaun finished off and ruled another line through his list of names.

'And?' Wendy said.

'Nah, Harry Henderson works for an ad agency. Said he's always had beamers – this is his fifth. Lives in a city apartment, doesn't use the car much these days. Said he prefers to ride his bike, instead.'

'Taking his life in his hands there,' Wendy quipped.

'Yeah, but probably gets around more easily than those of us who are car-bound,' Shaun said.

'Alright, finish your calls and we'll catch up after that,' Bec said and headed to her office.

She was still writing down her thoughts when the two detectives wandered in, notebooks in hand.

'Sarge, two not answering, but I reckon we can get through them today,' Shaun said, taking the seat closest to Bec.

She put her pen down. 'Any of them in company names?'

'Yeah, one in a company name, one private. I'll dig around for directors next,' he said.

'Okay. Carolyn Moorhouse said the file Kenny was after contained the only copies of documents Brereton needed to disappear, to make sure the system he used for his crypto scams wasn't recorded anywhere. That makes sense if he wanted to use it again.'

'He just stole the money from Nikki Cardone, though, Sarge. Didn't need a system for that.' Shaun turned sideways to Wendy, looking for agreement, but none was forthcoming.

'I think that was him being an opportunist,' Bec said. 'He was about to disappear as Mark Brereton forever. Nikki had outlived her usefulness and she had saved all this money, so he took it because it was there. No, the main scam for this bloke is the crypto one. He needs to protect that system from exposure.' Bec was thinking fast, trying to pull the elements together.

'Then how does he get Kenny back to breaking and entering?' Wendy said.

'I think, like Nikki, it was his unlucky day when his path crossed with this Mark Brereton.'

'But they met at different times,' Shaun said.

'Yes, I think Mark met Nikki and saw her as a perfect adornment: beautiful, famous, maybe even thought she was rich, and he liked having her around. Then he heard about her family – Kenny, Doreen – and all about Kenny's past activities.'

'Nikki said she had told him about it in the end, so that makes sense.' Shaun was nodding.

'Needs a little break- and-enter, and sees Kenny as his guy,' Wendy said. 'I don't get why Kenny would go back on his word just to help Brereton, a guy he hardly knew.'

'Remember what he told Ray Collier? The only thing that mattered to him was taking care of his mother.'

'That's my point, Sarge. Why help Brereton and risk going back inside and letting everyone down?' Wendy asked, confused.

'Okay,' Bec said, scribbling on her whiteboard. 'Brereton hired someone to steal the original file from the Sydney lawyer. He needs the other copy stolen, and here, magically, appears Kenny Smith.' She tapped Kenny's photo. 'Who only has two priorities in his sights, Doreen and Nikki. So, scumbag Mark thinks up a plan. He can't convince Kenny. We have security footage of them chatting, on numerous occasions, so let's say he tells Kenny that if he doesn't get the file, he's going to harm Nikki or Doreen or both? Brereton wants every written reference to himself and his scam to disappear. Then he changes his name so he can do it to some other rich patsies.'

Wendy shook her head. 'But there would be an electronic copy of the file, Sarge.'

'Just one. Moorhouse is old school. Hardcopy couriered from Sydney. Just the Sydney firm has the backup. Easy enough for Brereton to pay someone to delete it. Remember Carolyn Moorhouse said he asked for the code to delete her backup but she didn't have one.'

'Risky, though, isn't it?' Wendy still wasn't on board.

'Which part of this isn't risky? Brereton plays high stakes. Big money, big risks. That's who he is.'

Both Wendy and Shaun remained silent, waiting for Bec to continue.

'When was Nikki's money taken?'

'One day before Kenny's death,' Shaun said, without referring to his notes.

'We have Brereton's DNA on the rope that tied Doreen up on the night of the break-in, so let's imagine that after all Brereton's smooth-talking Kenny says no, I'm not going back. Brereton then says, well, Kenny, if you don't do this, bad things are going to happen to the two people you care about most in the world?'

'He takes Nikki's savings and holds Doreen prisoner till Kenny gets the file,' Wendy said.

Shaun was nodding. 'So, Kenny had no choice.'

'It's a theory, team. We have to find him and get him to tell us how it went down. But now, it fits all the facts we have. There are still a lot of jumps in it, so I won't be taking it upstairs just yet.'

'Brereton was in Doreen's unit regularly. If he came to the door, she would have let him in without qualm, so he had opportunity and motive. Let's find this bloke right now,' Shaun said, pumped.

Both he and Wendy headed back to their stations, leaving Bec to ponder the actions of one man and the trail of devastation he'd left behind.

Carolyn was only half right when she said Bec still believed the good in people to do the right thing. What she'd missed was that Bec also knew there were evil people in the world. People who would stop at nothing to get what they wanted. People who would think nothing of lying and cheating and doing any type of harm to their fellow humans for their own benefit. People like Mark Brereton.

*

It wasn't until Bec was driving home that she realised she hadn't spoken to Josh since she'd left his place yesterday morning. And he hadn't called her, either, which was confusing. One minute he was telling her she should move in, the next minute he couldn't find time to call her.

After a kilometre of building fury at him, she found herself laughing out loud at her own behaviour. She hadn't prioritised calling him, either, so it was a little rich to be mad at Josh. Especially as she hadn't even been able to say why she wouldn't move in with him.

Exhausted after a harrowing day, she decided a hot bath the minute she got home was the best option. Then she would call Josh to catch up. When making the final turn to her house, she saw his black jeep parked in the same place as last time.

She pulled alongside, wound her window down and stared at him.

'Hello, it's okay, I know the owner of the place.' Josh beamed at her.

'So do I. She's a cop, and she hates surprises.'

His tone was cheery. 'A mate of mine had to go to the airport, so I decided I could drop him and just keep driving.'

'Ever heard of this invention called a telephone?' Bec said, feeling so pleased to see him.

'I have, but the person I needed to call hardly ever picks up. And sometimes, it pays to ignore these modern inventions and take the bull by the horns.'

Without waiting for her to respond, he leaped out and was at her side in a minute. Opening her door, he pulled her out and into his arms. 'To be honest, I thought that if I'd called you'd have given me a million reasons not to come, so here I am.'

'You're becoming a little too sure of things, aren't you?' Bec just got the words out before Josh kissed her.

'Far from it, Rebecca. I'm here because I want you to be sure. When you left yesterday, I suddenly realised maybe suggesting you move in was too much pressure. I didn't mean to do that.'

'It's fine really. Well, it's terrifying, Josh, but that's me, not you.'

Josh looked around. 'It is lovely up here. I get why it's hard to give up the bush, the mountain, the cold, the pretty cottage, the company … Oh, did I mention the cold?'

Bec laughed. 'Sorry, let's get you inside to a heater, my rugged mountain man.'

Later, after the fire was burning, they sat together on the old couch, enjoying the silence. It was Josh who broke it. 'Maybe, Bec, there's a simple answer to it.'

She smiled. 'There aren't a lot of simple answers in my job.'

'Probably not, but let's go through it. I want to be with you whenever I can. You don't seem to mind hanging around with me. Point three, I have a lovely place in town where you are welcome any time. Point four, you have a lovely place up here.'

'A good summary.' Bec raised her wineglass to him.

'So, I give you the keys to my place, you give me a key for here. And we use this modern telephone thing you mentioned to decide where we want to be, and if you say let's go to the mountain, I can make sure there's food and proper coffee when you arrive.'

'And if it doesn't work?'

His eyes twinkled. 'Well, why don't we try it before you start making any dire predictions.'

Chapter 58

The search for the car owner continued, until Shaun announced, 'Gotta be this one.'

'Who is it?'

'Lucky last, city address and phone number. A twenty-six-year-old female owner named Josephine Walker. Didn't answer yesterday,' Shaun said, staring ahead.

'Go on, then,' Wendy said, 'make the call.'

Shaun picked up and pushed the number into the phone. 'Constable Hanley from homicide calling, I'd like to speak to Josephine Walker, please.'

A minute passed. Shaun tapped his fingers on the desk until a voice came on that sounded nervous. 'This is Josephine Walker. How can I help?'

Shaun calmly explained his reason for calling. 'I didn't mean to alarm you. I'd like to ask a few questions regarding your car.' He pressed 'speaker phone' to stop Wendy leaning over his shoulder.

'My car?'

'Yes, Silver BMW twenty-twenty, five series, number plates starting with the letters two-M-J. Have you recently sold a car of that description?'

'No, I've never owned a car, Constable, because I don't drive. Don't even have a licence,' the woman said.

'Well, according to VicRoads, you are the registered owner of a Silver BMW, registration two-M-J-six-K-D, listed under your name with this phone number.'

'That doesn't make any sense.'

A moment of silence.

'Unless …'

'Unless what?' Shaun asked.

'My ex had a BMW, and it was silver. But that was a while ago. And why would his car be in my name?'

'Would his car be a recent model, Ms Walker?'

'Call me Josephine.'

'Josephine.'

'Yes, but why would his car be in my name? I mean, he picked it up when we were together. No, it must be a coincidence or a mistake.'

'And what was your boyfriend's name, Josephine?'

'I'm sure he won't mind me telling you. He wasn't a boyfriend, just a brief encounter, really. Quite a talker, that one. Mark Brereton was his name.'

Shaun raised his arm, while Wendy raced off to tell Bec.

'And do you know what his occupation was, Josephine?'

'Finance broker. But I don't understand why Mark would put his car in my name.'

'We just need to find Mr Brereton as a matter of urgency.'

'Has something happened to him? You said you were from homicide.'

'I'm afraid I can't tell you any more at this point,' Shaun said. 'But we will need to talk to you in person and take a statement to the effect that this was not your car. Could you give me the best address, please?'

'I'm at work. I'm a travel consultant. I have an office upstairs in Collins Street, number one-three-zero. Is that necessary?'

'I'm afraid it is. We'll be with you shortly, and if in the meantime you think of anything at all you know about Mark Brereton, that would be helpful.'

'Now I'm alarmed, Constable.'

'You shouldn't be, Josephine. Our enquiry is only about Mr Brereton and the car.'

After he hung up, he and Wendy high-fived.

'Getting closer,' they said simultaneously.

Chapter 59

Nikki's nerve-endings were tingling like she was on fire. She was back. Interviews in the press about her new role, photoshoots – it was all thrilling. Her 'comeback', the journos were calling it.

Standing before the mirror, hot-curling long strands of hair into place, she could hardly believe her luck had turned.

'What a weird world this is,' she said to herself.

Kenny and Doreen, who she'd thought would be in her life forever. Her emotions surged when she pictured their faces, remembering how happy she'd been to find them. But they had been taken away from her. They'd been so kind. Now, she guessed that her mother would be in touch again, twisting the curling rod too hard.

Then, Cammy's words, 'This is everything you've worked for. It's your time, Nikki, show them all,' took over. She swallowed hard and recovered herself. Only herself to rely on from here on, and Cammy, of course. The agent who had believed in her and supported her through all the ups and downs.

Her thoughts whirling, Nikki startled at the sound of her phone. She glanced down. There it was buzzing away on her benchtop where she kept it so as not to miss any important calls. And when she saw who the caller was, she placed the curler back on its stand and picked up.

'Serge,' she said confidently, 'Tell me, have you found her?'

'Yes, I have.'

'Are you sure?'

'Of course I am,' he said, sounding cagey. 'Took a bit of digging, details not listed in the usual places. I tried every variation of names and addresses from the Nessy Johns name you gave me. But I have finally located an Agnes Johannsen, goes by the name of 'Nessy', and I think she's the person you wanted me to find. She was listed on the school records as the next of kin for Andrew Johns, his mother.'

'Where is she?' Nikki could barely contain the surge of energy that hit her body at hearing the name. Tony Packer had called him Andrew, mentioned the Manly school, and Nikki had put everything she remembered together. She had found him. The feeling was so strong her hands trembled, and her legs felt weak.

'Where you thought she might be, down on the coast.'

'Where on the coast?'

'Just past Frankston. Okay, so I've done what you wanted and found this woman. Your turn now to tell me exactly how it helps me. What's the woman got to do with it?'

Brereton had once mentioned his mother Nessy in passing, and later that he had to go 'down the coast' to visit her. Nikki had never forgotten. She had a hunch this might be where he had disappeared to. She wasn't about to tell that to Batrouny and risk him dumping her. She was keeping that information to herself for now. 'We have to talk to her in person,' she said firmly. 'Come and pick me up. I'll fill you in on the rest, and you can tell me exactly what you found.'

'You're not trying to trap me into something here, are you?'

'Don't be silly. I'm the girl from the peanut-butter ad, remember. How would I know how to do that?'

'Because you could be wasting my time. How do I know you're not still working with this bloke, blowing smoke to send me off on some wild goose chase,' the private investigator said. 'So, I'm thinking, I'll take it from here to find Brereton myself. I don't need your help to tag this woman you're so interested in.'

'That's true, but I think she might know where he is, so if you get there and you see some bloke, what do you tell your clients? There's a bloke living with an old woman just past Frankston who might be Brereton, but I'm not sure. Think about it, Serge. I can talk to the woman, and if we get any more information, I know exactly what he looks like. It'll be easier if I come with you,' Nikki said. 'Just come and pick me up, will you?'

He paused. 'Too late today, I'm too far away. It'd be dark by the time I get there and go back.'

'When can you come?' Nikki had an interview in the morning. Couldn't muck that up, Cammy would be mad.

'I suppose I could come tomorrow,' Batrouny said.

'Pick me up here tomorrow afternoon. Come on, Serge, you need me. I want to find him and so do you.'

He paused. 'Alright, makes sense given you know what he looks like,' he conceded, 'but I'm not a nice person to cross, okay?'

They agreed Serge would collect her at two o'clock the next day.

'Don't be late, or I'll go without you,' she warned.

'Sure you will.' He laughed.

With all other thoughts gone from her mind, Nikki put the phone down and took a deep breath. *I'll find you, Mark, even if no-one else can.*

Chapter 60

Bec had been going through Carolyn's statement over and over. And it was disturbing. High-profile woman being watched and studied over time. It was highly probable that Carolyn had even seen the man who'd threatened her, at some point, standing in the street maybe or rubbing elbows next to him in a bar.

Once they found him, Carolyn's situation would be assessed. She would likely be charged as an accessory to Aniken Smith's death. It would be 'under duress' because she was being threatened, but it was out of Bec's hands whether charges were laid or not. She heard footsteps.

'Did she have anything else?' was Bec's first question when Shaun and Wendy reappeared after their interview with the car owner.

'Not really. The time she spent with Brereton was brief. Not her type, she said. He did suggest crypto investment to her, but she wasn't buying.'

'Good for her,' Bec said. 'Anything else?'

'She didn't seem to know much about him, said they went out for about three months. He didn't seem to have any siblings, and once he said he couldn't come to a theatre show because he was on a boat with his mother and had to drop her home down the coast.'

'I guess that's something,' Bec said. 'Remember Avi's comments about the rope used to tie Doreen? This is the second mention of boats.'

'Yeah, the nautical theme Avi mentioned seems to be developing after all,' Shaun said.

'And now, we have the possibility of a mother living in the Mornington Peninsula.'

'I thought we were really onto something with the silver BMW,' Wendy said. 'Not much, is it?'

'Not yet, but we've confirmed the car is Brereton's. We got the rego. We know he was Andrew Johns at school, and we have a link to boats and a mother down the coast. The car has given us a strong lead to find this bloke who is up to his neck in everything. It's good work, Shaun, Wendy, both of you.'

'Is it worth putting a watch out for that car, Sarge?' Shaun asked. 'It might have been torched somewhere, but you never know. Sometimes these slime bags get too confident, and he might just still be driving it around.'

'Absolutely it is. Do that. Put out a car alert particularly for Mornington and Bellarine roads. He's already slipped up once, leaving the washbag with Nikki,' Bec said. 'And make no mistake, he will again.'

'How can you be so sure, Sarge?' Shaun said.

'Because they always do. Now, let's get to it.'

Wendy turned back from the door and said, 'Have you seen any of that media coverage for Nikki Cardone? She's back on TV, got a new series coming. I was starting to feel sorry for her. Don't think I do anymore.'

'She's certainly tougher than we gave her credit for. Bouncing back like that.'

Bec's internal phone rang. She picked up and signed to Wendy to close the door. 'DI Griffiths, good morning … yes, sir, I can.'

Chapter 61

Griffiths was forthright when she informed him of the circumstances.

'Hard, Rebecca, when it's a friend. Carolyn Moorhouse knows the law better than anyone and she will know that she must abide by it, too,' he said sternly. 'A man lost his life because of her. Then the young chap in her chambers, she let him go into remand and still she stayed quiet. She could have told you and avoided the whole mess.'

'Yes, sir, but the fact that her daughter was threatened ...'

'Yes, yes. In any case, it'll be up to the public prosecutor to decide whether we lay charges or not.'

'Shaun, have you got Tony Packer's phone details?' Bec asked when she came back downstairs. Right now, she and her team needed to pull out all the stops to find this mystery man of many names.

'Sure, here it comes,' he said, and a second later Bec's phone pinged.

'Anything you'd like me to follow up?'

'No, just thought it might be worth having a chat to see if he's remembered anything else.'

'Okay. No mention of our silver BMW in any road incidents, but the number is out there now, so cameras or highway patrol might turn something up.'

'Good, stick with it.'

Her adrenaline was pumping.

*

Bec punched in Tony Packer's number and waited.

'Hello, Tony Packer, dad's phone,' a young female voice said.

Bec introduced herself and asked to speak to her dad.

'Just a minute, he's manning the barbecue. ... Hey, Dad, you're wanted on the phone. It's the cops. You in trouble again?'

Raucous laughter coming down the phone told Bec she'd interrupted some sort of gathering.

'Hello, this is Tony Packer,' the man said apprehensively.

'Detective Sergeant Rebecca Harpin from Melbourne, Mr Packer. I'm sorry to be interrupting your lunch gathering.'

'Oh, that's alright, just burning some sausages, Detective. How can I help you?'

'If you could, I'd like to speak to you again about that incident on the Gold Coast you related to Constable Hanley about an Andrew Johns. I was wondering if I could ask you a couple more questions?'

'That's no problem, fire away. It was funny, you know, seeing an old school mate like that and him denying who he was,' Packer said. 'Couldn't stop thinking about it for a while. But then I thought, never mind, not one damn thing I can do about it. His problem, not mine.'

'Yes, I'm sure it was strange. But you are certain it was Andrew Johns?'

'Yeah, I'm sure it was him, sure as my arse points to the ground.'

'Thanks. I'm Rebecca, by the way.'

'Yes, got that, thanks, Rebecca.'

'I was wondering if he was such a good mate, can you remember anything about his family?'

'Like what?'

'His parents, for instance. Do you have any recollection of them?'

'Well, I used to call his mother Mrs Johannsen, if that's what you mean.'

'Yes, that sort of thing. Anything else?'

'I did used to hear the grown-up folks calling her 'Nessy' at the school. Never saw his father. No brothers and sisters, just him, Andrew. We figured he and his mother had different surnames because Johns was short for Johannsen.'

'Yes, sounds like it. And how many years were you in school together?'

'Two, maybe three. They moved away, never told us where or even that he was going.'

Bec smiled as she scribbled the details on a notepad, imagining how miners felt striking a rich vein of precious mineral. It would be just like this. *A name, a nickname, getting closer.*

'That's really good, Tony, thank you.'

'Is that it?'

'If you don't mind, would you know if Andrew was interested in the water, you know boats and the ocean. Manly sort of goes with the territory, doesn't it?'

'Oh yeah, we lived at the beach. Couldn't afford anything like a boat. Not enough cash. All us kids from that school were in the same boat.' He laughed at his own joke. 'We were forever telling each other that one day we'd own the biggest yacht on Sydney Harbour. Johnsie and I were going to win the Sydney to Hobart in our own boat. S'pose that's why it hurt. You know, him ignoring me like that. We were top mates.'

'Thanks, Tony, good to talk to you. You've been most helpful.'

'No worries.'

'If I needed a school class photo sometime, would you have one you could send?'

''Course. The wife just had all our old photos digitised into one of those digital albums that sit on the mantelpiece, you know the sort? I'll get one of the kids to send it right now if you want?'

'That would be excellent, thank you. I'll text my email.'

'No problem. Anything else, just give me a call, Rebecca.'

She disconnected and sat still for a second. For the first time since taking these cases on, Bec sensed strongly that the threads were starting to align and this investigation was coming together.

Chapter 62

The photos from Sydney arrived just as Bec was going through what she'd gleaned from the call with the team. Tony Packer had added a note as well, giving them the names of all the faces in the pictures.

'Not helpful, is it?' Wendy said, after studying Brereton's face.

'Well, at least we now have a photo of the bloke before he developed his allergy to being photographed,' Shaun said.

'Before he started ripping people off for a living – a long time ago, I reckon,' Wendy added.

Bec tapped the photo. 'We'll get him aged up and show it to Ms Cardone to see if it's a good likeness. Maybe get her together with one of the artists to fix it up. So, we have a name for Mark's mother – Mrs Johannsen, "Nessy". And we have our Mark character mentioning to the travel consultant, what's her name?'

'Josephine Walker,' Shaun said.

'That's it, Josephine Walker. Mark mentioned to her that his mother lived down the coast. He could have been lying about that to get out of a situation with her, of course. But what gives some weight to this is we know now from Tony Packer that Mark spent time near the ocean as a boy. And his confirmation that they both loved boats gives us another link to Avi's nautical connection.'

'Rich blokes who like boats. Should be easy, then,' Wendy said, voicing the frustration Bec could feel building.

'It's a step more than we had before, so first let's brainstorm Mrs Johannsen's first name, "Nessy". Short for Elizabeth, would you say?'

'Nah, that'd be Bessy, my nana's name,' Shaun said.

'Nanette, Antoinette or Vanessa could be Nessy,' Wendy said.

'Okay, keep thinking and we can work on that. Wendy, start with the electoral role and search Johannsen, any Christian names that could be made into Nessy. Start on the Mornington side, as far down the coast as you can, even addresses in Sorrento and Portsea. Then you can try the other side of the bay. You might see if someone at the electoral office can give you a hand with the search. Given your expertise with extracting information from them, that shouldn't be too hard.' Bec grinned. 'Tell them time is of the essence.'

'On it,' Wendy said and left the room.

'Shaun, you can start a search of all the boating clubs down the coast.'

'What are we looking for?'

'Any member by the name of Andrew Johns, or combination of his names, Andrew Johannsen, John Johannsen, John Andrews. Anyone on their list who is even connected to the club in some other way, we want to know. A name someone might know, a link, anything. Let's start joining these dots. I want to speak to Ms Cardone about getting her to look at the photo when we get it. Alright? Let's go.'

Chapter 63

Nikki was sitting in the back seat of an Uber when her phone rang. She saw 'police' and answered.

'Ms Cardone?'

'Yes.'

'It's Rebecca Harpin. Is this a good time for me to ask you a couple of questions?'

'Depends, I'm in an Uber on my way home.'

'Okay, I'll be quick. It's about Mark Brereton's cars.'

'What about his cars? I told you all I know.'

'Yes, thank you. We have located CCTV footage of Brereton and the silver BMW from your local strip of shops. We know it's the car you told us about, but I just wanted to ask if you know of a Josephine Walker?'

'Never heard of her. Who is she?'

'Well, it's a curious thing because we've discovered that the BMW you said you drove yourself sometimes is registered to a Josephine Walker.'

'It isn't Mark's BMW?'

'It does seem to be that car. However, it's registered in Ms Walker's name. Ms Walker has confirmed that she remembered Brereton buying the car but had no idea it was registered in her name.'

'So, this woman is a friend of Mark's?' Blood rushed to her cheeks.

'Yes, Nikki. She was his girlfriend at the time.'

'You're telling me I've been driving around in one of his ex's cars?' she said, her voice rising, tight with emotion. 'He told me it was mine to use any time, the lying ...'

Nikki saw the Uber driver glance at her in the rear-view mirror and stopped herself from saying more, although she wanted to scream out loud.

'Ms Walker didn't realise it was registered in her name and didn't ever drive it, so we believe the car did belong to Brereton. We think it was another attempt to hide his real identity.'

'Probably end up costing this woman money,' Nikki spat out furiously. 'Anyone who ever met this creep ends up losing something, don't they, Detective?'

'It does seem so, Nikki, yes, they do. That's why we're so desperate to find him, so I need some more assistance from you.'

Nikki was silent, so Bec continued. 'In the next day or so, I will have a photo of Mark Brereton that I'd like you to look at—'

'I have no interest in seeing a photo of the creep,' Nikki interrupted.

'I understand that, but we now have some younger photos of him that our computer team is working on to age him. And I'd like you to help us make it as accurate as possible.'

'Alright, but you'll have to fit in with my schedule. I have a very busy few days with my new series. Send me a message when you need me and I'll do what I can, okay?'

Bec agreed and they hung up.

She leaned forward and said to the driver in a nice voice, 'It's the second left after the lights.'

The driver nodded but kept his eye on her for the rest of the drive.

Once home, Nikki slammed the front door and burst into tears of rage. A short time later, her dark mood compounded when Batrouny called to change their arrangement.

'What's more important than this?' she said hotly. 'I thought you said this was urgent.' Nikki had already laid her clothes on the bed while running through vague plans in her head.

'Yeah, it is, but I have other clients, too, you know. Something's come up that I must attend to. Sorry. Tomorrow morning at eleven-thirty? Traffic'll be better anyway, all going the other way.'

'Lucky for you, tomorrow I don't have to be anywhere else,' she said. 'Just make sure you turn up this time or I'll have to make other plans.'

'Yeah, sure, find him yourself, will you?' She heard him laughing at her.

Nikki disconnected and sank onto her bed. 'I will if you don't front, Sherlock,' she said aloud.

Chapter 64

The mood was quiet and no-one was talking unless it was necessary. Bec and the team had been checking names on the electoral role and going through lists, and chatting to people at boat clubs all the way down the coast for the best part of the day. Mind-numbing but necessary work.

'I hope we're right about this nautical connection,' Shaun said.

'I do too, but we need to keep going regardless. Okay with that?'

'Yep.'

Bec considered herself lucky to have been given these two officers. The young constable could be relied upon for solid effort every time. And Wendy too was on track – if she wanted – for a good career in homicide. Her instincts throughout this investigation had been first rate.

'Feels like we're onto something. In fact, I'm sure of it.' The senior constable's voice cut through the air. 'Agnes! Of course. Agnes Johannsen, that'll be "Nessy" for sure.'

'Got an address?' Shaun stood up to see for himself.

Bec read aloud from Wendy's screen. 'Number five-A Gulls Way, Frankston South.'

'Down the coast, Nessy makes sense,' Wendy said, beaming.

'Looks promising,' Bec agreed. 'Get up a map of the area, would you? Let's see where this house is exactly.'

'Sure,' she said, and clicked until an overhead earth map filled her screen, with directions on how to get there.

The three police officers scanned the details.

'Sarge, it's only a stone's throw from the Davey Bay Yacht Club,' Shaun said, excited.

'Let's pick up our search there. Just because she has that listed on the electoral role, doesn't mean when we arrive she actually lives there. With this bloke, you can't assume anything, but the yacht club could give us another angle. That's our focus.'

Wendy was typing again. 'Here's the ad from when the house was last sold. Price undisclosed, but look at those views, will you?' she said, pointing at the photos she was clicking through.

'There's me when I win the lottery.' Shaun laughed.

'That's the only way any of us are going to live like that,' Wendy said.

'Great work, Wendy. Let's keep going and narrow this down. We want this bloke in an interview room.' Bec checked the time. 'Probably too late to visit the property before dark.' She considered sending a local car to door knock but ruled it out. She didn't want Brereton aware that they were close, just in case he or his mother did live at the address. From what Nikki had said about his style and taste, she had a strong feeling about it being Brereton's home. Obviously, he had a long track record of scamming to live that way. 'Okay, Shaun, get a title search of the house. And, Wendy, find us the quickest way to get there, will you?'

'Got it, Sarge.'

'Alright, make sure you know how to drive it. If we find Mr Brereton anywhere near this place, we'll need to get going fast.'

'Pretty nice yacht club,' Shaun said.

Bec looked over his shoulder. 'Bring it back to the contact page, would you, and I'll make the call.' Bec punched in the number and waited. 'Voicemail response,' she said, and disconnected. 'That's odd at this hour.'

'Maybe they're all out sailing,' Wendy chimed.

'There's a restaurant in that complex there,' Shaun said. 'Someone should be answering.'

'Give it a minute and we'll call again. If there's still no answer, we might have to wait till morning.'

'Here's the property search, Sarge. Owned by a company, no mortgage,' Shaun read out from the screen.

'Even more promising. If Brereton owns it, he wouldn't have used his own name. Company makes sense. Search the company name too. Okay, let's try the yacht club again.' Bec hit 'dial'.

After another three calls to the yacht club with no response, Bec said, 'Come on, you two. We can make a fresh start tomorrow, early.'

'Can't say I mind that,' Shaun said. 'Feels like a parma and chips at the local, I reckon. Anyone want to join me?'

'Why not after a day like this? Long as there's a decent dessert,' Wendy said, slinging a bag over her shoulder. 'A few more calories to get rid of at the gym, but who cares. We found Agnes!' She raised her flat palm to the air.

Bec waved them off and went straight to the lifts. If tomorrow morning panned out the way she thought it could, she would need to bring in help from the local station.

The DI's office door was locked and his lights were out. This was one occasion that she would break her 'never ring the DI out of hours unless the station was burning down', rule.

But first, she called Josh. 'Are those city keys still available?'

Chapter 65

Nikki had been ready for hours when she heard Batrouny lightly tapping on her door at 11.15 am.

'You're early,' she said, opening her door.

The big man gave her a head-to-toe and said, 'Who have you come as?'

'Come in,' she said, casting a quick glance to make sure there was no-one watching. She didn't want her neighbour, or anyone else, to notice Serge's comings and goings.

Batrouny was still staring at her. 'Seriously?'

'Yes, seriously, I have my image to protect,' she said patiently. Nikki had decided the best way for her to prepare for the task was an all-black outfit, pull on cap, dark glasses and runners. 'I'm about to start filming a new TV series,' she said. 'Too easy to recognise as myself. In case you hadn't noticed, my picture is everywhere.'

He shrugged. 'Whatever, you're just in my car. We're not robbing a bank. Anyway, let's get going.'

'I'm ready, let's go.'

He moved towards the door.

'Can you go first, make sure nobody's watching?'

'People are always watching,' the private detective said, adding, 'and I should know.'

Nikki had decided that Serge might solve some of his cases sometimes, but to her mind, he didn't seem to be the sharpest tool in the kit. She was confident that what she didn't have in size and strength, she made up for with savvy and strategy. And as she jogged along behind him, she was convinced the plan she'd come up with overnight was going to work. Ducking her head down to avoid cameras that recorded all comings and goings at the units, they approached the entrance and her attention peaked. She said a little hello to Kenny and his mother passing Doreen's door and whispered, 'I'm going to get him.'

'This is me.' Batrouny flicked open the doors to a large black four-wheel drive parked directly outside the entrance.

'You're not exactly inconspicuous,' Nikki said, climbing in. 'You'd be spotted a mile away in this.'

'Yeah, well, it does the job.

Batrouny appeared unconcerned whether she approved of his choice of vehicle or not.

'Oh wait. Bugger. I've got to go back.' Nikki was already out, head down, racing back to her unit. She wasn't about to tell Serge that she had found her key to Mark's BMW and had left it on the benchtop by mistake.

She zipped it into her top and was back at the monster vehicle. Strapping herself in, she fastened the seatbelt and said, 'Let's go.'

Chapter 66

By the time Shaun and Wendy showed up – sticking their heads through the door with a bright 'Good Morning' – Bec had been in for hours, going over different strategies and outcomes dependent on how the day panned out. With the photo-aging process still to come, she tried to imagine who Brereton was and what he might look like today. He was invisible to them. Harmful to anyone unfortunate enough to cross his path or be noticed by him. One of the sharpest legal minds around had fallen trying to defend herself and her family from his scheming. Nikki said he was charming. Bec could only feel frustration bubbling through her limbs. She had a strong feeling that the discovery of Nessy Johannsen's address would lead them directly to their mystery man. She knew that once they got to the house, the day could go in any direction. She had to be ready. Knowing nothing about the man meant she had no idea what he might do when confronted by the police at his door. Flexibility meant good decision making in any operation. She knew stuff-ups could still happen but preparing properly made it less likely. Before she made the call to the Davey Bay Yacht Club, Bec wanted Wendy and Shaun to be all over the location, too – entrance and exits from the house, the club, the area, shortcuts, anything that could save them time, give them the advantage and cut off any means for him to slip away.

'You been here all night, Sarge?' Shaun said with a laugh.

Bec shook her head. 'Preparation. Could be a long day if we can find this bloke. I'd like you both to come in once you've settled.'

The team came in a few minutes later.

'What's the latest on Moorhouse?' Wendy asked.

'Resting after her ordeal,' Bec said.

'I meant in the way of charges – she was involved,' Wendy emphasised.

'Nothing yet. We'll be speaking soon to the public prosecutor, who'll decide which course of action to take.'

Bec could see Wendy was itching to ask more. 'Did either of you get a chance to review the location last night?'

'Sure did,' Shaun said.

Wendy nodded. 'Even printed the floorplan, so I know it like the back of my hand.'

'Okay, no questions? Gull's Way, yacht club, back lanes, paths to the beach, all of that?'

'Locked in here, Sarge,' Wendy said, tapping her forehead.

Shaun nodded. 'All good here, too, Sarge.'

Bec picked up her phone. 'Okay, yacht club first.' She punched in the number for the Davey Bay Yacht Club and pressed 'speaker phone'.

'Good Morning, Davey Bay Yacht Club.'

Bec introduced herself and explained that she needed information about membership of the club, and about one name.

'Just a minute, Detective Sergeant, I'll put you through to the secretary. She happens to be in today.'

'Gladys Hinkley, Club Secretary,' a woman's voice said. *Older*, Bec thought, from her tone.

Bec introduced herself again, and went through the same spiel. 'I'm looking for someone who might be a member of your club.'

'I understand, Detective Sergeant, what's the name?'

'Do you happen to have an Andrew Johns on your books?'

'Just a minute, let me look. The name isn't ringing any bells.'

Bec waited.

'No, no-one by that name.'

'What about John Andrews?'

'That's good.' Gladys sounded amused. 'I can get names like that mixed up. Two Christian names can be confusing. No, sorry, no-one of that name, either.'

'What about Andrew Johannsen, anyone with that name?'

'Andrew Johannsen? No … oh, you mean Andre? We have an Andre Johannsen. Lovely fellow – a big financial supporter of the club.'

Bec gave a thumbs up to the team. 'Yes, maybe that's it, Andre Johannsen. And would you happen to know this Andre's occupation so I can be positive we're talking about the same man?'

'Is something wrong?'

'No, no, we just need to speak to him to check a couple of details.'

'Well, I hope everything is okay. I think Andre is some sort of finance broker. He's been a member here for years. Very generous man, buys all the raffle tickets and bids at all the auctions. He was here yesterday and he'll likely be about later today. He's been around more than normal in the last few weeks. I guessed he was on holidays. Shall I ask him to call you?'

'Thank you, Glady, but no, that won't be necessary,' Bec said. 'We know he's in Gull's Way, but do you have a number for him?'

'Let me look.'

Bec's foot was restless.

'Well, wouldn't you know. I don't have a current number listed for Andre. It's a TBA – to be advised. Must have changed.'

'Not a problem, Gladys,' Bec said smoothly to placate the woman's anxiety about there being no phone number in her inventory of members.

'It is something confidential, so I'd rather you didn't mention this call to him at all. I'm afraid I'm old fashioned like that, prefer to speak face to face.'

'Oh yes, I understand. I prefer the personal approach myself. Too much of this telephone messaging, I think. Anyway, it would be less of a disturbance for Andre if you spoke to him in person rather than me upsetting him, especially now.'

'And why is that?'

'His mother has just passed away. Told me the other day he'd been dashing back and forth to visit her – sometimes twice a day. He hadn't had a minute to take his boat out. Andre has a rather magnificent yacht, I must say,' she added, her voice drooling with envy. 'Anyway, I won't mention anything if I see him. Is there any more information I can help you with, Detective?'

'Thank you, but no, Gladys. I'll make my way to the clubrooms today and see if I can catch up with Andre. I'll pop in and say hello to you.'

'I'll look forward to meeting you, Sergeant,' she said. 'I'm glad I could be of assistance.'

'You've been a great help, thank you, Gladys,' Bec said and disconnected.

Shaun and Wendy sat staring at Rebecca. 'Fair dinkum, Sarge, you could talk anybody into anything,' Shaun said. 'The woman told you everything without the normal "privacy" concerns, confirmed the address and even thinks not telling Andre the cops had called was her idea.'

'Let's just hope her tongue holds,' Bec said. 'There are a few loose ends to tie up, and we'll head down there in about an hour. Wendy, you're the driver.'

Chapter 67

They'd been on the road driving for what felt like hours. Stop-start in heavy traffic. It wasn't until they were wheeling up the incline of Oliver's Hill, with sea views spreading out before them, that Batrouny finally told Nikki the address he'd found for Andrew Johns' mother. She didn't know how he'd found it and thought it better not to ask. Instead, she followed the house numbers, calling each one out loud until they arrived. However, Batrouny, making a pretence of visiting elsewhere, kept driving another fifty meters metres before he pulled over.

'Wow,' Nikki said, admiring the view. The location, high on the cliff top with an ocean view stretching out as far as the eye could see, beautiful marina to the left, sail boats skimming the bay, was stunning. 'What a beautiful place,' she said, imagining the beach below camouflaged by drifts of the same tea tree that surrounded the houses in this street. 'It's a good place for Mark to hide out,' she said. 'It's almost hidden by the shrubs and trees.'

'You wait here.'

'But ...'

'This is what I do, Nikki. Wait here and don't move. You see anything, text me. Okay?'

'But I can ...'

'Just do as I say,' Serge said firmly in a way that brooked no argument. 'I swear, anyone seeing you come down the driveway dressed like that would have to call the cops. You look more like a cat burglar than the real thing. Let me go first to check it out. I don't want you stuffing this up.'

Nikki watched him in the side mirror walking back up the hill, until he descended the other side and she lost sight of him.

At first, when they'd set out, she'd been uncomfortable being in the car with him. But after a while, she'd relaxed. His demeanour, negotiating disgusting roads and bumper-to-bumper traffic, had inspired something – not confidence exactly, but an assessment that he wasn't about to detour and make this about something else. Still, she had kept her pepper spray handy, just to be sure. The fact was that they were both after the same thing – Mark Brereton's head on a skewer. Which was why she was allowing Serge to direct their moves. He had found the address. And at one stage on the drive down, as a break from commercial ads on the radio, it'd even crossed her mind to ask him why he wasn't a cop anymore. But she'd decided against it. There was something about the man she certainly didn't want to get on the wrong side of.

He hadn't held back with her, though. 'What did this bloke do to you to chase him down, cheat on you or something? Is this some kind of vendetta?'

Nikki felt her blood start to boil. 'Cheat on me? What a pathetic, chauvinistic thing to say. No, Serge, he stole my life savings, he lied to me about who he was, even his name, and led me to believe he was in love with me,' she said heatedly. 'So, yes, it is some kind of vendetta, as you put it. I want this man to be held accountable.' She turned away and looked through the window to indicate it was her last word on the topic.

'He must be a talker, then. In your business, with your looks, you'll have come across a lot of snakes, but he fooled you, just like he did my blokes. And if it's any consolation, they're not easily fooled either.'

Ten more minutes elapsed before he suddenly reappeared, his head bobbing up first, until step by step his whole body emerged. She watched him walking purposefully along the footpath, until he abruptly turned left into a driveway, at just about where five-A was, and disappeared again.

It took every atom of Nikki's self-control not to launch herself out of the car and go in after him.

He finally returned and got back into the car. 'I think we'll go for a bit of a drive and come back in an hour or so.'

'Why?'

'Doesn't seem to be anyone home.'

'Isn't that a good thing? Can't we just sit here for a while and watch? Isn't that what's called a stakeout?' Nikki said.

Batrouny shook his head, bemused. 'You see that on TV, did you?'

'I played a cop once,' Nikki said, 'and before you laugh, we had advice from real cops on how to do it. So, yes, I've done a stakeout before.'

'Difference with us is we're not cops, so if someone asks why we're sitting here, we can't just flash a card and tell them to piss off, can we?' He checked his watch. 'We could sit here for a while, I suppose, but people don't like strange cars parked outside their houses, especially rich bastards, so my advice is we move on and come back.'

Nikki strapped herself back without saying anything more. Batrouny pushed the ignition, the engine turned over, and they were rolling back down the hill.

'We can go back to that last intersection,' he said. 'A few shops from what I saw on the map. Something to look at while we wait. Although maybe,' he gave her a once-over, 'you'd be better off staying in the car.'

'I'll buy a coloured shirt or something, then,' she said crossly. 'If it bugs you so much.'

'Couldn't hurt.'

'So, do you really think there's no-one in the house?'

'Pretty sure. Certainly, no movement anywhere. There is a car in the garage, but an empty spot as well. He could be on holiday, shopping, who knows.'

'A car?' Nikki said, controlling her reaction.

'Yeah, a BMW.'

'What colour?'

'Does it matter?'

'Not really, just curious. Mark had a silver BMW.'

'Yeah, well, could be his, then. Didn't get a good look to see the rego. That's something we can check when we go back.'

She was so close. Nikki's heart was thumping so much she thought Serge would be able to feel it from the driver's seat. She gently checked the spare key to Mark's BMW that was still in the belt pouch and pushing against her waist. Her brain had started working on fine-tuning her original plan. It was almost too much to hold in. A couple of times she almost blurted out, 'I've got the key to that car. I'm going to take it and not give it back until I get my money.' But she didn't.

She heard Kenny's words in her mind. *I don't know how I sired a beauty like you, Nikki*, he had said once, *but I'm very proud that I did.* Now, she wanted to say to him, *I wasn't expecting to have a break-and-enter guy for a father, but now I'm hoping some of those genes might come in handy for me.*

Chapter 68

At the last minute, as they approached their vehicle in the basement, Wendy threw the keys to Shaun. 'I'll drive back,' she said, 'you know the roads.'

Shaun pulled a face. 'Two years in Highway Patrol, happy to see the back of it, but okay, I'll drive.'

Progress was slow.

'This is taking way longer that it should,' Wendy said after forty-five minutes and fiddling with the Sat Nav. 'I forgot it was school holidays. Traffic will be like this all the way down. Are you sure you don't want to get the locals to pick up Brereton for us, Sarge?' She turned and spoke to Bec in the back seat.

'No, I want to talk to this fellow myself, but we do need them as back-up when we get there.' Bec stared out the window, running through her approach to interviewing Brereton.

'We could flash the blues, Sarge, get them to move over,' Shaun suggested.

'No, Shaun, I think we can save that for now. He doesn't know we're coming.'

'If the secretary at the boat club has stayed schtum,' Wendy said.

'Let's hope so. Otherwise, he'll be long gone.' Bec returned to her thoughts.

Finding an address for the bloke's mother was one thing, but apprehending him was another story. He had been disappearing for years.

She also knew that getting any charges to stick to Brereton was another challenge. He wasn't the one who broke into Barwick Chambers. The evidence against him for Doreen's death was strong but not conclusive. And the businessman and the politician would never agree to give evidence. Yet, it was one of those headaches Bec loved. Once he was in the interview room, she knew she had a good chance of getting him to confess. She just needed him in custody.

'Can't we go another way, get off the freeway?' Wendy said impatiently.

Focusing on the traffic, Bec saw they'd hardly moved.

Shaun waited before answering, 'Are you kidding, mightn't get there at all if we try that.' He put his head out of the window to see what was holding them up. 'There's been a pile-up further along. Our friends from Traffic are in attendance. I can see flashing blue lights just before the turnoff, but we're stuck for now.'

'Is it bad? Should we assist?' Wendy asked.

'No, looks like Traffic only, no ambos or fire trucks. Should be alright once we get past.'

'Just when we thought we had him,' Wendy huffed.

'I wouldn't be writing us off just yet, Wendy. Shaun, once we pass the accident and hit the next exit into Frankston, step on it, then we can use the lights to get clear.'

Chapter 69

Nikki felt like a cat on a hot tin roof. She wanted to get back to the house. She'd had to draw on all her skills to appear relaxed while watching Serge eat his toasted sandwich and she sipped her hot chocolate.

Finally, Serge looked at his watch and said, 'Time to go.'

Nikki didn't speak as she got up and started for the car.

'Just going to drive around, see what's going on. Anyone looks, we're just two sightseers, okay?' Serge didn't look at her.

'I thought we were going back to his house?' Nikki asked.

'We are. But if we found the address, I want to make sure the police aren't hanging around waiting for this bloke. Last thing we need. Won't hurt to kill a bit more time till the light goes.'

He turned the big car onto the beach road.

'You been down this way before?' he said, indicating a left turn.

'I might have been in Frankston as a kid, once,' Nikki said, making a note of which streets Batrouny was taking. 'But I don't remember much about it.'

'Just the beach,' he said.

'Yeah, just the train ride and the beach.'

He drove them around the streets near the house slowly, once, twice, three times, then circled back down towards the beach, where he pulled into a park and stared out at the ocean.

'Not too many willing to brave the cold at this time of year,' she said, anxiety mounting. *Fading afternoon light.* 'I mean, would you?'

'I'm gonna take a walk. You just stay here,' he said, and got out.

She watched him take the promenade; shoulders hunched, head down. And in the fading light, his dark figure quickly disappeared.

Frustrated, Nikki waited. She'd wanted to raise with him the prospect of whether they would call the police once they confirmed Brereton was living in the house. Again, her situation was freestyle, and she would play it by ear. Wouldn't DS Harpin be shocked when Nikki handed her Brereton's real name and address on a plate. Nikki smiled at the thought of making that call, then jumped when Batrouny pulled the car door open. She'd been watching the walking path, expecting him to emerge any minute, and hadn't expected him to approach from behind.

'Time to move, you ready?'

She nodded. *Ready? I really am ready this time*, she thought, gently letting her fingers touch the car keys in her pocket.

Batrouny fell silent as he focused on backing the car out and indicating right.

The big car churned along, but it wasn't until he took a right again at Pelican Point that Nikki breathed out, seeing that this time they really were heading back to the house.

Chapter 70

Late afternoon light dimming fast, they turned into Gull's Way.

'You check, see if there are any cars in the driveway or lights on in the house,' Batrouny said, driving straight past five-A again without stopping.

'No cars, no lights,' Nikki said, craning to see the whole property from the road. 'Nothing,' she said, 'no-one home, by the looks.'

Batrouny turned back and approached slowly this time, parking outside the house on the down side of the hill. 'Okay, doesn't seem to be any sign of life. Let's take a look,' he said and jumped out of the car. This time, Nikki followed. 'Stick close to me,' he said. 'I'll need you as the lookout. Just keep out of the way, and if I say go just go. Don't piss around. And put these on before you touch anything,' he commanded, handing her a pair of latex gloves.

'Anyone asks, we're visitors coming to see the owners,' Batrouny said as they walked as casually as they could side by side, approaching the house.

'Going in,' Batrouny said, glancing around before he turned into the driveway.

Nikki followed. 'Can't even see the garage from the street,' she said, panting to keep up with the big man, who was fitter than he looked.

A light flicked on.

Startled, they backed up against the house wall and waited.

'Someone home?' she whispered.

Batrouny shook his head and pointed up to sensor lights mounted under the eaves of the house, then signed that she should follow him. They slid along the side of the wall, keeping their backs against the house. A quick dash under another sensor light and they were at the side of the garage, set ten paces away from the house. A different light flicked on over the garage door.

'Lights up like Luna Park,' Batrouny hissed, tension in his voice for the first time.

They waited until they were certain no-one was reacting to the light coming on, Nikki peered through the smallish side window, shining her phone light in, and whispered, 'It's his car.'

'Okay.' He nodded. 'Can we get a closer look?'

'It's the one he drove,' Nikki said, 'I can tell.'

'We need to be sure.'

'Okay,' she said. 'You get that side window open, lift me up and I'll slide in. I can open the garage from the inside.'

'You can do that?'

'That door has a button to open it, and I know there's a remote in the car. I always wondered what it was for. I just need to get in there.'

Batrouny expertly used a small metal implement from his pocket and the window slid open. Nikki stepped on his bent knee, which he raised until she was able to slip through the space horizontally. Then the metal door started to roll upwards.

'That's the car and the number plate,' she said, shining her phone light at the registration. 'It's definitely his car. It wouldn't be here if he didn't live here.'

Batrouny ducked underneath the moving door. He pulled out his phone, snapped a photo of the number plate and walked around the car, using his own torch. He touched the bonnet. 'Hasn't been started recently, cold engine,' he said, looking at the empty space in the garage next to the BMW. 'He had another car?'

'Yeah, a Maserati. I never got to drive it,' Nikki said distractedly.

'Tyre marks look like he parks that here, too. I reckon he's out, so we need to not be here if he comes back,' he said, ushering Nikki out, before pressing the red button to bring the door down and stooping under it himself. 'We need to get out of here.'

Batrouny began retracing their steps up the drive in the dark, sticking close to the house to avoid the senor lights, assuming Nikki was right behind him.

Back on the street, speaking gruffly over his shoulder, he said, 'You ever need part-time work as a private eye, just call me, okay? Get in.' He jumped into the driver's seat, expecting Nikki to open the passenger seat door at any second. Nothing happened.

He peered out and waited. Still no sign of Nikki. And when she didn't come, he decided his headlights would pick her up on the footpath. But as his big black four-wheel drive crawled a few metres up the incline, allowing him to lean over and scan the empty expanse of footpath, his frustration escalated. Nikki was nowhere to be seen.

He shut off the engine. Through the side car window, he stared at the house, watching for any movement. Impatiently, he spun around to look through all the windows. Agitated, he got out of the car, and from the footpath dared to shine his phone torch down the driveway of five-A into the dim light. He whispered hoarsely, 'What the hell are you doing? Come on, we've got to get out of here.'

Nothing. Not a sound.

He got back into the car and furiously pushed her phone number.

'Hi, you've called Nikki, leave a message.'

He disconnected angrily and pelted his phone onto the seat where she should be sitting. 'What is she playing at?' he muttered to himself.

The front light – more like a spotlight – to the adjoining house, five-B, unexpectedly flicked on, illuminating the front garden and the footpath. He heard a man's voice say, 'Come on, Bruno, let's see what's disturbing you out here,' and saw the shadow of a tall man leading a large German shepherd up the pathway towards the road, and him.

Furious, Batrouny started the engine, planted his foot on the accelerator and roared off.

Chapter 71

'Here we are finally,' Shaun said, cruising slowly through the entrance of the Davey Bay Yacht Club carpark. The sight of masts, large and small yachts at anchor, a sprinkle of lights twinkling on the water and a clubhouse lit like a Christmas tree, was as pretty as a postcard. Gulls crying, and the smell of salt and sea air had already penetrated the inside of the car without them opening a window.

'Nice,' Shaun said. 'Wouldn't mind a slice of this lifestyle.'

'Right, on a copper's salary. You better start saving,' Wendy flashed back.

'Pull up here,' Bec said, poised to open her door. 'We can walk around to the front. Wendy, you come with me. It might be best if you stay with the vehicle, Shaun, in case we need to move fast.'

'Did you say the local station is on standby?'

'Waiting for a call from us. I asked for one car to be close here, and I've asked them to send another car to cruise around Gull's Way – to keep an eye out there, just in case Brereton shows up.'

'Might have been better to wait till morning,' Wendy said, observing the fading light. 'Took too long to get here,' she said.

'Not ideal, I know. But if this bloke is here, we want to make it as casual as we can. Let's try not to scare the locals. If Brereton will come in to answer a few questions, then we can do it gently. If not, then he's still coming with us.'

The police car was still idling when Bec and Wendy walked off towards the clubhouse. Only when they disappeared did Shaun shut the engine. He glanced around, getting his bearings, casually checking the local map on his phone, watching car movements in the park.

*

Bec and Wendy walked casually around the ground level of the clubhouse to get a feeling for the place, entrances and exits they might need to know. The club was a hive of activity. Barely an empty seat at the bistro overlooking the water, and people milling everywhere. The smell of food, the happy hum of voices talking, and glasses chinking reached outside where they were standing.

'Are these people retired?' Wendy said, checking her watch and nodding towards the queue forming for entry into the up-market restaurant.

'How the other half lives, Wendy,' Bec said, scanning around.

'Nice for some. Doesn't appeal to me, though, except for the fishing.'

'You fish on your days off?'

'As a kid I did, yeah, all the time. My whole family fished. That was how we fed the big family.'

Bec nodded, reminded of how different this senior constable's life was as a cop in Melbourne, compared with how her life could have been.

'Plenty of people fish along the coast here. You could buy yourself a little tinny,' Bec said, distracted by the movements of a man she'd been watching on the jetty.

Wendy laughed. 'A tinny, Sarge? Been there, done that. No, after I retire as police commissioner, I reckon I'll buy one of those "in your face" boats. Can't see anyone who seems to be in charge,' Wendy said, looking around. 'You reckon we'll find the woman you spoke to?'

'Gladys? Doubt she'd still be here.' Bec was focussed on a figure, sailor's cap, white hair, seated beneath a long line of overhead lights. The entire length of the jetty was illuminated as if it were a promenade. 'Let's have a chat with that bloke over there instead,' she said, heading in his direction.

The man was on his feet now, rolling up a long stretch of canvas. He'd been repairing sails with the paraphernalia lying at his feet.

He looked up, sensing their approach.

'Afternoon,' Bec called out.

He stopped what he was doing. 'Think you mean evening,' the man said amiably, and waited for them to reach him.

'Yes, evening to you. I'm looking for Andre Johannsen. Have you seen him about today?' The man stared at them. 'Detective Sergeant Rebecca Harpin,' Bec flashed her ID, 'and this is Senior Constable Santos.'

'No, I haven't, Detectives,' he said. 'Not yet anyway. He's usually here about now. Sounds serious. Can I give him a message?'

'Thanks, but that won't be necessary. But can you tell me, is his boat here?'

'Andre's boat?' The man pointed towards the end of the jetty. 'You can see it right down there at the end. The last mooring where the water is deeper. *Checkmate* is a beautiful vessel, sleeps eight. Andre reckons he'll sail it around the world one of these days.'

'Could he do that?' Wendy said.

'He'd need a pretty good crew, but yes, *Checkmate* could do it.'

'This yours?' Wendy nodded to the yacht moored next to where the man had been sitting.

'Yep, that's her. I've owned this little lady for close on twenty years. *Dreamboat*, she's called, and she is a dream to sail.'

*

Stake-outs were not Shaun's favourite part of the job, even with the extreme likelihood of apprehending their main suspect. He especially didn't like the responsibility of locking onto the details of every activity going on around the clubhouse with just one set of eyes. He didn't want to be the one to miss anything and get the blame if anything went wrong. His senses were in overdrive when he heard a rumbling sound. His years in traffic told him the sound was a luxury car, Italian. He scanned his mirrors just in time to see what could have been a silver car approaching the entrance to the carpark. The car appeared to slow and stop. Had the driver noticed his police vehicle parked at the side of the building? It was hard to see clearly. Before he could get a look at the plates, the engine revved, the car turned and drove off, gathering momentum as it sped away. Shaun grabbed his phone.

*

Bec's phone buzzed. 'Excuse me,' she said, leaving Wendy to carry on talking to the fisherman.

Shaun's voice was tight. 'Sarge, a flashy car, can't be completely sure, but I reckon could be a Maserati – light colour, maybe silver. It just came into the carpark, saw me, turned around and left. Do you reckon …?'

Bec held the phone away and spoke urgently to the man still chatting to Wendy. 'Excuse me, sir, do you know what kind of car Andre Johannsen drives?'

The man nodded his head. 'I do, Maserati, my dream car.'

'Silver?'

The man nodded again.

'That's it, Shaun, we're on!' Bec shouted and started to run back towards the carpark. 'Come on, Wendy, thank you!' she called back to the man, who was on his feet and whose open mouth and startled expression resembled someone watching a horror film unfurl in front of him.

'He'll be going to the house,' Bec said into the phone. 'Let's go there.'

Puffing hard, Bec and Wendy jumped into the car. 'Lights, no siren,' Bec said breathlessly, punching in the number for more local assistance, while Wendy gave Shaun the quickest route to Gull's Way.

'Do you reckon he's armed?' Shaun said, speeding through the exit, lights flashing.

'No idea,' Bec responded automatically. 'But be ready just in case.'

Chapter 72

Under cover of darkness, Nikki crawled out. After hearing Batrouny's car depart and the great beam of light that had been shining from the house next door flicked off, she made her move. He'd probably rung her phone, but she'd turned it to silent. Moving slowly, she made her way towards the back door. Up the steps, around the perimeter of the swimming pool, up two more steps, carefully keeping her phone torch pointed to the ground, making sure she wouldn't be seen. She'd hidden under a belt of tea trees at the bottom of the block, where she knew Batrouny wouldn't venture to look for her. She'd felt quite calm waiting under those trees on the sandy ground, to the sound of the waves lapping gently onto the beach in the background. It was a feeling that had come over her the moment she saw the car. She had planned exactly what she was going to do and exactly how she was going to do it.

Kneeling at the back entrance to the house, she unzipped the pouch belted to her waist, pulled out the keyring and shone some light onto it. One was obviously a car key for the BMW, but then there was this other key that she'd seen before but had never taken notice of. At least, not enough to wonder which door that key opened. Until now. Without knowing if the house was alarmed, she stood up, inserted the key and turned it. The lock clicked open. Her heart beat exploded.

Thank you, Mark whoever you are, for your house key!

With her pulse pounding, Nikki gently opened the back door, expecting at any moment that an alarm would start wailing, alerting the neighbourhood and maybe a private security company that someone had broken into the house. Nothing happened. Bolder now, she shone her torch around and edged forward. Quietly, she checked every room – utility kitchen and each enormous bedroom (she counted five). She tiptoed until she came to what looked like the main bedroom. Mark's room, by the look of the neatly folded familiar clothes laid out on the bed and the half-ready travel case packed with men's clothing – just waiting to be zipped. He hadn't even changed his aftershave. A faint waft of the scent drifted up her nose as Nikki moved across to the wardrobe and shone her torch around. More clothes, and underneath a carry-on case that she pulled out and opened. Part of her plan had been to try to find his bank statements or passport as extra bargaining power to get her money back.

She lifted the contents out: a cosmetic bag, change of underwear, a sporting jacket and cap, a passport folder in a plastic sleeve, which she slid out. *Andre Johannsen*, she read, with a photo of the man she'd known as Mark Brereton. Nikki almost exploded with anger seeing his face. She slipped it into her pocket. Feverishly zipping and unzipping side compartments, she realised that the whole top layer could be removed. She paused before pulling the larger zip around, but when she did, the sight of what lay staring back at her was such a shock that Nikki feared she might faint. Packs of crisp green hundred-dollar bills were piled up, layer upon layer, filling the whole base of the bag. *He's running away. This is his travel fund.* She fell to the floor, positioned her phone light, grabbed one pack, and started counting, ten thousand dollars per stack. *So much cash.* Nikki had never imagined it. There must be hundreds of thousands there. She was suddenly sure of her next step.

Rifling through the wardrobe until she found a shopping bag filled with new shirts, she upended it and then placed the shirts in the bottom drawer. Then she grabbed ten piles of the hundred-dollar bills and shoved the half-inch stacks as fast as she could into the bag. Ten packs amounted to 100,000 dollars – the exact amount Brereton had stolen from her. For a split second, it crossed her mind to take the lot, but *she* wasn't the thief here. All she was doing was taking her own money. It was only fair. *Call it a loan, Andre. Now, you're repaying it.*

She checked again, counting ten packs. She heard her meditation instructor's voice, *Be Calm. Just breathe* ... It helped. She felt like she was moving in slow motion. She'd only been thinking, at best, that she could take Mark's car to bribe him into returning at least some of the money. Maybe even take one of the artworks he was always talking about, but this was something else. Never in her wildest dreams did it cross her mind that she might be able to recover all her hard-earned savings. She jumped to her feet, and, emboldened by how the situation had turned out, switched on a bedside lamp. Rushing now, she tidied the room, feverishly straightening everywhere to appear untouched. When Brereton came back, he wouldn't pick that anyone had been here. Until he counted his cash.

She was making her way carefully out of the house when the sound of a car engine slowing outside stopped her in her tracks. She turned quickly and almost ran back along a wide passage to the front door. Praying it wasn't Mark, she peeped through the curtains covering the front windows. From the car lights, it appeared to be a large vehicle. It had to be Batrouny idling out front, looking for her. He would come in. He'd know she was still here, and the last thing she needed was for him to see the bag full of cash.

With her mind running a million miles an hour, she stared out. When she heard his car door slam, she would run out of the back door and return to her hiding place under the tea trees. As she wouldn't be able to use her torch, she tried to remember the way so she wouldn't trigger the lights or fall into the pool.

Still watching his car, her brain trying to decide if locking herself in was a better option, a flash of blue light broke through the darkness. She heard Batrouny's engine rev up and accelerate away. To her astonishment, she watched a police car cruise off after him.

Chapter 73

Nikki waited outside until she was sure both cars had gone before she made her move. She was through the garage window in no time. Leaping up, she got in unscathed, apart from a small rip in the left knee of her jeans. As soon as her feet touched the floor on the other side, she clicked the car open and slid into the driver's seat. The feel of leather under her hand and the smell of the interior was familiar; luxurious. She pressed the 'start' button, and the engine kicked over. The fuel gauge was three-quarters full. Her heart jumping out of her chest, her mind racing, she sat for a split second to calm herself down. This was the part of the plan she had considered. She was going to take the car. Having her funds back didn't change that. Reaching for the sun visor, she clicked the remote button and heard the garage door creak into action. She adjusted her driving position, trying not to look at the plastic bag full of money on the floor under the passenger seat, as she considered her next move. Batrouny might be waiting further up the street. He might see the car coming and try to stop her. The police might come back and see her. If that happened, they'd find the cash and arrest her for breaking and entering, stealing a car and she would lose everything, including her career. She looked at the bag on the passenger seat. 'Too late to pull out now, Nikki,' she said aloud, and putting the car into reverse, she backed it up the driveway, making sure the automatic door closed behind her.

Once she reached street level, she turned to the left and checked her right. All clear. She backed out across the footpath and waited, half expecting a car engine to start up, or headlights to flash in her eyes at any second. Batrouny's car was black, after all. It would be hard to see at night, even under streetlights. Still nothing. He could have given the police the slip. No sound. *Go.* Spinning around backwards onto the road, she flicked her headlights on, heart beating out of her chest, and took off.

In her rear-view mirror, she saw another set of headlights coming fast, and she thought, *This is it.*

Instead, the lights turned in to where she'd come from. She breathed again. Just made it.

Chapter 74

The police car gunned along Gull's Way, Wendy leaning forward to identify house numbers.

'That's it, five-A!' Wendy cried out. 'You've gone past, and there's a car in the driveway. Bet it's his car,' she yelled when they reached the top of the hill.

Shaun braked, spun the car around and swerved into the driveway without hesitation, lights on high beam. They drove straight in behind a silver Maserati. 'Mightn't need those road blocks, after all, Sarge,' Shaun said, braking hard, before shutting down the ignition.

'Wendy, you and me.' Bec indicated the front door. 'Shaun, you take the back, check all doors. And remember, weapons discharged only if fired upon. Let's go.'

When they reached it, Bec thumped on the front door. 'Police, Mr Johannsen.'

Wendy, hand on her pistol, moved back and forth along the façade of the house. 'Can't see a thing,' she said to Bec, 'curtains all drawn.'

'Open up, Mr Johannsen, police,' Bec said again.

'Clear,' Shaun's voice cut through the air, coming from the back of the house.

'Last warning, Mr Johannsen, open up, or we'll have to force our way.'

No sound.

'We're coming in!' shouted Bec.

But before Wendy put her shoulder to the door, Shaun's command came ringing up the drive. 'Stay where you are! Hands in the air. Do you hear me? Hands up! Face the wall.'

Bec and Wendy took off running down the length of drive. They arrived to find Brereton pinned to the wall next to a side door, hands in the air, bag at his feet, and Shaun putting his gun back into its holster.

'Mark Brereton?' Bec called out, shining her torch.

He made no move.

'Andre Johannsen?'

Silence.

She couldn't see his features. Her mind was racing. *Give me a look at his face.*

'Mr Johannsen,' she called out. 'I'm arresting you for the murder of Doreen Madden, and over your involvement in the death of Kenny Smith, together with blackmail and other charges still to be laid by the fraud squad and the NSW Police. Do you have anything to say?'

The man remained still and silent in the darkness.

'Read Mr Johannsen his rights, Senior Constable Santos, would you? And, Constable Hanley, cuff him.'

Johannsen seized the moment and lunged backwards, throwing his body weight at Shaun, then took off down the incline away from the light. They heard his feet pounding down the stairs, next to what was a large swimming pool.

'Take this!' Bec shoved her phone into Wendy's hand. 'You light the way. Both of you, follow me.'

'Sarge.' Shaun was on his feet again.

Bec and Wendy took the stairs, with Shaun just behind.

A shot rang out. They dropped to the ground, lying face down, eyes ahead, trying to see where the shots were coming from.

'Under those trees,' Bec whispered. Rolling to her side, she drew her weapon and engaged.

'Andre Johannsen, drop your weapon and come out!' she yelled.

Another two shots sounded. It was difficult to judge if he was firing into the air just to scare them or firing at them and missing.

'Mr Johannsen, this is no way to go about anything. Drop your weapon.'

Silence.

'Think about it. There will be thirty armed police here within ten minutes. The chopper lighting you up for a trained sniper. Do you really want to throw your life away?'

Shaun and Wendy had both activated their phone lights, scanning the tree at the end of the block. Beyond the bushy scrub, they could hear the ocean washing in.

'I'll give you one more chance to come out now with your hands in the air.' Bec got to her feet, weapon extended. 'Gun down, hands in the air!' she yelled, and stepped forward, every fibre of her body wired for action. If he fired again, so would she.

'Sarge,' Shaun whispered urgently. 'He's coming.'

'In the air,' Bec repeated. She could see him now. 'That's it. Step this way.'

Her weapon aimed, she watched him come into focus, hands high in the air, and for an instant their eyes met.

'Put it on the ground!' Bec yelled.

He placed his weapon down on the ground and put his hands up.

Shaun and Wendy pounced.

Chapter 75

Nikki checked her mirrors constantly, vigilantly. Anxious and watchful, she approached each intersection with caution, until somehow after a few wrong turns, she found her way back to the shopping strip. Cruising the esplanade along the beach, yellow lights, dark ocean, and lines of cars, any of which she imagined could be his, her pulse was racing. *Stick to the speed limit*, she warned herself when her foot threatened to floor the accelerator. *Slow down*. The last thing she needed was to be picked up for speeding.

Maintaining a good pace, she kept on and panicked only once as a large four-wheel drive started driving too close, tailgating, its blinding lights boring into her rear-view mirror. Fearing at first that Batrouny had caught her, the muscles in her arms released when the car roared past without a sideways glance in her direction.

Nikki knew she couldn't use the freeways. Too many cameras. And besides, she would be harder to track on the old roads. It meant the amount of time to get to where she was going would take a lot longer, but it was safer to stay away from too many prying cameras and tolled roads. Gathering speed, she followed the signs, and when she finally made it onto the road that would take her back to Melbourne, her breathing slowed. So far so good.

The drive would take three hours or more, depending on traffic, but she felt calmer now that she was clear of the beach area. She knew exactly where she was going. Her original plan was to take his car and hide it where it would take weeks to find, and if he wouldn't pay at least cause him a little pain in return for what he'd done to her. Hiding an expensive car was the hardest part of her plan. She had rejected the car park of her building out of hand, and then co-actor Bill James' lines flashed into her mind. 'You know the best place to hide a stolen car, Constable Nixon?' (That had been her character's name). 'No.' Not that Bill knew either, but the script writers supplied her answer. The memories flooded in, remembering how she and Bill used to run through their lines constantly to help each other memorise. He was in England now, working on a big soap over there.

An emotion like nostalgia, grief even, swept over her. Nikki realised how much she'd missed being in a regular series, the camaraderie, and how much she was looking forward to her new role. Being part of a team dedicated to the same outcome. A shiver ran over her as she thought about the ramifications of being caught in a stolen car with a bag of cash. It seemed that just trying to get even with Mark Brereton could harm her even more. She was determined that he wasn't going to damage her ever again, and the more she focused on that, the clearer her brain became. The police had told her the car was registered in Mark's ex's name, so technically, it wasn't stolen. It was her boyfriend's car. He had told her she could drive it at any time. Gave her the keys. She rehearsed the lines to herself.

And then to stave off any bad thoughts, she called upon an old trick. *Remember every good thing that has ever happened to you.* It was another line from her meditation classes, and more often than not, it worked for her in dark moments. She slipped into it. Thinking back on positive people and happy times: fan letters arriving, acting with colleagues, drinking cups of tea and laughing with Kenny and Doreen, Cammy, her agent, Smithy, the cat she'd had once, Kiri her schoolfriend, married now, her drama teacher, her first acting job. By the time she'd listed everything in her mind, including creating a website called 'Kenny's Kids', to find any other children fathered by Kenny as a sperm donor, her mood was upbeat again. The world was full of good possibilities, once more. She was even prepared to consider connecting with her mother and her new family.

After almost three hours of arduous motoring, Nikki's energy was starting to lag, and the positive happy thoughts were dissipating fast. She couldn't risk stopping. She was starving, but she didn't stop at any of the friendly looking cafés lining the beach road. Batrouny would be furious at her for leaving him like that. He wasn't the kind of man Nikki would choose to cross, but she had no choice. At least he could tell his clients he'd found an address. Then there was Mark himself. She had taken his car and his money. The thought of him steeled her resolve, once more. He had told her she could borrow the car whenever she wanted. Well, now she had. And as for the money, she had taken back what he had 'borrowed' from her. *Loan repaid in full, Mark! That loan anyway. I still owe you for getting Kenny involved in your schemes and that is going to be repaid the minute I get home and give the police your home address.*

Her brain flipped between anger at him and terror at being caught for the rest of the drive, finally relaxing a little when she saw low-flying monster aircraft lights glittering and flashing overhead. *Nearly there.* She drove the last stretch of road towards the airport bumper to bumper, eyes going everywhere, her insides knotted, feeling sick, focused on one thing only – survival. Whenever she saw a black four-wheel drive, her heartbeat soared, and she started to perspire. Her eyes were so blurred and fizzing with fatigue that when the sign leaped out of the darkness, 'Long Term Carpark', she almost missed it. 'Best place to dump a stolen car?' her actor buddy Bill James had told her all those years ago. *'Months before it's even noticed, long-term carpark at the airport.'*

She swerved off, causing the car behind to blast its horn and flash its headlights, and when she glanced over, someone was giving her the finger. She exhaled loudly. Following the winding road around to the entrance, she stopped, grabbed a ticket and waited for the gates to open. Not too many people around, luckily. At least until the next bus arrived. She idled in slowly, and continued past rows of cars until she found a perfect spot. Slowly edging her way in, she shut down the engine and sat completely still.

For an instant, inside the Silver BMW, a stream of blue light emanating from the overheads created an other-worldly atmosphere, making Nikki feel invisible, barely able to believe what she'd just done – the enormity of it. She sat for a minute, listening to the rise and fall of her own breathing. Then, suddenly, as if she needed to say the words out loud, in a clear voice she said, 'I told you I'd find him.'

Then thinking about all the things she'd done – breaking and entering, stealing cash and cars – she didn't know whether to laugh or cry. Was it good or bad? Would Kenny and Doreen be proud of her? In the end, she decided it was good because she had taken the action for herself, which could only be a good thing for her assault on Hollywood. And she deserved that after all her hard work.

*

Too scared to use her Uber account in case someone could track her to the airport, Nikki dutifully lined up for the bus, paying cash for her ticket.

She sat in the back seat, cap pulled down, bag of money in her lap, drawing her own energy inwards to ward off having to make conversation.

Once she was in the city, she felt confident enough to get a taxi home.

'Could you stop here,' Nikki said, a few doors from her unit.

'Here?' the driver said, pulling up beneath the canopy of a large tree, one of many in her street.

Nikki leaned over and handed him a cash payment, keeping her head down.

'Not many cash jobs these days, thanks, love,' he said, looking at her in the rear-view mirror.

Nikki leaped out, bag of money clutched to her chest, and in the darkness covered the short distance to her unit like her life depended on it. The way her limbs moved, running fast and smooth up the incline, desperation and adrenaline driving her, she might have been running on air. On full alert for a black four-wheel drive, she stopped under cover of a tree near the entrance, checking for a lurking Serge. Then seeing no-one, she ran through the entrance, past Doreen's door, and flew up the stairs.

Once she'd made back to her unit, she locked herself inside and put the security lock across the door. Her legs folded and she slid to the floor, where she stayed until her breathing returned to normal. Drained by her ordeal, she scrambled to her feet again and plugged her phone in. When the signal light came on, she punched in Batrouny's number and geared herself up. 'What the fuck? You left me down here! I saw you drive off,' she cried when the big man responded.

'What are you talking about? I'm still here waiting around the corner. There are cops all over the place.'

'Yeah, well, I'm back at home. I had to pay a fortune for an Uber when you drove off. Thanks for nothing.' She hung up before he could ask any questions.

She thought for a minute. Her next move was going to be to call the detective and give her Mark's address, but if the place was crawling with police, it meant they had already found it. They could only have been minutes away when she was in the house. Nikki felt a cold sweat break out again. She only just got out in time.

Chapter 76

Bec couldn't stop the words repeating in her head. They had finally got Andre Johannsen. The thrill of pulling off an operation like that without incident was reward enough. Still, Bec was wired the whole drive back from Gull's Way for reasons of her own.

Riding in the back seat alongside her cuffed and quiet, Johannsen, stared out of the side window lost in his own bubble of silence. No expression on his face.

Shaun was constantly glancing through his rear-view mirror checking on Bec and their suspect, Wendy, next to him, was paying attention to every activity going on outside the car.

Bec fell back to her own thoughts.

There had been times after counselling when she had wondered if she really was fit to be a police officer. Asked herself if she would react the right way in a tight situation. She had no doubt that their operation would be rubber-stamped by the people who reviewed these things and the shrinks. She hadn't had to fire her weapon, that was true. But she knew in her bones that she would have if the man hadn't surrendered. Acknowledging this was giving her a deep feeling of confidence and validation. She hadn't lost her nerve. She'd stayed on the front foot – under fire. No shadow of doubt, she was back and fit for the job.

'Now, getting the charges to stick …' she'd said to her team, as they'd high-fived away from prying eyes.

Chapter 77

Bec read the man his rights and the reason for his arrest under stark lighting; camera on, single glass of water on the table, Wendy in the interview room, Shaun and the DI watching from the viewing room.

'You've indicated that your preferred name is Andre Johannsen. Could you confirm that Andrew Johns, John Andrews and Mark Brereton are names also used by you?'

Johannsen acknowledged silently.

'Speak for the tape, you've been cautioned, Mr Johannsen. And you've refused the invitation to call a lawyer. Could you please confirm that?'

Again, head movement with no words.

'For the tape, Mr Johannsen has nodded his agreement. It would be easier, Andre, for you to say yes, rather than forcing me to interpret your non-verbal responses.'

Silence.

'You are charged with the murder of Doreen Madden and incitement regarding the actions of Doreen's son, Aniken "Kenny" Smith. We have also charged you with possession of an illegal handgun and using a firearm with intent to resist arrest. And there will be other charges in New South Wales and Victoria for blackmail, fraud and theft.'

More silence.

'I should tell you that in relation to the first charge, we have forensic evidence taken from the scene that puts your DNA at the scene of Doreen Madden's death.'

He smirked. And the way his liquorice-brown eyes stared confidently into Bec's; she saw that landing a conviction on this conman was not likely to come from a confession.

She continued to try to unsettle him by laying out the story they would tell. 'We have DNA from a hair found in the rope used to tie your victim. It matches the DNA sourced from a hair follicle found in your personal belongings left at the home of your partner, Nikki Cardone.'

This mention of Nikki seemed to surprise him and drew his first words.

'Of course my DNA would be in Doreen's flat,' he said in a smooth, urbane voice that surprised Bec. 'I visited the sad old girl on numerous occasions. She was a friend of, how shall I put it? Someone I was screwing at the time, oh yes, Nikki Cardone.' His lip curled scornfully. 'Saying she was my partner would be stretching it, Detective. Seriously, if that's all you have, then my solicitor, when I call her, will have me out of here in ten minutes.'

Bec held his gaze. 'Then I suggest you call your lawyer and we'll see.'

Johannsen shrugged, then suddenly became talkative. 'Oh, not yet, Detective. I'll hold off, thanks, so you can tell me more about what I'm meant to have done. Then I'll decide whether I need to call her.'

'Alright, then, Mr Johannsen. You have again declined my offer to have your lawyer present, so we will continue.'

His lips turned up at the corners gave him an appearance of permanent amusement.

'Ms Cardone will be most disappointed in your description of your relationship with her, particularly in light of the hundred thousand dollars taken from her account.'

'Come on, Detective, do you think even if I took that money that it could ever be traced to me? No. I think you'll find that silly little Nikki gave that money to her crook of a father and now wants to blame me for losing it.'

'So, you admit knowing Kenny Smith, your partner's father?' Bec pressed.

'If you insist on calling her my partner, then yes, but I'm not sure being a random sperm donor really makes you a father, does it, Detective. Not anyone's view of parenthood, I would think.'

'You used the term "crook of a father", Mr Johannsen. So, Ms Cardone explained her father's background?'

He snorted. 'Background? Is that the new woke term for extensive criminal record and jail sentences? Yes, I was aware of his background.'

'That does seem an awful lot of detail for Ms Cardone to share with you, if she was just a woman you were having sex with, Mr Johannsen.'

'People tell me things, Detective. It must be my honest face.'

'Alright. Let's leave that. Ms Cardone has given a statement that she knew you as Mark Brereton rather than Andre Johannsen. Can you confirm that?'

'Yes, Detective, I admit to lying about my name to a pretty girl. Is there actually a charge for that?'

'No, there is not. Although, a jury may not see it from your angle. We also have a senior businessman and a leading politician who say that as Mark Brereton, you defrauded them out of a substantial amount of money.'

His demeanour didn't change. 'Even if that were true, which I deny, there is no way those two would give evidence. Showing the public that they are stupid enough to be taken in by some crypto scam – it'll never happen.'

'Again, you seem to be aware of details that only someone involved in the crime would know.'

'Just intuition, Detective.'

'I understand your confidence,' Bec said. 'It is improbable that the two businessmen concerned will give evidence. But this is where our view of the future takes a different turn. You see, Andre – you don't mind if I call you Andre, do you?'

He raised one shoulder, as if he could care less.

'We don't intend to call your victims, directly.'

This time, he shifted slightly in his seat, the same half-smile on his face.

But Bec saw that he was listening. 'We intend to call their solicitor in Sydney, who will give evidence that his file setting out all the evidence against you was stolen from their office. Then we'll call the barrister in Melbourne he briefed. The barrister who had the only other copy of the file. The one you threatened unless she cooperated with you, and whose chambers Kenny Smith broke into on the night he died. Under legal privilege, these lawyers can give their evidence without being compelled to disclose their clients' names, but they can disclose your role as Mark Brereton, and then Nikki Cardone will give evidence that you were known to her as Mark Brereton. So, you can see that I won't need your fraud victims to testify.'

He leaned forward to speak. Bec put her hand up to stop him. 'No, Andre, if you don't mind, I might just continue for a moment.' She gave her broadest smile. 'You probably can convince a court that you didn't steal Ms Cardone's funds. But our job, Andre, is to convince a magistrate that you should face a trial.'

Johannsen stared at her, fiercely.

'Let me tell you about magistrates, Andre,' Bec continued. 'They don't have time for complexity. After we present forensic evidence that puts your DNA on the rope Doreen was tied up in, we show your link to Kenny and the stolen files, you stealing money from Nikki and that you live an incredibly high life despite the fact that you haven't filed a tax return in over ten years, my prediction is that a magistrate is going to shrug and say too hard for me, I'm sending you off to trial. And you know what happens then? We get to present all that again in front of a judge and jury.' She paused. 'And what they want to hear, Andre, is a story. That's what will convict you. A story that connects all these events with you as the star player.'

From the look of absolute loathing that came over his face, Bec saw the man laid bare. No sign of the amiable yacht owner, the charmer who could convince Nikki that he loved her, or persuade businessmen to hand over their money. No sign of that person. There was just the lying, scheming con artist he was, glowering at her from across the table.

'Let me tell you how that story will go, Andre,' Bec said, shuffling her paperwork, sensing her advantage, and hoping she might yet be able to cajole an admission from him. 'You've been doing this for a long time. But in your efforts to find rich victims for your schemes, one fine day you came across a beautiful actress, who was also successful and therefore a potential target herself.'

Johannsen turned sideways away from Bec, crossing his legs.

'Now,' she continued, 'the thing with Nikki was going along – you are playing the gallant boyfriend, using her as … what's that term … "eye candy" – when you heard that your most recent victims had decided to take action against you. That made you nervous. No-one had done that before. But then you heard they had gotten cold feet. All you needed to do was make sure all the evidence against you disappeared before they changed their minds again. So, a hired gun breaks into the law firm in Sydney and steals a file. One file. A mistake, I think, Andre. I think you should have paid them to take more than one, so it wouldn't be quite so obvious to the court.'

'No court will listen to any of this wild theorising.' He spun back to face her.

'Oh, I'm not worried about that, Andre. The people lapping this up are the jury. All leaning forward, wanting to know what you did next,' Bec replied, not breaking her stare. 'And this is where you decided your charmed life had delivered again. Not only was Nikki beautiful, but one night, in a heart-to-heart, she reveals the truth about Kenny. He's her natural father, but this is where your brain goes into overdrive. Good old dad has just been released from jail after a lifetime of break-and-enter crimes. Just the man you need to recover the last remaining copy of your file, sitting right in front of you at the coffee shop.'

He made a scoffing sound that Bec chose to ignore.

'Now, you hit your first problem. You schmooze Kenny in your proven manner, but Kenny says no. Says he has retired once and for all. He's got his old mum and his newly discovered daughter to worry about now, so he's not doing anything that means he would ever go back to jail.

'But that's where you come up with your stroke of genius. You realise how to force Kenny to break in and retrieve your file, and even better, it won't cost you a cent. Of course, you have to disappear afterwards. Well, Mark Brereton does anyhow, so as a parting gesture to Nikki, you clean out her bank account. Just because you can.'

'My lawyer will pull that apart in a minute, we both know that,' Johannsen said, his voice dripping derision.

'Oh, but do we, Andre? Just look at the jury's faces. How did he do it, they're all wondering.'

'Bollocks,' Johannsen raised his voice.

Bec had put the story together how she thought it could have happened with the evidence they had so far. His angry reaction told her that she was on the right track. So, lifting her own delivery she said, 'Well, ladies and gentlemen of the jury, Mr Johannsen explained to poor Kenny that unless he carried out this robbery, he would never see his mother alive again. And just for good measure, he'd keep her tied up in her own flat until Kenny brought the file back.'

He stared at Bec, oozing hostility.

'Now, tying her up is not supposition, Andre. You see, your hair was found on the rope around Doreen's wrists, and as we speak, a forensic team is dismantling your boat, where I'm sure we will find matching rope.'

For the first time, Johannsen's façade altered. Shifting uneasily in his chair, he said, 'I think now would be an appropriate time to call my lawyer, Detective. I won't say another word until she's here.'

'We will organise that, Mr Johannsen. But why don't I continue with the story until she gets here. And you don't have to make any comment.'

Bec pushed on. 'You gave Kenny a deadline, file in your hands by 8 pm or his mum disappears forever. But unfortunately, Kenny encounters someone in the barrister's offices, falls and dies. Not that you know that. You start to threaten Doreen, who can't answer you because you had gagged her, but if she could have spoken, she would have begged for her asthma spray. Without it, with her terror, she panics; she can't breathe, stress brings on a heart attack and because she is not attended to for many hours, she dies.'

Bec paused. 'And there is the story that will convict you, Andre. Your premeditated actions caused Doreen Madden's death. Tied up and gagged by you to incite her son to commit a crime, plus fraud and theft.'

He waited for a minute. Bec could almost hear his brain ticking over. 'If any of that happened, Detective, or even if it didn't but the jury falls for it,' he said, 'the old woman is manslaughter at worst. The son had nothing to do with me. Incitement … maybe. Fraud … won't happen. A loan from a girlfriend, no crime there. With good behaviour, I'll be out in two to three years tops,' he finished smugly with a smirk, his old demeanour fully restored.

Bec closed the folder she had in front of her. 'I wouldn't be too sure about the fraud, either Andre. Then there's the Proceeds of Crime Legislation, which would enable us to seize your assets so that when you get out, you won't be able to sail off in that magnificent yacht of yours or live in Gull's Way.'

'Perhaps if any of those assets can be linked to me, you would be correct, but they can't be. Check all you like. I own nothing. Just the clothes I stand up in.' Relaxed again, he leaned back and smiled brazenly.

'Oh, did I mention that we have the tax office and Federal Police fraud team tracing the trust your mother's house was moved into? They are very good these days, Andre, so I guess we'll have to see on that topic, won't we?' Bec stood up and straightened, her shoulders aching, the muscles in her legs strung like wire. 'You'll be held in custody overnight and appear before a magistrate first thing tomorrow,' she said. 'And we'll oppose any application for bail,' she added over her shoulder as she exited the room, leaving Wendy to terminate the recording.

At least she'd wiped the smirk from the man's face.

*

Fourteen hours later, the sound of shuffling feet and voices became louder as Johannsen was led into the courtroom. Taking his place in the dock, he looked over briefly at where Bec was sitting. She was struck by his presentation; beautifully cut dark suit, crisp white shirt, conservative striped tie, hair swept back, shiny under lights. Seriously, who did he call in the middle of the night to scrub up like that? Johannsen looked more like someone on a red carpet rather than an accused murderer standing in the dock of a court of law or the ruffled figure they'd cuffed in Frankston. Bec sat still to quell the anxiety taking hold of her stomach. Would the case they'd built be enough to get the result they needed for this man?

Thankfully, the hearing was over quickly. After a bit of argy-bargy from Johannsen's lawyer, the magistrate set down a short timetable for the committal hearing, and after the police prosecutor objected to bail, the magistrate remanded Johannsen in custody until the next hearing. Bec breathed a sigh of relief and turned around to find Wendy and Shaun sitting two rows back, their serious expressions mirroring her own thoughts. This was only step one. The road to conviction was long. One wrong fact, one technical detail incorrect, and the case could be dismissed.

On her way her out, Bec was startled when she saw Carolyn seated in the back row of the courtroom. And next to her, the older man and younger woman she'd seen going into her hospital room. Carolyn waved for Bec to join them.

'Rebecca, I'd like you to meet Ian, and our daughter, Merrily. Ian, Merrily, this is Detective Sergeant Rebecca Harpin, the one I've been telling you about. My solid-gold friend.'

Bec smiled a greeting and shook their hands.

Carolyn's face was thinner. Her manner less intense.

'Ian found the listing. I couldn't resist coming along to see what he looked like,' she said quietly. 'Ian thinks I'm crazy to want to see the face of the man who terrorised me. But I wanted to. No matter what happens.'

Bec knew Carolyn was referring to whether the Crown prosecutor was going to have her charged over withholding information.

'Know thy enemy, Mum, I agree,' Merrily said, putting her arm around Carolyn's shoulders.

Carolyn smiled at both, and from the loving expression on her face, Bec had the distinct feeling that Carolyn's daughter and her ex-husband had arrived at exactly the right time. There seemed to be a connection between them that was warm and real. From how he looked at her, Ian was obviously still besotted with his ex-wife.

'Will you join us for dinner, Rebecca? Merrily is a fine cook, and she's doing one of her Nigella dishes tonight.'

'Oh, Mum and Dad make such a fuss over the few things I throw together because neither of them can boil an egg,' Merrily said, smiling bashfully.

'That's very kind of you, thank you, but can I take a raincheck? I'm afraid I still have some matters to take care of. It's been a long week.'

'Of course, another time,' Ian said civilly.

'Lucky you, you've been saved,' Merrily joked.

Carolyn stepped forward and hugged Bec, whispering, 'Thank you' in her ear, then asked, 'Do you think you've got enough to put him away?'

Bec drew back and couldn't help but smile. The old Carolyn was still in there.

'Hope so. I'll let you know.'

Chapter 78

Nikki had hardly slept. She'd collapsed into bed but woke in terror every hour or so, expecting Batrouny, or worse, Mark the scumbag, to be pounding on her door wanting his bounty back. And every time her eyes flicked open, she had got up to check that her cache of money was still in its hiding place, on top of her wardrobe.

She'd even devised a plan of how she would get the cash back into her bank account. Being cast in a starring role for a new series, she realised, had come at exactly the right time. It meant that depositing a few thousand at a time wouldn't raise any eyebrows anywhere. Most people assumed TV paid the same as a Hollywood movie. So, of course she would have money to deposit.

At 9 am, after tossing and turning, and jumping in and out of bed, Nikki finally gave up on sleep and decided to treat herself to breakfast at her favourite café. She almost jumped through the hall ceiling with fright when her neighbour suddenly appeared just as she was turning the lock. *How did that woman always seem to know when she was going out?*

'Nikki, there you are. I was hoping I might bump into you,' she said warmly, brushing down the front of a floral dustcoat worn to protect her clothes underneath. So quaint. 'I simply can't wait for your new series to start,' she said excitedly. 'I'm your biggest fan, you know.'

Nikki thought she might have blushed at the pleasure of hearing those words. 'We haven't begun filming yet, just the promos, but it's not far away,' she said, in full PR mode easily making the switch from performer to publicity with filming about to start. 'I'll tell you when. It is exciting.'

'And I did want to say goodbye.' Her neighbour gestured to the boxes Nikki now saw piled inside her front door. 'I told you I was going to move, didn't I? It just doesn't feel safe here anymore, not after what happened to poor Doreen.'

'Where will you go?' Nikki said, momentarily taken aback.

'I'm going for a change of air,' the woman said, 'found a nice little unit down in Beaumaris by the sea.'

'That's nice,' said Nikki replied, and meant it.

'I'll be able to tell my new neighbours that I knew that lovely TV star once, Nikki Cardone. Had many a cup of tea with her, I'll say.' She patted Nikki on the arm.

'Thank you, that's so nice.' Nikki said genuinely.

'Now you take care. Can't be too careful these days.'

You don't the know the half of it, thought Nikki, as she bent to hug the tiny woman.

'I'll be watching,' Nikki heard her call out.

*

Her neighbour's decision to change her life impacted further on Nikki's mood as she settled into a back corner table at the café. It was deeply unsettling for her to realise that her relationship with the man called Mark Brereton had wreaked havoc on so many lives. Dear sweet Doreen and Kenny, and now even her kindly neighbour was upending her life because of him. She didn't look up as the waiter put her breakfast down, so he couldn't see her watery eyes. As a way of avoiding thinking too much about the effect the man had had on everyone she loved, she picked up her scripts and began reading through them, preparing for her breakthrough role. Not only because she had to, but because it stilled her mind to immerse herself in her character's journey, rather than focusing on her own life.

Deeply absorbed in this task of being her character, Nikki was startled when her phone buzzed. She glanced down anxiously, her heart pounding as she answered.

'Nikki, it's Rebecca Harpin,' the voice said. 'I need to speak to you about a couple of things. Is this a good time? Can I come out now, are you at home?'

'Hello, yes, I'm just finishing breakfast out, but I can be home in about twenty minutes, if that suits you,' she said as casually as she could, denying the hard beating of her heart.

'Good.' Harpin sounded pleased. 'I'll see you soon, then.'

Nikki couldn't finish the meal in front of her. If the police had been watching Mark's house, they would have seen her driving out. She imagined they would have tracked her driving to the airport and found the car.

Reluctantly, her heart filled with apprehension, she headed back to face whatever was going to happen. How could she have thought she would get away with taking the money and the car? People like Mark could lie, cheat and steal their way through life, but not people like her, even if she was just trying to take back what was hers in the first place.

*

Ashen-faced, Nikki answered the door to Bec and Shaun.

'Nikki, just a few matters to clear up,' Bec said, and sat down.

Nikki watched and waited for them to announce that she was being arrested.

'I have to inform you that yesterday evening'

Here it comes, thought Nikki.

'… we arrested Andre Johannsen, known to you as Mark Brereton, at an address in Frankston and he's been charged with several offences, including the murder of Doreen Madden and incitement over Aniken Smith's death.'

She saw both officers watching for her reaction.

'We hope to charge him over his theft of your savings, but that will be your decision. We also believe we'll be able to charge him with both fraud and deception over his various cryptocurrency schemes.'

'He killed Doreen? Incitement over Kenny? How? What?' Nikki couldn't grasp it.

'It's a long story, but we believe he was holding Doreen hostage to force Kenny to carry out the crime. Unfortunately, when Kenny fell and hit his head and the deadline passed, Doreen was so panicked at being tied up by Johannsen that she had a massive heart attack.'

Nikki shook her head, overwhelmed. 'Oh, poor, poor Doreen,' she said breathlessly. 'Are you saying Kenny had to do it to save Doreen? That he didn't break his promise to me?'

'That's certainly what we think, Nikki. That he had to break that promise to save Doreen.'

Nikki wiped her tears away when Bec spoke again, and this time a chill went right through Nikki's body. 'There is one other thing I need to talk to you about.'

Nikki could only stay silent to see just how much trouble she was in.

'You understand that during our enquiries, we took a sample of your DNA to rule you out when we were looking for Mr Johannsen?'

She nodded weakly. She'd obviously left her DNA in Mark's house or car.

'Well, there was no need to tell you at the time that your DNA was a familial match with both Kenny and Doreen. However, given neither has any other family that we could find, that makes you their next of kin.'

'What does that mean?' was all she could manage.

'It means, Nikki, that when the coroner releases their bodies, you'll have to organise what must be done for funerals and the like, but it would also seem to me that as their sole surviving family, you'll be the only person to inherit their estates. In Doreen's case, her unit in this building, and in Kenny's case, a bank account holding a not insubstantial sum.'

Nikki's eyes, stinging with tears again, blurred. Why had she not realised this? That she would be the one who had to take responsibility for her donor father and her unexpected grandmother. Because she'd never thought they'd be dead within months of meeting her, that's why. Picturing how Kenny and Doreen had been when they'd first met, so happy to claim her as their blood connection, the beloved grandmother, the proud father, her heart ached. They should have had years together, not weeks. Overwhelmed with the emotions flooding through her, her mind blanked. She could cry a river.

'Do you understand what I'm saying, Nikki?' Bec said.

Nikki pulled herself together, and with a choked throat said, 'I think so. I'm sorry, I didn't mean ...'

'It's a stressful time, and you'll need help with dealing with the inheritance. I have a barrister friend who does a bit of work in this area. She owes me some favours right now, so if it's okay with you I'm going to use one of those favours to get her to help you.'

Nikki looked at the policewoman who had initially terrified her. 'You'll help me like that?'

Bec smiled at her. 'Let's just say that I'll ask for a favour, Nikki. I can't put everything else back together. This man took almost everything from you, but maybe this way you get your chance to make it in Hollywood like you explained to us.'

A nod from Bec, and the constable stood up with her.

'That's all I can tell you now. Johannsen is in custody, and we will need to know at some point if you want to proceed with the theft charges against him. We'll let you know when the full committal hearing is, but in the meantime, good luck.'

It wasn't until she saw their car drive off that Nikki finally collapsed onto her bed. She just lay there, unable to cry, hearing Kenny and Doreen's voices telling her how happy they were to all have each other.

Chapter 79

Bec could hear music playing inside, so she rang the doorbell for a second time.

To everyone's relief, the Department of Prosecutions had decided not to press charges against Carolyn Moorhouse. It had apparently been a close-run thing, but as an acknowledgment of the duress she'd suffered, she was allowed to walk away. Bec was able to deliver the good news in person to Carolyn and her family.

Merrily answered the door in the East Melbourne apartment where they were still camped. 'Do come in. I rushed out to get some little cakes to have with our tea to celebrate, or commiserate,' she said, throwing the door open wide. Merrily was a happy spirit, like her name implied. She took Bec's arm before they proceeded through to the sitting room. 'Update. Mum's drying out,' she whispered. 'Cold turkey with the pills, too. Just so you know.'

'Thanks for telling me. That's a good thing.' Bec smiled.

'Yes, she's doing well.' Merrily beamed. 'I'll go and get her.'

The music was turned off, and the place went quiet, suddenly. Bec could hear a man's voice – she presumed was Ian's – on the phone in another room.

Bec hadn't seen Carolyn since she'd come to the courthouse for that first hearing, and she hadn't heard a word from her family, either. But now, Merrily explained, Carolyn was undergoing the necessary treatment.

The minute Carolyn appeared with Merrily, she rushed forward and grabbed both of Bec's hands in hers. 'Rebecca, it's so good to see you,' and to her daughter she said, 'Can you leave us for a moment, darling?'

'Sure thing, I've got tea and cakes to sort.'

'Come, let's sit down here.'

Once they were comfortably seated, Carolyn, looking and sounding more like her old self, said, 'I've wanted to call …'

'And I wanted to tell you in person,' Bec said. 'Good news. No charges.'

Carolyn sat back and breathed out loudly. 'And Juan?'

'Good news for him, too. No charges. Smith's death was deemed as accidental. Juan acted in self-defence. Has to be signed off by the DPP, but that's the word. He can finish his time at Barwick Chambers,' Bec said.

'Not with me, Bec. Ian has organised for Juan to finish his time with another barrister. He needs a clean break. As I do.'

'You don't need to tell me, Caro.'

'This "event" has brought a lot of things to the surface. Work mounts up, drinking escalates, the years pass, you're not the young thing anymore, and before long …' She didn't finish.

Bec said nothing but agreed with Carolyn's sentiment. There was no immunity from those pressures in any occupation, even a female cop.

'I let so many things slip in my attempt to be a hard-driving barrister,' Carolyn continued. 'I've had a crappy relationship with Ian until now, and my relationship with Merrily wasn't much better, either, until now. I haven't been much of a friend to you, especially over this, and yet, despite my worst efforts, here you are. I don't deserve any of you, I know that for sure.' She beamed a warm smile that wiped the lines from her face.

Bec smiled. 'You don't, and yet here we are.'

Carolyn reached across and put her hand on top of Bec's. 'Thank you, Bec, for everything.'

For a moment, neither spoke.

'Ian has been marvellous, you know, and my daughter, who is a fine young woman, seems to have forgiven me for my shortcomings as a mother. Which were many, I can guarantee. Anyway, we're going to France together, all of us, to spend some time getting to know each other again. Merrily will be studying a little, too, but that's fine. Bec, I still don't think my guys will give evidence against Johannsen.'

'Aaron is working on that for us, so you shouldn't worry about it, Caro.'

'Is he? He's a good stick that Aaron.' She paused. 'I thought about leaving my practice, you know,' Carolyn volunteered, 'but I'm not done yet, Bec. I still have a lot to offer. Only this time, I'll make sure I look out for my family and friends. And other young women coming behind, who hopefully can use some of my wisdom and experience.'

'Pretty soon, I won't recognise you.' Bec laughed.

'Not the old me, Bec, I hope she's long gone. But what about you? You can't just keep saving your friends. What about your life?'

Bec thought about it for a moment. The case had changed her. Seeing what Carolyn's single focus on her career had done, then the damage Johannsen had wreaked in so many lives, especially to Nikki Cardone, leaving her completely alone, Bec had acknowledged to herself that she did want more than a career, and Josh was a big part of that. 'My life is looking up too, Caro. I've taken a leap of faith and moved in with my boyfriend, Josh. So, I guess we're both changed women.'

Placing the back of her hand on her forehead, Carolyn feigned a headache. 'Oh, this might be more information than I can process.' Then seriously, 'I'm so pleased for you, Bec. It's important to have someone to love. You especially after all you do for everyone, me at the top of the list. I'd like to meet this Josh. Just to run my protective friend's eye over him.'

Bec smiled at that. Josh would have a field day. She could see Carolyn eating out of his hand in mere moments.

Merrily entered the room pushing a rattling trolley: tea pot, cups, saucers, milk jug, sugar bowl and a plate piled high with brightly coloured cakes. 'High tea is being served. Are you coming, Dad?' she called out, edging the trolley into position.

Carolyn leaned across the coffee table and said softly, 'Even with the new us, I'm sure we'll both be riding back into battle on our white horses pretty soon.' She squeezed Bec's hand and turned to her daughter. 'That looks beautiful, darling.'

Ian appeared, looking anxiously at Bec and Carolyn, and causing Carolyn to turn and smile at Bec. 'You'll be pleased to hear that Rebecca has come to tell us that there'll be no charges laid.'

After a split second of silence, Merrily rushed to hug her mother, and Ian joined in.

Merrily served tea and cake, and conversation around the table was bright and friendly.

'One thing before I go,' Bec said.

'Yes?' Carolyn looked mildly apprehensive.

Bec briefly explained the Nikki, Kenny, Doreen situation to her and Carolyn smiled. 'Who knew you already had the white horse saddled up and waiting. Of course, I'll help the girl. It'll be my pleasure.'

Ian thanked Bec profusely and insisted on accompanying her back to her car. She thought he must have something on his mind, so she let him talk.

'It hasn't been easy over the years, I'm sure you can see that, but Carolyn means the world to me, and I just want to thank you again,

Rebecca, for being a friend and for doing what you have. Anything you need, anytime, just call,' he said, vigorously shaking her hand.

Bec drove away smiling. She and Carolyn had been talking easily, as if the wind had suddenly blown away all the deep concerns. They weren't back to where they had been before Kenny Smith's death, but maybe there was a road back, after all.

Chapter 80

Six Weeks Later

Bec was waiting outside the courtroom when her name was called. She made her way to the stand, confident that the evidence she and Avi presented today would see Johannsen committed to trial over the death of Doreen and incitement over Kenny. Even if the last time she'd discussed it with the pathologist he had been worryingly circumspect.

'It's not a given that it will go to trial, Rebecca, from what you've told me about this Johannsen frequenting the poor dear's home prior to the event of her death. But I can tell the court that the follicle was embedded into the rope, and it's unlikely that would have happened accidentally.'

Bec's optimism lifted at his final remark. But still, there was no way of knowing how the magistrate would see it.

After she was sworn in, the prosecutor took her step by step through her investigation. First, Doreen Madden's death and the evidence they'd gathered from the scene. The prosecutor planned to work backwards from Doreen to Kenny, and then link the two deaths so the magistrate could put it together piece by piece. So, question by question, Bec went through it all in detail.

Doreen's body being discovered tied up: the rope with the hair embedded, the asthma attack, the heart attack, her son, Kenny, her newly discovered granddaughter, Nikki Cardone. Then Johannsen's involvement with Nikki, Kenny and Doreen, and the DNA link through evidence provided by the granddaughter.

Bec could see Johannsen's legal team scribbling frantically with each piece of evidence discussed.

She'd been surprised when Nikki had informed her that she'd decided not to press charges against Johannsen. Wouldn't be good for her image, she'd said, now that she was back on TV. The angry young woman Bec had first met, given half a chance, would have drawn and quartered the man. But who knew how the showbiz media would cover it? Perhaps Nikki was right, and it would be detrimental for her career. Bec had decided to let it go and she'd accepted Nikki's decision without trying to persuade her otherwise.

The defence barrister was studying her notes, closely. She glanced briefly at Bec before opening with her first question. 'Given Mr Smith was a man already convicted for break-and-enter crimes, do you have any evidence at all to prove that my client put Mr Smith up to breaking into the barrister's chambers on the night of Smith's death?'

'Only the evidence I have presented to the court,' Bec countered confidently. Her role was to answer the questions without embellishing in any way. No matter how much more she wanted to say, she cautioned herself to remain steady. And after a few more questions, the magistrate finally released her, thanking her for her evidence.

The pathologist took his time getting to the stand, and when he stood tall and gave his oath, Bec smiled at the immediate authority Avi brought to his presentation, correcting the prosecutor when he referred to him as Mr Ahern.

'I believe my role entitles me to the honorific of professor, but I'm also quite happy with my professional qualification of Dr Ahern. Just for the court's reference, Your Honour.'

Avi carefully answered each question with absolute confidence, including questions from the defence about the hair and rope. He admitted it was possible that a stray hair from Mr Johannsen might have been caught in the rope bindings used to tie Doreen, but pointed out that although his team had not found any other rope in Doreen's flat, they had found matching rope on their later search of Mr Johannsen's yacht.

It was during closing arguments that Bec started to feel confident Johannsen would be going to trial.

As both barristers finished their summation, the magistrate looked up at the clock and called the lunch adjournment, announcing he would hand down his decision after the break.

Bec and her team waited as Johannsen was taken back to the cells.

'Did you see him just sitting there all dressed up? Butter wouldn't melt in his mouth. Couldn't you just—' Wendy stopped when Bec turned to her.

'You're a cop and you're in public,' Bec said quietly.

'Sorry, Sarge,' Wendy whispered.

'Off the record, we all agree,' she returned softly.

Out on the street, Bec saw Avi and hurried to catch up. 'Avi … I mean, Professor,' she teased.

'Still Avi to you, dear girl. Sometimes, these barristers need to be reminded of their manners.' He smiled brightly at her. 'Hopefully, we will be able to repeat our performance in front of a jury very soon.'

A car pulled up next to them.

'Here's my car,' Avi said, 'and with any luck, I have a lovely long lunch waiting. So, I will bid you farewell. Let me know the outcome, please.' And he climbed into the back of the waiting car.

Bec and her team strolled off to find a local coffee shop. And by the time their coffee and sandwiches arrived and they'd eaten, over an hour had passed since the adjournment. Bec's phone rang with the junior barrister's number.

'Committed to trial, Detective Sergeant. Well done,' he said without preamble. Bec gave her team the thumbs up. 'Arguments about bail starting any moment. I'll let you know,' he added, then hung up.

Another round of coffees, and they were each engrossed in their mobiles reading emails, when Bec's phone rang again. This time, it was the prosecutor himself, who rushed his words.

'His Honour decided against our strongest arguments that Mr Johannsen was a flight risk and granted him bail until the trial.'

Bec glanced quickly at Wendy and Shaun.

'Not the outcome we wanted or that your work deserved, I must say,' the prosecutor continued in a friendly but impersonal way, like someone accustomed to compromise. 'We did get some onerous reporting conditions, but he'll be out tonight,' he finished flatly.

'Not what we were hoping, you're right,' Bec said.

'Sorry about that, but we can be very confident that he'll be facing jail time once we get him in front of a jury.'

As soon as she thanked him and hung up, Bec shrugged.

'I don't believe it. He got bail?' Wendy exploded. 'The bloke's loaded and has his own ocean-going yacht, for heaven's sake. How can he not be the biggest flight risk we've ever seen?'

'Wendy's right, Sarge. He even had licences and passports in other names.'

'Which we now have. We just focus on making sure everything is watertight when we get to the trial,' Bec counselled, feeling as furious as her team.

'Won't help if the scumbag is sunning himself on some Greek island under another name, will it?' Wendy said fiercely.

'We got the main result today. Our work got him committed – that's our job and we did it. Let's enjoy that victory for now.' Bec thought her words sounded hollow, but she believed what she said, even if she still wanted the bloke under lock and key.

*

The DI was sympathetic.

'Hard to take when it goes like that. Who knows what goes through the minds of these magistrates? But this was fine police work, Rebecca. Chasing all these connections, putting it together. Old-fashioned grind.' He paused and looked squarely at her. 'I'm glad you were the one leading it. And on that topic, the officer whose job you're covering has let HR know that there are a few complications with the bub. Nothing serious, apparently, but enough for Sally to resign. HR being HR, they've offered her another twelve months of unpaid leave, which she has accepted, so I need to cover her role for that time.'

Bec nodded.

'It's not ideal to be acting in a role for that period, but it's yours if you want it.'

'Thank you, sir. I do enjoy it here. I was hoping for my next role to be a permanent one. But thank you, I'd love to be part of your team' she said.

'I understand. As I said, it's not ideal, but I can assure you that if Sally decides to make her leave permanent, and I'm told she will, soon, the role is yours. You have a first-rate high-solving record, Rebecca.' He stood and extended his hand. 'I'm very pleased for you to be staying. There'll be an announcement in the usual manner.'

Bec left the meeting feeling elated. Just weeks before, Griffiths had told her he was giving her enough rope. Now, he 'was pleased to have her'. Smiling to herself, she pushed the lift button to return to her office.

Got any champagne? she texted Josh.

Chapter 81

It was late. She and Josh had enjoyed a perfect evening together, and now each nursed the last mouthful of a wonderful Italian red Josh had opened earlier.

Bec loved the fact that they could sit together so comfortably, relaxing on the couch, gazing at flames from the gas fire casting dark shapes over the walls.

'A penny for them ...' Josh said quietly, and she realised he was studying her.

She smiled at him. 'A million things.'

'Like?'

'Very uncop-like things. How the universe seems to do its own thing when we least expect it.'

'I can't disagree with that. Any examples you want to share?'

'Well ...' Bec tried to put her thoughts into words. 'Look at the actress Nikki Cardone. One minute she finds not just a father but a grandmother and a boyfriend she adores, then ...' she flicked her hand wide, extending her fingers, 'all gone. But then her acting career takes off.'

'Then Carolyn, who one minute is a leading barrister, role-model, next thing, suspect in a suspicious death and evidence appears that could destroy her reputation and her life, then ...' she made the same hand movement, 'the universe decides she can come out the other side not just with her reputation intact but with her family wrapped around her.'

'I'm not sure that one was only the universe, babe. I think the outcome of that may have had some help, from the snippets you've let slip.'

'I couldn't have helped if a couple of things had gone another way, but they didn't. So, okay, I might have helped, but I think, no matter what Caro did, the universe said, *You've got some credits so we're going to let you off. Go back to your family and friends and let this be a lesson for you.*'

'What, you think there's a record of good and bad that the universe keeps?' Josh asked seriously.

'I think there must be, mustn't there?'

Josh pulled her against him. 'We must have built up plenty of credits, then. Otherwise, how could this feel so right?'

Bec snuggled in. 'But do you think the universe keeps score?'

Josh was quiet for a moment, then kissed the top of her head. 'Yeah, I do.'

The moment was shattered by the incessant buzzing of her phone.

She picked up. 'DS Rebecca Harpin.'

'Sergeant John Wheeler from the Frankston station calling, Detective. Sorry to disturb you at this hour, but I wanted to let you know. It's about the premises at Gull's Way. I'm told you were the arresting officer for Andre Johannsen.'

'Yes, that's right.'

'Don't know if this is good news or bad news, but we've just found the body of Andre Johannsen floating face down in the swimming pool at that address.'

Bec sat straight up, pressing the phone to her ear. 'Are you sure it's him?'

'Yes, the body was identified by the same neighbour who called it in. Said there has been suspicious activity going on at that premises for months.'

'What happened, do you know?' Bec asked, ignoring Josh's miming about coffee.

'Doesn't look suspicious. Empty alcohol bottles by the pool and evidence of drug use. Looks like he was three sheets to the wind, tripped and hit his head on the edge of the pool – fell in unconscious and drowned. Forensics will give us more when they're done.'

'Anything of concern?'

'Not really, the same neighbour said his dog was barking at something all night. When he went to check, there was a big black four-wheel drive parked in the shadows at the end of the street. Reckons he's seen it a few times, recently.'

'Relevant?' Bec asked.

'Dunno, couldn't see the plates. Could be a couple of kids parking. It's a bit of a lover's lane at the beach end of the street, so who knows.'

'Well, if I have to be disturbed at this time of the night, Sergeant Wheeler, I would rather hear that news than having to drag myself off to some crime scene. Thanks for letting me know.'

She heard Wheeler laugh. 'Silver linings, eh? I reckon he's saved everyone the cost of a trial, at least.'

'True, thanks, Sergeant, let me know if there are any developments.'

'Sure thing.'

Bec disconnected, then lay back on the couch and stared up at the ceiling, a multitude of feelings flying through her body.

'Nothing too serious?' Josh asked from the kitchen door.

'No,' she replied, her heart swelling at the sound of his voice.

Josh wandered in with a coffee, placed it on the side table and flopped down next to her. 'Then why do you have that bemused smile on your beautiful face?'

'I think the universe just balanced a ledger.'

The End

Acknowledgements

To Gregory, my first reader and champion who sees all and has my heart - no love big enough for all your encouragement and positive input since the first word.

To editor Alexandra Nahlous, I was so pleased to work with you again. Your suggestions on my previous two books made them so much better. Now 'One Night' has benefited from your enormous skill as well. I love working with you, and your instinct for story is second to none. Special thanks.

To author Anna Romer, thanks so much for your friendship and support. Your helpful comments and long chats about everything under the sun, but mostly books and writing are a treasure. It really helps to exchange thoughts about the Indie Hybrid author experience and to support each other in this ever-changing environment.

To Victoria Police Film and TV Services Luke Western, a huge thank you once again.

To Designer Nick Castle thanks for another fabulous cover! And for being patient. Love your work.

For my friends who are so encouraging and happy to read my stuff and do so with care and attention, thank you. You are the best!

The bloggers and reviewers who read up a storm and comment on new books all the year round. What you do keeps interest in reading and books running high. Your enthusiasm and support for authors is special.

To all librarians and booksellers who never lose their passion for books, readers, and authors, huge thanks. Where would we be without you? I would say that of course - my first paid employment was trainee librarian in a public library. But seriously, this is important work.

And my biggest shout out goes to readers and booklovers everywhere, thank you! And please, if you enjoyed 'One Night' or if you read 'Making Up Amanda' where DS Rebecca Harpin made her first appearance, it would be wonderful if you could reach out and leave your feedback on Amazon, Goodreads or whatever platform helped you find 'One Night'.

I would also love to hear from you so please feel free to get in touch via my website. It means the world to me to know that my stories connect with you. If you visit my website you'll also find a link to sign up for my newsletter and I'll send you a free DS Bec Harpin short story set in the aftermath of the dramatic ending of 'Making Up Amanda''.

www.rozzibazzani.com